THE ASSISTANT

Syno Oslo, 1938. War is in the air and Europe is in turmoil. Hitler's Germany has occupied Austria and is threatening Czechoslovakia; there's a civil war in Spain and Mussolini reigns in Italy.

When a woman turns up at the office of police-turned-private investigator Ludvig Paaske, he and his assistant — his one-time nemesis and former drug-smuggler Jack Rivers — begin a seemingly straightforward investigation into marital infidelity.

But all is not what it seems, and when Jack is accused of murder, the trail leads back to the 1920s, to prohibition-era Norway, to the smugglers, sex workers and hoodlums of his criminal past, and an extraordinary secret.

SPECIAL MESSAGE TO READERS

THE ULVERSCROFT FOUNDATION
(registered UK charity number 264873)

was established in 1972 to provide funds for research, diagnosis and treatment of eye diseases. Examples of major projects funded by the Ulverscroft Foundation are:-

- The Children's Eye Unit at Moorfelds Eye Hospital, London
- The Ulverscroft Children's Eye Unit at Great Ormond Street Hospital for Sick Children
- Funding research into eye diseases and treatment at the Department of Ophthalmology, University of Leicester
- The Ulverscroft Vision Research Group, Institute of Child Health
- Twin operating theatres at the Western Ophthalmic Hospital, London
- The Chair of Ophthalmology at the Royal Australian College of Ophthalmologists

You can help further the work of the Foundation by making a donation or leaving a legacy. Every contribution is gratefully received. If you would like to help support the Foundation or require further information, please contact:

THE ULVERSCROFT FOUNDATION
The Green, Bradgate Road, Anstey
Leicester LE7 7FU, England
Tel: (0116) 236 4325

website: www.ulverscroft-foundation.org.uk

KJELL OLA DAHL
Translated by Don Bartlett

◆

THE ASSISTANT

Complete and Unabridged

LARGE
PRINT

ISIS
Leicester

First published in Great Britain in 2021 by
Orenda Books
London

First published in Norwegian as *Assistenten*
by Aschehoug, 2020

First Isis Edition
published 2022
by arrangement with
Orenda Books
London

*A catalogue record for this book is available
from the British Library.*

ISBN 978–1–78541–987–4

Published by
Ulverscroft Limited
Anstey, Leicestershire

Printed and bound in Great Britain by
TJ Books Ltd., Padstow, Cornwall
This book is printed on acid-free paper

KRISTIANIA, MAY 1924

I

Time is headstrong; it rolls on relentlessly and never looks back. But Jack can. He likes the early-morning stillness of Sundays in the spring, when the sun has already risen and people are continuing to enjoy the sense of innocence or are just sleeping off the night's excesses. His footsteps are all that can be heard, and he remembers how bored he felt as a young boy on days like this, because no one else was up and he ran a stick along the railings, just to make a noise. Now he is doing the same along the wooden fence, with two fingers, but he stops by the entrance and realises it isn't the sound he wants to recreate but the feeling. He takes the key from his pocket and unlocks the doors. The hinges screech as they swing open.

On the gravel inside there are two dry birch skis he uses as props to keep the doors in place. The lorry is in the yard, a green Ford TT with a tarpaulin over the back. He unties a corner to check that everything has been strapped in tightly, then does it up again and turns the crank handle three times to prime the engine. Then he climbs onto the running board, reaches through the window, turns the key, pushes the gas lever forward a couple of notches and adjusts the spark advance. Then he jumps down again, cranks the up engine with a swing of the handle, clambers into the cab and adjusts the throttle until the engine is in the sweet spot.

It is half past seven by the time he turns into Stu-pinngata, which is a narrow, uneven street. You can barely manoeuvre the lorry between the houses and the fence. A thin, gangly man, wearing a faded-blue cotton jacket and worn trousers of the same material, is sitting on an upturned cart beside the water pump. He has a hemp rope attached to the belt around his waist. Johan is no more than twenty-three, but already his hair is thinning.

Jack stops, rolls down the window and asks him if he is going to church. After all, it is Sunday.

Johan shakes his head.

'Perhaps you and I are working together today, then?'

Johan lifts up a lunch box and nods. Jack leans across and opens the door. Johan climbs up, wriggles in and places the lunch box on the seat between them.

'Amalie at home?'

Johan shakes his head, then stammers: 'J-just G-gran.'

Jack nods. Give Johan time and he can answer fine without too much stammering.

'Amalie's working.'

Jack takes a pack of Golden West from his jacket pocket. Taps out a cigarette for himself and holds the pack in front of Johan, who hesitates, scowls down and peers over at the house to check that no one can see them. Doesn't Amalie like you smoking? Jack asks.

Johan shakes his head.

'Gran doesn't like it?'

Johan nods. At that moment the toilet door behind the fence slams. The grey hair of Johan's grandmother appears above the wooden boards.

'Let's drive for a bit first, then.'

2

Jack accelerates and turns into Langleiken and then along Smedgata. There, he pulls the lighter from his pocket.

They set a course north. People are getting up. Windows open and young kids slowly emerge from house entrances. Most of the conversation is a monologue from Jack. His helper is quiet, but Jack knows Johan will thaw eventually. Jack is in a good mood. There isn't a cloud in the sky. The sun will warm the day.

Soon they are out of town and passing farmsteads. Apple trees in the gardens are in blossom and lilacs are coming into leaf. They drive past cows lying majestically in the fields, chewing the cud, paying no attention to either them or nearby insects. They pass Grorud and the quarries. Jack likes to sing and he breaks into a song he knows Johan is fond of. Johan smiles and taps his foot on the floor to the beat.

'I should've brought my accordion,' Jack says.

'You couldn't have driven, then,' Johan says.

'You're dead right there.'

They pull in by Sveiva general store, where a lean shopkeeper with a white beard stands waiting on the front step, his back bent, thick woollen socks in black clogs. Jack tells Johan he can stay in the lorry. 'This man doesn't want much.'

With that he jumps out, unties the tarpaulin and unloads a couple of metal liquor cans, which he carries down into the cellar through the door at the back of the house. Then he settles up. Afterwards he ties the tarpaulin back and they drive on. The trip takes them over Gjelleråsen Mountain, to Lunner and Hadeland. Next stop is Grindvoll general store. There is less life here. Jack has to walk down the side of the shop and bang on the window. At length the shopkeeper appears on the front step: an overweight man with a walrus moustache and bushy eyebrows, braces hanging down and a serviette round his neck, like a bib. He doesn't take to having his Sunday breakfast disturbed, which he makes abundantly clear, before unlocking the shop door. The two of them carry the cans up the steps and inside. Slippers shuffle as the shopkeeper staggers over to the cellar trapdoor and bends down, stiff-kneed. His balls are outlined in the crotch of his trousers as he leans over, grabs the ring and lifts the trapdoor. Jack steps onto the ladder and carries the cans down into the cellar. Johan hesitates.

'Aren't you going to carry anything?' the shop-keeper asks.

Jack is on his way up again. 'Johan doesn't like the dark.'

'Are you afraid of the dark?' The shopkeeper still has a brusque tone.

Jack is annoyed. 'Are you hard of hearing? Johan doesn't like the dark. It isn't a phobia.'

Johan turns and walks out. Jack removes the cork from the last can and tips it up to pour some into the cup the shopkeeper passes him. The fat face above the bib slurps the liquor. Jack sets down the can and holds out a hand. The shopkeeper gives a contented nod before opening the cash till and taking out the banknotes. Jack counts carefully, then stuffs the money into his wallet, making his way to the lorry while motioning to Johan, who clambers into the cab.

They continue northward. Johan eats his packed lunch. Hard- boiled eggs and sliced bread. Jack asks him who made it. 'Was it Gran or Amalie?'

Johan concentrates before answering. 'Amalie did it yesterday,' he says and takes a smaller packed lunch from the box. 'For you, Jack.'

'For me?'

Johan nods. 'From Amalie.'

'You're lucky, Johan, to have a sister like Amalie, but I'll eat it later.'

★ ★ ★

It is afternoon, and the tarpaulin over the back of the lorry is lower now as they drive along the western side of Lake Mjøsa and see the farmhouse and long barns reflected in the pale-blue water. Jack is on his home ground. A little later he pulls into the area in front of Hans's general store. The shop is a white Swiss-style chalet with a single petrol pump dominating the forecourt. Hans appears in the doorway and trudges down the front steps, a man with a square jaw and eagle eyes, who wheezes as he speaks. Jack has heard that Hans has only one lung. He lost the other while undergoing an operation for TB. Hans says they can put the cans in the room housing the bakery oven, and points to the cellar entrance on the river side of the house. 'I'll fill you up in the meantime,' he says. Then he shouts for Alvhild, the young housekeeper, who brings the keys.

Alvhild fumbles with the bunch. Jack knows her: a dark-haired girl, a contagious laugh, tall and long-legged, and bounteously equipped by nature. Alvhild giggles as she tries the keys, none of which goes in. 'Maybe you have more experience of finding holes than me, Jack!'

Alvhild laughs aloud at her own joke, but shuts up when someone calls her name.

An elderly woman has stopped on the road. 'Are

you working on a Sunday, Alvhild?'

'No,' Alvhild shouts back, and Jack realises it is her mother standing there. He sends her a nod.

'Mamma and Hans are not getting on so well at the moment,' she whispers, and at last finds the right key. The door screams as it opens.

Jack asks her to take Johan into the kitchen and make some coffee while he brings in the goods.

'What about you?' she asks, glancing with a furrowed brow at her mother, still watching from the road. 'Aren't you hungry?'

Jack says he will be along soon and goes to the lorry to get more cans.

Hans has finished filling the tank under the seat, screws the lid back, puts the seat down and closes the cab door. He stands and watches Jack running with two cans in each hand, but then, after the third or fourth trip, Jack notices that Hans has opened one of the cans on the back of the lorry to sample the contents. Jack is not best pleased, but he suppresses his annoyance and asks Hans if he is satisfied.

Hans nods and bangs the cork back in.

Jack asks why Alvhild's mother is angry with him.

Hans tells him about his wife, who died of TB when he was having the operation on his lung.

'Alvhild's mother thinks I'm after her daughter.'

'You are,' Jack says. 'Everyone can see that.'

'She thinks I'm too old, just because she and I were in the same class at school, but that's how it is, Jack. Some go for the mother, others go for the daughter. No point fighting nature.'

Jack looks at the woman with the scarf over her hair as she hurries towards the farm near to the shop. 'She saw you tasting the booze.'

6

'So what? The old dear barely knows who she is.'

'Why did you have to sample the booze in full view of everyone?'

Jack moves in front of the pump and sees that Alvhild's mother is almost by the farm's storehouse, which stands on pillars across the road.

'She's going to beg for some food,' Hans says. 'From the farm.'

'They've got a phone.'

'Do you need a phone?' Hans says. 'I've got one too.'

They go inside. In the kitchen Johan has a cup of coffee and is eating while Alvhild is spreading butter and syrup over more slices of freshly baked bread.

Jack asks Johan if the syrup is good.

Johan bares his horse teeth in a broad grin and struggles to say the word until it arrives: 'Terrific.'

Jack asks Alvhild to pack them a couple of slices. 'I suppose we'll have to be off soon.'

The telephone on the table behind the comfortable chair in the parlour rings.

'It's not for me,' Hans says. 'It always rings when someone calls the operator. That's how Alvhild knows all the village secrets.'

Alvhild turns to him, mock-offended. 'Me? You're the one who eavesdrops on people talking on the phone, Hans.'

Jack goes over to the telephone and picks up the receiver. Everyone is silent as he puts it to his ear. Johan stops chewing.

Jack hears a woman's voice talking to the operator. The woman asks to be put through to the local police. Their phone rings. The *lensmann*, the local police chief, answers. The woman tells him that Hans Dahl has a store of illegal alcohol in his shop.

Jack cradles the receiver. 'She's called the police. Why did you have to open the booze in front of her?'

Alvhild is uneasy. 'You'll have to pour the booze into the river, now, Hans.'

Hans tells her to shut up and turns to Jack. 'Take it easy. The *lensmann* knows what potato farmers are up to. He knows what the distilleries in Toten are doing. Do you think he'll saddle up and come over the mountain because of some old crone?'

Jack is annoyed. 'What will you do if he does?'

Hans grins. 'Perhaps I'll offer him a dram.'

Jack's annoyance grows. 'I only had one delivery left to do.'

'Where?'

'Bøn.'

'What will you do?'

'Come on, Johan,' Jack says, already on his way to the door.

★　★　★

Jack concentrates on driving, and Johan holds on tight to the strap by the door. They are racing along. They don't talk. The road winds around the side of a mountain, which falls steeply to the lake. The lorry is supposed to be able to reach fifty kilometres an hour, but the gravel track is narrow and bendy, and they still have some cargo on the flatbed. Jack keeps checking in the mirror to see if it has shifted. He isn't taking any chances. He wants to go south before the police have time to react. Why didn't he listen to the end of the telephone conversation? Alvhild's mother may have said something about the lorry. But, he calculates, the

8

lensmann will have to cross the mountain anyway, and what can he actually do? He doesn't have a car, only a horse and cart. Will he contact other forces further south? If he does decide to act, it will probably only affect Hans. So the question is whether Hans is able or disposed to keep his mouth shut.

They reach Minnesund, and Jack turns off for Kristiania. He accelerates. Johan lets out a holler every time they round one of the small hilltops because he has stomach cramps.

On the bend by Stensby Hospital barriers have been set up on one carriageway, and at this very moment the other one is being closed — a Black Maria is moving into position.

Jack jumps on the brake pedal and pulls the handbrake as hard as he can. Tries to do a U-turn, almost careering into the ditch, but just manages to keep the vehicle on the gravel. Rams the gearstick into neutral and presses the reverse pedal. Reverses. Back into neutral and forward. Accelerates. As he hauls the wheel round with both hands he sees a sturdy-looking uniformed policeman step over the barrier. The man has round shoulders, a big beard and a pipe hanging from the corner of his mouth.

Jack wrenches again at the heavy wheel. Manages to turn and shifts the accelerator lever to full speed ahead.

Johan is nervous now. 'Wh-what's ha-ha-happening, Jack?'

'We don't want to go to prison, do we, Johan?'

'Will we have to go to p-p-prison, Jack?'

'Ludvig Paaske's after us.'

'Who's he?'

'Paaske's the cop from hell.'

9

Jack sees in his mirror that the Black Maria is leaving the road block to take up the chase. The siren sounds behind them. Jack is going as fast as he can, but the police vehicle is catching up with them.

Johan looks over his shoulder, through the rear window. 'I'm s-scared, Jack. I don't w-want to be arrested.'

Jack doesn't answer. He has no answer. They are approaching the turning they took before. Jack gets ready to branch off, but, ah, no, this road is being blocked as well. Uniformed men are rolling barrels onto the carriageway.

They are caught in a rat trap. There is only one road free now. It leads to the quay in Minne. They would be trapped there. The choice would be between driving the lorry into the strait or being arrested by Paaske and taken to prison by the Oslo police. Nice choice, he thinks — death by drowning or imprisonment.

There is no time for reflection now. He is forced to make a decision, but there is only one option: to drive down to Minne. The trap is set. Should he stop the lorry and tell Johan to leg it? There are two of them. It might confuse their pursuers if they run in separate directions, but Johan is not like other people. Johan is frightened and slow, he will cower in fear, allow himself to be arrested and, furthermore, let the cat out of the bag afterwards.

'What the hell do I do now?' Jack yells. So loudly that Johan shrinks in fear in his seat.

At that moment the lorry meets the first bend on the last steep hill. Jack isn't concentrating properly. He is going too fast for the hairpin bend. The lorry ploughs straight on, following an overgrown path leading to the railway line. There are bangs and scraping sounds as branches beat against the cab. Now the decision is obvious. Either get stuck in the scrub or turn left. Jack wrenches at the wheel with all his might. The lorry mounts the railway track and comes to a halt.

There is no way back now. Their pursuers have stopped on the bend. Doors open and uniformed men sprint towards the railway line.

Jack drives. The lorry picks up speed, heading for the railway bridge over the strait. The whole vehicle is shaking. The wheels thump over the sleepers.

Johan screams in terror. Jack wrestles with the steering wheel. The lorry is shaking more and more, and Jack can see in the mirror that the cargo at the back has broken loose. The cans are rolling around under the tarpaulin. The rear of the flatbed is slanting to the left; the rear wheel is on the edge of the bridge. Worse, however, is the sight of a column of grey smoke heading in their direction from behind the mountain in front of them, on the other side of the bridge. He forces his eyes away from the smoke, twists the wheel as far to the right as he can and gives it full throttle. It is at least twenty metres down to the strong current. Plunging into the sea would be certain death.

Johan rolls down the window.

Jack shouts that he shouldn't look, but to no avail. Johan holds the door tightly with both hands to see. 'We're going to f-f-fall into the water. I can't s-s-swim. I don't want to die, Jack.'

Then a shot rings out. In the mirror Jack sees a police officer standing on the railway track behind them. The man is holding a revolver with both hands and kneeling with the weapon pointing at them. Another shot rings out.

Johan screams again.

'Be quiet, Johan. They only want to puncture the tyres.'

Johan lets go of the door on his side and tumbles against Jack, who has to use both hands to push him away. The steering wheel spins. There is a bang on the chassis. Now the front left wheel is also out of position. Jack extends a fist to shift Johan from his body and the steering.

A loud whistle permeates the cab. The noise frightens Johan enough to crawl back and stay quiet. He looks through the windscreen ahead of them. Jack does, too. The train has rounded the mountain. The black locomotive is eating up the metres and making for the bridge at great speed.

Johan slides down onto the floor. There, he sits in a huddle, his eyes closed and his hands over his ears. The train whistles again. Now there are no more shots coming from behind them. Their pursuers can see what they can see: the train bearing down on them, brakes squealing. Steam and black smoke seethe around the massive locomotive as it pulls wagon after wagon of heavy goods. The train fills the whole of the Langset bend, tons and tons of steel hurtling towards the bridge.

Stopping now would mean certain death. They have only one chance. Through misty eyes Jack can see land coming closer as the distance to the train decreases with every second. He pinches his eyes shut, counts to three and wrests the steering wheel hard to the left. The lorry leaves the railway track with a crash and Jack waits for the floating sensation, the weightless free fall, but it doesn't come. The vehicle judders to a halt and stands still with terra firma beneath its wheels. They have made it. The same second that he realises this, the giant steam locomotive thunders past, onto the bridge and towards the two policemen running for their lives on the other side. Jack gasps for air. His heart is pounding like a sledgehammer, and he can taste blood as wagon after wagon clanks past. His back is soaked in sweat, and the knuckles of his hands on the wheel are white. His gaze is still misty. The silence in his head is deafening.

Johan crawls up onto the seat. Now he doesn't stammer as he shouts in wild excitement: 'You did it, Jack! We're alive! We did it!'

Jack doesn't answer. He is thinking about his late father. He can see him clearly standing there, saying that Jack should learn from watching running water. *Water doesn't choose the shortest path, Jack, but the easiest.* Jack is struck by another thought now, an incontrovertible truth: water always runs downwards. It occurs to Jack that God might be playing with him now, playing and laughing.

Johan nudges him in the ribs. Jack looks into his elated face and tries to dispel his sense of unease. Glances left and over to the other side of the strait. A man is standing by the Black Maria puffing on a pipe.

Jack rolls down the window and waves.

Ludvig Paaske doesn't wave back.

Jack wants to drive on, but the lorry doesn't. The rear wheels spin round and round. The lorry has landed in wet grass. Jack pushes the throttle lever again. The wheels spit grass. The lorry rocks; the rear end slides. It rolls backwards. Throttle. Slowly, slowly, he can feel the wheels finding traction. They are moving, down the cutting to the cart track, and they follow it to the crossroads, where he swings north.

13

Soon fifteen minutes have passed, then twenty. Still he can't shake off his unease and he scans for new barriers at every bend. In the end he turns off, into a road leading up the mountain. There are still more than a hundred litres of booze on the back. They have to get rid of the cans.

He stops and jumps down from the cab. Climbs up onto the flatbed. Two of the cans have broken open. The lorry is soaked in alcohol and you can smell the stench miles off. The cans that are still whole he tosses down the slope.

There is a knife in the cab toolbox. He cuts some branches from the spruce trees and drags them back to the slope. Lays the foliage over the cans, in case he is able to come back to retrieve them later.

Afterwards Jack reverses down the hill and onto the gravel road. Now it doesn't matter if anyone stops them. The stench of strong spirits is suspicious, but it isn't evidence.

II

It is night, but almost as light as day. The surface of Lake Mjøsa is black with shiny edges. The spruce twigs crackle as they burn on the fire, and midges buzz through the air. They share the food Amalie made for Jack — *lefse* with herring — and the slices of bread Alvhild spread with butter and syrup, heat them over the fire, and drink water from the stream running into the lake and smoke cigarettes to deter the insects.

'The bridge saved us both from a spell behind bars,' Jack says. 'Do you realise?'

Johan nods.

'We were close to death, Johan. We were so close to death.'

Johan nods again. He blinks.

'It was God who decided our fate, Johan. God wanted us to live.'

Johan climbs onto the back of the lorry. He stretches out using his jacket as a pillow and the tarpaulin as a duvet.

'Promise me one thing,' Jack says. 'Don't breathe a word of this to your sister. Don't say a word to anyone.'

Jack lights another cigarette and squats down. Throws pebbles and sand onto the embers of the fire and looks over at the hills across the lake. Tries to locate the cleft in the hill you have to go up to reach where his mother now lives alone. But it is dark, the black wall of trees is all-encompassing, and again he thinks about his father, who died three years ago from terrible abdominal pain, while Jack was away whaling. The doctor had diagnosed it as volvulus. His father's sudden passing is a sorrow that Jack carries inside him. There is so much he should have spoken to his father about. And he is tormented by the thought that his mother, the next time she is in the local shop, may find out that Jack was there and didn't drop by. Then she will be depressed again, and Jack promises himself he will soon go and visit her. Chop some winter wood. Repair the leak in the roof of the little log cottage. Soon.

He walks down to the water. Flicks his cigarette end. It rises in an arc and dies with a short hiss.

★ ★ ★

15

Early the following morning, he removes all his clothes and wades out into the lake to wash. Johan is sitting on the back of the lorry watching, his horse teeth bared in a grin. The sun is shining on Skreifjellet Mountain, which towers over the west of the lake. It looks like it is going to be another beautiful spring day, but the water is ice-cold. Jack tries to encourage Johan to undress and have a wash, but he shakes his head. Johan is anxious; he doesn't like water or being naked. Jack comes ashore and dries in the sun while Johan eats the remains of the food. Jack makes do with a Golden West, then looks for a quiet spot between the trees.

It is such a good feeling that afterwards he has to announce it to all and sundry. 'Nothing quite like a shit in God's open nature, Johan. On your haunches, surrounded by bird song, the scent of fresh air and forest in your nostrils, not the stench of the privy at home mixed with the tang of toxic smoke along the river Akerselva. Do you know what tops this experience? Wiping your arse with soft moss instead of old newspaper that is so hard and dry it cracks when you fold it.'

Johan doesn't acknowledge this truth straightaway. He says there must be some wipes that are softer than moss.

'Such as what?'

'Newly hatched ducklings.'

Johan bares his teeth in a broad grin.

'You're one of a kind, you are, Johan. You really are. Shall we go home?'

★　★　★

Jack has dropped Johan off in Enerhaugen and is alone in the lorry as he leaves Drammensveien at Høvik and continues through the woods on the idyllic old cart track down to Villa Strand in Holtekilen bay. The house is like a little fort at the water's edge, towering over an orchard and a quay at the end of the bay, no neighbours, no prying eyes.

Climbing down from the lorry, Jack hears the rhythmic chug of a fishing cutter on its way out. The skipper of the cutter, Arbostad, has already delivered the goods. Everything is on the lawn, partially covered by two tarpaulins. Jack lifts a corner and sees a pile of boxes of original spirits and liqueurs, and cigars. The second tarpaulin covers a tower of liquor cans. This is going to require several lorry deliveries.

Standing in the doorway is Arvid Bjerke, a man with a narrow face, slicked-back hair, deep eyes and fleshy lips, which open in a winning smile dominated by strong, white teeth.

'There you are,' Bjerke says, walking ahead and sitting down at the large dining table in the living room. 'Arbostad's just been and unloaded the stock. We have to get it shifted to the warehouse in Grønland.'

Jack nods and says he has some bad news. 'The shop in Bøn didn't get the goods. I had the police on my tail in Minnesund and had to improvise.'

Bjerke grins, picks up the newspaper that has fallen on the floor and calls Amalie, who comes in from the kitchen.

Amalie is a sight. Slim and lithe with unruly hair, a pronounced nose, a dress that is glued to her body and curves that ripple as she bounds across the floor. Bjerke reads aloud from *Aftenposten* about the lorry carrying contraband alcohol across the railway bridge.

17

'Here he is, the hoodlum who was behind the wheel.'

Amalie pretends she doesn't see Jack, and this provokes him, but he ignores her too. He tells Bjerke the police probably saw the lorry's registration plate. 'They'll trace you, and come here and investigate. I don't think it's a great idea to have so much stock standing around.'

Bjerke puffs out his cheeks. 'The *lensmann* in Hurdal doesn't have any contact with Paaske. Paaske's the one in charge of the force here.'

'Precisely,' Jack says. 'The officers that were after me were Oslo police.'

'What do you mean?'

'I think it was Paaske. Bearded guy smoking a Sherlock pipe.'

Bjerke gesticulates. 'You left them standing. We don't give a shit who you escaped from, so long as they're gone.'

Jack passes him the money. The banknotes form a thick, solid wad, held in place by two elastic bands. It is like a brick.

Amalie squeals at the sight.

Bjerke laughs. 'Amalie's always so happy when she sees money. Here you are.' He pulls out a few notes and passes them to her. Amalie goes to grab them. Bjerke retracts his hand. Amalie lurches forward to hold them and almost falls over. Bjerke smiles and proffers the wad of notes again. She makes a grab for it. He pulls it back. She runs after him as he teases her. In the end he lets her take the money. She puts it down her blouse.

'Some for you too, Jack.'

Bjerke passes some notes to Jack and tries to stuff the remaining wad into his pocket, but there isn't enough room. He takes out his gold pocket watch and lays it on the table. Now there is.

Amalie goes into the kitchen and returns with a frying pan. She serves them both with bubble and squeak. It contains pork, peas, bits of potato and sliced carrots. Jack scans her face, attempting eye contact, and is successful. Amalie is the only girl Jack has ever seen with one brown and one blue eye. Nevertheless it is perhaps the last thing you notice about her. Amalie offers a lot for the eye.

She puts the pan on the table. 'How was Johan when you had to sleep in the forest? Was he afraid?'

'Your brother used the back of the lorry as a mattress and the tarpaulin as a duvet. Johan's never slept so well, but he was petrified when I drove up onto the railway bridge.'

Jack can barely watch Bjerke eating. The tip of his red tongue flashes out with every mouthful he takes and reminds Jack of a snake or a lizard. Instead, Jack looks at Amalie, who finally looks back and acts as if she is angry. She stands with her fists clenched and plants one on each of her rounded hips.

'Jack Rivers,' she says firmly.

Jack can't help but smile.

'Come here. I have a few serious words to say to you.'

He gets up, with a mock hangdog expression.

Bjerke shakes his head as Amalie drags Jack into the little parlour. She closes the door and leans back against it. They look into each other's eyes, both suddenly embarrassed by the intimacy the closed door affords. Jack raises his hands and holds her cheeks.

'You know Johan isn't like other people,' she says, affecting an accusatory tone.

19

'You aren't like everyone else either,' he whispers. 'You have one brown and one blue eye. Who are you? The cold blue one or the passionate brown one?'

They meet hip to hip, but her back is soft and rests in his arms. The only sound to be heard is the clink of Bjerke's plate in the adjacent room. Jack kisses her, and she lets him, but her breathing is deeper and more hurried.

'Bjerke will be angry with you now.'

'But will you say anything?'

Hesitant, she eyes him for a few seconds, stretches her neck up and plants another kiss on his lips. It lasts, and her eyes are closed as she embraces him.

'That's all you're getting, Jack. And it's for Johan.'

As she says her brother's name, there is a bang outside.

Jack lets go of her and rushes to the window.

Amalie straightens her dress and grabs the door handle. 'What is it?'

The figures that storm through the trees are wearing uniform. There are many of them, and at least two are armed.

'Police,' he says, and follows Amalie, who has already left the room, but stops as she opens the cellar trapdoor, darts down the stairs and closes it after her. Jack scans the room for Bjerke, but can only see the gold pocket watch on the table and his jacket over the back of the chair.

Only now does Jack make for the trapdoor. Too late. There are footsteps on the stairs outside. The front door bursts open, and a policeman is suddenly in the room, holding a revolver. Jack raises his hands over his head and backs away. The policeman grabs Jack by the lapels and kicks him. Jack falls to the floor. The

20

air is knocked out of his lungs, and he is gasping as he tells the man to calm down.

'Turn around!'

Jack obeys and rolls onto his stomach. He lies like this, by the cellar trapdoor, his fringe in his eyes, a knee in his back as the man breathlessly gropes around for his handcuffs. There is a click as they close around his wrists. Roughly. It is painful, but he says nothing. Lying there, unable to move, with a knee in his back. If Amalie is lucky she will leave the house through the cellar door at the back.

From the corner of his eye he sees more uniformed officers entering the house. A voice shouts into his ear.

'Where's Bjerke?'

Jack says, quite truthfully: 'I don't know.'

They go up the stairs to the floor above. A voice shouts from up there: 'There's no one else in the house.'

The policeman helps Jack to his feet and calls for Paaske.

It is obvious who the boss is. Paaske is perhaps ten years older than Jack, in his late thirties. A pretzel-like beard grows around his mouth and chin.

'Who are you?'

'Jack Rivers.'

'What are you doing here, Jack Rivers?'

'I drive for Arvid Bjerke.'

'You're the lorry driver, are you?'

'No.'

'No?'

'Mostly I drive buses, but now and then lorries too. The boss asked me to come here to pick up a vehicle. I caught the train here, but I didn't see a soul when I

21

arrived, so I went to the loo, but before I had a chance to have a leak, I heard some shots and I ran in here.'

Paaske stares at him without saying a word. At length he opens one of the cigar boxes on the table, takes out a Cuban, runs it under his nose and sniffs.

Paaske turns to the table. 'A meal for two,' he says. 'One plate's been used and the other's untouched. Someone's eaten, but that cannot be Jack Rivers because he's only just got here. Someone's made the food. That can't be Jack Rivers, either.'

Jack doesn't answer.

Paaske takes the gold pocket watch from the table. Opens the lid and reads the name engraved there.

'Bjerke left his watch then. I assume it isn't yours?'

Paaske turns to Jack and swings the watch in front of his face.

Jack says nothing, and Paaske puts it back on the table and pours himself a glass of whisky from the bottle. Tastes it, smacks his lips and gives a nod of acknowledgement.

Jack likes Paaske's style.

'You came here to transport contraband alcohol, did you?'

'I don't know anything about contraband alcohol.'

Paaske smirks. 'So you didn't notice the piles of illicit hooch outside?'

Jack doesn't answer.

'If you came from the station, as you say, you must've walked past the biggest collection of moon-shine I've ever seen.'

An officer enters the house. Paaske turns to him.

'The cellar door on the north side of the house is open. Bjerke probably escaped that way.'

Paaske nods. 'Then he isn't too far. Start searching.'

Paaske turns back to Jack: 'Why did he leave you here?'

'I've just arrived and was alarmed when I heard the shooting. I don't know about any of this.'

Paaske sits down at the table, lifts a fork and tastes the food on the untouched plate. 'Good,' he says. 'Bjerke might be a good cook, but he's married, and his wife isn't here, either. Where's Bjerke's wife, Jack?'

'I don't know.'

'That's true,' Paaske says. 'Julie Bjerke's with her parents in Hadeland. Are you wondering how I know?'

Jack shrugs.

'The moonshine and all the rest will be confiscated,' Paaske says with his eyes still fixed on Jack. 'You're under arrest.'

Paaske takes a deep breath. 'Take this man to Møllergata 19.'

OSLO, 1938

I

Meltwater runs down the gutter and gathers in a pool, which the wheels of a passing car shower over the pavement, forcing a pedestrian to jump back against the wall, narrowly avoiding the spray. Some also falls on a little boy sitting on the rubbish bin outside the patisserie, but he doesn't react, he just sits there with his eyes closed and the spring sun on his face. The man who saved himself from a drenching may have been tempted by the cakes in the window, because he turns, opens the door and goes in.

Ludvig Paaske watches the scene from his office window on the third floor of a building called Majorstuhuset. Paaske has to smile at the boy enjoying the warmth of the sun, indifferent to the traffic, the busy adults scuttling up and down the pavement, or indeed the world in general. He takes his pipe from his waistcoat pocket, turns away from the window, sits down at a desk and opens a tin of Capstan. An open newspaper lies on the writing pad, beside a photograph of his daughter, Edna, on the day of her confirmation.

He tamps tobacco into the bowl with his index finger as he finishes the newspaper article, in which the head of the crime division comments on the sentencing of a man who abducted, abused and killed a young girl. Paaske knows nothing about the case, but he does know Reidar Sveen, the crime boss, and finds himself wondering whether he misses life in the police station. Poor girl: first abducted, then abused and killed. Paaske thinks about how terrified she must have been. He looks across at the photograph of Edna and muses that we never stop worrying about our children, even when they are adults.

As he is about to strike a match and light his pipe, there is a knock at the door. A woman of around thirty is standing in the doorway, obviously unsure of herself.

'Come in,' Paaske says, getting up and moving towards her.

The woman closes the door after her, takes off her coat and folds it over her arm. Paaske offers to take it from her, but she waves him aside.

'Don't worry.'

Her mouth is heart-shaped, with full lips, her nose sharp, without dominating her face, and her complexion clear and white. He catches a glint in her eyes, from under the small veil attached to a hat the size of an ashtray.

'Vera Gruber,' she says, shaking his outstretched hand.

'Ludvig Paaske.'

With his pipe, he indicates that she should take a seat.

She lays her coat over the back of the chair. Her dress is simple, with a belt that accentuates her narrow waist and full bosom. The hat, dress, gloves and shoes are all the same lilac colour. The heels emphasise her willowy back. When she sits down, she pulls off her kid gloves and folds her hands in her lap. She has a plain wedding ring on one hand and a ring with a precious stone on the other. The woman, who now looks up at Paaske, is wreathed in the scent of fresh flowers, and the aura of discreet wealth.

Paaske takes a sheet of paper from the desk drawer, chooses a pencil from the holder and checks that it is sharp enough to take notes. 'And what can I do for you, fru Gruber?'

'What kind of…?' She tries to find the right word, displaying the same initial nervousness as so many of his clients; '… jobs do you take on?'

'What do you mean?'

'What I am about to ask concerns my private life.'

'Many of our jobs are to do with people's private lives, fru Gruber. In fact, most of them are.'

The woman looks down again. Still groping for the right words. 'What I mean is that I need to know that you can show the utmost discretion.'

'Discretion is a matter of honour, my good lady.'

'This concerns my husband.'

Whatever she is about to tell him is not easy to articulate, but Paaske is patient. Most of his clients struggle to say why they are there.

It is as though she has had to muster all her strength when she finally spits it out: 'I think he's seeing other women.'

Paaske gives her the time she needs.

'I'd like to have this confirmed or disproved,' she adds, eyes downcast.

'And what makes you think this?'

'Bernhard is out a lot. Often for a long time. And he never says what he does when he disappears like this. Our marriage isn't what it used to be. We've drifted apart, and he refuses to tell me what he's up to.'

Paaske clears his throat and takes a deep breath.

She inclines her head and arches her eyebrows.

26

'And do you think you could still love your husband?'

She sits up in her chair. 'What kind of question is that?'

'To be frank, my advice is that you should think this through one more time,' Paaske says, looking her straight in the eye. 'As I'm sure we both know, in every marriage there are good times and bad. And you wouldn't be the first to sit in that chair regretting ever starting out on this business.'

She looks away, clearly wrestling with her conscience. 'I've thought about it long enough. I can't bear the indifference any longer. This stagnation while my life's on hold. That's the long and short of it. I want to know who he's meeting and where, then my lawyer can deal with the rest.'

Paaske sits quietly for a few moments, watching her, before his lips eventually break into a smile. 'Of course. Your name, Gruber, doesn't sound particularly Norwegian?'

'My husband's originally from Germany.'

'And what does your husband do?'

'Bernhard's an agent and he works from home.'

'Have you been married long?'

'Five years. I had a job in Hamburg, and we met there. But Bernhard loves Norway and only wants to live here.'

'A job?'

'Theatre. I worked in theatre at the time.'

They look at each other, and she lowers her eyes. Paaske is still curious, but she clearly has other things on her mind than her personal history.

'What exactly is it that he's done? What is it that's aroused your suspicions?'

'He goes out, is away for several hours and won't tell me where he's been afterwards.'

'In the evenings?'

'Most often during the day.'

'Could it be work?'

'As I said, he works from home.'

'Could he be out on business?'

'Then he'd have to go to Germany. Believe me, these outings are nothing to do with work.'

'Is there anything else that's aroused your suspicion?'

'You mean lipstick traces on his collar, or long, blonde hairs on his shirt?'

Paaske shrugs. 'For example.'

Vera Gruber shakes her head, but puts a hand to her heart. 'This is something I feel, herr Paaske. A wife knows.'

'You say you think he's meeting other women. Do you have anyone in particular in mind?'

'There's no one to my knowledge.'

'Someone in your circle of acquaintances whose company he particularly enjoys?'

'Not that I'm aware of, and this is driving me to distraction.'

Paaske gives an understanding nod. 'It would be useful to have a photograph of your husband.'

'I thought you might ask.'

Vera Gruber opens the small handbag she has been holding on her lap. She takes out a photograph and hands it to him. A man sitting on a bench on what resembles a veranda. The man is looking up at the photographer. He is in his forties and balding. He has an oval-shaped face. His lips are full and his eyes deep-set. His determined brow completes the impres-

28

sion of a man with authority. The photograph makes Paaske think of a revolver bullet.

'What if he doesn't have a mistress, but is just out with friends?'

'I want a detailed report, herr Paaske. I want to know what he's doing, who he's meeting and where.'

'Do you want to know even if there are no women involved?'

'A wife knows when she's no longer loved, herr Paaske. I want to know what he's up to, no matter what.'

'What's your address?'

Once again she delves into her bag and passes him a piece of paper. 'I've written down all the practical details here, but please don't contact me at home. I require full discretion.'

'Of course.'

'I have to be absolutely certain.'

Paaske nods several times and rounds off her reasoning for her. 'Should it transpire that your suspicions are misplaced, it would not be good if he then discovered you'd employed someone to investigate the matter.'

She lets out a long breath, obviously reassured.

Paaske takes a folder from the desk and pops the piece of paper and photograph of Bernhard Gruber inside. 'I charge by the hour. There will, of course, be some additional expenses, as it'll be necessary to follow your husband over a period of time. And we normally ask for a token advance payment, as proof that both contracted parties are in agreement.'

'Of course,' she says, and once again delves into her bag and produces a banknote. One hundred kroner. 'Will this be enough?'

29

'Absolutely. More than enough, fru Gruber.'

Paaske remains seated as she closes the door after her. Vera Gruber has left behind a lilac fragrance, which makes Paaske decide not to light his pipe. The scent finds a resonance in him. He takes a cash box from a drawer, opens it and drops in the banknote, thinking about the ease with which she parted with it. But it tallies with his overall impression of her generosity and good manners. Paaske is surprised to catch himself feeling a little sorry for her. It is often the generous and the good-natured who are deceived.

II

Jack steps onto the running board at the back of the tram as it pulls into the stop on Kirkeveien. He steadies himself and then jumps over the stream of meltwater running down the kerbside. Crossing the road, he passes a sports car parked by the steps up to Majorstuhuset. An Adler Trumpf Junior. Jack stops to admire it for a few seconds. He likes cars, and this one is special, more than just a car with front-wheel drive. The long bonnet and rounded back make it especially attractive. The Adler is feminine in many ways, yet it oozes power.

As he goes up the steps to the entrance, a woman comes down with her coat folded over her arm. Jack stops and his eyes follow her. She crosses the pavement and gets into the Adler. Initially, he waits for the purr of the engine, but then he finds himself focusing on her profile. She pulls out from the kerb. He tears himself away and carries on up the steps into the building.

Jack decides against the lift and instead takes the

stairs up to the third floor. He is out of breath but not perspiring when he opens the door. He stops and theatrically sniffs the perfumed air.

'You missed her,' Paaske says, folding the newspaper on the desk.

'I saw her though,' Jack replies, and he describes the woman he met coming down the steps. Her figure, the dress and the little hat with the veil.

'Fru Gruber,' Paaske says.

'There was something familiar about her.'

'She said she used to work in the theatre.'

'Did she have one blue and one brown eye?'

'In fact, she did, yes.'

'I was once involved with her. A few years ago now.'

'You know Vera Gruber?'

'Is her name Vera? Then it's not her.'

Jack goes over to the window. He stands looking out. 'But she was remarkably like her,' he says pensively. 'I don't think many people have eyes like that. It's called heterochromia. It's one of the few Greek words I know, and I learned it from the woman I once knew.'

III

Ludvig Paaske gives fru Gruber a ninety-minute head-start before he gets into his car. A quarter of an hour later he parks his Opel P4 behind an overturned horse-cart in Båhusveien. The piece of paper she gave him says that she and her husband live in number twenty-two, which is a newly built, five-storey apartment building. The top two storeys have long balconies with steel railings. Paaske settles back in his seat, prepared for a long wait. Every now and

31

then the front door opens — largely housewives on their way in or out, either carrying a shopping bag or a laundry basket. Sinsen is a peaceful residential area, apart from the construction work on the northern side, which is almost finished.

For all he knows, Bernhard Gruber may already be out, but then, just before midday, the front door opens and a man who is remarkably similar to the husband in the photograph comes out and strolls towards Paaske's car. Gruber is a stout fellow, with a buttoned-up coat and a scarf around his neck. Paaske readies his Voigtländer Brilliant and snaps him as he passes by. Gruber continues on down the pavement. He doesn't appear to have a car. The man walks briskly and swings his arms. Paaske puts the camera back in his briefcase, then gets out of the car and follows him.

Gruber strides down Trondheimsveien, crosses Carl Berners plass and carries on towards Lakkegata School and past the Botanical Gardens. It is proving to be quite a trek. Paaske is a little surprised that he didn't choose to take the bus or a tram, but he appears to know where he is going. The route takes him through Grønland. They pass a gravel playground with a seesaw next to a metal merry-go-round. Two small boys are kicking it round and cheer as it picks up speed. An elderly man is sitting on a stool on the grass, feeding breadcrumbs to the pigeons that flock around his feet.

Gruber crosses the marketplace in Grønland, with people milling all around the stalls, but he clearly isn't interested in shopping. He carries on across the Akerselva, past Oslo East Station, all the way to the quay called Langkaien. A small forest of cranes and cables stretches upward to the sky over Oslo Port. The place

32

is teeming with life. The jib of a huge crane swings out over a vessel and lowers an empty net into the hold. The stevedores wrestle with the steel cables and yell up at the crane driver.

Paaske ducks behind a parked lorry as Bernhard Gruber stops to observe the activity. He eventually tears himself away and the trek continues. Gruber decides to walk along the quays below Akershus Fortress. He then carries on past the construction site in Pipervika, between the workers with wheelbarrows full of cement by Hønnerbrygga wharf. The new city hall rises up like a gigantic shadow behind the latticework of scaffolding outside. Gruber proceeds past Akers Mekaniske Verksted shipyard. There is even more activity here than on the city hall building site. A new ship is being built. The workers are crawling over the scaffolding like ants. Welding torches flare brightly, and the air rings with banging and hammering. Gruber doesn't appear to be interested in what is going on there and heads up a side street to the back of the shipyard, towards Filipstad quay, where a ship is docking.

Gruber stops to watch. The long hull glides slowly towards the quay, and black smoke spews from the funnel as the engine locks into reverse. The problem for Paaske is that he has nowhere to hide. So he slows down while walking towards Gruber, who still doesn't move. A group of stevedores approaches quickly from behind Paaske. He joins them and passes Gruber. He has no option but to carry on, and makes for the bathing house at the end of the quay. As soon as he is hidden behind it, he opens his briefcase and takes out the Voigtländer. Gruber seems to be waiting for someone, as he keeps looking at his watch.

The flag on the stern of the ship is red with a black swastika inside a white circle. So, the boat is German. A sailor up on the poop deck throws down a line. One of the stevedores catches the monkey's fist knot and pulls the hawser ashore. The quay is swarming with life. A uniformed customs officer is waiting to go aboard and there are stevedores everywhere.

Gruber is talking to a man who is pointing. Paaske has them in the mirror of his camera and snaps them. The two seem to be dis- cussing something. Another man joins them. Gruber and the new man walk away. They are coming in his direction. Paaske changes the film roll. They are even closer now, but then decide to walk onto Brannskjære pier. In front of the banana-ripening building, they stop and talk. Paaske could not have a better view. Only a few metres of water separate him from the men he is photograph-ing. The two men shake hands, then walk back and go their separate ways.

Paaske packs away his camera and follows Gruber, who turns first into Munkedamsveien, then Ruseløk-kveien and along past the bazaars beneath Victoria terrasse. Perhaps the man has now decided that he has had enough exercise, because he joins the bus queue at the Drammensveien crossing. Lots of people are waiting. A bus pulls in. They all wait to get on. Gru-ber has a bus pass. Paaske has to buy a ticket from the conductor. The bus is packed, but Gruber manages to find a seat. Paaske has to stand in the aisle.

They go through the city centre, heading first east and then north. Passengers alight and new ones get on, but there are noticeably fewer the further they are from the centre. Paaske spots an empty seat and notices Gruber's eyes on him as he sits down. The bus

34

approaches Sinsenterrasse. Gruber pulls the cord and the bell rings. The bus stops.

Paaske lets a couple of ladies with net bags full of shopping get off before he steps down himself and follows Gruber.

Gruber walks straight home. Paaske gets back into his car to continue his surveillance, but Gruber doesn't come out again. Nor is there any sign of his wife.

At around five in the afternoon, the passenger door opens. Jack slides in and takes over. He sits in the car all evening, keeping his eyes trained on the apartment building in Båhusveien, but there is nothing to report. At almost half past ten, he calls it a day. Most of the lights are out in Båhusveien 22, so he drives to his little flat in Rødfyllgata for a few hours' sleep before returning first thing in the morning, equipped with Paaske's Voigtländer, his own binoculars and a packed lunch.

IV

It is not yet half past seven as Jack drives the Opel into Båhusveien. The apartment buildings are waking up to a new day. Men, and a smaller number of women, hurry to catch a bus or tram. A little later, schoolchildren burst through the front doors, their rucksacks bouncing on their backs, and then the buildings settle back into tranquillity.

All is quiet until eleven. A taxi pulls up outside number twenty-two. Jack gets out his binoculars. The front door opens and a man who looks very much like the one in the photograph of Bernhard Gruber stops in the doorway while buttoning up his coat.

Gruber slips into the taxi, which then drives off. Jack quickly turns the key in the ignition and follows. First they head towards Torshov, then to Bjølsen and on to Sandaker. Here the taxi pulls into the side of the road and stops. Jack parks about fifty metres behind.

Bernhard Gruber gets out of the taxi, which drives on. He then walks back along the pavement a few metres to another taxi. He opens the rear door, gets in and the taxi pulls out and drives off.

Jack starts up the car and follows. To his surprise, the taxi goes back to Sinsen. But this taxi had been ready and waiting, Jack thinks. So Gruber is probably not alone with the driver. If he has a lady friend he meets, he may be with his lover in the taxi now.

Bizarrely, the taxi returns to Båhusveien and stops outside the same front door. Gruber gets out and goes into number twenty-two. The taxi turns and comes towards Jack.

He catches a glimpse of someone on the back seat. He now has to decide whether to stay here or try to find out who was in the taxi with Gruber. The answer is obvious. He follows the taxi with the unidentified passenger.

The taxi turns left down Trondheimsveien towards the city centre. Jack stays on its tail.

At Carl Berners plass, there is a policeman directing the traffic. The taxi with the unidentified passenger pulls in and stops just before the crossroads. And Jack has no choice but to carry on. Beyond the crossroads, he finds a space between two cars and parks, his eyes fixed on the rear-view mirror. Behind him, the rear door of the taxi opens and a man gets out.

Jack grabs the camera from the back seat, rolls down the window and takes a couple of pictures before a

36

tram gets in the way. It stops. Jack waits for it to move on. When it does finally set off, the man is no longer anywhere to be seen. Jack looks back at the tram stop, without seeing the man. Presumably he caught the tram.

Two conclusions form in his head at this point. One: Bernhard Gruber knows someone is spying on him; and, two: whatever he is up to, it doesn't seem to involve a woman. This conclusion reminds Jack of the woman he saw coming down the steps in Majorstuen, the one who bore such a resemblance to Amalie.

He looks in the rear-view mirror and waits until there is no traffic. Then he does a U-turn and drives back to Sinsen, where he stops outside the apartment block in Båhusveien to see if Gruber will leave the house again. Nothing doing. Until four in the afternoon. And then he appears, ambling down the road towards number twenty-two. Jack spots him in the mirror.

So the whole taxi business was a ruse to shake off any following cars. When he went out that morning, the plan must have been to lose Jack. When the second taxi dropped Gruber off, he must have gone into his block and waited behind the front door until Jack drove off after the taxi. And once Jack had gone, he went out again.

Not only did Gruber know that someone was tailing him, he was also a man who knew how to lose unwelcome interest.

Once at number twenty-two, Gruber turns and stares at the car where Jack is sitting. Jack wonders if he should wave to him, but decides against it.

★ ★ ★

A couple of hours later, the passenger door opens and Paaske gets in. Jack tells him what happened.

'I think Gruber and the other man were making a plan in the taxi. They shook me off first and met up later. There's something going on, and my gut instinct tells me that whatever it is, it's not legal.'

'And what kind of illegality might that be?'

Jack shrugged. 'No idea, but he's behaving like people used to during the prohibition days, when we had police and customs officers hot on our heels.'

Paaske looks at the house entrance before replying: 'Did he see *you*, or just the car?'

'Just the car. I haven't left it.'

Jack opens the door on his side, but then turns back to Paaske before getting out. 'I haven't seen his wife all day. Did you see her yesterday?'

Paaske shakes his head. 'Why?'

'It's probably nothing,' Jack says.

V

Paaske doesn't sit outside the apartment building for long. Gruber has been out for several hours today, and according to his wife, he rarely goes out in the evening. After staring into the air for about an hour, Paaske starts the car and drives a short distance, then does a U-turn and heads home. Dusk is falling. As he comes to a halt by the crossroads onto Trondheimsveien, he looks in the mirror and sees a parked car nearby turn on its headlights. Paaske drives on, but keeps an eye on the rear-view mirror. The car behind is tailing him. It is a Chevrolet. The grille, with its vertical ribs and bow-tie emblem, is unmistakeable.

Paaske pulls in and stops. The car behind him slides

in right behind. Paaske leaves the engine running. Even though it isn't particularly dark, he is blinded by the headlights in his mirror from the car behind. It is impossible to see how many people are in it. Paaske sits quietly for a few moments, but nothing happens. Exhaust fumes seep up over the sturdy bonnet. He takes a deep breath, opens the door and gets out. At that moment the car behind revs up, swings out and speeds past him.

He stands there and watches as the car turns down towards the city centre. He hurries back to his own car, gets in and pulls away from the kerb. He turns left, in the same direction as the Chevrolet, but the street is completely deserted. The car has vanished. So Paaske turns into another side street and heads for his flat in Fayes gate as he ponders the significance of someone following him like this. There is a strong possibility that Gruber is behind it.

★ ★ ★

It is so hot in the small bathroom that Paaske has to unbutton his shirt. The bathroom is doubling up now as a darkroom. The developer, stop bath and fixer trays stand in a row on a board resting on the sink and a plant stand he has brought in from the living room. He has changed the yellow light bulb for one painted red. The enlarger is on a stool beside the toilet. Once again he curses himself for not having put up a permanent shelf in here, so that he can use the enlarger without having to crouch down. Paaske is careful to step across the cables and not to trip over them. He places the negative in the film carrier and concentrates on the faces in the photograph. Makes them as large as he can without them becoming blurred. Sharpens the focus. The Voigtländer was a good investment. It has the best optics. Even when pictures have been taken from a distance, the faces can be enlarged without losing any definition. He removes the red safelight and lets the yellow bulb shine on the photographic paper for five short seconds before replacing it with the red filter. Then he washes the paper in the developer. Watches as the facial features slowly appear. He then puts the sheet in the stop bath and finally in the fixer tray. After the fixing is finished, he pegs the photos to a wire he has run up beside the drying line. He studies the pictures but is none the wiser.

Paaske hangs his own shots on the drying line and Jack's on the other cord. The man getting out of the taxi at Carl Berners plass is the same one that Gruber spoke to at the docks. He looks rather ordinary — a clean-shaven man in a winter coat with a broad-brimmed hat. He has a strong chin with a small cleft in the middle. The man is gesticulating as he talks to Gruber.

It is cooler in the living room than in the small bathroom. So he buttons up his shirt again as he stares out of the window. It is a quiet evening. An ambulance races past, on its way from Ullevål Hospital to a patient somewhere in town. Paaske absent-mindedly fills his pipe. Glances to the left. And then he sees it: a black Chevrolet Master. The grille, the wheel arches, the bow-tie emblem, so unmistakeable. It is parked behind his Opel, about a hundred metres further down the street. It could just be another parked car, but Paaske is not happy to see it here. He backs away from the window and goes to a cupboard at the end of the hall. Finds a pair of binoculars. Turns off the light in the living room and goes back to the window. Studies the car. The registration plate is at an angle. Only the letter A is visible, not the number. When he focuses on the car windows, he wonders at first if the shadow he can see is the steering wheel, but no, there is someone sitting in the driver's seat.

It could of course be a coincidence, but he knows that it is not. Paaske goes back into the hall, puts on his coat and stuffs his feet into a pair of wellingtons behind the door. Goes out and down the stairs. Emerges in the yard, turns left and rushes through the covered gateway to Fayes gate. The black car has disappeared.

VI

From a distance, Jack sees Bibbi getting off the tram in Stortorget. She looks around, but gives a start when he sneaks up behind her and taps her on the shoulder. She laughs and gives him a gentle dig, pretending to be annoyed.

Bibbi's real name is Anne Britt, but her father gave her the pet name of Bibbi. And then her friends followed suit. She is of slight build, with silken blonde hair that falls down to her shoulders, and is so kind and friendly that Jack can't recall ever seeing her angry or upset.

They have a drink at Stortorvets Gjæstgiveri first, and when Jack again asks if she has heard anything from Oddmund, she shakes her head and looks away.

Bibbi's fiancé is a sailor, whom Jack got to know in his youth through Oslo Chess Club, but it is a long time since he and Oddmund have played chess. Oddmund signed aboard a Fred Olsen ship, but then quit in Barcelona and volunteered to fight for the Republicans in the Spanish Civil War. Oddmund had always been a passionate socialist, first as a shop steward for the Norwegian Seafarers' Union, and now as a soldier in the International Brigades. The fact that the Norwegian government had made it illegal to fight for the Spanish Republic poses a serious problem for Oddmund. He is risking his life in Spain, but if he comes home, he faces being sent to prison. It is now several months since anyone has heard from him.

'I keep writing,' she says, and wipes a hand across her cheek. 'But I still haven't heard anything, and now I want to have fun, so let's talk about something else.'

The conversation turns to films. *Gypsy* is showing at the Eldorado, made by the same man who was behind *Two Living and One Dead*, a film that they have both enjoyed.

★ ★ ★

The queue down Torggata is long, but they manage to get tickets. After they have found their seats, Bibbi asks Jack if he has managed to get his motorbike started. Jack has to confess that he hasn't. The bike is a three-year-old Nimbus, which he bought with the wages he had accrued when he signed off as a seaman a little over a year ago. He promised he would take Bibbi for a spin, which she never fails to remind him about. 'It's just waiting for warmer weather,' he says, 'and for me to get round to fixing it.'

As the lights go down, she takes his hand. He glances over at her, but Bibbi has eyes only for the screen. And when he forgets his hand is in hers, she pulls it over. He looks at her again, but her eyes are still on the film.

Afterwards, they walk slowly, side by side, towards her flat. Jack says that he likes Guri Stormoen, who is big and fat and witty. Reminds him a bit of his own mother — when he was a boy. Bibbi tucks her arm in his and says that she's read somewhere that Guri Stormoen and Alfred Maurstad really did fight; it wasn't just cinema when they were going for each other.

'That would be something for you, Jack, rolling around on the floor with a fat lump.'

She sends him a practised smile, and she reminds him of a graceful cat, he thinks. She has small hands, small feet and a silky gait.

They turn into Pilestredet and arrive at her block. As always, they stand outside, in an awkward silence.

'Can I offer you anything?' she says, at length. 'A cup of something?'

Jack would love to go up and enjoy everything she has to offer, but Bibbi is engaged, and the resignation in her eyes tells him that she knows what he is thinking.

'Another time perhaps,' he says, kisses her goodnight on the forehead and waits until the door has closed behind her. A tram rattles past. Jack lets it go and walks quickly back the way they came.

VII

There are a lot of people out and about. The pavements around the bazaars in Kirkeristen and Storgata are crammed with people. Nevertheless he recognises a figure in the throng.

Vera Gruber is with a man, and this man is not Bernhard Gruber. Her companion is tall and thin and lame. He has a game leg.

They walk slowly beside each other, talking. It is a chilly evening, and Vera Gruber is wearing a tight-fitting coat with a leather collar. Jack can't take his eyes off her undulating hips and the way she holds her head. There is something so familiar about the bearing of the woman calling herself Vera Gruber, and the feeling that he knows her compels him to follow them, keeping a distance of fifty metres. Jack forgets about all his intentions of going home.

The couple stop by the entrance to Dovrehallen, and then go in. Jack does the same and is met in the doorway by a wall of dance-hall noise: music mixed with the sound of heels shuffling across the parquet floor, the drone of voices, laughter and clinking glasses. A five-piece band is playing, and there are several couples on the floor, dancing. He waits until Vera Gruber and her companion have gone into the main hall before he leaves his coat in the cloakroom.

Once in the main hall, he takes a few moments to look around. The place is almost full. Cigarette smoke hangs like a bank of cloud under the ceiling. Then he sees them. They are sitting at a table next to the dance floor. Most of the tables are taken, but he spots a man he knows sitting at a table for two, over by the wall. Vidar is a former Norwegian wrestling champion, but now mans the cloakroom at Theatercaféen. Vidar has seen him and points to the free chair. Jack sits down and they give each other a friendly slap on the shoulder. The music is too loud for any kind of conversation. Vidar stubs out his cigarette in the ashtray, winks at Jack and stands up. He makes his way over to a woman in a group sitting closer to the door. He bows to her, and then Vidar and she move onto the dance floor. Jack takes Vidar's chair and now he has a perfect view of the couple he is shadowing. He can't understand how this woman could be anyone other than Amalie. He hasn't seen her for years, but the face and the figure, the way she holds herself — he sees Amalie in every movement Vera Gruber makes.

The man she is sitting with cranes his neck. He has thinning hair, a small chin, a prominent Adam's apple and a pointed nose — and is presumably looking for the waiter. Yes, indeed. He raises a hand in the air, but the waiter doesn't notice him.

The band starts to play another song. The rhythm is enticing. It is a hit most people know. A woman in a long, slinky dress sings in front of the band. More couples flock onto the dance floor, which makes it harder for Jack to see the couple, but he catches a glimpse of Amalie and her gentleman friend on their way to the floor. He stands up and asks a blonde at the next table if she would like to dance. The blonde leaves her two friends, takes his hand, and Jack leads her out.

They dance well together. She is dangerously young, with a slim waist and a graceful neck. The girl hums and smiles as she swings round. *'Again I'll explain, it means you're the fairest in the land...'*

The dance floor is heaving, but Jack still manages to manoeuvre himself and the blonde towards the other couple. The man's game leg is probably quite a hindrance. They hold each other rather than twirl around. Jack finally makes eye contact with the woman who resembles Amalie. She looks away immediately, but Jack is certain now. It has to be her. She recognised him.

When the song is over, Amalie and her companion

go back to their table. Jack thanks the blonde for the dance and overhears Amalie and the man speaking German together. The man says he thinks the service here is bad, he will have to go to the bar himself to get them a drink. He stands up and heads towards the bar as the band strikes up again. As quick as lightning, Jack is in front of her and bowing.

'Amalie?'

She studies him without showing any sign of recognition.

'Long time, no see,' he says and holds out a hand.

She looks at it, but doesn't budge.

Jack gives a final flourish of his hand. With a faint smile, she takes it. This is something else. It feels like a return to the landscape of his youth. Jack and Amalie have danced together before, and both of their bodies know it. They dance without talking. There is no need to say anything. Their bodies are talking, and his is bold. The woman at the microphone sings: '*So — when you hear it thunder, don't run under a tree, there'll be pennies from heaven for you and me.*' Jack thinks the words suit Amalie, in an odd way. The poor girl who appears to have been reborn in a higher class, who would now make others bow and scrape wherever she goes. Jack squeezes her hand and looks at the slim fingers. No ring. He looks her in the eye, and she reciprocates, without ceding ground. After the song is over, he holds her for a few seconds longer. Amalie waits patiently, but she is stiff, like a good-natured cat waiting for its owner to let go. When Jack finally does, she turns towards her table, where her companion is standing, watching them. Jack holds her back, wanting to puncture the aloofness in which she has immediately enveloped herself.

46

'Can I get you something, Vera?'

Then there is a reaction. Her eyes are like daggers.

'Because that's what you're called now, isn't it?' Jack says. 'Vera Gruber?'

Her expression is hard to read, but she spins on her heel and goes back to the man standing by the table with a drink in each hand. They speak together briefly in German, and then leave.

VIII

Jack hands over his cloakroom ticket as soon as Amalie and her suitor have gone. While the female attendant searches through the line of garments, he sees the couple getting into a taxi. Jack is given his coat and hat, and he leaves a coin on the counter. He goes out into Storgata and casts around for a free cab, but there are none to be seen.

It is raining now. The couple have not gone far. The taxi stops at the crossroads. There is a police officer in black oilskins directing the traffic.

At that moment, a taxi pulls up in front of the entrance to Dovrehallen and a couple get out. Jack asks the driver if he is free. The driver nods and Jack jumps in.

The taxi with Amalie and the lame German is still waiting at the crossroads. Jack's taxi is now two cars behind. The windscreen wipers arc slowly back and forth. The driver lights up and offers a cigarette to Jack, who declines, as he has his own. He asks the driver to follow the car at the head of the queue, but at a distance. The driver rolls down the window a couple of centimetres, and chuckles: 'One of those rides, eh?'

Jack doesn't reply.

They don't drive very far. The couple's taxi stops in Karl Johans Gate, outside the Grosch building and Hotel Westminster. Jack pays and gets out of the car. He wants to give the couple some time, so he sticks close to the wall to avoid the rain and ends up studying the window display for Myhre & Co: pipes and lighters and advertisements for various kinds of tobacco. When a car door slams ahead of him, Jack stays where he is. Only when the taxi drives off does he hurry over to the swing doors and go in.

The receptionist in Hotel Westminster is a man in his thirties, dressed in a dinner jacket, with a moustache as thin and curved as a plucked eyebrow. His hair is slicked back and as shiny as the lapels of his jacket. There are some keys hanging from a board behind him. Most are in place. Jack says that he saw an old friend of his, Amalie, come in here. Is she staying in the hotel? The receptionist tells him he must be mistaken. No women have come in. The only person to come in recently, just a moment ago in fact, was Herr Krause.

'Krause, is he Norwegian?'

'German.'

'Does he drag one leg?'

'I beg your pardon?'

'Has he got a limp?'

'Yes, but what is that to you?'

Jack thanks him and leaves. He stands outside and looks up towards the Royal Palace. So only her companion got out here. The taxi went off with Amalie in it. Where did she go? To Bernhard Gruber in Båhusveien, or somewhere else?

Why has she suddenly reappeared in my life, he wonders, and why does it make me uneasy?

48

KRISTIANIA, MAY 1924

I

The Black Maria races along, and Jack presses his feet down on the floor and his back against the wall so as not to slide off the bench on the bends. He ought to be terrified out of his wits, he thinks, he should have been sweating blood when they arrested him, but he isn't frightened at all and he obviously isn't sweating blood. All he can think about is how Amalie made a beeline for the cellar, dashed in and closed the trap-door after her. Bjerke must already have fled down there, before her. Jack looks between the bars over the door and onto the winding road, thinking about all the illegal goods on the lawn outside the house. For a brief moment panic surges through him: perhaps he alone will be left to face the music.

Jack has lost all feeling in his hands, but when the vehicle stops he is ordered out, still wearing the cuffs. They go up a staircase and into a building. He is placed on a chair in front of a counter. It is cramped and warm inside. The officer behind the counter is plump, and his combed-back hair falls over his fore-head whenever he searches for a key on the typewriter. The man strokes his fringe back and squints as he looks for the next letter. Eventually the typewriter bell rings and the man hits the lever for a new line.

It is a long time since Jack has felt so small and insignificant. He feels like a louse, a piece of dirt that has been collected and swept into a corner, a persona non grata, someone who is just a pest. He sits there, his hands numb, ignored, except for contemptuous glances from uniformed officers brushing past, in and out through the counter.

Finally a lanky uniformed officer comes and tells him to stand up. Jack obeys and follows the policeman into a room where he has to stand facing a white wall. Here he is photographed, from the front and in profile.

'How long do I have to wear the cuffs? I can't feel my fingers anymore.'

The policeman emerges from under the cloth over the camera. Takes a key and unlocks the handcuffs. Jack rubs his hands. The pain is worse now, his fingers tingle and he rocks his upper body to stop himself screaming. But before the pain has gone, he has to have his fingerprints taken, to press one white finger on an inkpad and afterwards onto paper.

'Name?'

'Rivers. Jack.'

'Jack with CK?'

'Yes, and Rivers with an R.'

'Shut up, Rivers.'

The door opens and a policeman sticks his head in. 'Jonny,' the man says, 'Ludvig's waiting.'

The man called Jonny grabs Jack under the arm and leads him down a long corridor and opens the door to a closet of a room. Inside, Paaske is sitting on one of two straight-backed chairs, reading some papers. Paaske has put his hat on the table and tells Jack to sit down, but he remains standing.

'Are you hard of hearing?'

Jack sits down.

'We have nothing on you. You have a clean record.'

Jack nods.

'Your family are solid, working stock. Shame you had to tarnish their name, Jack.'

'I haven't done anything. I went to Arvid Bjerke's house in Høvik to pick up a lorry. I work for him.'

'I know you work for Bjerke. I know you're the man who's worked longest for him. You were with him when he started his transport business. You were with him when he started smuggling. You're the man Bjerke relies on for everything. I know you aren't as innocent as you make out, so don't annoy me with any more lies. I might lose respect for you. It won't do you any good.'

Jack is silent. He meets Paaske's intently staring eyes.

'Have you heard about the Bridge of Sighs?'

Jack doesn't respond.

'Next time, Jack, next time you're near contraband, take a walk over the Bridge of Sighs.'

Jack rubs his hands, which are still tingling. Quiet jubilation is growing inside him. Paaske is talking about next time. So he will be released this time.

'For me you're a minnow, Jack. I want the kingpin behind this racket. I want Arvid Bjerke. Looking at you, I know how I'll catch him, and you're going to help me.'

'I don't understand what you mean.'

'I think you understand all too well, but I'm still going to indulge myself and tell you, so that you and Engineer Bjerke have something to discuss the next time you meet.'

II

Jack feels a responsibility for the lorry and gets up early to catch a train from Oslo West to Høvik to pick it up. He walks through Akersgata, with its newspaper buildings, and stops in front of the windows. The police raid on the smuggler gang in Holtekilen is a front-page spread over several columns. Jack reads about the huge quantity of goods confiscated and the smuggler gang that has been 'bust'. Almost thirty thousand litres of raw alcohol and tens of thousands of bottles of original spirits are now in the hands of the authorities. Jack shakes his head. The numbers can't be right. Arbostad cannot have unloaded that much onto the grass outside the house. The paper writes that this is the biggest seizure of illicit alcohol in Norway's history. The assumed ringmaster — Engineer Arvid Bjerke, the owner of Bjerkes Bilcentral — has gone missing. When the police stormed the house, Bjerke is supposed to have left in haste 'without his jacket and gold pocket watch'. Jack reads that one man was arrested in the house, but that this 'driver' was later released. It isn't known how many smugglers escaped when the police struck.

Many people are standing, reading the news and discussing it. Many are intrigued by how Bjerke disappeared and launch their own theories. Some seem to know he is out of the country. Most are impassioned about prohibition and furious with the police for pouring away great quantities of valuable drink. Why should there be a ban on spirits? After all, you can be served beer and wine quite legally. The authorities are creating a crime wave for no reason. Think of all the capital flowing between the criminals just because of Christian hypocrisy. Priests serve stiff drinks at daughters' weddings, too.

A short man in a long coat and a bowler hat weighs in for the opposition: 'Strong drink is to blame for

52

everything. It's Satan's henchman and it rains misfortune down on homes. People struggle to find work, they can barely feed their families and then they buy expensive spirits. Why should their money go into the pockets of riff-raff and rich businessmen when it could feed their children?'

Jack walks on before the man starts brandishing a Bible. There are roadworks in Grensen. The unemployed have been drafted in. Some of them are working in hats and coats. A man pushing a cart can't get past. Jack grabs hold of it and helps the man to pull the cart onto the pavement. He hurries on. In a strange way he feels important. It is not a feeling he knows how to respond to. The fact is that he is crossing Studenterlunden Park while many of the other people walking there at the same time are thinking about him. They have opinions about his character and his activities, not knowing who he is, not knowing why he does what he does, not knowing what happened in Holtekilen and not knowing anything about Arvid Bjerke. They conjure up images of swarthy armed men running the devil's errands, but Bjerke is a likeable chap with a contagious laugh, maybe a little overweight and a clumsy clod on the football pitch, but people thrive in his company.

At the ticket window in Oslo West Station Jack buys a single and runs through the concourse to catch the Drammen train, which is ready to depart. He sits beside a family of four. The two children are shy and whisper to each other and their mother while sending him glances. When he gets off at Høvik, both girls stand with their faces glued to the window and wave to him in a fit of exuberance. He waves back and they laugh out loud and retreat back into their compart-

53

ment and the warm embrace of the family.

Jack continues on foot towards the sea and thanks his lucky stars he left the key in the lorry when he went into the house the previous day. If Paaske had found the key in his pocket Jack wouldn't be walking through the trees and listening to the birds today.

On his way down through the forest he wonders whether the police have posted guards around the house. They could have done, as Bjerke has disappeared, but he can't see anyone. The contraband on the lawn has gone. The front door of the house is closed. The Ford is where he left it.

The house looks locked. Nevertheless he runs up the steps and knocks on the door. No one answers and the door is locked. So Julie Bjerke isn't at home. Perhaps Paaske was right. Perhaps she is still in Hadeland.

After cranking the engine into life he drives back to Kristiania and heads for Sagene and the Rivertzke Complex. Rivertz the architect is related to Jack in some way or other, but Jack and the architect spell their surnames differently. That is all Jack knows about these buildings and the architect who designed the quarter.

Outside the bus depot he sees Bjerke's wife on her way in. Julie is beautiful, but also appears fragile; there is something very vulnerable about her mouth and her shy gaze. Jack has never understood why Bjerke has such appeal, and he certainly doesn't understand why Bjerke can be bothered to chase other women when he has a wife like Julie.

Stopping by the side of the entrance, he rolls down the window.

'Julie.'

'Jack.'

'I thought you were at your parents' place in Hadeland.'

'Why?'

'I was arrested yesterday,' he says, jumping down from the cab and banging the door shut. 'Arvid has disappeared, but you probably know all that. The papers are full of it.'

Julie just stands staring at him. Jack looks back. She has the same beauty as elegant, expensive porcelain, he thinks. As though it wouldn't take much to break her. It is as if the real Julie is hiding inside. Beneath the white skin and behind the veil of charm there resides a different woman looking out at the world, frightened that the veneer might crack and she will have to reveal herself. This is a Julie he has never seen and perhaps never will.

At length she raises the papers she is holding.

'Do your job and you'll be paid for your labour, Jack.'

'Where's the old man?'

'I don't know.'

Julie turns her back on him and walks into the depot. Jack follows her. They both go to the duty office, where Jack hangs the key from the lorry on the board.

'Here,' she says, flicking through the pile to pass him a job chitty.

'A bus?'

'The Overland.'

III

Jack takes the chitty and goes to look for the car, thinking all the while that Paaske is a clever bugger, knowing that Julie Bjerke was in Hadeland the day before. At the same time he wonders what is going on in Julie's head, glances back at the office window and meets her gaze as she sits watching him. It is none of your business, he tells himself. It is none of your business what married couples get up to.

After reversing the car out of the huge garage he jumps out to fix the folding top. Jack likes this car. It is a red Overland 1923 Tourer. The steering column is the same green as the seat leather. The accelerator is located in the middle between the clutch and the brake. There are twenty-seven wild horses beneath the bonnet, squeezed into a purring four-cylinder engine. The bodywork is warmed by the sun in a cloud-free sky.

After securing the top he drives down to Skansen restaurant in the Kontrasjæret area, where his prospective passengers are waiting for him. There are three of them. They are young and good-looking, and they have money; refined folk who don't have to work. A young man in a straw boater waves a walking cane. Behind him are two women. They are going to a seaside hotel in Drøbak. The man is wearing a striped jacket and white trousers, but can barely be more than twenty years old. He has pimples on his temple and a moustache of uneven provenance. Jack holds the door open for the ladies, who climb onto the back seat. They smell of wine and giggle, and one leans heavily on Jack in the process.

When Jack is behind the wheel again, the moustachioed stripling wants him to speed up. Jack shouts to the ladies at the back that it will be blowy. They should tell him if he is going too fast. They hold on tight and squeal with delight as he accelerates. Jack looks in the mirror at the one who leaned on him. Her cheeks are powdered and her lips are as red as blood. When she laughs, she reveals pearly-white teeth. Her hat fits tightly and frames her oval face. Her eyes meet his, then she leans forward and taps him on the shoulder.

'Have you got a cigarette?'

Jack produces a packet of Golden West from his waistcoat pocket and throws it behind to her. She catches it in mid-air.

The young man takes out a hip flask and passes it round. Jack declines the offer, but is moved to comment and shouts over the noise of the engine: 'So you have spirits. Where did you get hold of it?'

The young man shouts back: 'Where there's money, there's liqueur, chauffeur.'

He turns to the young ladies. 'Liqueur. Chauffeur. It rhymes.'

The man snorts with laughter and repeats the rhyme. Then he shouts that he is renting a car from Arvid Bjerke, you know. The engineer should know where you can get spirits.'

There is a pothole in the gravel road ahead of them, and Jack lets the front wheel go in. Everyone jumps in their seat. The women scream, but the cavalier's laughter stops at once. His boater blows away in the wind.

'Jesus, man, can't you drive?'

Jack stops. The man jumps out and runs after his hat. As he bends to catch it, there is a sudden gust of wind and it takes off again, as if escaping. Now the women are in fits of hysterical laughter. Jack also allows himself a smile. The cavalier grabs the hat and returns, brushing the dust from it.

'It was because of the speed,' Jack says, and adds:

'Perhaps I'd better slow down?'

The women at the back sing in unison: 'Please do!'

Peace and silence reign among the travel companions as the journey proceeds. The two women smoke and chat to each other.

One taps Jack on the shoulder again.

'Apparently one of Bjerke's drivers was arrested and then released. It wasn't you by any chance, was it?'

Jack meets her eyes in the mirror and holds them without answering. At the same time he feels the eyes of the young man on him. Jack concentrates on driving and silence descends over the car. The atmosphere has changed. No one says anything. It is only when they are passing Bunne fjord that the young man clears his throat, turns round and points to a house, and says that his uncle lives there. The two women don't answer. Jack looks in the mirror. They are whispering.

When Jack drops the party off at Reenskaug Hotel, she stands by the car with a serious expression on her face. 'Are you staying for a while?'

'I have to go back. Other clients are waiting.'

'What's your name?'

'Jack Rivers.'

'Sure you don't fancy some fun, Jack Rivers?'

'Another time, perhaps,' he says, and asks what her name is.

She smiles sadly and strokes his hand.

'Another time is usually too late,' she says, ascends the steps and enters the hotel without a backward look.

IV

At half past seven the following day Jack appears in Holtekilen, liveried and in the Overland. Julie comes down the steps alone. She gets in at the rear and fills the car with the scent of cinnamon and flowers. They exchange looks in the mirror.

'Just drive,' she says. 'No one else is coming.'

It is not only this that is different, he thinks, driving towards Oslo. There is an atmosphere. It is as though there is a magnet in the mirror, which he avoids, because whenever he does look, he meets her eyes.

Today he hasn't been given any of his usual bus jobs, either. Instead he has to go on little errands for Julie. First, a trip to Hansen the baker to buy cake. Jack uses the opportunity to drop by the shop in Sagene and buy a cone of sugar candy and camphor lozenges. From there he continues to Enerhaugen. A throng of kids in tattered clothes run after the car as he turns into Stupinngata. Jack throws the sweets at them and finds Johan by the water pump. He asks after Amalie, but Johan hasn't seen her. Not for some days.

The next day his job is to deliver two of the mille-feuilles from Hansen's bakery to Julie's parents. This will be a long trip, as the wholesaler and his wife have moved to their summer house in Vestfold. After parking where the road ends and trudging over the hills to the white house set picturesquely between the sea and steep sea-smoothed rocks, he stands holding the cake box while a nervous uniformed maid runs to find the lady. The girl doesn't return. Instead the wholesaler himself fractionally opens the terrace door. Julie's father, one eye pinched around a monocle, is wearing a dinner jacket, short trousers and black walking shoes. Without saying a single word he takes the box of cakes from Jack. The door closes and Jack realises his audience is over.

On the return journey he starts thinking that Julie

is crazy, but it is no skin off his nose. He likes driving in the country, hooting at cows, which bolt away as he comes round bends, throwing five-øre coins to kids on gate duty, hanging with their bums out as the gate opens, but a trip like this takes time. The working day is almost over when he turns off by Skillebekk and heads for Sagene. As he rolls into the depot the other drivers are on their way home. They wink at Jack and ask if it has been a long day. Jack winks back and sits down with a cup of coffee to wait for orders. When Julie decides that her working day is over too, she comes out of the duty office.

'Get your livery on, Jack. We're off.'

Jack goes to the changing room and dons his uniform jacket and cap. Julie likes sitting at the back of the Overland — a babe dressed in a fur collar and sleeveless dress, with a private chauffeur in an open car. Julie instructs Jack to drive down Karl Johans gate, where people turn and gaze at the beauty ensconced on the back seat wearing a blasé expression. This is what Julie wants: to be the mysterious, wealthy wife driven around by her liveried chauffeur. Jack brakes as a cyclist shoots across the street. He stops and waits for a mother holding her little son's hand to cross into Studenterlunden Park.

As soon as they are out of the centre, she feels cold. He pulls in by Skøyen and puts up the top. Julie doesn't say a word, nor does she when he gets back in. Once again there is a kind of magnetic silence between them, a silence it seems unnatural to break, but which he still feels as pressure from over his shoulder. Jack turns off by Høvik, drives through the forest on the cart track and parks in front of Villa Strand, which announces its presence with a glass veranda

60

and the noise of sawing in the garden. He jumps out and opens the door for her. Her hand searches for his and she almost falls against him as she finds it. Julie laughs at herself, and he smiles back.

'Don't go away, Jack. I may need you.'

With short steps and swaying hips she makes for the house. Julie looks good, but standing there, outside Villa Strand, Jack's uppermost thought is what it was like when the cops stormed the steps, kicked him to the floor and cuffed him.

It is warm although it is almost evening. The sun hangs low in the cloudless sky. Jack puts his jacket and cap on the car seat, rolls up his sleeves and walks to the quay. There is a ladder down to the sea at the end. Bjerke's boat is moored beside it — an open double-ender with a square engine casing, measuring maybe twenty feet. The paintwork is shiny. There is a bailer floating in the bottom of the boat.

He sits down on the edge of the quay and takes in the atmosphere. The ripples of water lapping against the side. The screaming gulls. A magpie couple making a nest in a maple tree. One flies up with a twig in its beak, leaving it for their partner in the half-built home that has already begun to take its chaotic form. A white wagtail jumps from the lawn to the quay. It stands there, justifying its name.

Time passes. The sun is setting behind the mountain ridge to the west, and Jack wonders if he should knock on the door and say he is going home, but he doesn't move. Finally the front door opens. He gets to his feet. Julie is standing in the doorway.

'Jack,' she says. 'Come inside.'

She has changed clothes now. The dress has been exchanged for a kimono knotted around her waist.

Her hair is hanging loose over her shoulders. She is barefoot and has a little sore on her instep. The red mark with bits of scab makes him see her with new eyes. This aloofness and distinction she always strives to assume has been peeled away, and he sees she is only a woman alone in a house that is far too big. As they exchange glances he can read her, which immediately makes him hesitate.

'Come inside,' she repeats.

Jack hesitates for a few more seconds, then goes inside, and has to brush past her as she is leaning against the door frame. The dining table is set for one person. Open sandwiches. One with cheese and one with ham. Julie must be preparing the food herself, now that Amalie has disappeared.

'Eat,' she says, and pulls out the chair.

Jack sits down and watches her go to the corner cabinet and take out one glass amid much clinking of bottles. He realises she is unsteady on her feet.

'What can I offer you? Whisky? Gin?'

Jack is impressed. She has managed to conjure up original spirits in this house, even after everything has been confiscated. 'You decide, Julie.'

The bottle glugs as she pours. She takes her own glass from a smaller table and fills it. An auburn liquid with water. This isn't her first stiffener. Jack takes a mouthful of the sandwich and realises he is hungry. Julie sits down at the table and looks at him.

They look into each other's eyes. Then she raises her glass. 'Skål.'

Jack follows suit. They drink. Bread and whisky don't go together that well. Besides, he has a suspicion he knows what she is after and isn't too enamoured of the idea. At the same time he is frightened he might have misunderstood, frightened to judge her without sufficient grounds.

At length she gets up and stands behind him. When she rests her hands on his shoulders he gets up too and turns to her. They are standing close — too close — but if he wants to retreat he will have to shove the whole table back.

'Kiss me,' she whispers.

This moment has been in the air all afternoon, and Jack knows in himself that he has seen it coming, even if this isn't somewhere he wants to go. Searching for words to defer all this, to slip away without offending her, he finds he has none and ends up blaming himself for walking into this situation with open eyes. The scent of her perfume is heavy, and she loosens the knot of her kimono. It opens and she is wearing nothing underneath. He breathes harder, and she takes his hands, raises them and places them on her breasts. Everything male in him reacts. She notices. Her hands grope, her fingers find the buttons on his trousers. They are both panting. Then he grabs her hands and restrains them.

They stand like this, looking into each other's eyes until he turns away and leaves the house. Closes the door after him. Stumbles down the steps. Stands gasping for breath by the car. Faces the front door. It has stayed closed. She is drunk, he thinks, drunk and desperate. I may be the biggest idiot in the world, but I am who I am.

V

The next morning Jack is outside Villa Strand with the Overland at the usual time, but Julie doesn't appear.

After waiting for a few minutes in the car, he ambles up the steps and knocks on the door. No reaction. He feels the door. It is locked, and all he can do is drive to work alone. As he enters the garage he sees she is already there. She is sitting inside the duty office and still hasn't taken off her hat. This attractive young woman doesn't fit in here, he thinks, remembering the sight of her white skin and the raspberry-red nipples stiffening under his fingers. He is dreading meeting her, but forces himself to. He goes into the office and hangs up the car key.

'Rivers,' she says, swivelling round on her chair.

'My lips are sealed. With seven seals. What happened yesterday has already been erased from my memory.'

Julie says nothing. She just smiles weakly and looks down.

'Rivers,' she repeats. 'The situation is tricky now with Arvid and the police and all that.'

Jack nods.

That vulnerable mouth of hers is still smiling weakly. Again he has the impression that she is a doll, controlled by a motor hidden deep behind her blue eyes.

'I'll send for you when there's a call for you, Rivers.'

At first Jack doesn't answer. She has never spoken to him in this manner. He isn't quite sure what she means and feels he needs some clarification.

'What do you mean?'

'I mean what I say. You will be contacted when we need extra drivers.'

'Have I been sacked?'

'There isn't much work now.'

'The buses have to run, don't they, even if Arvid's

away?'

Julie closes her eyes as though she can't bear any more of this. 'I'll contact you, Rivers. If your presence is required.'

'The pleasure's all mine,' he says, and leaves without looking back. He isn't aware of any reaction from her.

OSLO, 1938

I

Jack follows the woman, who rushes off. The click-clack echo of her footsteps resounds loudly against the high walls. As he moves closer he can see she has used slides to put up her hair. One lock coils down her smooth neck. Jack wants her to stop. Wants her to turn around. So he makes a lunge, launches himself forward, and taps her on the shoulder. At that moment he opens his eyes.

Awake. He is lying in his own bed beneath the window, which is slightly ajar. He can hear the cart men shouting to each other. The privies in the yards are being emptied. Another cart is taking bread and beer to the corner shop. There is a racket every morning when lorries, horses and carts have to pass one another outside Rødfyllgata 18, where Jack has a shoebox on the first floor.

He gets up and heats a pan of coffee over a gas flame. It is chilly in the little flat, but he has to leave soon and can't be bothered to light the wood burner. It is six o'clock. The five hours of sleep behind him seem like an eternity. He woke up and dreamed, woke up again and continued dreaming. Now he allows himself half an hour. Drinks a cup of black coffee as the pan heats some water for a shave. At half past six he has packed his own camera, a Certo Dolly, in a briefcase.

With the briefcase under his arm he walks across

Grønland to Oslo East Station and then up Karl Johan. His breath is frozen, and he digs his hands deep into his coat pockets. As he rounds the mound between Øvre Slottsgate and Akersgata, the morning sun gleams on the paintwork at the top of the flagpoles along Studenterlunden Park. The benches in front of the pavilion beside the theatre are unoccupied. They are wet. In the nearest rubbish bin he finds an old newspaper. He puts this on the seat and sits down. He puts the camera on his lap, concealed beneath his coat. Afterwards he buries his hands in his pockets again while keeping an eye on the entrance to Hotel Westminster. The swing door rotates now and then. A bellboy runs an errand to the newspaper kiosk. One person enters, carrying a suitcase. A couple of other guests come out, wait until a taxi pulls in. Jack's stomach rumbles, but he stays where he is.

At last he sees a figure dragging one leg emerge through the swing door. The German who was with Amalie in Dovrehallen buttons up his coat and crosses the street, comes into Studenterlunden and passes Jack, who clicks the camera. Then the German takes the path to Stortingsgata. Jack packs away his camera and stands up.

The man goes into Theatercafé. Jack allows him enough time to find a table, then goes in himself.

Vidar is in the cloakroom, and Jack thanks him for the seat the previous night in Dovrehallen. Vidar asks where he went. Jack was gone before they'd had a chance to exchange a single word.

'I was on a job,' Jack says.

Vidar asks if Jack is going to have breakfast because, if so, his coat is free.

Jack shakes his head. 'On a job now, too. The German, that chummy with the game leg who just came in.'

Vidar nods.

'Is he here often?'

'Breakfast. Only for breakfast.'

'Every day.'

Vidar nods.

'Alone?'

'Every day, alone.'

'How long has he been doing this?'

'A week maybe. Five to six days anyway. No more than six.'

'Chatty?'

'Just good morning and thanks. I'd guess he's a rep.'

Vidar beams a broad smile over Jack's shoulder. Jack steps aside. A man with a bowler hat and a camel-hair coat has come in and hands both to Vidar, who takes care of them. While he is doing that he fiddles with another coat hanging further up.

The new customer goes into the restaurant, and Jack walks back to the counter. Vidar shows him what he has found in the coat pocket. It is an ID card with a photo. Amalie's escort is a German police officer. The card was issued by an authority calling itself the 'Geheime Staatspolizei'. His name is under the photo: Werner Krause. Jack and Vidar exchange glances. Jack nods and Vidar replaces the ID.

II

Ludvig Paaske's only child, Edna, is living in Paris for the moment. He doesn't know much more than that, except that she spends her time painting. He doesn't even have her address. Edna will be twenty-nine in

68

a week. He has sent off a parcel, the way he always does. Poste restante.

Life can often tinker with elements of our existence and displace them in such a way that the poor soul trying to navigate their way through can find the world unfamiliar and difficult. Ludvig and Edna have a complicated relationship. Her mother died from Spanish flu when she was nine years old. He himself hovered between life and death for a few difficult weeks in the winter of 1918, but he survived. As did Edna.

Without Margrete, Ludvig was left a single father with a very demanding job, and he needed a housekeeper. Frøken Dybvik was a slim, red-haired woman from a good family in Fredensborg, but she was better with children than she was at housework. Edna and she were inseparable. It was frøken Dybvik who brought out Edna's quirks. At that time they lived in Colletts gate, and the walls of the flat were always covered with Edna's vivid drawings. Frøken Dybvik, however, was a dreamer. Paaske discovered too late that she always took Edna with her to town and her lover's atelier. Here Edna was given a brush and palette while the two adults locked the door to the parlour behind them. When Paaske finally learned about what was going on, she had to resign her post, but Edna retained her passion for art. In addition, she also kept up contact with frøken Dybvik and her circle. When she travelled to Berlin, Edna followed — the day she turned twenty-one. Paaske didn't like this, but his daughter was of age, and he had the money to let her go. Afterwards he regretted his decision, because Edna left a deafening silence behind her. At least she wrote letters at that time. Even before the Nazis won the election in 1933, she wrote in harsh terms about the man who hated everything she loved about the Weimar Republic. This man, who had even been a painter earlier in his life, infected the country with his hatred. The authorities began to regulate art. Modernism, Dadaism and Constructivism were hit hard. Artists who didn't paint the way the Nazis wanted them to were persecuted. They set fire to books by writers who didn't conform to their way of thinking. Being different had become a crime in Germany. The letter from Edna was furious, but Paaske was pleased because he hoped it meant she would be coming home. However, she didn't. Instead she went to Paris.

Now she doesn't write letters anymore, but occasionally she paints a watercolour and glues it to plywood. Then she saws it into small pieces and sends them home to her father. After toiling over the jigsaw puzzle for hours to reproduce the watercolour before it was cut into pieces, Paaske sticks it to cardboard and hangs it on the wall. There are two pictures hanging above the sofa, one on each side of his old national championship boxing diploma. These puzzles are a fine way of keeping in contact with his daughter. Participating in what she sees, with the same concentration and focus on detail. To assemble the picture is to recreate her gaze in his, to share her frame of mind and observation. There is a message in the pictures, and without the time it takes to complete the puzzle, he might not be able to immerse himself deeply enough in them. The last puzzle arrived a week ago. Its motif is the metropolis. Paaske has managed to put together parts of Notre Dame Cathedral and a chunk of the river Seine. A woman very much resembling Margrete, Edna's late mother, is leaning against

70

a fence. There is something on the surface of the water he hasn't been able to identify yet; the sky is immense, the blocks of flats are identical and the pieces many.

On his way out he can't quite let go of the picture; he stares at the table and sees a piece with a dark shade of blue. He picks it up and slots it in. Very pleased with himself, he puts on his coat.

Outside, he looks for a black Chevrolet Master and can't see it.

III

Paaske is in luck; he finds a bench with a view of the relevant house entrance. He sits down with the morning paper. When Bernhard Gruber comes out and sets off towards the city centre, he folds the newspaper and follows. Soon he has a feeling that Gruber has an inkling he is being followed, because now and then he stops in front of a street-level window and stares. Paaske guesses that he is studying his pursuer. Paaske hangs back further and is outmanoeuvred. Gruber turns into Grønlandsleiret, hails a passing taxi and gets in.

Paaske is forced to watch Gruber disappear into the distance. Unsure what to do next, he walks on. And eventually decides to follow up on the events of the first day by investigating the activity on Filipstad quay. So he casts around for a telephone box. As always there is a queue outside — two women. The door opens, a man comes out and the first woman goes in. There is a clink of coins as she puts them down, but she ends up gazing at them with an expression of resignation. Presumably she can't get through, so she picks up the coins and comes out again. The woman standing in front of Paaske says he can go before her.

'I always talk for so long,' she says with a laugh.

Paaske goes in, inserts his coins and asks the switchboard to be put through to his office. Jack answers, and Paaske tells him Gruber has given him the slip.

'There's something about this job that isn't right,' Jack says.

'What do you mean?'

'We can discuss this when you get here.'

'In the meantime,' Paaske says, 'it would be good if you went to Sinsen and took over. I lost him when he hailed a taxi. He may've gone home. Take the Opel. The key's on the left-hand front tyre, under the fender. And Jack, if you see a black Chevrolet Master, either outside my place or in Sinsen, note down the number.'

★ ★ ★

Paaske carries on walking to Filipstad. There are several boats moored, and the quay is heaving with stevedores equipped with carts and lifting straps. The German motor vessel he and Gruber watched docking is still being loaded. The coal crane is in operation. The electric motor with the cab on top glides forward on the gigantic rails. The iron jaws are lowered into the cargo hold behind the foremost mast. The bucket lifts up a black mass, and the crane glides back. Some of the coal dust showers down onto the harbour before the load is dropped into one of the coal wagons queueing on the railway line. Paaske approaches the ship. There are loudspeakers on the deck. Presumably they are broadcasting a radio programme, because the song is interrupted with news — in German. Paaske is standing too far away to catch much. But he does pick up '*Anschluss Österreichs*'. Paaske knows of course that the German authorities have been striving to incorporate Austria into Germany. Whatever is said on the loudspeakers, the news is popular among the German crew. They shout and cheer, but the same news is obviously not so popular with the dock workers. One of the stevedores drops his cart, drags his knuckles on the ground and makes ape-like grunts. One of the ship's officers reacts. There is a scuffle. Men run over to part the combatants.

Paaske uses the opportunity to slip past them and ascends the gangway with long strides. On the deck he stands for a few seconds, looking around, before heading for the ladder leading to the bridge wing. He climbs up, opens a door and peers into what has to be the mess. An officer is talking to a girl cooking by a stove. She is young and attractive, wearing a flowery apron and a kerchief over her hair. The officer speaks German to her, but she isn't very interested and backs away from the man. She stops in front of the portrait of Hitler mounted on the bulkhead between two portholes. She says to the German officer in Norwegian that she thinks Hitler is a poof.

'His moustache looks like a piece of shit he got from sniffing another Nazi's arsehole,' she says.

The officer grins and tells her to speak German because then he would understand her.

Then she forms a gun with her hand and pretends to shoot the Führer and blows on the index finger representing the barrel. It would be hard to find a more offensive insult to a German, Paaske thinks, and admires her courage. The officer doesn't. He loses his

73

temper, grabs her arm and drags her over. The girl reacts by striking him in the face with her free hand. Claws him. The man howls and raises a hand to punch her. Then Paaske steps over the threshold and asks what is going on. The German presses a hand-kerchief against the claw marks on his cheek and forces his way past him and out.

'What happened?' Paaske asks when he is alone with the girl.

She answers by telling Paaske to mind his own business. 'Haven't you got a job to do? I have.'

Then she goes back to the saucepans.

'You haven't signed on, have you?' Paaske says.

'I cook for the men doing the loading.'

What a wildcat. And what an unpleasant atmosphere on this boat.

Paaske goes back on deck. Stands by the railing and looks out. The red flag with the black swastika flutters in the breeze. Things seem to have quietened down on the quay. The loudspeaker on the deck is playing music again. The large crane on the rails glides back towards the ship. The iron jaws are lowered into the hold once again. Then Paaske notices a gang of dock workers with neither carts nor lifting straps and watches them. They are moving towards a man. He looks like the one Bernhard Gruber was talking to by the banana-ripening building. The man is talking to these stevedores. One might expect him to be a foreman, but he isn't. The man isn't wearing overalls or a peaked cap, but a dark coat and walking shoes.

The mess door opens with a bang. Now the girl is carrying a bucket of slops, which she lifts onto the railing. The potato peel and other waste splash into the water, then she places the empty bucket back on the deck. Paaske points to the man and asks her if she knows who it is.

'What's that got to do with you?' she says. 'Why are you so nosy? Who are you, anyway, and what are you doing here? Are you a spy?'

Paaske has no option but to shake his head. He can see there is not much information to be gleaned here, so he climbs down the ladder, past the open hold and down the gangway. On the quay he looks for the man the stevedores were flocking around, but he is nowhere to be seen. Paaske decides to walk to Olav Tryggvasons plass.

Something makes him turn back towards the boat. He sees the girl still on the deck, but now she is talking to stevedores and pointing at Paaske.

IV

Less than half an hour later he gets off the Holmenkollen Metro at Majorstuen Station. As he is walking into the entrance of Majorstuhuset itself he hears the click-clack of heels on the steps up from the street. He turns and catches sight of Vera Gruber.

'Herr Paaske,' she pants. 'I was in the area anyway,' she continues and pats her hair with gloved hands. 'I've just had my hair done and was thinking I should pop by to hear how things were going, and then I saw you.'

Paaske invites her to go up to the office with him.

Standing side by side as they wait for the lift, he glances at her, once again struck by both her beauty and her elegance. Her red hair has been styled into a becoming bob. He is reminded of the housewives he has seen frequenting the block of flats in Båhusveien and thinks she stands out in more ways than one. For example, she goes to the other side of town to have her hair done.

The lift arrives and the attendant opens the doors. Inside they stand in a kind of repressed silence as they are hoisted through the floors. The attendant pulls the scissor gate open. Paaske lets fru Gruber exit first.

'I was wondering if there has been any progress,' she says.

Paaske unlocks the office door. And closes it behind her.

'So far your husband hasn't been in contact with any other women, from what we have established.'

Paaske goes over to the filing cabinet, pulls out the top drawer and flicks through until he finds Vera Gruber's file. A chair scrapes as she takes it from under the table and perches on the edge, as before, without removing her gloves.

'As I said, your husband doesn't appear to be particularly interested in other women.'

'What does he do?'

'He goes for walks along the quays.'

'What on earth does he do there?'

'Talks to people.'

Vera sends him a look of incomprehension.

'From what I can see, he talks to people who have some connection with the work being done there.'

'Who?'

Paaske opens the file and shows her a photograph of the man Gruber was talking to in front of the banana-ripening plant. 'Him, for example.'

Vera squints as she looks at the picture. 'Who is he?'

Paaske opens a desk drawer, takes a magnifying glass and passes it to her.

Vera studies the photograph through the magnifying glass. 'I have no idea who this person is. Why is Bernhard talking to him?'

'You'll have to ask him. For all I know, it could be business, but so far we haven't seen anything to suggest your husband is involved with any other women.'

She places a gloved hand on her ample bosom and closes her eyes. 'Thank you,' she says. 'It's a relief to hear your words.'

When she opens her eyes again she looks around his office, at the empty desk at the other end. 'You don't work alone?'

'I have an assistant.'

'Who's that?'

'Why do you ask?'

Vera Gruber laughs. 'For no other reason than I'd like to know who's working for me.'

'My assistant's name is Rivers.'

'That's an unusual name.'

Paaske cannot comment.

'This Rivers, where is he now?'

'Right now he's keeping an eye on your home in Sinsen.'

'Where does he live?'

'You're asking me where my assistant lives?'

Fru Gruber doesn't answer, just tilts her head and looks back at him with a raised eyebrow.

'Jack lives in Rødfyllgata in Vaterland, but I can't see how that has any bearing on our work.'

'Of course not,' Vera Gruber laughs. Her beautiful face becomes even more alluring. 'It's neither here nor there. It's just me bumbling. Please forgive me.' She looks down at the photograph again. 'So Bernhard meets this man on the quayside. Does he meet any others?'

Paaske answers with a question. 'Does he drive a car, your husband?'

'Bernhard doesn't like driving. I'm usually the driver.'

'I was wondering if he occasionally drives a black Chevrolet.'

She shakes her head.

'Anyone you know drive a Chevrolet?'

'No. How so?'

'I was just wondering,' Paaske says.

Fru Gruber is still studying the picture with the magnifying glass. 'Who is this man?'

'I haven't managed to identify him by name, but we will.'

'Don't worry,' she says, putting down the magnifying glass and the picture. 'I'm reassured. It's a relief to know that Bernhard is still the man I married.' She rummages in her bag for some money. 'It was probably stupid of me to engage someone to spy on him. How much do I owe you?'

'You wish to conclude the commission?'

'Now you've told me what the situation is, I feel stupid and base getting someone to sneak around after him.'

'Of course,' Paaske says, taking a pencil and totting up the hours.

A slim hand in a white glove lays some banknotes on the desk.

'Is this enough?'

'More than enough, fru Gruber.'

She collects the photos. 'May I keep these?'

'Naturally, but as I said before, if you and your husband are to be reconciled without suspicion and accusations, I'm not sure you should tell him you hired a private investigator to follow him.'

'You're absolutely right.'

'Vera,' Paaske says, standing up as the elegant lady is about to leave. He passes her a receipt for the fee he has received and concludes their business.

V

Jack sits for ages in Paaske's Opel P4, waiting outside the house entrance in Båhusveien. Bernhard Gruber hasn't appeared, and Jack is thinking to himself that this surveillance is a waste of time. Nevertheless, he waits a little longer without anything happening. In the end he looks at his watch. Paaske usually eats at this time.

Jack decides to talk turkey with his boss, starts the car and moves off. Heading towards Majorstuen. There, he parks in Bogstadveien, outside Den Gamle Major restaurant, and goes in. The tables are covered with white cloths. A drum kit and a couple of music stands stand in lone majesty on the small stage. Paaske hasn't arrived yet. Jack orders a beer, and when his boss comes in shortly afterwards, he motions to the waiter for another.

'I think, as I said, we have to talk openly about this job,' Jack says.

'No need,' Paaske says. 'Fru Gruber came by. We've finished.'

'Today?'

Paaske nods with a smile playing on his lips. 'The fact is we've never earned so much money so fast.'

He laughs heartily, but Jack can't join in.

'What is it?'

'Why did she want us to stop?'

'I don't know.'

'What does your gut instinct tell you?'

Paaske pauses to think. 'I think she came to her senses and realised her husband wasn't unfaithful after all.'

Jack shakes his head condescendingly.

'What is it?'

'An old flatfoot like you having the wool pulled over your eyes.'

Paaske doesn't understand what he means.

'I saw her last night,' Jack says. 'She was with a German I didn't recognise at Dovrehallen.'

'Fru Gruber?'

Jack nods. The waiter comes and places Paaske's tankard on the table.

'Bit odd, isn't it? She comes to you and complains that her old man is having affairs, then she goes dancing with someone else.'

'What was he like?'

'In his thirties. Tall, red hair. With a game leg.'

Jack places a roll of film on the table and pushes it towards Paaske. 'I went to the trouble of preserving his picture for posterity.'

Paaske doesn't take the roll. Instead he starts to fill his pipe.

'You don't want it?'

'The job's over, Jack.'

'He's a policeman.'

'How can you know that?'

'Vidar at Theatercafé.'

'A German policeman holidaying in Norway,' Paaske says. 'Surely he's allowed to do that?'

'One who goes to dances with our client, who lies

about who she is?'

Paaske doesn't answer.

'I asked her to dance.'

'Vera Gruber?'

'The lady's name is not Vera Gruber. I knew her once. Her name's Amalie. I haven't seen her for a few years, admittedly, and since then she's climbed out of poverty and scaled new heights, but it was her alright — I had my suspicions confirmed.'

Paaske keeps his own counsel and lights his pipe while they look at each other in silence.

'That doesn't concern us,' Paaske says, breaking the silence. 'This woman had a hidden agenda, just like most of the people who give us commissions. Now she's paid us, and handsomely. I assume we'll never see her or Bernhard Gruber again. We can advertise and we'll get new jobs.'

'When she came to you with this job, did you notice if she was wearing a wedding ring?'

'As you say, I'm an old flatfoot. Of course she was wearing a ring.'

'She wasn't yesterday.'

Again Paaske is silent.

'This lady's pulled a fast one on you,' Jack says. 'We've been used for some skulduggery or other. We've *allowed* ourselves to be used.'

Paaske is still silent.

'There is an explanation as to why,' Jack continues. 'I think the answer is to be found in the harbour. The only point of interest about this Gruber is that he's preoccupied by whatever's going on in the harbour. I fancy doing some digging there.'

Paaske shakes his head. 'You see this woman in town, follow her and ask her to dance. Now the job's over, you want to continue investigating. What is this, Jack?'

'It's my past.'

'What about it?'

'Have you never had someone throw your past in your face?'

'I have no past to be ashamed of.'

'This isn't something I'm ashamed of. I just want to know why this lady in particular has reappeared in my life and why it's tied to someone's illegal activities.'

'You don't know if Gruber is doing anything illegal.'

'It's as plain as day.'

Paaske raises his glass, drinks and smacks his lips. 'How long have we been working together now?'

'Soon be a year.'

Paaske nods. 'We want to continue working together, don't we?

Don't you agree?'

It is Jack's turn to nod now.

'The first commandment of this game is to keep your distance.

You mustn't get involved with clients.'

'I don't, but this case is special. The lady calling herself Vera Gruber is a girl who once lived in Ener-haugen and her name's Amalie Iversen. We carry out surveillance on Gruber, her so-called husband, who has some mysterious intentions in the harbour and behaves like a man with plenty to hide. It's obvious he's frightened of being spied on. So he immediately gives us the slip. When he spots us he behaves as if he has the devil himself on his tail. Then I confront his alleged wife with the truth about who she is, and the first thing she does is to come to you and bring the job to a close. We've been taken for a ride. You know we have, if you think about it.'

'Forget it, Jack. The job's done and filed, and we have our money.'

'She doesn't live there, in Sinsen.'

'No?'

'We hung around there for hours. The only women I saw there were housewives knitting and darning stockings. Amalie dresses like a film star. She drives around in a roadster, an Adler, which was parked outside here when she booked us. I saw her drive away in it. Have you seen anything like that car parked in Sinsen?'

Paaske doesn't answer.

Jack stretches out a hand to take the roll of film, but Paaske snatches it and puts it in his pocket.

Jack smiles weakly. 'The man I photographed coming out of the taxi in Carl Berners plass, you say he knows stevedores in Filipstad. I went to sea for some years. I know people. There are lots of stevedores who were at sea. I can sniff around, talk to them.'

Paaske releases a heavy sigh and leans across the table. 'This lady gave me a commission. I've done it. If you're unhappy about this case, it's up to me to make you happy.'

The waiter comes with menus. Jack holds up his hands defensively. 'I'm not hungry.'

'I'll have the usual,' Paaske says, handing back the menu to the man, who bows cursorily and departs.

'He knows what I want,' Paaske says. 'Medium,' he shouts after the man who makes the effort to bow cursorily once again before disappearing into the kitchen.

'What did you say about the car?'

'Which car?'

'The Chevrolet. You asked me to look for it.'

'Have you seen it?'

'No.'

'It was probably nothing.'

'Why did you ask me to look out for it?'

Paaske inhales. 'Forget it. The job's over.'

'Has the car got anything to do with Gruber?'

'I thought it was following me when I left here.' Paaske looks down. Then up again and meets Jack's eyes. 'What is it?'

'Chevrolet Master. Black. The police do surveillance work in cars like that.'

Paaske cuts a sceptical grimace.

'You've been thinking the same yourself,' Jack says. 'This job isn't over. You know it isn't.'

Paaske takes another deep breath, but he doesn't get as far as saying what is on his mind.

'They're having a party at Folkets Hus,' Jack says. 'The Stevedores' Union is inviting family and friends. You can go in and listen to what they're talking about and do some digging on the guy who met Gruber.'

'Or ask what the German boat being loaded in Filipstad is up to,' Paaske says. 'I'll take care of this one. Then I'll tell you afterwards what I find out. Are you happy with that?'

KRISTIANIA, MAY 1924

I

There is a letter in the post box, without a sender's name on the envelope. Jack tears it open. The letter is from Arvid Bjerke. Presumably the engineer doesn't know what his wife has decided to do, as he asks Jack to go up to a cabin. Bjerke writes that it is near Holmsbu. He has attached a map. If Jack doesn't have a car, he is welcome to take the boat moored at the quay in Holtekilen.

At the crack of dawn the following day Jack catches the train to Høvik and strolls from the station across Drammensveien, through the forest down to Villa Strand. He has no idea whether Julie is at home, and, what is more, he has no wish to know. He walks straight past the house, continues onto the quay and jumps aboard the double-ender. He lifts the lid above the motor. It is a simple hot-bulb motor. He unscrews the lid on the tank and checks the petrol. It is full. The blowlamp is in the space under the aft thwart. With it he heats the motor, which starts in neutral without a problem. Afterwards he crawls forward in the bow and unties the mooring rope. Drags the anchor on board and, as the boat reverses out, he casts a last glance over at the house.

Julie has come out onto the steps wearing a white dress, white stockings and an equally white hat. She is a perfect match for the house, Jack thinks. Or perhaps the house is a perfect match for her. Jack pushes the tiller as far as it can go to turn the boat slowly. When he raises his hand to wave, she is as motionless as before.

Jack speeds up and enjoys the feeling of standing aft in a motor boat on the fjord. The lake is as calm as a pond. The two-stroke motor chugs away and the sun burns down on his forehead. On land, some children are jumping between the rocks. One of them waves and he raises his arm in greeting. One day, when he has enough money, he will buy a boat, he thinks. Then he will fish for his own food from a boat of this size, light a fire on the shore, boil coffee over it and sleep in the boat — or under canvas on land.

Or if he had even more money, he could buy one of the fast, low-slung speedboats. Then he could go to Torbjørnskjær and beyond, load up with liquor cans and have enough power to outrun the customs boats on the way back. And put by enough money to do something he still hasn't dreamed about.

Jack passes Drøbak with all the bathers. An artist is standing in front of an easel on a lawn, and Jack scans the shore. Catches himself looking for a woman with short, blonde hair and blood-red lips, but there are many blonde heads among the rocks. On top of that, it is several days since he dropped off the party of three at the seaside hotel.

Jack kicks off his shoes and rolls up his trouser legs. Sitting on the rear thwart with his feet on the middle one, he sees a long, slim speedboat he assumes belongs to smugglers. The noise attests to a powerful engine. There is a man sitting at the helm, a guy in a blue blazer, white trousers and dark glasses. The man cruises past without paying any attention to the double-ender chugging towards it. Jack casts a long stare at the wake from the speedboat, thinking this is exactly the kind of boat he would buy if he had enough money.

After passing Filtvet and Tofte, he reaches Drammensfjord by Rødtangen and goes on to Holmsbu. When the small cabin comes into sight, he turns starboard, stops the motor and moves forward to the bow, standing with the rope in his hand as the boat glides the last few metres to an anchorage pole set in a rock. He clambers ashore and ties the rope with a half hitch. Jumps back into the boat, throws the anchor into the water, makes sure the line is taut, then steps onto the rock and walks barefoot to the brown cabin by the water. He knocks lightly on the door, opens it and goes in without waiting for an answer.

There is a stale smell of sleep and frolics inside. Amalie is sitting on a chair in just her petticoat, filing her nails. The straps of the petticoat are thin and it is clear that is all she has on. She has wound her hair into two long plaits and she seems neither embarrassed nor surprised to see him. They clock each other without saying a word.

Amalie gets up and goes into what has to be a bedroom and closes the door behind her. Jack stands looking at the overflowing ashtrays and empty bottles between the chair and the sofa. Shortly afterwards she comes out again. She has loosened her plaits and put on the dress she was wearing when the police raided the house a week ago. With her back to Jack, she asks him to pull up the zip. He does so. Roughly.

'Ow,' she says, spinning around angrily.

'Where's Arvid?' he says.

'In the loo,' she says, pointing to the window.

The loo is a little shed with a red heart on the door.

Jack taps a cigarette from a packet of Teddy lying on the bench. Lights up. She takes a cigarette from the pack too and puts it between her lips. Comes very close and uses the glow of his cigarette to light hers. Looks him in the eye as she puffs her cigarette into life. Puts it down on the edge of an ashtray and rolls a stocking up her leg. Lifts her dress to attach it to her suspenders.

Jack stands watching her with the cigarette in the corner of his mouth. They exchange glances as she drops her dress and rolls up the other stocking.

The toilet door bangs. Jack turns to the window. Bjerke is buttoning up his trousers. A powerfully built man in patent leather shoes, black trousers with creases, a stained singlet and braces. The engineer is beginning to thin on top and fill out in the middle.

'Why are you doing this?'

Amalie doesn't answer.

'What's the point?'

'Of what?' she says, taking her time to attach the other stocking.

'He's married. His wife's young, stylish, attractive and rich. From a cultivated family. Do you think he's going to divorce her for you?'

Amalie drops her dress. 'You can fetch some wood,' she says. 'I'll fry us some eggs.'

At that moment the door opens. Bjerke comes in with an armful of wood. His face splits into a broad smile at their reunion. 'Jack, my trusty friend,' he says, trapping the log box with his foot and dropping the wood in it.

'You'll soon be forty,' Jack says. 'Amalie's eighteen.'

'Don't say anything to Julie.'

'Julie already knows,' Jack says, meeting Amalie's

eyes as she kneels in front of the stove and lights the fire.

Jack sits down by the little dining table. They both look at him.

'How are things, Jack? What happened?'

'Don't you read papers?'

'They know nothing about me, yet all they write about is me. What I want to know is what happened.. I want to know what happened. What did the police do?'

'What do you think? I was arrested and all the goods were confiscated. I was driven to Møllegata 19, but they released me the same day. Julie has taken charge of the business and the buses run as usual. The first thing she did after you scarpered was give me the boot. Apart from that, everyone's waiting for you to come out of your hiding place. That's what the police are waiting for. Your wife's waiting. The journalists, too. Normal people talk about nothing else but how the smuggler gang was busted. Who owns this cabin, by the way?'

'A pal. The police let you go the same day, did they?'

Jack flashes a weak smile. Typical Arvid Bjerke, listening only to what he wants to hear. 'I'm here,' Jack says. 'Paaske let me go because he wants to summon me as a witness when they bring you before the judge. Paaske says I'm the lead in his gun. He's going to use me to trap you. I'll be the case's star witness.'

Bjerke's expression hardens. 'Have you blabbed?'

Jack shakes his head. 'I haven't said a word about anything, but Paaske says I'll have to stand as a witness. If I hold my tongue or lie in court, they'll bang me up.'

'Court? Don't they realise I've gone underground?'

'You have a business, you have a wife and you have

a house. Paaske's just waiting for you to show up.'

Jack walks to the door, opens it and gazes out at the fjord and the afternoon sun playing between the trees.

'What are you going to say to the court if we get that far?'

Jack bends down and stubs the cigarette out on the flagstone, goes back in and puts the dog-end into one of the already full ashtrays. 'I'm not going to say anything, but Paaske wants me to stand in the witness box before a judge and reckons I'll be forced to reveal why I was in the house, where I'd come from and what I know about all the goods that were confiscated. He says he can prove that there were more people in the house than me when they broke in. You live there. Your gold watch was on the table, and your jacket was hanging from the back of a chair. Paaske wants me to spill the beans. You're the man who buys the booze and sells it on. The police have a lot on you and they've been working for quite a while to nab you. Paaske was in Minnesund when I lost the police. The same lorry that went over the railway bridge was in your garden. In his opinion, I'm the only person who could have driven the lorry, and he wants to use me as a battering ram in court. If I refuse to answer the judge's questions I'll be convicted. I'll have to do time.'

'Shit,' Bjerke says angrily. 'Why didn't you make a run for it, Jack?'

'I did try, but the queue outside the cellar trapdoor was too long. When they caught me, I lay across the door so that they couldn't run after you two. I gave you a head start so that you can sit here on your fat arse instead of in a cell in Møllegata 19.'

Bjerke makes no comment.

Amalie has been quietly listening to the conversa-

90

tion. Now she hides her hair under a kerchief, cracks some eggs into a frying pan and kneels down to add more wood to the fire. The room is warm and warmer still where she is. The fly strip over the stove is black with insects. The eggs in the pan are beginning to simmer. Amalie sets the table while Bjerke is still deep in thought.

Jack takes a ladle and fills a saucepan with water from the bucket on the bench. Finds a packet of ground coffee in the cupboard and pours some into the pan.

The silence persists.

Jack looks at Amalie, who is standing with her arms folded looking at Bjerke. The coffee rumbles as it boils and Jack removes it from the most intense heat.

Bjerke is still reflective.

Amalie and Jack sit down to eat.

'How did you get away?' Jack asks.

'By train,' Amalie says with a grin. 'We watched the cops running between the trees and calling. Not one of them thought to walk up to the platform before the train came.'

'Man and wife on a day out?'

'Father and daughter, weren't we, Pappa?' She glances at Bjerke with the same sly smile on her face.

Bjerke pours coffee from the pan into a cup, then from the cup into a saucer and slurps it down.

Amalie tells him to stop. 'Surely you can drink from a cup like a normal person, can't you.'

'Pappa does what he likes,' Bjerke says brusquely.

Amalie rolls her eyes in Jack's direction, who now feels like a spectator to something he doesn't quite understand.

Bjerke lowers both cup and saucer and says: 'I'm

91

going to hand myself in.'

'Hand yourself in? We were going to travel.'

Bjerke slurps down more coffee. Looks out of the window, taking no notice of her.

'You promised.' Bjerke doesn't answer.

Now she starts sobbing like a resentful little girl. 'Pappa.'

'Another time.'

Amalie's back straightens. She is furious, but silent. Then she gets up and leaves the table, pours water from the bucket into a large pan. Places it on the stove and adds more wood. 'If you hand yourself in, what am I going to do? Your wife hates me. She'll give me the sack. I know she will.'

'We can work out something together,' Jack says. 'Julie's already booted me out.'

II

When Jack and Bjerke are set to go down to the boat, Jack ends up walking ahead and stepping into the boat alone as the other two stand at the door snapping at each other. Bjerke tells her she has to stay and clean up, but Amalie refuses to slip back voluntarily into her role as maid. She slams the door in his face. Bjerke stares at the door, perplexed for a few seconds, then turns, lumbers down to the boat, casts off and jumps on board. As the boat drifts he stares at the cabin, still in the slightly cowed pose of a wounded rooster. Finally, he turns and asks Jack why he hasn't started the motor.

'I've been given the boot,' Jack says, which is the truth. 'If you don't want guests on the trip, you'd better put me ashore.'

Bjerke eyes him inscrutably, but at length lifts the lid and starts up the motor with the blow-torch.

Soon the regular chug of the two-stroke engine is all that is heard. It is evening and the landscape has turned dark, with no sharp contours. Jack wonders if he should say what he feels like saying and glances over at Bjerke, who seems taciturn and lost in thought as he sits holding the tiller.

'Amalie's right,' Jack says at last. 'Nothing's changed. Why do you suddenly want to hand yourself in?'

'That bloody Paaske. He thinks he can storm my house and get away with it.'

'Have you forgotten what you had on the lawn? The biggest haul that has been made in the whole of the prohibition era — on your property.'

'That shit cannot claim that I had anything to do with it.'

Jack doesn't answer. 'There's one thing I haven't told you.'

'Tell me then.'

Jack braces himself. 'I think it was Julie who told Paaske that your Ford lorry would be going past Minnesund, loaded with booze.'

Bjerke falls silent.

'They were waiting for me. They knew about the lorry. They'd blocked off half of the road. When they saw me coming, they blocked off the other half.'

'You escaped,' Bjerke says eventually. 'If it was Julie who put the bastard on my trail, why do *you* have to testify? Why not Julie?'

'For all I know, she will have to appear in the witness box as well.'

It is so dark that Jack can't interpret what is going on in Bjerke's face.

'Paaske knew that Julie was away when they arrived and arrested me. He said she was with her parents in Hadeland. How could he know that?'

'Why would she do such a thing to me?'

'Perhaps because you sleep with her maid.'

Bjerke spits over the side. 'Fuck her,' he mumbles in a low voice, clenching his fists. 'Fuck the lot of you.'

Jack doesn't see any point arguing with him and keeps quiet. Julie's mother might also have tipped off the police, he thinks, or Julie's father. At any rate, someone wanted them to be caught. Someone didn't approve of their activities.

'You're barking up the wrong tree,' Bjerke says, as though he has been reading Jack's mind. 'No one in Julie's family would do anything like this to me.'

There is no point discussing this. Jack is sick of both Arvid Bjerke and his wife. One left him in the lurch to avoid being arrested. The other sacked him as thanks for his sacrifice.

'I think Julie's right that you and I shouldn't have so much contact in the future,' the man at the helm says.

Jack doesn't answer. Actually, he has always known what a selfish bastard Arvid Bjerke can be. So Jack has no job, but he needs one. He won't bother to ask the engineer.

Land towers up in front of them. It must be the island of Håøya. In Drøbak lights shine in windows. The wind has picked up and Jack buttons up his jacket, not that it helps much against the cold.

III

The next morning Jack boards the train to Eidsvoll. The journey is about seventy kilometres and takes a

94

couple of hours. In second class he finds a free bench and falls asleep quickly. His body knows this journey, knows the bends and the stops. When he wakes up, the train has stopped in Bøn station. Jack yawns and looks out at the shop that didn't receive its delivery of hooch when he had to flee from the police. A pair of boots and a tray of corn-cob pipes can be made out behind the display window. That makes him think about the cans he and Johan hid under spruce branches near Strandlykkja. He ought to rent a car and pick them up, he reflects. The cash would be handy now that he no longer has a job.

In Eidsvoll he gets off, follows the throng to the paddle steamer and goes on board. He sits down on a bench along the railing on the foredeck. It is a lovely day, and although there is a light wind, he is not cold. When PS Skibladner passes under the railway bridge in Minnesund he leans back and looks up at the rails, wondering if he and Johan would have survived if the lorry had fallen off. Probably not. They would have been knocked unconscious when the vehicle hit the surface of the lake. The water would have forced the doors in, and the current is wicked in this strait. The paddle steamer, which is flat-bottomed and barely has a keel, is being harassed by the current and moving forward in a crab-like way. Johan and he would have drowned in the lorry and might never have been found.

Now he is standing by the railing and trying to make out the road on the eastern side where he and Johan had been driving. Trees and rocky ridges obstruct his view. Soon they will be passing Fagerneset on the western side and approaching the first stop. A lot of passengers stand waiting as the steamer docks at the quay. Jack gets off and nods to the old boys in the horse-drawn carts queueing outside the mill. Jack knows most of them, but can't see any of them going west. In other words, he will have to walk, so he strides out alongside the river. He considers dropping by Hans's shop, but gives it a miss, as actually he isn't interested in hearing how things went when the police were informed. Instead, he trudges past and up over the mountain ridge.

It is a tough walk, and at first he is warm, then sweaty. Water gurgles as he jumps from tuft to tuft in a marsh along the path. Soon he can hear the noise of a waterfall. Shortly afterwards he reaches the top of Kastet and crosses the bridge over the river. A stooped figure is sitting on a flat rock between the two steepest slopes.

Alf is sleeping with his rucksack between his legs. Jack taps him on the shoulder and the old man gives such a start that his rucksack clinks. Even though Alf has so much chewing tobacco in his mouth that slime is running down his chin, Jack sits next to him and offers him a cigarette, out of politeness.

'You know, Jack,' Alf says, 'he who sits on a rock is happy twice, as they say. Once to sit down and once to get up.'

He spits out tobacco and takes a gulp from a bottle he produces from his rucksack. Jack raises a defensive palm when Alf offers him a swig.

'How much does Hans charge per litre?' Jack asks.
'Five kroner.'

Jack has to shake his head, impressed. What a bloodsucker, he thinks. He buys a can of spirits for five kroner and sells it for fifty.

'This stuff is better than what I make myself,' Alf

says. 'It's festival quality.'

'Every day is a festival,' Jack says.

Alf nods and offers him the bottle again.

Jack declines politely and gets ready to move on.

'Sobriety's a fine thing,' Alf says, his arm raised in a farewell wave.

Jack carries on. He frightens a herd of sheep and stands still until they have calmed down and continue grazing. Then he tears himself away and follows upward the summer path along the river. By the rock-fill dam he cuts north, and when the clearing appears between the trees, at first he just stops and stares. It gives you such peace to see your homestead. There is a kind of secure permanence about the fence rail, the grassy bank and the little log cottage. It is a peace he allows himself to wallow in.

Strangely enough, his father settled down here after being at sea for more than twenty years. The seaman found love and harmony deep in the forest. With logs from it he built a small cowshed, a smithy and a hay barn. Using an axe, one night, he managed to chop a finger from his left hand. Jack has always known his father as a man with nine fingers. Now that Jack can feel such peace coursing through his body, he doubts it will be enough to keep him here in this place. Should he ever succeed in finding love, he doubts it will spread its roots here.

With that he strides across the clearing and goes to find his mother. He meets her as she is coming out of the shed, where she has been milking the cows. With a smile she comes to a halt and puts down the bucket.

'Have you come to repair the leaking roof?'

'Shouldn't be a problem,' he answers. 'Anyway, I was thinking of making a start with the winter wood.'

Jack nods towards the pile of birch logs at the top of the hill, the ones he had chopped the last time he was here.

He hands her the fee he received for his last trip for Bjerke and carries her milk bucket. They walk slowly towards the house. His mother struggles to breathe. She wheezes as she breathes in. Jack slows down and looks at her with new eyes. Realising that her health has gone downhill. Her back is more bent, her hands are thinner. Now he regrets not stopping off at Hans's shop and buying something for her.

'Getting old is a curse,' she says with an apologetic smile.

'Think I should give it a miss, do you?'

'Will you stay a few days this time?' she asks, squeezing his hand.

Jack is quiet. He doesn't like to disappoint her. Instead of answering he opens the door for her and they go in.

OSLO, 1938

I

The asylum resembles a wealthy estate. Expansive red-brick buildings with no plaster and roofs covered with grey slate stand on either side of a clock tower with a verdigris copper dome, which towers above the mighty treetops framing the whole site. Between the road and the main residence there is a field that is almost free of snow. Another field must be pasture land, where yellow tufts have a touch of green in them. The asylum appears to run a farm.

At first, Jack watches the taxi drive off. When he turns to the main entrance, he sees a woman running to hide. He catches only a glimpse of a skirt and a head concealed by a kerchief before she disappears around the corner. He is about to go and ask the way when a man dressed in a white coat and dark trousers walks over with bouncing strides.

'Can I help you?'

'I'm looking for someone who knows the patients here.'

'Ødegård,' the man says, proffering a hand. 'I'm in charge of the hospital. I should be able to help you.'

Jack tells him he has been at sea for the last six years and would like to meet an old friend he thinks might be here.

Ødegård nods as Jack is speaking. The hospital director knows all about Johan Iversen. In fact, he was speaking to him only an hour ago.

They walk down a gravel path to a huge cowshed. Ødegård explains that many patients work with animals and on the gardens. They also have a smithy and a carpentry workshop.

'The farm is one large enterprise,' Ødegård says. 'We produce milk, meat, vegetables, summer flowers for ourselves and people living around us. We have our own nursery.'

'Johan joins in with all this?'

'He's a bit hit and miss. Johan belongs to the group of passive patients, but I'm afraid to say that occasionally he has to be moved into another department, if he becomes excited.'

Jack is both surprised and impressed that the top boss of such a large set-up as this can afford the time to help find a patient, but Ødegård is a nice man. The head consultant has an alert, friendly expression beneath luxurious hair, which billows back across his crown.

'So you were at sea?' Ødegård repeats.

'I was in the Caribbean recently.'

'My uncle was a seaman. I always dreamed of going to sea when I was a young boy.'

The smell of the cowshed hits them as Ødegård opens the door. Immediately there is an inferno of mooing. There are long lines of animals chained on both sides of the food trough. They pull at the chains and screech. One cow lifts its tail and expels a thick, dark-yellow stream of piss into the slurry channels. The noise in here is unbearable. Ødegård grins as Jack holds his ears.

'It's feeding time for the cows soon,' he shouts. 'They think we're going to feed them.'

They scan the shed, but there is no one inside, so

they back out again.

Jack says, and it is the truth, that he is surprised and impressed that this is a hospital — such a large expanse of land with animals and corn and vegetables.

Ødegård tells him that country life is the best medicine for anyone suffering from mental illness.

'How ill is Johan actually?'

Ødegård says that unfortunately he has been very ill. 'Johan hears voices, and then he can be anything from desperate to angry and uncontrollable. When Johan has such bouts he has to be transferred to Department E. They have to strap him down so that he doesn't hurt anyone else or himself, but generally he quietens down quickly. Now he's better and can work outside. Johan always makes good progress when his sister's in Norway.'

They are walking now towards a whitewashed greenhouse.

'I remember Amalie,' Jack says. 'Doesn't she live in Norway anymore?'

'His sister's married and lives in Germany,' Ødegård says. 'Whenever she comes to Norway she calls in here, and that's good for Johan. It's just a shame she isn't here more often.'

Ødegård opens the greenhouse door and they walk in.

The air inside is fresh, and the windows in the roof are open. Ødegård has stopped and nods to a stooped figure further in. Ødegård whispers: 'That's him. I'll leave you two alone.'

After Ødegård turns and leaves, Jack walks between the rows of tables covered with small potted plants. Johan has changed. His facial expression seems more slow-witted, and Jack catches himself wondering why, until he realises that Johan has no teeth and is chewing his gums the way that people with no teeth do. His lower lip juts out and reaches up to his nostrils. In addition, he has lost more hair. His monk's tonsure is complete. He has heavy shoulders and shuffles along, his back bent, carrying a tray of seedlings to a table. His clothes are as they always were: blue cotton jacket over a burlap shirt and blue cotton trousers.

'Johan,' Jack says.

Johan stops and raises his head. Chewing his gums, as his irises flicker to and fro beneath half-lowered eyelids. He shows no signs of recognition. Jack clears his throat and sings in a low voice:

'*Whenever*
an accordion plays, so fast or so slow,
every girl's heart burns with a glow,
and to a dance she won't say no ...'

Johan stamps the beat and then bares his gums in a toothless grin. 'I kn-know you. You're J-Jack.'

Jack takes a pack from his pocket and offers him a Blue Master. 'Do you remember, Johan, when you slept on the back of the lorry that night?'

Johan holds the cigarette between his thumb and forefinger. The tips of his fingers are yellow, and the nails long and dirty. Jack flicks his lighter and Johan puffs his cigarette into life over the flame.

'What are you doing now in the garden?'

Johan explains that he is pricking out beetroot and celery plants. They will be sold on vegetable stalls in the market square this autumn.

'How are you, Johan? Do you live here full-time now?'

Johan nods. He is fine. Lives in Gaustad. He is happy here.

'Did Amalie get married?'

Johan doesn't answer.

'Do you visit her sometimes?'

Johan nods.

'So you know where she lives?'

Johan nods again.

'Are you going to tell me where she lives?'

'Jack,' Johan says, concentrating. 'Let's sing a bit more.'

'Perhaps you and I should go on a trip again, Johan? Rent a lorry and sing, and when we stop, light a fire and make coffee over it and fry fish we've caught in the river?'

'I wish we could do that.'

'Can't you ask the doctor for permission? I could come and pick you up, like in the old days.'

Johan does a little jig, claps his hands and turns a pirouette, his gums bared in another toothless smile.

Jack has to smile back. 'You can say this to Amalie when she comes next time,' Jack says. 'Do you remember the address? The street she lives in?'

Johan just looks at him, still smiling.

They smoke in silence.

Then the door opens and a small but strong, red-haired man wearing a blue coat pokes his head in. 'Are you loafing about, Johan? Get down to some work.'

'Johan has a visitor,' Jack says. 'I've cleared this with Ødegård.'

The gardening foreman appears to be miffed by this information. 'No one's allowed to bunk off work. You can come during visiting hours like everyone else.'

The man slams the door behind him.

'I'll leave you to your work, Johan,' Jack says. 'It was nice to see you again.'

Johan just stares at him, disappointed.

'Say hi to Amalie from me.'

Johan grabs his arm. 'Don't go.' Johan's fingers are long and bony with long nails, and his grip is firm. 'Don't go!'

'Let go, Johan.'

Johan doesn't.

Jack tries to wriggle free, but his arm is held tight. Like in an eagle's claw, Jack thinks, and uses his other hand to detach each finger individually until his arm is free. 'You have to work, Johan.'

'Don't go!'

Johan's knuckles whiten as he holds the edge of the table. His fingers claw at the cloth and his shoulders slump. It is more like a growl than a shout. His voice is desperate. There is a crash as the table falls and the trays of seedlings tumble to the ground. Johan stamps on the pots and smashes his fists into the greenhouse walls. The glass splinters and blood runs from his knuckles.

Through the hole in the whitewashed glass Jack can see the shadow of a figure. It is the muscular foreman returning. Jack doesn't wait to see what happens; he backs towards the door at the other end of the greenhouse and leaves. Carries on towards the main entrance at a faster rate, cursing himself for not asking Ødegård about Amalie's new surname and address. Then he is struck with horror by what he might have set in motion. He turns, walks back a few steps, but he can't see what is happening through the whitewashed windows. He can only hear Johan's howls increasing in volume.

104

'I can't do anything about this,' he tells himself, but still he hesitates. Another man runs over to the greenhouse. This one is wearing a white coat. He disappears through the door and soon all the cries are silenced. All is quiet. Eerily quiet.

II

Paaske studies the latest photographs hanging from the drying line. Touches them lightly. They are almost dry, so he unpegs them. The man going through the swing door of Hotel Westminster is tall and thin. His face is narrow and he has almost no chin. The profile reminds Paaske of a gallinaceous bird, a pheasant.

Paaske dislikes what he is doing now, dislikes going back on a decision and dislikes carrying on with a job that has been terminated. Furthermore, he feels unsure about Jack. When he took him on in the business a year ago, it was mostly because they knew and respected each other. Jack had gone off the rails, but he has behaved. Besides, he has always been a decent, resourceful person. Despite this, Paaske is struggling now to accept Jack's contention that fru Gruber is a fraud. But why? The answer is obvious. If she is a fraud, all his experience as a policeman must have let him down when she came to his office and gave him the commission. The question is whether Jack is lying. If so, it would be serious, a betrayal. The next question is: why would Jack lie about his past with this woman? Is this his old criminal past catching up with him?

Paaske could go down to the hotel and confront the German face to face, but such an initiative would embarrass the woman, and himself in particular.

Paaske decides that his best option is to continue investigations in a more discreet way — even if he is uncomfortable with the idea of doing it. Nevertheless, it has to be done, he reflects, if for no other reason than to dispel the doubts he now feels about his assistant.

★ ★ ★

The Stevedores' Union has a meeting at Folkets Hus in Nytorvet. Paaske passes the fire station in Youngs gate and joins the crowd going in. Songbooks are handed out at the entrance. The hall is almost full and still people are coming. Both men and women are in attendance. Workers with partners, wives and children pack the place. The men have coarse hands and weather-bitten faces, workers who today have donned their best suit and a white shirt. The red flags hang down over the rostrum. The union flag is attached to the wall behind. *Solidarity is our Strength* is the motto. Most people know one another, greet others with a raised hand and chat in small groups. Small children run, zigzagging through the adults, and laugh when one of them collides with another. Curious gazes follow Paaske, quite probably because he is new and unknown, but people are polite and he assumes most imagine he is related to a member of the union.

A man ascends the podium and waves the songbook. With that the audience breaks into song. Paaske joins in. 'Forward, Comrades' has a catchy, rhythmical melody. Paaske likes to sing, and now it is very much like singing in a choir.

The audience claps when the song is over. The chairman on the rostrum introduces the evening's speaker: Martin Hjelmen. To deafening applause, a smiling, athletic man steps up. Hjelmen is clearly a workman, in his early thirties, with short, blond hair parted at the side above a high forehead. His eyes are deep set and he has a determined jaw.

'Comrades,' Hjelmen says, pausing dramatically and scanning the auditorium, 'a year ago Justice Minister Trygve Lie enshrined a ban in law. From that moment on we've been forbidden from fighting for the Spanish Republic. The bourgeoisie decided that fighting for the Red Internationale was a criminal act.'

Hjelmen clearly comes from Vestland. His accent is melodious with a rolled 'r'. Paaske looks around him. The audience's attention is focused on the rostrum, and people are quiet and attentive.

'But the government cannot forbid solidarity,' Hjelmen continues, 'just as they cannot forbid charity. There was no ban on fighting for a good cause two years ago when the generals started their treachery and had the army open fire on their own com-patriots. When our boys travelled to Spain in 1936, they left as heroes, but then the government turned these same heroes into criminals overnight. On the twenty-second of January last year we were forbidden from fighting for Spain's legally elected government. What a betrayal. What treachery against our comrades, who risk their lives on a daily basis.'

Hjelmen takes another pause for dramatic effect.

'At the same time the right-wingers in Høyre demand that Norway should acknowledge Franco as Spain's leader. Høyre talks up the fascist cause, and the government is about to do the same. It's so easy to forget that the Spanish Republic came about as the result of a free, democratic election. For generations we working people have fought for the right to vote. Acknowledging Franco is like throwing everything we workers have fought for decade after decade onto the scrapheap. It's like embracing Hitler's and Mussolini's imperialism; it is like acknowledging Salazar's fascist regime.

'The government talks about halting militarism, as though the fascists' lethal actions are mechanical movements performed by a system without a face and a will of its own. Nothing could be more wrong. When Hitler's bombers dropped their deadly loads over Guernica in April last year, it was on his orders. An order that killed hundreds of civilians.'

Hjelmen waves a newspaper in the air. 'But it didn't stop with the destruction of Guernica,' he says. 'We're reading about it today. It happens all the time; it's happening now. Mussolini's bombers have been dropping their deadly cargoes over Barcelona for two whole days. So far, two thousand bodies have been found, and there are thirteen hundred wounded.'

As Martin Hjelmen pauses, Folkets Hus is utterly silent. When he opens his mouth again it is to repeat the figures.

'Two thousand dead and thirteen hundred wounded. All civilians. The entire population of a small Norwegian town. Two thousand murdered men, women, children, grandparents. They were all innocent. Death rained down from the sky and wiped out whole families. They sit watching without saying a word: France, England, Belgium, the Netherlands and of course the Nygaardsvold government. They wash their hands of it and approve the execution of Spain's children by German and Italian armed forces. Hitler uses Spain as a training ground for his most brutal weapons. In the meantime our comrades are being arrested when they join up to fight the fascists. The Nygaardsvold government has even deliberated how help from outside Norway's own borders can be stopped. It's happening in Denmark and the Netherlands, too. The government has positioned agents on Spain's borders to pick out and punish honourable comrades who travel to Barcelona to defend democracy. Parliament and the Nygaardsvold government are punishing the Norwegian working classes for holding up what they call a neutral flag.'

Martin Hjelmen pauses again for dramatic effect.

'*Neutrality*,' he says as though it is a slimy, revolting word.

'Being neutral in international politics is about taking the side of the strongest party. Norway's government has chosen to kneel to evil and let it prevail. Nygaardsvold's neutrality is no more than being an errand boy to the dictators Hitler, Mussolini and Salazar.

'Long before you and I started school we were taught to stand up for the weak. We learned that keeping your mouth shut was the same as giving your consent. The fight for working people is fought every day and it is fought during your working day as much as it is on the battlefield in Córdoba. The fight for Spain is our fight; it is the workers' fight. It is our historic duty to fight for the values in which we believe.'

Paaske looks around him, at the faces staring up at the speaker. Messages invoking a religious awakening or a political one are surprisingly similar he thinks to himself. It is no more than a year since the government in Spain began to fight against its own people, the more moderate socialists, accusing them of Trotskyism, and killed and arrested them. Why doesn't Martin Hjelmen mention these facts?

At the same time he notices that he is being observed. Slowly he turns his head to the left and recognises the girl who was cooking in the mess on *MS Claus Böge*. She is attractive; a curvaceous figure in a blood-red dress and without a kerchief over her hair today, but it is her, no doubt about it. Now she is standing with two men of the same age, and all three of them are eyeing him intently. Paaske doesn't like them showing such an obvious interest in him. It makes him realise that Jack was mistaken. This is not a suitable place to grill dock workers about Bernhard Gruber or anyone else. If it has to be done, it should be done where meetings between dock workers and Gruber take place — on the quay. Paaske decides to leave.

Hjelmen is still talking as Paaske makes for the exit. As he opens the door there is a thunderous applause in the auditorium, and he stands on the steps for a few seconds, breathing in the chilly evening air. From inside comes another rousing song: 'The Internationale'.

It is only when he is crossing Nytorvet and casts a glance over his shoulder that he sees them. It is the same two. They are both young and strong, wearing their best suits and peaked caps. They are following him with a purposeful stride.

III

After turning into Elvegata, Jack first passes the queue outside the entrance to the Café for the Unemployed, then continues over to the entrance of Rødfyllgata 18. He stands here for a few seconds and observes life on the river. An elderly man is tying up a rowing boat and climbing onto the quay. The man queues in front of the café. He knows people and scrounges a cigarette. Jack is still thinking about his meeting with Johan. He already knew that he was mentally ill, but he had never seen him like this. When he knew him, he never heard of Johan behaving in this way. When did he change?

Jack turns away from the river and changes his plan. He is still restless and upset, and feels a need to calm down. Instead of going up to his flat he opens the door to the low wooden house nearby. There is no electricity inside, but the windows give enough light, either daylight or from the street lamp outside at night.

Inside, he has fitted the place out as a private workshop, and on the floor of this old sack factory stands his pride and joy: a four-cylinder Nimbus 750, which Jack calls the Bumble Bee. It has a top speed of well over a hundred kilometres an hour — if it starts, that is. Jack is the first to see the irony in this, and is tired of being teased by Bibbi and others. He intends to use the bike this summer. So he will have to make an effort, and he may as well start now as later. Once again he stands on the kick start, but without success. Afterwards he reflects, looks for a bowl, which he fills with petrol and places on the floor. Then he unscrews the carburettor and washes it, along with all the filters, in the petrol.

Finally, he screws it all together again with fingers greasy from the petrol and oil. He dries his hands on a cotton rag. Moves the bowl of petrol away. Unscrews the plugs and checks them. Scrapes off the soot, measures and adjusts them, screws them back in. Goes over to the bench by the wall, taps out the last cigarette in the packet. Uses the lighter, but it doesn't spark. Removes the screw at the bottom and changes the flint. Spins the wheel and it lights. Jack is excited now. If the Bumble Bee still refuses to start after all this loving care and attention, he will chuck the whole pile of crap in the river.

Reverently, cigarette in the corner of his mouth, he grasps the handlebars and kicks down hard. The engine starts at once. Jack can't help but grin and congratulate himself. He twists the throttle and enjoys the magnificent roar, but pinches his eyes shut when the smoke begins to sting. Twists again. Beautiful. He lets the engine idle while he washes his hands.

As he switches the engine off, he hears the sound of a car stopping outside. He walks over to the window. It is the roadster that was parked in Majorstuen a few days ago. Jack opens the door and goes out. No one is in the car, but as he peers inside, he hears his name being called by a voice he hasn't heard for a long time.

Jack straightens up and turns.

Amalie is standing by the entrance, wearing a white outfit: a short waisted jacket over a skirt.

'So, at last you've come.'

'I'm here to tell you something,' she says. Her voice is dry and controlled.

Jack knows her anger, the sound of her voice and the expressions she uses when she is at boiling point. Knows it all too well.

'Keep away from Johan, Jack. You keep away from him.'

'Nice to see you again, Amalie. I'd been looking forward to seeing you this evening. I went to Gaustad to smoke you out. You just disappeared from Dovre-hallen. Why couldn't you let us have some time for a chat?'

'Don't change the subject. You leave my brother in peace.'

'Why so angry? I'd planned to offer you something. Talk about old times.'

Her eyes flash. 'Offer me something? In this hole? I must say you've done well in life. You lived in a dump before, and this is worse. The river stinks. The whole place stinks. You stink.'

Amalie strides past him, opens the car door and gets in.

'Johan was my friend and he still is,' he says.

'You're no more his friend than you're the King of Portugal. You haven't shown your face for how many years? And then you turn up at the hospital and confuse him with all your talk and all the dirty past you represent. Now he's strapped down, just because you got him agitated. You keep away from my brother. That's all I have to say.'

'What if I don't?'

'Then I'll kill you,' she says, slamming the door, starting up and driving off.

Jack stands watching the car for a few seconds. Blaming himself for not asking the crucial question — why she is pretending to be someone else — but the fish isn't off the hook yet, he thinks, spinning on his heel. In the sack factory he puts on his leather helmet and goggles. Shrugs on his leather jacket and rolls the bike into the road. When the engine roars, he feels an invisible surge of energy, mounts it and flicks the gear into first.

There is no sports car to be seen anywhere, but Jack guesses that it would be hard to hide one like a Roadster, certainly around here, in the slums by the

Akerselva. Jack speeds up the side streets and sees it heading west along Grønlandsleiret. He turns to follow, staying some distance behind.

★ ★ ★

The journey takes him past Majorstuen and on to Smestad. As the car rounds the hairpin bends up the mountain, he is still a long way behind her. After passing Besserud, she turns into Doktor Holms vei and the drive of a detached house. People live well here. These are houses with piped running water and indoor toilets. There is enough fresh air and a lot of forest all around.

Jack rides past and stops in a clump of trees beside a house further up. Here, in the trees above the road, he walks slowly back to her house.

You can't complain about the view either. The Oslo pot, as it is called, the houses and streets surrounding the harbour basin. Street lamps blinking like chains of luminous pearls.

The sports car is parked in front of an almost square house on two floors. The windows are rectangular, with the curtains drawn to the side.

Amalie appears in the middle window. She is alone and in a living room. There is a low suite of furniture in front of a book case with no books. A sofa and two armchairs are placed around a low table. Amalie sits down, stretches her legs and kicks off her shoes. There is total silence, and Jack has the feeling he is watching a silent film, crouched down in the forest and staring at the panoramic window as if it were a cinema screen.

Then a door closes. The sound comes from a house

further up the road, closer to where he left his motor bike. He hears footsteps. A figure is coming down the road and appears between the houses and is gone again. It is a man taking a dog for a walk, a poodle. It has been clipped; parts of its torso and legs are shaven. Its small, stubby tail is standing up, and its legs are going twenty to the dozen as it pulls at the lead in front of its owner. The footsteps stop.

Then something happens on the cinema screen. Amalie gets up, goes over to a staircase in the corner, descends the stairs and is gone. Jack hears a door open and then voices. A door closes. In the room behind the window, the poodle comes bounding up the stairs. It flits around, sniffing chairs and table legs. Two people walk up slowly. Amalie first. She turns and speaks to the man gesticulating back to her. Jack knows the man. That is, he used to. Jack would have recognised Arvid Bjerke anywhere on the planet. It is Bjerke who is speaking now, but this meeting doesn't seem to be very cordial. Suddenly he slaps her. She turns away from him, steps away and points to the stairs. The man is talking in a loud voice. Jack can hear him through the window, but he can't distinguish the words. The dog sits down and watches them. Bjerke attaches the lead and drags the dog down with him. Amalie doesn't accompany them. The door slams. Bjerke and the dog continue down the road. Amalie disappears through a door to another room.

The stage is empty. The film appears to be over, so Jack sets off back to his motor bike. He wonders if Bjerke is still married, and casts a glance to the right when he is level with the house that Bjerke left. He gives a start and comes to a halt. She is standing in the window looking out. The window is so large that he can see the whole person. Julie Bjerke is as attractive as twelve or thirteen years before. Dark-haired, in a tight-fitting dress, one hip bent, she stares at him as he stares back, motionless. Jack imagines she has been observing him and knows who he is, so he expects her to raise an arm and wave, but she doesn't. For a tiny eternity they continue to stare, then she turns and goes into the room and is out of sight.

He goes back to the Bumble Bee and starts it up. As he swings into Holmenkollveien he sees Bjerke gazing into the air while the dog sniffs at a lamppost. Jack rides past without making his presence known and returns the way he came. The wind in his face is wonderful. It is as though it is trying to caress away his sense of unease.

IV

Paaske walks in the middle of Torggata to stay close to people and reach Stortorvet in one piece. Casting another glance over his shoulder, he sees that the two pursuers have now become three. Paaske strides out, turns down Kirkeristen, wondering where the police are when you need them. Not a policeman in sight. When he hears his pursuers walking faster as well, he breaks into a run, turns into Skippergata and sprints until he can taste blood in his mouth, but the footsteps behind him are closer, and ahead of him he sees only darkened house walls.

He stops, turns and meets them face to face. One of them lets fly. Paaske ducks away from the first punch, but can't avoid an uppercut into the ribs. The pain shoots up along his spine. This guy is good. Paaske retreats with his guard raised. The man comes closer.

116

Paaske ducks again and twists at the same time. He invests all his weight into a punch to the man's temple. The man staggers and his knees buckle. Paaske was once well known for this combination: first a right, then a straight left, but as the left strikes home, everything goes black. Unaware of what hit him, Paaske sinks to his knees. Through the mists he sees a man raising a plank of wood for another blow. Paaske ducks, but can barely stay upright and keels over. The man kicks him. Paaske remains on the ground, huddled up, his arms folded around his head to protect himself.

In the distance he hears voices. The kicking has stopped, but he remains in this position in case there is more to come. When someone next touches him, it is with a wary hand. Someone is speaking — in a foreign language. Paaske frees his hands and looks up into a face he has seen before. Bernhard Gruber's unknown interlocutor is kneeling beside him and asking in German how he feels. Paaske checks. Struggles to his knees. Answers in English that he is not sure. The first assailant is leaning against the wall. He is pale and has lost his cap; his blond hair has fallen over his forehead. The cap is lying by the kerb.

Paaske brushes the dust and dirt from his clothes. Finds his hat and suddenly feels his senses reeling. The foreigner grabs him under the arm and helps him to keep his balance.

'I'm sorry about what happened, but the guys are on their guard. We're living in worrying times.'

Paaske is still brushing down his clothes. He touches his face with his fingers. He doesn't seem to be bleeding. Nevertheless, he runs a hand across the back of his head. There is a huge bump. Luckily for him he was wearing a hat when the man hit him with the plank, but he feels battered and bruised. But then he was, and he is.

Paaske looks around for his assailants and notices them standing a short distance away. They turn and walk off.

'Who are those two?'

'Ordinary working people who believe in their cause.'

'That one has a good left on him,' Paaske says, pointing.

'He's a southpaw,' the foreigner says, and asks Paaske if he feels any pain when he breathes.

Paaske draws air into his lungs and shakes his head.

'No broken ribs then.'

Paaske's whole body still hurts as he and the foreigner walk down Skippergata. There is no one around and it is quiet. They stop, and Paaske checks himself over again. They are outside Kafé Grei, which is still open. A waiter in a white jacket towers up behind the counter. The sight of him reassures Paaske.

'What's your name?' he asks the foreigner, happy that his voice carries.

The foreigner shakes his head.

'You owe it to me to tell me your name,' Paaske says.

'I owe you nothing. I stopped you from being beaten up.'

'Actually I *was* beaten up,' Paaske says.

They stand eyeing each other without speaking. Paaske is still waiting for the man to introduce himself.

Instead the man opens the café door. 'Let's go in, and you can have something to raise your spirits.'

They find a table at the back of the chic establishment. The foreigner holds two fingers in the air and soon the waiter brings them two mugs of beer.

The foreigner waits until the waiter is back behind the cash till before raising his mug to Paaske, who only now realises how thirsty he is and knocks back half of the beer.

'Tell me why you're spying on us.'

Paaske puts down the glass and decides to play with an open deck.

'I'm a private investigator. I was working on a job. A woman introduced herself to me as Bernhard Gruber's wife. She commissioned me to follow him, saying she suspected him — that is, her alleged husband — of cheating on her with other women.'

'So this woman was lying? It wasn't Bernhard's wife?'

'No.'

'What do you know about her?'

'In fact, I don't know anything.'

'You take on a job tailing someone without knowing anything about your client?'

'In my line of work trust is as important as not asking too many questions.'

'Was she Norwegian or could she have been German?'

'The lady was as Norwegian as I am.'

The foreigner turns pensive. 'What did you find out?'

'What are you?' Paaske says. 'A journalist? Give me something in return.'

'If I do, I first have to know what happened.'

'Gruber goes to meet you, and you two don't wish to be seen together.'

'So you decided to go to the Stevedores' Union meeting?'

'You and Gruber are more than slightly interested in the unloading going on in Oslo harbour. I visited the stevedores because I'm trying to get some sort of handle on the game I've been used in. That's also the reason I want to know who you are, what your name is.'

'You obviously have no idea what you've got involved in. I can't say anything about it, either, but I do need to know everything about this woman who gave you the job.'

Paaske has his ethics, and he is under no obligation to tell this man anything, but to move on he needs to play one card.

Paaske takes a deep breath and takes out the photograph he has in his inside pocket. Places it on the table.

The foreigner studies the picture. A fierce grimace forms on his narrow lips. 'Werner Krause,' he says.

'So you know the man?'

The foreigner nods. 'Know is not the right word.'

'Is he a policeman?'

The foreigner nods again. 'What has Krause to do with the woman?'

'They've been seen together.'

'Where was this photo taken?'

'In Oslo's promenading street, Karl Johan.'

'When?'

'Yesterday.'

The foreigner studies the picture again. 'Krause is walking through a swing door. A hotel?'

Paaske nods. 'Hotel Westminster. Who is he?'

'Werner Krause works for the German secret services. The Gestapo.'

'What's a German policeman doing in Norway?'

'I can promise you one thing: Krause's not on holiday, and his intentions are not good.'

Paaske waits, but the foreigner says nothing else.

'Who's Bernhard Gruber?'

The foreigner gets up.

'What's going on between the stevedores and Gruber?'

The foreigner gazes at him in silence. 'I had hoped you wouldn't ask such questions.'

'Why?'

'It could be dangerous for you.' 'Is that a threat?'

The foreigner closes his eyes for a few seconds before answering. 'Not for the time being, but the less you know about this, the better for you. I would advise you to keep well away. For your own safety. You should forget Werner Krause. Forget Bernhard Gruber. Forget me. Unless you do, I can almost guarantee you'll end up in trouble, but the next time it's not certain I'll be able to help you out of a tight spot. Do you understand what I'm saying?'

As Paaske doesn't answer, the foreigner swivels on his heel and goes to the counter. He pays before leaving.

If I were ten years younger, I would have stood up and gone after him, Paaske thinks.

The pain in his ribs is still there. He puts the photograph of Werner Krause back in his inside pocket and finishes his beer. Although he feels weakened, his desire to find out more is strengthened. Paaske wants to know why he in particular was used, even though now he knows no more than what Jack told him earlier in the day. All he has achieved today is to provoke an assault. Paaske feels a fury he hasn't felt for many years, and takes out his pipe. There is a plug of half-smoked tobacco in the bowl. He pats his jacket for a box of matches without locating it, then notices the waiter standing beside the table — a pale man with a flat nose. In the white jacket and the black trousers he resembles a penguin.

'Another beer?'

Paaske shakes his head

The man delves into a pocket and passes him a matchbook advertising the café.

Paaske stands up. 'I have to find a taxi,' he says.

'Oslo East Station,' the man says. 'There's usually one in the taxi rank.'

V

Jack grabs a bottle of beer from the line on the window sill, opens it with his teeth, takes a swig and examines his universe: the little room with a sink and a primus stove on a worktop. The bed in the corner. The little table with a chair and a stool. The radio. The shelf with two books: one about chess and a large atlas. He tries to be displeased, to see the place through Amalie's arrogant eyes, but cannot. Instead he sits at the table with the chessboard. It has been set according to the Immortal Game, the classic between Adolf Anderssen and Lionel Kieseritzky. Jack has always had a tendency to support losers and tries yet again to see the moves Kieseritzky could have made to turn the game.

After unsuccessfully trying to think about chess, he gets up, goes over to the window and looks out. Arvid Bjerke must have been very angry with her. They live in the same street. The Bjerkes and Amalie. They know each other so well that she lets him in when she is at home alone, but she must have done something to him, which makes him yell at her first, then hit her.

The telephone in the corridor rings, but he doesn't move from the window. It seldom rings for him. In the end the neighbour takes pity on it. Her shuffling steps are unmistakeable. Jack hears her say her name and mumble a few phrases, then hang up. There is a knock at the door.

'Rivers. Phone.'

Jack steps into the corridor, but waits until his neighbour has closed the door behind her before he lifts the receiver from the wall mount.

'Amalie here. Let's talk.'

Jack is not sure what he expected. You know that something will happen when you lift a telephone, but you never know what.

'Have you changed your mind?'

'It was stupid of me to shout at you, but I was so desperate because of Johan's relapse. I apologise for my behaviour, but I think it's important we talk.'

'Talk away, Amalie.'

'I want to see you when we talk.'

'When?'

'This evening. I'll drive to Bygdøy. Let's meet there. In Oscarshall.'

'Why there exactly?'

'I don't want to be seen with you, Jack. Please don't misunderstand. It's important for me not to be seen by anyone.'

'When do you want to meet?'

'Ten o'clock maybe?'

After ringing off, he feels increasing suspicion

creeping up his spine. He speculates on the paths that life can take. Amalie. Johan. Bjerke and his beautiful wife. He has never had any wish to retrieve them from his memory, nor any recollections or emotions associ- ated with them, then all of a sudden there they are — and at the head of the queue are the lies.

★   ★   ★

When the government bought Kongens gård, the royal estate in Bygdøy, to place it at the disposal of the ruling monarch while the land around it was laid out as a park for the people, the king's pleasure palace came as part of the deal. The garden inside the surrounding wall, with gravel paths, a fountain and the terraced flower beds, constitute one part of the park. During the day Oscarshall is like a fairy-tale castle towering up on the hill overlooking Frognerkilen bay. It is a small, neo-Gothic building with a tower and secondary buildings, architecturally inspired by castles in Potsdam and Bavaria, but having been built long before electricity, nothing but a wall of dark trees can be seen from the town side this evening as Jack alights from the metro at Skarpsno Station and crosses the park in front, to carry on down to the ferry jetty.

It is not a quiet evening. Behind the Kongen restaurant there is a racket coming from the fairground attractions in the VI KAN exhibition. Now and then you can hear the screams of people being flung around on the swing rides, but the ferry landing area is quiet.

Jack finds the ferryman in the little kiosk beside the quay. He is an elderly, bearded man, in coarse woollen clothes with a cap on his head. From the corner of his mouth hangs a yellowing Meerschaum pipe. Jack

124

asks if there are any more ferries.

'You're in time for the last one,' the man says, lighting his pipe with a large match, opening the kiosk door and coming out.

The boat is small and round, at the bow and the stern. It is like a covered barge with a chimney going up through the roof. Jack buys a ticket and boards the ferry, the only passenger. A young man with a peaked cap casts off. Thick mist hangs over Frognerkilen this evening, but the crossing takes no time at all. It is only five hundred metres from Skarpsno to Bygdøy. As they approach the quay here, a figure gradually emerges in the grey mist. There is someone waiting for the boat. It is a man. Jack looks at his wrist- watch. It is a quarter to ten.

The young man jumps ashore and holds the hawser while the engine is still running. It is chilly, and the plank that functions as the gangway is damp and slippery. The man on the quay waits until Jack is on land. Then he boards the ferry. Jack notices that the man has a game leg.

The gang plank has already been dragged back on board. The boat starts its return journey. Jack moves to the edge of the quay.

'Herr Werner Krause!' he shouts.

The German turns to Jack, but just stands still on the foredeck without answering.

The ferry glides into the mist. The man on the deck slips slowly into the grey murk. As does the boat. Jack is left alone. Soon the engine can't be heard anymore, but he has a bad feeling. The sight of the Gestapo man has given him a shock.

The lights of the VI KAN exhibition glow, causing the mist above the water to shine yellow rather than grey, but when he turns, the darkness is almost impenetrable. Only the outline of the grand entrance into the garden is visible, the so-called Cavalier Building.

Walking through the gateway he can barely see his hand in front of his face, so thick is the darkness. He stops and waits until his eyes have become accustomed to it. At last he can make out the path leading up to the main building. He slowly makes his way up to the plateau with the fountain beside the smokers' pavilion. Once there, he feels the first drop of rain and sticks out a hand. It has started to drizzle. It is so dark he can hardly see the low wall around the fountain. There isn't a sound to be heard. It is too early in the year for the palace gardeners to open the taps. The pillars of the smokers' pavilion glow a matt white in the pitch-black. Jack moves under a roof and is blinded by the flame of his lighter as he lights a cigarette, then continues up to the pleasure palace at the very top, deserted and blacked out.

He carefully climbs the steps to the terrace in front of the castle- like construction. There is still nothing to hear but the drip-drip of the rain. At the top he finishes his cigarette, drops the stub on the ground and watches the red glow die in the rain. Then he raises his head and can see the gateway between the tower and the main building. Makes his way there and into the area on the opposite side. Here, he trips over something and almost falls headlong. He squats down, searches the ground with his fingers and feels cloth. He gropes further. There is a body outstretched on the gravel. It is limp and lifeless.

Jack rummages through his pockets for his lighter and sparks a flame, which dimly illuminates the corpse.

KRISTIANIA, 1924

I

The light under the roof vault dims as the thunder starts. The big mirror running from the edge of a ring up to the ceiling rigging is illuminated in all the colours of the rainbow. This is a Theatre Moderne revue stage in Christiania Tivoli. Soon the audience can see themselves in the huge mirror: row after row of heads in the auditorium. Jack tries to catch a glimpse of himself, but in vain, several bright lights come on too quickly, and the mirror becomes a blank, shiny surface. Jack has to squeeze his eyes shut so as not to be blinded. The band plays a fanfare, and at that moment water rushes down the mirror like a waterfall while Indian squaws throng around both sides of it. Their black hair is plaited, with long feathers threaded through. The fringes of their native dresses reach down to mid-thigh. They all run barefoot round and round the ring, which is filling with water.

'This is Niagara!' an excited voice calls out from behind Jack. 'The great North American Niagara Falls.'

People shush the man, but Jack can understand the man's excitement. After all, the audience is inside a Tivoli theatre and they are sitting in front of an artificial waterfall. This must be a masterpiece of engineering. Water cascades down, the noise of it and the pump machinery almost drown out the big band, while the squaws are soon sailing around the ring in small boats. A man in front of Jack jumps to his feet and claps and cheers. Another pulls at his jacket to make him sit down while others also stand up. Soon the whole auditorium is on its feet, applauding the magic waterfall that is soaking the beautiful women through to the skin.

Then he sees Amalie, in her fringe dress with a feather in her hair, drenched. The band strikes up again. Bangs on the timpani and drum rolls ricochet between the walls of the Theatre Moderne. The lights change colour and from the water a platform rises. On it the squaws perform their evocative dance. The throng divides; like two broad wings the dancers glide apart and in the middle the diva steps forward. A woman in green, Tivoli's great star, Hansy Petra, who sings a song about wild Indians.

Jack sinks back in his seat, but without paying any attention to the star. Instead, he is following the woman in the back row. Amalie is unsure of herself, but he can also see how much she likes being in the spotlight, until she suddenly takes a wrong step and quickly glances at the others to see if they have noticed. The little mistake only makes her more attractive in his eyes. There is something genuine and endlessly honest about her performance. It makes her vulnerable and transparent, and it strikes Jack that now he sees her as her mother probably would: alone, slightly gauche in a role she hasn't yet mastered, but she is sticking with it. Seeing her like this, Jack passionately wants her to succeed, and for a few brief seconds he feels he is the only person in the world who can really see her — without any artifice or pretence. It is an intense moment, a passing glimpse, it doesn't last long.

Jack realises that he can now see beyond the distorting mirror of emotions that wrap themselves around

the object of one's love. At the same time he realises something obvious: Amalie is just a very ordinary
girl, lurching between jobs, men, and she is doing the
best she can. In Benno Singer's Theatre Moderne
she is in the back row, one of many attractive women.
Surrounded by them she is somewhat anonymous.
Amalie is one of the faceless women in the crowd,
there to make the diva stand out and shine. However,
his brain is not capable of taking on this new insight.
His brain wants the distorting image back; his emotions are thrashing around, like a cat in deep water,
struggling back to shore.

In the interval he gets up and whispers to the vendor walking between the rows, selling flowers. He
buys a bouquet of roses and writes on the card. Afterwards he goes to one of the attendants and sends the
bouquet with him backstage to Amalie.

After the performance he goes backstage. Squaws
are running around semi-naked, some with wigs,
some without. They are breathless and euphoric.
They hug each other in their excitement at the
crowd's deafening ovations. Jack asks after Amalie,
but the girl he asks can't hear him. The next one just
shrugs. They don't know one another, and if they
did, they haven't got the time to search. Most of
them are already dressed and on their way out. In
the end, Jack has to accept that Amalie isn't there.
His roses lie untouched on the bench under the row
of anonymous lockers.

II

The newspapers are full of speculation. The great
puzzle is where Arvid Bjerke stayed during the days

129

after the police raid on his house — until he strolled into a police station and handed himself in.

The engineer's statement has been leaked to the press. Bjerke claims that some time ago, on a street in Kristiania, he met a German ship's captain he had met earlier in Hamburg. This captain is supposed to have asked if he could rent a couple of rooms in Bjerke's house in Holtekilen. Bjerke saw no reason to reject his request. With that, the captain moved in, although he wasn't often at home, but one morning Bjerke is supposed to have got up and, to his horror, noticed a stack of illegal spirits and other goods in the garden outside his house. Bjerke was very upset and confronted the tenant. The German captain told him to calm down. Bjerke told him to pack up the goods and find himself a room elsewhere, but then Bjerke heard shots being fired in the forest. He fled in haste, because he thought it was contraband raiders or some other criminals coming to loot. The newspapers are full of stories about armed robbers dressing up as police to confiscate booze from smugglers. It was only several days afterwards that a maid told him it had been the police who had come through the forest. He immediately gave himself up to the authorities.

Bjerke has no answer to where the mysterious German captain was when the police raided the house, which makes the police suspect the whole story is a pack of lies.

However, he refuses to reveal where he stayed after the police raid. The engineer also refuses to reveal whether he was alone or with others.

Bjerke is asked if he read newspapers in the place he was staying. His disappearance was front-page news for days. How come a maid told him he was wanted by the police when every newspaper in the country had been speculating about his disappearance?

Bjerke has no answer to this, either.

Apparently the police consider Bjerke's story comical. Jack thinks the same, but Bjerke has played a trump card: the captain's name. Bjerke insists the captain called himself Lehman. The police may not know it, but the smuggler Herman Jehle goes under the name 'Lehman'. Jack doesn't approve of Bjerke machinating in this devious manner. Jack would never have believed that Bjerke would be such a rat, even though he understands Bjerke's thinking. There are very few people who know who the real Lehman is. Bjerke is relying on the judges knowing about the rumours of a Captain Lehman, the captain who is supposed to be the mastermind behind a large gang of smugglers. Bjerke's lawyer also emphasises this point to the press. He maintains that the police would be better off searching for Captain Lehman rather than harassing his client, a respectable businessman who has built up a transport firm that is entirely legal, necessary and socially useful.

Jack is aware that his respect for Arvid Bjerke is not as wholehearted as it used to be.

★ ★ ★

Jack retrieves the booze hidden next to Strandlykkja and lives well for a few weeks on the profits. When the money eventually runs out, he takes a few one-off jobs from his cousin, Ole, who has a grocery store in Geitmyrsveien. Actually, Ole has no need of any help, but he lets Jack stack shelves and carry goods from the lorries into the warehouse. Ole is engaged to

Petra, who, together with three other women, works in the shop. Jack's job is done in a couple of hours every Monday, and the money he earns can be viewed as sporadic alms. Jack calls on Antonisen, the smuggler in Slemdal, and asks if he needs anyone. He doesn't.

★　★　★

The trial against Bjerke starts on 1st August. Jack is dreading it. Bjerke, for his part, is probably expecting him to make himself scarce. Paaske, however, has threatened him with a fine if he doesn't show up. Jack doesn't want to snitch, but running away from the police, without knowing what the consequences will be, goes against the grain. On Sunday morning, the day before the trial, Jack is more nervous than he has ever been. He has barely slept a wink, and the summons to testify is on the kitchen table. The letter is open, and he has read it several times.

Early in the morning, several hours before the churches have rung for mass, there is a knock at the door. Amalie is wearing a light-blue dress with a rose in a buttonhole in the collar. Over one arm she is carrying a basket, as though she is going into the country.

Jack is so surprised that he doesn't know what to say, but holds the door open.

She comes in and looks around. Takes in the little flat, which looks more like a single room. Jack sees his home through critical eyes now: the full ashtray on the table, the bed that hasn't been made yet, the glass of water on the floor, the dirty plates and cups on the worktop. He feels an urge to tidy up, but his feet are rooted to the floor as he watches her.

Amalie puts down the basket and walks over to the

window. She looks out as she informs him she has been lent a cabin. Then she turns, goes to the table and helps herself to a cigarette from the packet. Holds it between two fingers of her right hand and tilts her head.

Jack collects himself, takes the lighter from his trouser pocket and lights her cigarette.

'A cabin?'

'You've been there before. It's the one by Drammensfjord. Holmsbu.'

So she is talking about the cabin that she and Bjerke borrowed. And now she has been lent it again. Today of all days.

Amalie pouts and blows out the smoke. 'Feel like coming?'

'You and me?'

She nods.

'No one else?'

Amalie shakes her head and takes another puff. Everything Amalie does is thought through.

'Why?'

She comes close to him. 'Don't you like me, Jack? You did send me flowers.'

'You didn't want them.'

'They're in a vase at home in Stupinngata, all except this one.' She takes the flower from her buttonhole and smells it. 'They were lovely, Jack.'

'That's six weeks ago. The flowers must be keeping incredibly well.'

'Wow, have you got running water?' she says, going to the sink and turning the tap. She watches the water stream into the sink. Holds the cigarette underneath. It goes out, drips water and disintegrates. Then she turns off the tap.

'A girl has to be careful,' she says, facing him. 'You can't be careful enough. The world's full of dangerous men. I didn't see the card, so I only took the flowers the following day after I'd read on the card who'd sent them.'

'Great performance,' he says, mostly to make her talk about something else.

'I've finished with them.' 'How come?'

'The water scene. I caught a cold.'

She doesn't sound as if she has a cold, but she has stopped working at Tivoli, and now she has been lent a cabin that Bjerke had borrowed from someone. Jack has a glimmering that someone is standing above them and pulling strings. He wonders when he became a marionette moving its arms and legs whenever someone pulled the strings.

'I'm starting at the new restaurant in Klingenberggata in a couple of weeks. The Rainbow.'

'Dancing?'

'I have some lines as well.'

Now she is standing right up against him, smelling of lilac, and he can feel her breasts against his chest as he looks into her brown and blue eyes.

'Who gave you the cabin?'

She stares at him for a long time before answering. 'The owners. Who else?'

'I have to go to court tomorrow. It's not a good idea to go to Holmsbu today.'

Amalie wraps an arm around his neck, pulls him down and kisses him. A silence surrounds them as he feels her soft lips and brazen tongue.

At length they stop to draw breath, and she whispers: 'It's summer. We can go swimming. There's booze at the cabin. We have food.'

134

'Why today of all days?'

'Let's have a bit of fun,' she says, holding her hands around his back, pressing against his groin and leaning backward.

'We can take Bjerke's boat.'

Jack smiles. 'We can take the boat, but I don't want to go to the cabin.'

'Why not?'

Jack doesn't reply.

'The boat's in Holtekilen,' Amalie says. 'We can take the Drammen train. You get off at Høvik, take the boat and pick me up from Kadettangen in Sandvika.'

'Why don't you come with me to the boat?'

'Fru Bjerke doesn't like me.'

III

Her red hair is bleached by the sun, as are the two blonde feathers that are her eyebrows. Amalie sits on the middle thwart. She gathers her hair in her hands in front of her and holds it in place with a slide so that it doesn't fall over her eyes. As they pass Tofte, Jack holds a steady course straight ahead.

'You have to go up Drammensfjord,' Amalie says.

Jack grins. 'I know where the cabin is.'

'Where are we going?' 'Somewhere else.'

Amalie pretends to be offended. It won't last long. She likes surprises. The place he has decided on he has visited many times, both from the sea and land. He has delivered spirits there, and cakes. The summer house is owned by Julie's father, a wholesaler. He seldom uses the house, and Jack knows where the key is kept. As soon as the red tiled roof comes into view from behind the rocks, he steers into the gently slop-ing bay with white sand. Amalie jumps ashore with the mooring rope in her hand and ties it to a knee-high bog myrtle shrub growing at the water's edge.

'Where are we going?'

'It's a secret.'

As the tide is rising, he grabs the bow of the boat and pulls it half onto land.

'Tell me,' she says.

'First I want a swim,' he says and walks towards the rocks.

$\star \quad \star \quad \star$

After the dip they wade back side by side, looking for shells. Amalie's bathing costume is sleeveless and fin-ishes mid-thigh. The sun casts a yellow grid across the sandy sea-bottom as she picks shells, uses her finger-nail to coax out the mother of pearl and studies their colours. Jack catches a little crab that almost merges into the sand. Amalie squeals hysterically when he drops it on her shoulder. Then she covers her mouth with her hand and laughs at herself.

They clamber up the smooth rock. Jack looks across at the white summer house and checks that it is unoccupied before leading her down to the sea. Here they find a hollow in the rock. Sheltered from the breeze, they lie with their eyes closed and feel the wind caressing their eyelashes as the sun bakes down on them and water ripples and laps against the rocks.

'There's no one here,' Amalie says, standing up. 'My costume's itchy.'

Jack lights a cigarette and watches her undress. Amalie gives a faint smile, folds up her bathing costume and winds her way down the rock feet first. Her body glistens and gleams as she lies in the water on her back. Then she comes back up. Searches for a hold with her fingers in the slippery rock. Crawls on all fours. Laughing at herself. Stands up and straightens her back. Lifts both hands and wrings the salty water out of her hair. Jack watches her and she looks back. At the same moment they realise they are being spied on by two small boys from behind the bushes. Amalie giggles and says she thinks they are sweet.

Jack says: 'Get your clothes on.'

He yells at the boys, and they run off.

Amalie laughs and pulls her dress over her shoulders.

Jack finds his wristwatch in one shoe and puts it on. 'Let's go.'

'Where?'

'Come with me.'

Her dress has dark patches of damp as they walk hand in hand over the grass to the white house wedged between rocks. Jack finds the key under a pot by the gatepost. Soon he has the door open.

Amalie stops inside. Looks around, impressed. 'Who owns it?'

'A client,' he says, making an amorous move.

She wriggles out of his arms. 'Jack, it's broad daylight, no.'

With that she runs through the folding doors to the next room, but comes to a halt when she catches sight of a gramophone on the table. 'It's a portable.'

Amalie carries the gramophone to the terrace. Runs back into the sitting room. Sees some records in a low cabinet beside the sofa. Reads the labels. 'Isham Jones' Orchestra.'

Jack finds two garden chairs in the patio shed and unfolds them by the stone table while she puts a record on the gramophone and cranks it up. They exchange glances as the sounds of the orchestra stream across the patio. Amalie dances barefoot over the slate floor. Stretches out her arms for Jack, who holds them and dances with her. They dance well together. He swings her round first once, then again, and again and again, faster and faster. Amalie leans back and looks at the sky as they swing round.

'Again! Again!'

In the end they both collapse in a chair.

Amalie's smile dies and she glares at him.

'What's the matter?'

She doesn't answer. Instead she gets up and walks to the patio gate. She stands there with her back to him.

Jack smokes a cigarette while she mopes. Stubs it out in the ashtray on the table. 'Are you hungry?'

Amalie fries sausages and potatoes, and Jack slices some fresh bread. They have a beer with it, and by the end of the meal she is back in a good mood. Jack finds some gin and vermouth in the sitting-room cabinet. Amalie has taken another record from the pile. When Jack carries the drinks onto the patio, Amalie is singing the words of a Swedish song:

'The truth does you good, and it is true,
that in this country if you shun the rest
and don't do
as all the other chicks in the nest...'

She takes one of the glasses from him and does a couple of dance steps. The song continues, and she

138

wags a finger, like a school- teacher, as she sings along:

'but go your own way, however far,
rejecting the drab for all the fair,
then some old hen is going to declare,
how terribly frivolous you are.'

Amalie does a few more dance steps when the song is over. She laughs in delight and asks if the person who owns the house is rich. Jack says he is sure he is.

'Is he richer than Arvid Bjerke?'

'No idea. I don't give a shit how rich they are.'

'What do you care about?'

'I care about you. *Now* I do.'

'And what about tomorrow?'

Jack shakes his head. 'I care about this. This moment, the sunshine, the heat, the music, the aromas.'

Once again Amalie searches through the pile of records. Soon the gramophone is playing 'Who's Sorry Now?'. It is a slow song and she is affected by it. She falls back into a chair, blinks and appears to be asleep.

Jack shakes her shoulders, but she is fast asleep. Then he goes back to the gramophone and lifts the stylus.

Amalie opens her eyes, sits up and stares at him with a strange expression. Then she gently gets to her feet and goes inside.

Jack remains in a chair with his legs resting on the patio fence. Asking himself why he decided to go with her. She only creates trouble for him. Because now he is going to make things tricky for himself. He won't make it to the court tomorrow. Using the wholesaler's summer house and drinking his booze doesn't compensate for how bad he feels. Alone on a summer evening, he feels stupid, simple-minded, and a fury is churning through his body. He thinks about other women, about Julie Bjerke. He should have done it with her. He should have spread her across the table; he shouldn't have been loyal to the husband who danced to her tune when he was given the sack.

Amalie is away so long he wonders whether she has gone to bed.

Then at last the patio-door hinges squeak. Amalie is standing in the doorway, wearing a skin-tight silk dress.

'Does it suit me?'

He has to smile. Amalie has been going through the wardrobe, trying on Julie's dresses without realising whose they were. 'Everything suits you.'

'Why don't you buy me clothes like these, Jack? Why don't you buy me rings like Bjerke does?' She shows him the ring with the jewel she is wearing. Kisses it, sashays across the floor and cranks up the gramophone. Marion Harris sings 'I'm Just Wild about Harry'.

Amalie moves awkwardly in the tight dress. It is as though the fullness of her body is protesting; her breasts don't want to be imprisoned. Jack gets up and goes over to the table with the bottles and mixes another drink. Amalie dances across the slate patio alone, slowly and dreamily, in large circles. She sings along to 'I'm Just Wild about Harry', but exchanges Harry for Bjerke. Jack leans against the rails and looks at her.

'Bjerke is wild about me.'

Jack can feel the fury growing and is aware she knows and likes it.

She holds up her arms and sways, swings her hips, then laughs, and wriggles away when he makes a grab for her. Bjerke's lover in Julie Bjerke's dress is acting like Julie Bjerke, and has enticed him out of town when he should have been meeting the police. At last he catches hold of the dress and pulls hard. She turns to face him, her eyes flashing. The material is torn from the neck down. She takes both halves and rips the dress apart, steps out of the rags that fall to the floor, naked. When he hooks an arm around her waist she slaps his face. Now he really is angry, locks her wrists with one hand, pushes her, stumbling, to the chair, lays her across his lap and spanks her bottom. She laughs out loud and shrieks. This makes him hit her harder.

'Not so hard!'

'I do what I like.'

'Do you? Me too.'

His blood is boiling and he doesn't think, he stands up and carries her like a bundle through the door and throws her down on the sofa. She lands on her back and now it is not frivolity driving her. Her eyes are hungry as her body edges backwards while he undoes his belt. Jack can feel the madness in him and does as he wants, but when he rolls her onto her stomach, it is she who is the wilder of them. When she lets out a loud scream, there is no way back. They both fall, their bodies entwined. She is trembling and looks at him with eyes from another world.

He gets up and walks onto the patio. His anger has turned and he despises himself. He tries to lay the blame on the alcohol, the trial, her caprices. It doesn't help. The feeling of shame weighs down on him and he blames himself to such a degree that he can't bear to go back in. He stands naked in the chilly summer evening, trying to concentrate on the moment, the gentle breeze and the melody of a blackbird singing in the tree behind the house. After a while the sounds are broken by a low squeak of hinges. Amalie is leaning heavily against the door frame. Her brown eye is glowing like a lump of coal, and the blue one is glinting like mountain water as her voice whispers:

'You and I could make an attractive couple, Jack. Pity you're not rich. Just such a terrible pity you're not rich.'

IV

When he wakes, light is breaking. It is the magical hour between night and morning. There is not a sound to be heard through the open window. No gulls screaming, no wind, no chug of fishing boats on their way to the horizon. Amalie is lying beside him, sleeping with her thumb in her mouth. He gives a start at the sight, and then she whimpers.

Soundlessly, he gets out of bed. With the sun rising behind his back, he looks at the naked girl before tiptoeing out of the bedroom and going downstairs. The first step creaks. The morning sun hangs low over the sea-smoothed rocks to the east. The light pierces the window panes, and the conches displayed on the window sill cast shadows across the floor.

For a long time he stands wondering what to do. Go? Leave her? Stay? Stay here until she wakes up or go back to bed?

The same step creaks behind him.

Amalie is on the stairs: 'Shall we go for a swim?' she says.

They walk onto the patio and continue across the chill, dewy grass, gently holding hands, over the gravel and onto the narrow jetty. Amalie scans the water for jellyfish before she jumps in. Jack follows her.

It is the crack of dawn, the water is as soft as silk and suddenly he feels her hands, legs and chest as she clings to his back, she squeezes her legs hard around his waist and her arms around his neck. Their bodies are entwined, and he breathes out. They sink, but Amalie doesn't let go. His chest hurts through lack of air, but they rise, infinitely slowly. They break the surface of the water and both gasp for air before sinking again. The less air Jack has, the greater the thrill he feels. He sucks air from her mouth and she from his, and finally they rise again. As their bodies break the surface this time, he takes a firm grip of the jetty and holds tight as she bites his neck and shoulders.

Afterwards she doesn't let go. He holds on to the jetty; she holds on to him. When she eventually opens her eyes, she asks:

'Do you think dying would be different from what we experienced just now?'

'I don't want to give an opinion.'

'Why not?'

'I'm not ready to think about death, not yet.'

They clamber up onto the jetty. He lies back. Amalie sits looking at him. Anger is radiating from her eyes. This is so different that he sits up.

'What's the matter?'

'You think you own me now, don't you.'

He doesn't answer.

'No one owns me.'

'Not even Bjerke?'

'No one!'

Jack lies back down with his arms outstretched. 'Come here.'

She doesn't move, but in the end edges over and lies down with her head on his arm. Soon he falls asleep, but wakes up when Amalie says she is hungry. Her lips taste of salt. They stroll back. Amalie enters the house like the owner, and Jack wonders what Arvid Bjerke or Julie would say if they knew what their lackeys were up to. He stands looking out of the window. Fishermen are on their way to make their daily catch, and he can feel that he likes standing here like this, listening to the chug of the two-stroke engines and gulls screaming in the wake of the boats.

★ ★ ★

There is a clinker-built dinghy moored to a buoy some distance from the jetty. Jack swims out and climbs on board. The sail is wound around the boom and there are oars at the bottom of the boat. With the oars he manoeuvres the boat back to the jetty. In the boat-shed there are some line winders for sea-fishing, which they pack up and take with them. Amalie battles with the oars while he fixes the sail. When the wind fills the sail she lays down the oars. The wind is the sunrise breeze, and the dinghy soon picks up speed. Amalie lies in the bow, which rocks gently in the heavy sea. She appears to be asleep. Jack lets her be and concentrates on the wind. The boat is moving fast now. When the wind drops, he reefs the sail and ties it to the boom, then he casts a line and waits for a bite. Amalie is asleep with her mouth open and her eyelids half closed. He can see only the whites of her eyes through the narrow crack. Her lips seem bloodless. That is how she will look when she is dead, he thinks. Not a pretty sight.

144

There is a pull on the line. He hauls it in. He manages to grab a nice saithe before she wakes and sits up.

'What's the time?'

'No idea.' Jack squints up at the sun. 'Maybe one or half past.'

'Bjerke's in court now.'

'Perhaps it's already all over.'

'Do you think he'll be convicted?'

Jack shakes his head.

'Why not?'

'Because I'm here.'

They exchange looks. She says no more. Some things they can talk about, not everything though.

Amalie looks around. 'Where are we?'

'At sea.'

'I can't see any land.'

Jack can feel that he likes her to be anxious. 'Perhaps I'm kidnapping you,' he says, pulling in the line.

'I don't like not being able to see land.'

'You're thinking about the black depths beneath us? The endlessly cold, black depths?'

'Don't speak like that.'

'Perhaps I'm behaving like you now. Luring you into paradise.'

'Jack, turn back now.'

It is obvious that she is not only afraid but angry.

He keeps pulling in the line. Fastens the hooks to the bottom of the winder one by one. After the lead sinker hits the side, he puts the winder at the bottom of the boat, but keeps her sitting there, boiling with anger, keen to see how she will cope with being trapped by fear and anger while dependent on him. In the end, her fear wins.

'Turn back,' she pleads meekly. 'Please, Jack. I'm scared.'

Jack forces her to wait a few more long seconds, reads the terror ravaging her face, raises the sail and moves the tiller so that the boat turns and the boom swings. Then he tightens the ropes until he can feel the sun on his back. Gradually he heads back to land, ruminating on why he enjoys her feelings of fear. Or maybe it isn't the fear he likes, he realises the next minute, but the crack in her mask. He likes her fear because it is genuine.

V

As evening approaches, Amalie runs to the shop to see if they have any afternoon newspapers. When she returns it is with vegetables and potatoes in a cloth bag, and an open newspaper in her hand.

''Key Police Witness Missing'. Is that you? 'Police went to court to convict the mastermind. They returned empty-handed. As a result, it is widely expected that Bjerke will go free.''

'Are you happy, Amalie?' Jack smiles. 'Bjerke will go free.'

She nods.

'Do you think he'll get divorced for you?'

Amalie laughs. 'Jack, I don't want to get married, at least not to Bjerke.'

'So what do you want from him?'

'I want money; I want to live well. I want clothes and food, and I want some help for Johan.'

'What kind of help?'

'A dentist. I've spoken to a doctor who works at the asylum. He says Johan will be fine if his teeth are extracted, but it has to be done properly, by a specialist.'

'Did he say why he needs to have his teeth extracted?'

Amalie nods. 'The pus and crap that comes with toothache can enter the bloodstream. That's how you become like Johan. His blood isn't clean.'

'So Johan hasn't always been like this?'

'He became like he is when Mamma died. He started to hear voices in his head, but they'll go again if he gets help.'

Jack looks at her sceptically. 'Are you sure?'

'I'm sure, but first of all he has to go to a hospital that has a specialist who understands this kind of disease.'

'Can't all dentists do it?'

Amalie shakes her head. 'That's what's so annoying. There are only one or two in the whole country who can make Johan well, and they cost a hell of a lot of money.'

★ ★ ★

The following morning they sail back to Kristiania. He sets a course up the Akerselva and drops Amalie off on the stone steps of Grønlands torg. Afterwards he goes back alone to Bjerke's quay in Holtekilen.

As he is mooring the boat, he can feel he is being observed. This feeling won't leave him, not when he is walking towards the house, either. It looks quiet enough, but it isn't empty. Jack can feel that in his bones. They are in there watching him. The high and mighty are watching the pauper who saved their skins.

Without a sideways glance, he passes the house, thinking that now they are probably breathing a sigh of relief. They were happy enough for him to help them out of a tight spot, but they don't want close contact. He walks at a sprightly pace through the forest, making for Stabekk Station.

A car stops on the road in front of him. The man who opens the door on the driver's side is Paaske, and he gets out.

'Thought it was you, Jack. Been at Bjerke's?'

He shakes his head.

'You didn't turn up at the trial,' Paaske says, puffing life into his pipe.

Jack has nothing to say. He has no wish to say anything, either.

'You can run away from me, but you can't run away from a bad reputation.'

'What do you want?'

Paaske opens the passenger door for him. 'Hop in. I'm going to town anyway, and you have to go home, I assume?'

Jack walks around the car and gets in.

Paaske sets off. 'Bjerke'll go free,' he says, 'but my guess is the public prosecutor will decide to appeal. The German captain story.' Paaske shakes his head and grins. 'You'll be summoned when the public prosecutor appeals. Furthermore, you'll be fined because you failed to appear this time.'

'A big fine?'

Paaske shrugs. 'It'll hurt. That's the idea, but as you're in league with the wealthy, you can no doubt afford to pay.'

VI

After a week Jack can't be bothered to wait any longer and catches the metro to Sagene. From there he wanders between the farms in the Rivertzke quarter and ends up at the bus depot. Arvid Bjerke sees him approaching from a distance and goes out to meet him.

'Are you coming here?'

'We have unfinished business.'

A chauffeur is standing on the running board of the Overland. The man is holding a cloth in one hand and a tin of polish in the other. He stops polishing and watches. Jack doesn't know him, but nods a greeting anyway.

Bjerke tosses his head. 'Let's go inside.'

They enter the duty office. Inside, Bjerke's voice is more like a hiss. 'You can't come here.'

'Why not?'

'There's an appeal.'

'So what?'

'It means that they'll summon you as a witness again. They won't be fooled by an Amalie number a second time.'

Jack doesn't like the expression. An Amalie number. 'I'll turn up.'

'Are you out of your mind?'

Jack likes to hear the desperation in Bjerke's voice. 'I'll get a fine for not turning up this time,' he says. 'If I fail to appear next time, they can put me behind bars.'

'They won't, but they will fine you. I'll pay the fine. Rest assured.'

'I want to move on from this. If you're acquitted in the next round, they won't have finished with you. They'll appeal again, and I'm the one left sitting in the shit. I've been thinking about this. For me it's best to get it all over and done with.'

Bjerke drums his fingers on the table. Jack can see

he is searching for words, and wonders when the man is going to understand why he is here.

When Bjerke does finally speak, it is with an intense, almost imploring voice.

'Jack, I trust you. It will stop with the jury. If I'm acquitted, that's the end. You can't appeal against the jury's decision, but if I'm found guilty, I'll be convicted. So this is just a little favour. You've already saved my skin once. I'm grateful.'

'Are you?'

Bjerke angles his head, a little perplexed.

Jack says nothing. Waits. Either Arvid is utterly stupid or he is acting stupid. Jack comes to the conclusion that he is pretending so that he doesn't have to go any further. After a long, unpleasant silence the slippery crook finally goes to the safe in the corner and turns the combination wheel. He opens the steel door and removes two fat wads of banknotes.

'I *am* grateful, Jack. You can see that, can't you?'

Jack takes the money without answering. Slips off the elastic band and starts counting.

Bjerke watches as Jack flicks through the money. Jack looks up. Bjerke fetches another wad and passes it to him.

'Still unhappy?'

Jack doesn't answer. Instead he weighs the money in his hand. The wads are compact. Heavy.

'Your gun,' Jack says. 'Do you need it now that you're a law-abiding citizen?'

Bjerke stares at him. 'Close the door,' he says, turning to the display cabinet.

Jack stuffs the notes in his pocket and closes the door.

Bjerke opens the safe again. Turns and places it on

the table, the revolver he won in a poker game with a police officer a few years ago. 'It's yours, Jack.'

Jack takes it. The revolver is nice to hold. 'Ammo,' he says.

Bjerke inhales with a resigned shake of his head, bends down to the safe and takes out a box, which he lays on the table.

OSLO, 1938

I

A raindrop lands on the lighter flame, which goes out. Jack shields it with his other hand, but he has to flick the spark-wheel several times before it ignites. It casts a flickering light over the body on the ground. The man is dressed in a dark suit and a lighter-coloured coat. His hair is dark. He has lost his hat in the fall. Jack shakes his shoulder, but there is no sign of life. A thin line of blood has trickled from the corner of his mouth down to his chin. If he isn't dead, he definitely isn't conscious.

Jack extinguishes the flame and pockets his lighter. The rain is heavier now. It drips from the brim of his hat onto the man's face. Jack straightens up and can barely see the outline of the darkened buildings. He thinks about Werner Krause, who boarded the ferry. The German has something to answer for now, but he can't leave this man lying like this.

Jack seems to remember there is a covered walkway in front of the tall windows in the main building and can just make out the contours of the arches. At least there is some shelter from the rain. With the man's hat under his arm, he grabs the body beneath the shoulders and drags it under cover. Lays the body on the stone surface. As he struggles with the body he can feel one hand is wet. It is a dark liquid. Blood. Jack steps out into the rain and wipes his hand on some leaves on the ground. It still isn't clean, so he uses the tails of his coat. Then he goes back to the man. Searches for a pulse in his neck. The body is warm, but he can't feel any pulse.

Presumably the man has been killed, and Jack should notify the authorities. Once again he uses his lighter and illuminates the man's face, which is an anaemic white and set in a rigid grimace. He can't work out whether he has seen this man before or not.

There is supposed to be an elderly woman living in a little house here somewhere, a caretaker who keeps an eye on the palace when the royal family isn't in residence, but where does she live?

To the north and west all he can see is black tree-tops, while to the south the planted area is lower. He walks in that direction and collides with a post. His fingers find some wire netting. The smell is unmistakeable: this must be a chicken run. Behind the fence he can make out the ridge of a roof against the grey sky. There he sees a flickering light in one of the small windows. At last he finds the front door and knocks. Not a sound. He knocks again.

Eventually he hears some shuffling steps behind the door, which opens a couple of centimetres. Jack notices a chain on the inside and behind it a wrinkled face. A trembling hand is holding a candlestick with a tallow candle.

'Have you got a telephone?'

The woman doesn't answer, only shakes her head.

'I need a phone,' Jack says. 'There's been a murder.'

As soon as Jack utters the last word, the door closes. There is a rattle of metal as she locks up.

Jack knocks, but nothing happens. The door stays closed. 'Please open the door. Have you got a boat I can row over to town to inform the authorities?'

Not a sound.

Again he activates his lighter and holds it over his wrist watch. At least ten minutes have passed since Amalie should have been here.

Then he hears something he does not like the sound of. It is low and far away, but the sirens are growing in volume. Soon he can discern car lights behind the line of treetops to the west. Jack has no wish to meet the police, at least not beside the body of a man who has been murdered. So he hurries down the slope, slips, manages to stay upright, and comes down the narrow path leading him away, north towards the end of Frognerkilen. A few hundred metres down the road, he glances over his shoulder and sees the cones of light from two cars travelling at high speed. They are already on their way up the little hill to the palace. Jack hurries on, and as the sirens are switched off, he breaks into a run, panting for breath. He notices it has stopped raining. Visibility is now so good that he can see the boathouses at the end of Frognerkilen. At the same time he hears barking behind him. Just his luck. The police have brought dogs.

Jack crosses the field taking him to where the road leads back to town, but the sound of baying dogs is like something from a nightmare. Soon the yapping stops and that can mean only one thing: the dogs have been let loose. Jack trips and almost falls, but recovers and sprints alongside the sea towards the street lights further ahead.

While he is running, he looks down at his coat. There are dark stripes on it. Blood, he thinks, and rips it off his back. By the water's edge he stops to find some rocks to put in the pockets so that it won't float to the surface. He is standing with the coat in one hand and a rock in the other when he hears paws beating on the pavement. As he turns, he sees only the shadow of a dog in flight with its jaws bared. Jack holds the coat in front of him like a shield. The dog's jaws close around the material. It tries to snap at him, but the coat is in its mouth, so Jack wraps the rest around the dog and falls on top of it with his full weight. Its teeth tear at the coat. The dog is a bundle of muscle, impossible to hold, its head jerks from side to side and its jaws snap at him without cease. He feels the pain from the bites to his arm first, then to his hand. His grip on the dog slackens and he groans as it sinks its teeth into his calf. Now the dog has a hold on him. It jerks and growls as Jack fumbles for the rock and finds it. The rock is heavy, but not so big that he can't get his fingers around it. He aims a blow at the dog's skull and there is a crunch of bone. The dog bites harder. Jack hits it again. And again and again. His arm goes up and down like a crankshaft. Until it lets go of him.

He is left struggling to breathe and gasps for mouthfuls of air. Crawls onto all fours beside the dead dog, inhaling deeply. Eventually he manages to raise himself. Looks down at his clothes. There are streaks of mud down one trouser leg; the other is torn.

He stands there, a dead dog on the ground and a dead man's blood on his coat. Try and explain that to the police, he thinks, and realises he can't feel any pain, only the pounding of his heart. He has to get away. The police probably don't know where the dog has gone. He puts the rock in a coat pocket and looks for some more, stuffs the pockets full of stones and pebbles and throws it as far as he can into the sea. Then he grips the dog by its rear legs. It is heavy, but he swings it around like an Olympic hammer and throws it in the same direction. There is a loud splash as its body hits the water. Looking up to the ridge of the hill, he can see torch beams roaming around up there. They are searching for the dog and him.

Jack steps backward. He sidles alongside the wall in front of Brown & Boveri and climbs the slope to Bygdøy allé. It is late and he would prefer not to bump into the police now, bearing in mind the state he is in. The torn trouser leg flaps as he hurries along. Then he hears the sound of an engine. The black outline of a car is on its way down the hill. It has the massive bodywork of a Black Maria.

Jack dashes towards the nearest tree in the street. And makes himself as thin as he can. Stands motionless behind the tree trunk as the police vehicle slows down for the crossing. The beams from the headlamps pick out the tree and he sees his shadow against the wall behind him.

The vehicle has stopped. Jack imagines the driver has noticed his shadow and realised there is a man hiding behind a tree. Jack waits for the doors to open. Waits for shrill commands to be shouted and gives a start when the siren lets out a wail. His legs give way and he thinks he is lost, but no. The vehicle sets off down Bygdøy allé and accelerates. It is probably heading for Oscarshall. Jack waits until the Black Maria is out of sight before continuing up the hill. Another siren rings out. He sneaks behind the hedges at the crossing. A police saloon screams past. When the car has passed him, he runs on and sees a taxi parked at the top of the hill, in front of Frogner Church. He makes for a covered gateway to regain his breath.

He waits there until his breathing has calmed down. As he is about to walk to the taxi, he hears footsteps and peers out. A police officer is coming up the street and stops at the crossing.

Jack slides down the wall inside the gateway so as not to be seen. The silence is unbearable. Then he hears the footsteps again. The man is coming towards him, stops by the taxi and glances in through a side window. Straightens up and walks on. Jack has cramp in his thigh and has to stretch his leg. He scrapes a heel as he does so. The officer stops and looks in Jack's direction. Jack closes his eyes and waits, but hears nothing. In the end, he can't stand it any longer and opens his eyes. The policeman is nowhere to be seen.

Then he stands up, peers out and spots the back of the police officer further down the street. Jack strikes out for the taxi. Sees the driver in his seat asleep. His hat has slipped down and the brim is resting on his nose. Jack tears open the rear door and gets in. The driver sits up with a start and straightens his hat. Jack tells the man to drive to Åkebergveien. He doesn't want to give away his address, not in his present predicament.

The driver turns on the ignition. He is the garrulous type and talks about the big news, that Austria has been annexed by Germany.

'Hitler's from Austria, as you know. The papers said he drove through Braunau in an open car and people went crazy. They were shouting '*Heil Hitler*' and saluting. There's talk that Munich might become the new capital. What do you think?'

The car is nearing the fortress, and Jack looks out onto streets that are quiet, deserted almost. 'I don't think Hitler's the kind of man I'd get involved with,' he replies diplomatically. Jack would have liked to dis-

157

cuss the matter, but he wants to remain anonymous. He doesn't want this man's attention attracted to anything about him.

The driver says that *Aftenposten* thinks that Czechoslovakia can relax.

'But they won't. Hitler's a bastard, if you ask me. I'm glad that Nasjonal Samling and Quisling haven't made any inroads in Norway. You see, I have Jewish roots. It's impossible to be a Jew in Germany. They're not allowed to have a passport or work. They have their properties confiscated. Jews are beaten up in the streets and arrested illegally. If you have a grandmother who's half Jewish, you're no longer considered German. Whenever something happens, they blame a Jew — a Jew or a communist.'

The silence is oppressive when the driver goes quiet.

'Why don't they like the communists?' Jack asks to keep the man talking.

'It's because they think communists support international worker solidarity and prioritise it above everything else, but the Nazis are no better, if you ask me. The difference is only that they classify people by race and not by class.'

At last they have reached the intersection between Grønlandsleiret and Åkebergveien. Jack digs in his trouser pocket for coins, pays, gets out and waits until the car has driven off before limping through the side streets home.

Jack knows in himself that he did the right thing running away from the crime scene. He already has a conviction. He is what they call 'an old friend of the police'. They would lock him up without a second thought. If Amalie confirms his story they might let him go after a few days on bread and water, but he cannot muster any confidence that she would con-firm anything at all. Jack remembers her eyes and tone when she threatened him earlier in the day. Later she lured him into meeting her at a place where her gen-tleman friend committed a murder. As such thoughts race through his mind, he tries to rein in speculation and suspicions, but he has been on the run before. Instinct tells him not to go to his flat this time. Instead he opens the door of the abandoned sack factory in the neighbouring house.

Here, he makes a bed on the floor, beside his motor-bike. A burlap sack serves as a pillow and a tarpaulin as his mattress. Light from the street lamp in Rød-fyllgata enters through the window.

Fully dressed, he lies, staring up at the dark ceiling. The wound to his calf aches. He hears the scurry of little feet alongside the wall. Probably a mouse or a rat. Unable to distract himself from thinking about the dead man, he lies with his eyes open in the dark-ness. The man's body wasn't even cold, but Jack can't remember having heard a shot. Could he have been stabbed? The man might have been killed while he was getting off the metro in Skarpsno. Jack sees the silhouette of Werner Krause on board the ferry as it slips into the mist, then his thoughts go into a whirl again, out of control, until they merge into a dream. It is still night when the police stomp up the stairs to the first floor of Rødfyllgata 18. Jack lies still staring into the pitch-black. The police seem to be most inter-ested in waking up the whole neighbourhood. They yell. They pound on doors. He looks from under the engine of the motorbike — at the front door. This old wooden house is unoccupied, but do the police know that?

159

Then someone hammers so hard on the door that the windows rattle. Jack's sole thought is that the door is unlocked, takes a deep breath and stays still. The policeman keeps hammering.

'Open up! Police!'

Another thump on the door. Jack prays to God that he doesn't try the handle. There is absolute silence outside. Then the door bursts open and hits the wall with a bang. A black figure is silhouetted in the doorway. A man in a police uniform and hat. A hand gropes for a light switch. Jack holds his breath. The policeman's hand doesn't find one, so he turns on a torch instead. A torchlight flickers across the walls, finds the motorbike. Shines on it.

Jack doesn't think he is visible behind the bike and looks down himself. My shoes, he thinks. His shoes are sticking out from behind a wheel. If the man in the doorway moves the torch a tiny bit to the left, he will see his shoes and legs. Jack holds his breath and beads of sweat form. The man comes in. There is a crunch under his boots. Shines the torch across the wall. The man's foot kicks something. There is a clatter and the man swears, no more than two metres away now. The torch beam sweeps across the floor.

The man is fidgeting with something. Another shadow appears in the doorway.

'What are you doing?'

'Shh,' says the man with the torch.

Jack can hear it too. A rustling. The torch beam runs along the wall. It finds a rat frozen for a few seconds before darting off.

'That was his cousin,' the man standing in the doorway says. 'Obviously no one lives here. This is an abandoned factory.'

'Factory? This shack?'

Both of them grin.

The man with the torch makes for the door. 'He isn't here.'

Jack lies as rigid as before, staring at the two silhouettes in the doorway. Not daring to move a muscle.

There is a shout outside. The door closes. Footsteps fade into the distance.

Jack still doesn't move. *He isn't here.* So, they *are* searching for him. They were searching for him before — in Bygdøy. It was right to make a run for it. They knew he was there. No one else but Amalie could have told them he was there.

'What are you up to, Amalie?' he whispers to himself. 'What are you doing to me and why?'

Jack stares into the darkness. Still he can hear banging and yelling, but it isn't as loud now. Only after a very long time is it as silent as before.

It is impossible to go back to sleep. In the end, he gets up. His leg is stiff, but mostly because of his trousers sticking to the blood on his calf. When he looks from the door, he can't see anyone. He sneaks up to his flat. The steps creak on the staircase, but no doors open. People here hate the police, and if the cops are sniffing around the premises, they want to know as little as possible.

His flat door has been kicked open. There is white wood where the door strike used to be. *Upholders of law and order, my arse*, he thinks, and walks in. Switches on the light. Fortunately, they haven't destroyed anything, but they have emptied cupboards; there are clothes, kitchen utensils and chess pieces scattered all over the place. Jack searches through the mess until he finds a pair of trousers he can wear. He examines the wounds to his leg. They aren't too deep. There are several bite marks, but not many deep gashes. With his foot in the sink, he washes all the cuts and lacerations, and bandages them. Changes into clean trousers. Changes his shirt. Packs his shaving gear, some extra clothes and the bare essentials into a bike pannier. Hurries. Finally, he runs down the stairs, out and back to the wooden house.

He lies down on the same tarpaulin and stares at the ceiling. He doesn't fall asleep, he listens, first to the usual morning sounds: draymen yelling, horses clip-clopping over cobblestones and a two-stroke engine on the river. Beer bottles clinking as a horse-drawn cart passes. As soon as his watch shows that newsagents have opened, he gets up and walks down to the kiosk by the Tomtegata crossing. Luckily, there are lots of people around, but in the pile of newspapers there is only *Tidens Tegn*. Jack picks up a copy and waves to the vendor behind the counter. Leaves the coins on the pile of papers. Walks back to the shack, reading it.

There is no report on Bygdøy or Oscarshall. Most of the news is about Hitler and Austria. Otherwise there is an article about bank robbers in Horten, who, the police suspect, are day labourers from Oslo. There is some debate about whether the Workers' Fund money should be used to increase the old-age pension. A boat has sunk off the coast of Jutland. Why isn't there anything about a dead man in Bygdøy? Could the police have been investigating anything but the man's death? Jack doubts it.

Back in the sack factory, he accepts the reality of his situation. This isn't somewhere he can stay. First, he goes to the work bench with all the tools. The top drawer is locked. The key is in a cup on the shelf. He unlocks the drawer. Has to remove pliers, spanners and a mini anvil before he finds the cloth bundle at the bottom. He places the bundle on the bench and unrolls the cloth. The steel of the revolver gleams in the light from the window. Jack rotates the cylinder. It needs a spot of oil. On the shelf beside the cup there is a little can of gun oil. He slants it over the gun, drips oil over the movable parts and greases everything until it runs smoothly without any friction. Next, he rummages a bit further in the drawer to find the box of ammunition. Loads all the chambers. Places the box back in the drawer and the revolver in his pannier. Adds a suit jacket as well, together with the items he packed in his flat. Attaches the pannier to the bike and dons his motorbike jacket. Finally, he has a peep in the mirror above the workbench. With his leather helmet and dark googles on, not even his mother would be able to recognise him.

The petrol can is in the corner. He fills the tank, then opens the door and trundles out the bike. Closes the door after him. Sits on the bike, starts up and twists the throttle, out of the yard and past the queue outside the Café for the Unemployed.

The first priority now is to find somewhere else to live. The police drew a blank yesterday, but they will definitely be back. So he sets a course for Pilestredet to see Bibbi before she goes to work at *Telegrafen*. Asking Bibbi if he can stay with her for a few days will be crossing a line, but she is the only person he knows who is sure to say yes without asking any questions. Afterwards she will keep her mouth shut if he asks her to.

A police constable is directing traffic at the St Olavs gate crossing. Jack brakes and stops behind the flatbed of a lorry at the front. From here he can make out the entrance to the block where Bibbi and Oddmund live, and he can see he is too late. The woman with the blonde hair coming through the entrance is unmistakeable. The officer lets the traffic go. Jack accelerates and is about to wave to Bibbi when he sees that she isn't alone. She is waiting for someone, and behind her a man comes through the entrance. They walk together, arm in arm. The robust figure of Vidar, the wardrobe man at the Theatercafé is not to be mistaken either. Jack doesn't know what pains him most — Bibbi abandoning Oddmund or missing the bus as far as finding a bolthole is concerned. Neither of them notices him as he whizzes past.

Jack carries on, his mind vacant, mostly because he has no idea what to do next. Soon he is in Drammensveien and turns off at Sjølyst, passes the field where he escaped from the police the previous evening, then rides between the trees until he reaches the slip road to Oscarshall. Here, he stops the bike and leans it against a tree so that, under cover of the forest, he can sneak up on foot and venture as close to the pleasure palace as he dare without being seen. The palace looks peaceful and pink, like the scenery for some romantic adventure. The sight makes the night's events seem like utter fantasy, until he discovers that the area is now under guard. A uniformed police officer is leaning against a tree and smoking a cigarette. A twig cracks beneath Jack's foot. The policeman immediately straightens up and stares towards the trees the sound emanated from.

II

Everyone has secrets. Some people have secrets of such dimensions that you cannot imagine them. Paaske accepts this; man is a complex creature. Secrets are bound up with strong emotions, such as shame and honour. Paaske accepts that people fight their demons with a variety of methods, but he doesn't like being either tricked or beaten up. There is a difference between fighting your own fight and using others. In this particular case he feels more used and exploited with every day that passes.

After parking outside Båhusveien 22 he takes a deep breath, grips the door handle and gets out of the car.

A small piece of cardboard has been attached to the doorbell on the first floor: Gruber. Paaske rings, but nothing happens. He tries again, and at length the door is opened by a pretty woman in her mid-thirties, wearing an apron typical of women in this area. Her hair is light blonde, curly, with a side parting and held in place by a slide. She has alert blue eyes, and asks how she can help.

'I'm looking for fru Vera Gruber,' Paaske says.

'That's me,' she says with a weak smile. 'That is to say, I have kept my maiden name: Vera Halvorsen. My husband's name is Bernhard Gruber.'

Paaske is astonished and not a little perplexed.

'What do you want from me?' the woman says. 'Who are you?'

'My name's Ludvig Paaske. I have an important message. Above all, for Bernhard Gruber.'

'My husband isn't at home.'

'When do you expect him home?'

'He's on a business trip.'

'Where?'

'What's that to do with you?'

Paaske says he has something important to discuss with her husband.

'There's only me here. You'll have to discuss it with me.'

'I'm a private investigator. A woman pretending to be you, Bernhard Gruber's wife, came to my office and engaged my services.'

Now he has the woman's full attention.

'The job was to track your husband's movements and circle of acquaintances.'

Paaske has no idea what sort of reaction he expected, but it wasn't silence and an expression of deliberation. Paaske clears his throat and says the woman introduced herself as fru Bernhard Gruber and used Vera as a Christian name.

'So someone has been conspiring against you and your husband. I'm sure you appreciate that it's very important that I talk to your husband.'

Even now she says nothing. She merely eyes him up and down.

Paaske strokes the bump on the back of his head carefully and feels like shaking her, forcing her to tell him where Bernhard Gruber is.

'Have you got any ID?' she asks before he can say another word.

Paaske rummages through his inside pocket and passes her his card.

She reads it and says, 'I'll tell my husband to contact you as soon as he's back.'

Then she closes the door.

Paaske doesn't move for a few seconds. His fingers are burning to ring the bell again, but he rejects the idea, turns and walks slowly down the stairs and out to his car. From the driver's seat he looks up at the façade, at the first-floor windows. The same woman is standing in the window looking down at the car, alone, so she was probably telling the truth when she said her husband was travelling.

Should he make another attempt? Go back up, describe the fraudulent fru Gruber and ask if they know each other? Paaske rejects this, too. Instead, he starts up and drives off.

It is only when he is changing down gear on the hill in Griffenfeldts gate, on the way to the Geitmyrsveien intersection, that he notices he is being tailed. A glance in the mirror and he recognises the car. The grille with the vertical grooves and bow-tie emblem. A black Chevrolet.

III

Jack is rooted to the spot and holds his breath as the policeman stares up at the trees where he heard the crack of a twig. Jack uses his hunting experience: Never look straight at an animal. There are forces in eye contact, forces that are appraised by the object of your gaze. So he stands still while the policeman moves. The man takes a few steps and disappears behind some vegetation. Jack still holds his breath. He can hear the crunch of gravel underfoot. When the policeman reappears, Jack is still looking down at his side. The man stares into the trees for a long time. At last he drops his cigarette on the ground and

167

crushes it with the tip of his boot. Shortly afterwards he squats down and faces the opposite direction.

Jack still doesn't move. He looks for signs that the police may have positioned more guards around the crime scene, but he can't see anyone else apart from the young man, who is yawning now, clearly bored. Then Jack slowly retreats to where the undergrowth is thicker. From here he moves towards the palace to gain a better view. It is quite apparent now: there is no body lying in front of the tall windows where he dragged it last night. Again, Jack thinks about Amalie, who didn't turn up as arranged, and then he takes a long detour back to his bike.

He heads north and turns off by Smestad. He leans his bike against the station building in Besserud, removes his helmet and the dark goggles, and ambles up to the house. Her car is parked by the fence in front of the entrance. So Amalie is at home. Jack walks along the stone path between the berberis bushes. The sign beside the door is made of porcelain. The name is German and painted in black. Von Schiller. Above the sign there is a single bell with a pull handle. He pulls. The bell rings, but nothing happens. He pulls again. Steps back a pace and peers up at the window on the first floor. He catches a glimpse of her as she quickly backs into the room. Jack goes to the door, listens and hears footsteps inside.

'Come on, Amalie!' he shouts. 'Let me in. I know you're there. We have to talk.'

He hears something brush against the door inside. Presumably she is leaning against it. The magnets in his skin are never wrong. She is there. Only a few centimetres of wood are separating them now. He knows that with every fibre of his being.

'You know as well as I do that we have to talk,' he says. 'Let me in. I haven't come here to do anything to you. I went to meet you last night. You never showed up, but there was a man lying dead where we were supposed to meet. I want to know what happened. I want to know what you're up to. I have a right when it's me that's affected.'

Nothing happens behind the door.

'I left before the police got there, but sooner or later I'll have to speak to them. When I do, I'll send them on to you.'

Still nothing inside.

Annoyed, he bangs his fist on the door. 'Surely you must understand that we have to talk.'

The silence is total, and he can no longer feel the magnets in his skin. There is no point banging on the door anymore, but he does go to the bother of walking around the house. He passes a glass patio door and walks on to the garden, which has a long wall bordering the forest behind the house. Over the wall, between the trees, he finds the place where he was the previous evening, but now he can't see into her house. She has drawn the curtains in every window, even though it is the middle of the day.

IV

While Paaske still has his eyes glued to the rear-view mirror, the car behind him performs a manoeuvre. It accelerates past. As it does so, a uniformed arm shoots out of a window holding a stop sign. Paaske pulls in and comes to a halt.

He looks at the vehicle parked in front of his. A policeman steps out. Paaske recognises him by his

169

blond hair and sharp features. It is Johnny Moe, whom he doesn't particularly like. Moe and Paaske have had many disagreements over the years.

Paaske rolls down the window. Moe has bushier eyebrows than the last time they met, but his lips are as thin and severe as ever.

'I'll drive in front,' Moe says. 'There's something I have to show you.' He goes back to his car and gets in.

The police vehicle turns left into Geitmyrsveien, and Paaske follows him. It is making for the city centre. Soon they are in Kristian IVs gate and finally pass through the gateway behind the university hall. They park side by side.

Paaske follows Moe, who leads the way. The scissor gate in front of the door to the Medicine Faculty's Anatomical Institute is pushed aside. Moe knocks on the door. It is opened by one of the technicians, a red-haired man wearing a butcher's apron and gloves. Paaske nods to him and walks in. He has been here before. Now he is apprehensive, but remains patient.

The smell of chemicals in here is strong. Moe leads the way. They pass the brick tanks filled with dead bodies donated to science, carry on past the electric band saw, which, with the steel head over the blade, resembles the silhouette of an executioner. They pass shelves of jars containing dead animals in chemical liquids. One jar contains something that looks to be a human brain. A human embryo floats in another. Paaske checks his emotions as he walks these corridors again, to see if he likes this reunion or not, but cannot make up his mind.

Moe walks up the narrow, winding staircase first. They continue in file down the cramped corridors, where a smell of alcohol and formalin hangs in the air

170

like damp mist on a rainy evening. The wood creaks as they ascend another narrow, steep staircase. The door at the top leads into a little auditorium, where the chemical stench is now mixed with the smell of flesh and butchery. The auditorium has no windows. The rows of seats cladding the walls are in darkness.

In the middle of the floor there is a solitary zinc table. A naked light bulb hangs over a body on the table. The body is covered with a linen cloth. Moe waits for Paaske to come in. Then he closes the door, but doesn't bother to switch on more lights. Instead he walks over to the table and removes the cloth. The dead man's stomach has been opened. The innards have been sorted and placed in a variety of vessels and glass tubes in front of the lectern by the blackboard. So, a dead man is lying here on a zinc table in the auditorium of the university's Anatomical Institute — presumably the focus of the lecture, but what troubles Paaske is that, bending over and looking at the body, he actually spoke to him not that long ago. The dead man on the table is the person who stopped the stevedores beating him up. It is the man who spoke to him in Kafé Grei.

'Seen this guy before?' Johnny Moe asks.

Paaske straightens up. 'Why do you ask me about a corpse?'

Moe turns to the auditorium seats and rotates a switch on the wall. Lights come on over the rows. A familiar figure is sitting in the third row. Reidar Sveen is still wearing his coat and holding his hat in his lap. The crime division boss raises a hand in greeting and stands up. The sturdy figure edges out from the line of seats and comes down.

'How long have you been sitting in the dark?'

171

'I wanted to see your reaction,' Sveen says, turning to the zinc table. 'This body was found in Bygdøy yesterday evening, outside Oscarshall. He'd been shot and killed. I had a feeling you'd seen the man before.'

Paaske doesn't comment.

Sveen raises the jar containing the man's heart. 'We still haven't managed to locate the cartridge. My theory is that there isn't one because he was shot with a revolver. The gatekeeper out there tells us she was in bed when she heard a shot fired. A little afterwards a desperado was banging at her door wanting to get in. Naturally enough, she didn't let him; however, she did get a good look at him. I've also spoken to the crew running the ferry between Skarpsno and Bygdøy. They remember the passenger on their last trip very well. I showed them photos of ex-convicts. The gate-keeper, the ticket man and the skipper pointed out the same man.'

Sveen puts down the jar containing the man's heart, digs a hand in his pocket and holds up a photograph. It is a police mugshot, but the likeness is striking.

'That must've given you a good laugh,' Paaske says. 'That one was taken more than ten years ago.'

'1924. Fourteen years ago.'

'What made you go so far back through the files?'

Sveen smiles archly. 'They picked him out, Ludvig. Not one of them has a shadow of doubt. You and your assistant occasionally carry weapons.'

'That's true.'

'What kind?'

Paaske understands where Sveen is going, and tells him the truth. 'I have a Smith & Wesson. Jack Rivers has a single-action Nagant. Neither of us carries a gun on a daily basis, and when I saw him yesterday, there

172

was nothing to indicate he was carrying a revolver.'

'So you don't know if he was or he wasn't.'

Paaske is forced to agree.

'The patrol attending the scene had dogs with them. One dog tracked your assistant, but didn't return. Today the dog was found dead among the rocks in Frognerkilen. A coat was also found, stained with blood.' Sveen takes a deep breath. 'Why did Jack Rivers catch the ferry to Bygdøy last night?'

'Ask him and he'll tell you.'

'We've spent all night and many hours today searching for him. He's disappeared off the face of the earth. Now you're here, and you've seen the man before. Tell me when you met him and under what circumstances.'

Paaske tosses his head towards Johnny Moe. 'Why are you involving other departments in a murder?'

'Johnny represents Surveillance in this case.'

Paaske looks from Sveen to Moe and back. No form of explanation is forthcoming. Johnny Moe works in Surveillance. That is new. All Paaske knows is that the Surveillance Department is new too, and he finds it a little strange that Moe has been given such a post. Moe was born a sack of shite and it has taken him more than forty years to make something of himself. Now both Sveen and Moe are eyeing Paaske as though they are expecting him to cast some kind of definitive light on the circumstances.

'You've been shadowing me for quite a while already, Johnny.'

Johnny Moe doesn't answer.

'You followed my car not so long ago, and you were parked outside the block where I live.'

Moe is still silent.

Sveen clears his throat.

Paaske turns to him.

'I want to know what you know about this man,' Sveen says.

'Why's Surveillance spying on me?'

'Johnny,' Sveen says.

'I'm not spying on you, Ludvig.'

'Your car followed me.'

'Must be a coincidence.'

'It was parked outside my block in Fayes gate, but shot off when I showed my face.'

'I would've known that, if it'd been me who was in the car. What day was it? I'm not the only person who drives that car. I can look into the matter.'

Paaske turns to the door to leave.

Reidar Sveen stands in his way.

'Please step aside,' Paaske says.

Sveen shakes his head, and they look each other in the eye. 'You aren't a police officer anymore. Right now you're impeding my investigation. That's against the law.'

Paaske smiles at the threat, not that the smile softens Sveen. He stares back with an equally inflexible expression.

'Can you tell me what job Jack Rivers was on in the place where this man was killed?'

'Can you tell me why he would want to take the life of this man?'

Sveen pulls something from his pocket. A brown wallet. 'This was found a few metres from the body. An open, almost empty wallet. All that was in it was two tram tickets. Jack Rivers was alone with this man, pulled a gun and wanted his money. The man put up a fight and a shot went off.'

'Do you think my assistant would commit an armed robbery and kill the poor devil afterwards?'

'I don't think anything. I'm pursuing my investigation.'

'You're drawing hasty conclusions.'

Sveen shakes his head. 'I'm taking it one step at a time, and I always keep an open mind. Remember Mary Olsen?'

'The girl who disappeared? What has she got to do with this?'

'I would never have cracked that case if I hadn't kept an open mind.'

'An open mind? You spoke to clairvoyants and spiritualists.'

'Public opinion demanded it. We didn't want to leave any stone unturned, but it was honest, hard police work that meant that after four months we found her remains in a sack by the quay in Tjuvholmen. It was unrelenting graft that led me to the neighbour who killed her. No one had the slightest idea that he was such a simple-minded character, but it turned out that he was, despite a number of good references. A few days ago he was convicted. You can tell that to Jack Rivers when you see him: I never give up. If he's guilty, he'll go down. That would be true, of course, whether Rivers was on your payroll or not. How come you employed a criminal?'

'Friendship survives the ravages of time as well as gossip and nasty rumours. Jack Rivers served his sentence.'

Sveen looks at him as though he can't believe his ears.

Paaske stares back.

Sveen and Moe exchange looks. It is barely noticeable, but Paaske notices and feels the condescension that follows, the little union they form between themselves and against him. At the same time he can feel how sick he is of his ex-colleagues' arrogance, how sick he is of having to accept their condemnation. Accordingly, he looks Sveen straight in the eye, ready for confrontation and ready to clear the air once and for all.

'What's the problem?' he asks provocatively.

'I have one thing to say with regards to this body,' Sveen says. 'I'm going to solve the case. Jack Rivers is a key player, whether he's your friend or not. He knows something about this murder. I want to know what he knows.'

They stand weighing each other up, until Paaske gives way and nods towards the dead man. 'You said Jack was the only passenger on the ferry, but the victim travelled there. Did he have a car?'

'There was no car at the crime scene. If he'd taken a taxi, the driver would've called us sooner or later.'

'It hasn't occurred to you that the victim could've met the murderer before the last boat left for Skarpsno?'

'You don't work for the police anymore, Ludvig.'

'Then *someone* contacted the police,' Paaske says, 'and I doubt it was Jack, as you're searching for him. Nor the old dear in the gate-keeper's cottage. So, *someone else* knew what had happened. Let me guess: an anonymous caller? And they gave you the name of Jack Rivers? It's the only logical explanation for why you went back fourteen years in the files to find a photo of him. There's someone out there, at least one person, who knows a lot. For all you and I and Johnny know, this is precisely the person who shot and killed the man.'

'The police get a tip-off about who is at a crime scene,' Sveen says with annoyance. 'It turns out to be true. I want the man's statement, but he runs away, kills a police dog that was chasing after him and then goes underground. What would you do in my shoes? Stop looking for him?'

Paaske glances across at Johnny Moe. 'Why's the Surveillance Department interested in a murdered robbery victim?'

'I need to know the victim's identity,' Sveen says. 'There was no ID on him. Even the labels have been cut off his clothes.'

'A spy?'

The two officers exchange glances once again, and Sveen says: 'You know something about this man, Ludvig. Please share what you know with me now.'

'I don't know anything about the man, but I have spoken to him once. I was convinced he was German.'

'What did the two of you talk about?'

'The man claimed that the German security services had an agent in town, and he suggested this agent was after him, despite the fact that he wasn't a criminal. It was all very bizarre.'

'The German police have no agents here,' Sveen says.

Paaske turns to Johnny Moe. 'This German was supposed to be working for a department called the Gestapo. Apparently they run surveillance, like you're doing now, Johnny. So what does the Norwegian Police Surveillance Department say? Does the Gestapo have any agents here in Norway?'

Johnny Moe doesn't answer.

They both look at him, Paaske and Sveen, but Johnny still won't answer.

'The murder victim knew the name of the German agent: Werner Krause. I know he's staying at Hotel Westminster in Karl Johan. All you have to do is knock on his door and haul him out.'

Paaske turns to Sveen. 'My advice is: talk to Werner Krause. He knows all about the victim. I don't.'

V

It is many years since Jack has been to Arvid Bjerke's depot in Sagene. Now he notices that the company has a new name: *Ingeniør A. Bjerkes Buss Centrale*. Jack stops outside the wall, under the sign, gets off his bike and pushes it onto the stand, then walks in through the broad gates as he takes off his leather helmet and goggles.

There have been changes here. The depot is larger, the buses are more modern. They all look the same now — green — but the duty office is the same. The light is on, but there is no one inside. Jack carries on in, between two buses towering side by side. Soon he hears a familiar voice. A couple of legs are protruding from under a bus. It is a mechanic lying on a car creeper. A strong man in a dark suit is talking to the mechanic.

Bjerke is so unchanged that Jack is almost moved by seeing him again: the white smile, the rascally expression and the big fist pumping his hand.

The booming voice is also the same. 'What are you doing here, Jack? Looking for a job?'

Jack shakes his head. 'I was in the area, then I saw your big sign. *Hell*, I thought, *I spent my younger days in this place. Perhaps I should have a word with Arvid and rediscover my youth.*'

'We've grown, Jack, expanded.'

Jack nods and looks around feigning that he is impressed. Bjerke has expanded too. His stomach is big, his double chin wobbles, and his thighs are so fat he has to find his sea-legs when he walks.

'Those were the days, Jack.'

'All gone.'

'Do you remember driving the model T across the railway bridge? A T-Ford lorry?'

Bjerke talks to the mechanic under the bus. Bjerke kicks the creeper. 'Bjarne, this guy drove over the railway bridge in Minnesund in a bloody T-Ford.'

The man on the board wriggles out. He is wearing a Standard cap and oil is streaked across his cheek. He dries his hands on some cotton waste.

'Today you can drive over Minnesund in a car beside the railway track,' Bjerke says. 'That wasn't there when this guy crossed on the rails.'

'Must've been hairy,' the mechanic says.

'Johan was with me,' Jack says.

'Johan?' Bjerke is lost.

'Amalie's brother.'

'Oh, Christ, yes, Amalie. Do you remember her, Jack?'

Bjerke wraps an arm around his shoulder and leads him to the office.

'The girl with one blue and one brown eye,' Jack says.

Bjerke grins. 'Amalie. The best lay I've had in my life, but don't say that to the old girl.'

'What happened to her, to Amalie?'

'She moved to Germany.'

'Ah, of course, I knew. I saw her off on the train.'

'She got married in Germany,' Bjerke says. 'To a

German who speaks Norwegian.'

Now, as in the old days, there is a pallet in front of the door as a step. They go in. The same low sofa is there by the wall. The same worn chairs on the other side of the table. The gas stove on the corner table is new. The office door is open. Inside, Julie used to sit organising bus schedules and doing the accounts.

'Take a pew, Jack, and I'll fix us some coffee. How come I haven't seen you for several years?'

'I've been to sea. Signed off last year.'

'Where?'

'Just about everywhere, from North Africa and the Med, Suez and the Indian Ocean, the Persian Gulf, Japan. The four winds and the seven seas, like in the song, but mostly between the Caribbean islands.'

'Right,' Bjerke says, guiding a big pan over the gas flame. 'I've been here, working with transport the whole time, while Amalie finally found what she was looking for, a guy with gold up his arse. Love cars. Love fast cars, good food and lovely ladies.'

'Have you kept in contact with her?'

'With Amalie? No. I happened to bump into them once.'

Jack has to smile at Bjerke's amateur dramatics.

Bjerke smiles back. 'They were with a delegation from a German airline when we met. Lufthansa. There was a seminar on Gressholmen island. It's a few years ago now. It was when Oslo municipality bought Snarøya in connection with the planned new airport out there. I'm going to start a bus route when the airport opens. Have to think of the future, you know. That's why we're setting up a bus route to Fornebu. I've bought a plot in Skøyen, by the way. For a bus depot. They start building this autumn. The day the new airport opens is the day we run buses to and from the airport.'

'We?'

'Wife and I. You know. Julie's got money. I'm responsible for the practical side.' Bjerke grins. 'Yes, Amalie's husband was interested in investing in transport.'

The pan rumbles as it heats up. Bjerke fills two cups and passes one to Jack.

The coffee is not bad. It is strong and has probably been reheated a few times.

'And did he? Invest?'

'That was why he came. Germans, you know, they can't get enough of Norway.'

'When was this?'

'Maybe five years ago. It was just after the fire in Berlin. This man's high up in the state apparatus and talked all the time about the Jew who set fire to the Reichstag. He and Amalie were pretty angry about the Jews. She's often in Norway. Because of her brother. You know Amalie's always been crazy about her mad brother.'

Bjerke holds a sugar cube between his lips, pours coffee into a saucer and slurps it up.

The door opens. A woman comes in, wearing a Persian coat knotted around the waist and high, laced-up boots. Her black hair cascades down her back from under an elegant hat she uses both hands to remove.

Julie Bjerke angles her head and recognises him, he can see, but for some reason, she doesn't want that to be known. 'Do I know you?' she says with her eyebrows raised. They resemble two fine pencil strokes.

'Julie,' Bjerke says. 'This is Jack, of course. Don't

181

you remember Jack Rivers from the roaring twenties?'

Still she is silent, and Jack doesn't understand why.

He decides to play along. 'I was marginally involved in driving buses, but mostly transporting goods.'

'Transporting goods.' Bjerke grins. 'Bloody hell, you can say that again. I miss you already, Jack.'

Julie Bjerke turns her back on them and walks out. The door closes behind her.

Bjerke winks at Jack. 'Women, you know how it is. Once a month. Hell. I can see you don't wear a ring. Wise. Never get married, Jack.'

Jack watches her through the window. Julie has removed her coat, and she looks good in the dress. As though she has noticed his eyes, she glances over her shoulder. They appraise each other for some long seconds.

'She looks after herself,' he says.

Bjerke boxes him lightly on the shoulder. 'You too, Jack. You don't look a day older. Unlike me.'

Bjerke pats his stomach and laughs. Ever the charmer. His laughter is infectious.

Jack smiles back, polite, but pensive. He has missed the bus as regards begging for a bed at Bibbi's. This is plan B. And now, sitting here and gazing into the toothpaste-white, Yankee grin of Arvid Bjerke he can feel he likes the plan better and better.

'Arvid. I need a bolthole. A few days, that's all. Until the worst heat has passed.'

Bjerke's soft, fleshy face changes in an instant. His mouth becomes a tight line, and a deep frown has appeared on his forehead. 'It's been a few years since I cut corners and messed with the law. I'm a respectable man now.'

Jack nods. 'I can see things are going really well.

Good job you got off the hook that time. I seem to remember the key police witness never showed up. If he had done and if he'd said who brought in the goods and how they were distributed, you would've spent a few years in Botsen prison, and your future prospects would've been far murkier than the ones you're sunning yourself in now.'

Bjerke's lips are still tight. The silence between them quivers for a few long seconds.

'I seem to remember I was grateful, Jack.'

'Now I need somewhere to lie low. Just for a few days.'

'We were quits, Jack. Today you'll have to go elsewhere.'

Jack nods.

Bjerke grins again. Clearly thinking the battle is over, but this time Jack doesn't smile back.

'I haven't been quite honest with you, Arvid.'

Bjerke's smile fades.

'I've had a bit to do with Amalie recently. Now she's got a house in Doktor Holms vei.'

Bjerke sends him a stiff glare.

'The same street you and Julie live in. You and Julie and the dog shorn like a sheep.'

Bjerke says nothing.

'Yesterday I was above the house where Amalie is staying. Big windows. When it's dark outside and light indoors, it's like a cinema.'

'Are you a Peeping Tom?'

'I'm not so good at labelling people. Don't want to speculate on what's wrong with you, either.'

'She's divorced,' Bjerke says. 'Amalie. Just divorced her husband, but lives in the house, when she's in the country, to visit her brother.'

183

'You keep her company?'

Bjerke doesn't answer.

'Relations weren't so cordial last night. Had she done something to you?'

Bjerke doesn't answer.

'Perhaps best to ask Amalie? Or maybe your wife?'

Bjerke gets up and goes to the key cabinet on the wall.

'Being married is a much more complex and complicated business than you read about in novels, Jack.' Bjerke holds up a key. 'I don't need any help from you to make this business any worse than it already is. The house in Holtekilen is empty. Keep a low profile, and when the heat's off, as you put it, you can leave this key in the post box outside here. I never want to set eyes on you again.'

Jack takes the key, turns his back on Bjerke and leaves. Jack has never understood people who feel the need to say aloud what they are thinking.

VI

Arvid Bjerke stands watching through the window as Jack walks through the depot and disappears behind the bus nearest the gates. Then he takes a deep breath and has the unpleasant feeling that he has been used. What started as a warm reunion has turned into something quite different. This guy shows up after all these years, exclusively for his own benefit. Arvid dislikes such situations and such people. So he wishes he hadn't given in to him. In addition, he doesn't like himself now, his weakness. He dislikes the reunion itself, while also wondering why this ghost of the past is suddenly spying on the

184

people in the street where he lives. He is so immersed in his own thoughts that he isn't aware of Julie's presence until she closes the door after her. Then he turns and looks at her.

'Fancy that,' she says, walking past him into the office.

He follows her. Stops in the doorway and watches her sit down at the desk, holding her hair with both hands and securing it behind with a slide.

'The world's full of surprises,' he says.

'So, you were surprised, were you?' Julie asks, opening a drawer and taking out the ledger. Opens the next drawer, where she finds a pen and checks the nib.

'Weren't you?'

'Jack's a man in his best years. Or did you perhaps imagine he was dead?'

'What were the theatrics about? You recognised him alright.'

Julie doesn't answer. Stiff and inaccessible, she sits as she did before. The Ice Queen enters numbers in the ledger.

Arvid breathes in and looks at the clock. 'I'm late,' he says and makes a move to leave.

'What did he want?'

Arvid turns again to the Ice Queen, who is still concentrating on the figures. She is using blotting paper now, without looking at him, without looking up. Places the blotting paper before writing any further. Only the scratch of her nib can be heard.

'Julie!'

'Just answer me. What did he want?'

Arvid stands in the doorway staring at her back, feeling how sick he is of having to weigh his words judiciously, of having to walk on eggshells, of Julie's inability to be more pragmatic. Arvid wonders how much longer they will be like this.

'He asked me about somewhere to stay for a while,' he says.

She flicks through the invoices. Punches holes in one. Turns for a file on the shelf by the wall. Inserts the invoice and replaces the file. 'Why?'

'I don't know,' he snaps.

At length she gets up and eyes him. 'You couldn't say no, could you.' 'No, why should I?'

They glare at each other, and he realises he doesn't have the words to confront her frigidity.

'I gave him the key to Villa Strand. It'll only be for a few days. I'll make sure the place is cleaned and tidied properly as soon he's gone. Is that OK with you?'

Arvid doesn't wait for an answer. He leaves and slams the door hard behind him.

VII

Jack rides off, unable to stop thinking about this strange couple. The well-fed businessman who at first rejects him, then hands over a key. Julie, who probably remembers Jack as well as she remembers she is a woman. Although feigning something else. Jack doesn't understand it.

From some distance he sees the car parked on the cobblestones in Rødfyllgata. The silhouettes of the men sitting inside are like pawns on a chessboard. Police, no question about it. Jack is glad he is wearing a leather helmet and goggles as he roars past.

★ ★ ★

It is afternoon by the time he has manoeuvred the motorbike down the gravel drive and stopped in front of the darkened house in Holtekilen. He pushes it up onto the stand and removes the pannier hanging over the wheel. At first he stares up at the house. Quite a bit has happened in the last fourteen years. The paint on the south wall is peeling. A plank in the staircase is rotting.

Jack turns and gazes across the sea. The old boat is moored at the quay, as before. It lies well in the water and the paintwork gleams. Some people look after their boats better than their houses.

Jack finds the key and lets himself in. The house smells of dust and stale air. So he leaves the door wide open. It feels strange to walk into the house; it is almost like visiting a stage in a theatre where you once performed a role you don't remember much of anymore. The house still isn't on mains electricity. The paraffin lamps in the ceiling are the same as those before. He cautiously touches the glass tube as he checks the oil level and the wick. The dining-room table is where it had been many years ago. The same wood stove is in the corner of the kitchen, but is now supplemented by a gas stove on the worktop. He continues up the stairs to the first floor. The beds are in the same places, with duvets and embroidered quilts. He opens a window to allow air to circulate and then goes down-stairs to the living room. The furniture has been covered with large sheets. He removes them one by one — the sofa, the armchairs, the table — thinking how time can go round in circles. Now he is back in this house, folding large sheets, the master of the place where he was once a servant.

He releases the catches on the panoramic win-

187

dow in the living room. It is stuck. To loosen it he has to bang gently — first at the top, then at the bottom — and repeat the process several times. When the window finally opens, he fetches the pannier with his cigarettes. Sits down on a chair and rests his feet on the table. A current of cold air runs through the room. He painstakingly gets up from the chair, goes into the hall and closes the front door.

OSLO FJORD, MAY 1925

I

The bow lies deep in the water. Jack has stowed the liquor cans in the forecastle under the foredeck, knowing that when he starts the main engine, *Gloria* will still easily be able to rise in the sea — if he wants. It should be a quiet trip back. The wind has picked up now, in the Grisebåene shallows, in Swedish waters, south of the Torbjørnskjær lighthouse. If the bow bangs up and down too much, the cargo can loosen.

Jack undoes the mooring ropes holding *Gloria* to the German cutter. Starts the main engine and waves to the crew leaning on the railings a couple of metres above him. The captain has shoved his cap back and raises a hand as Jack reverses the boat. *Gloria*, a twenty-four foot *plattgatter*, built in shiny mahogany at Helle Boatbuilders in Arendal, turns. Now she is calm as Jack shifts the gear into neutral.

Jack loves this boat. It is long, narrow and has a prow that is longer than half the hull. Under the deck there is a 180-horse-power engine. It acts as reserve to a Napier aircraft engine aft. *Gloria* has a total top speed of close on forty knots — if there are two people on board, but Jack no longer has a mechanic. Without him it will be hard to start the extra engine, but he believes in *Gloria* anyway. He thinks he can easily outrun *Rappen* — the customs and excise racer. The only fear he has is their armed cruisers. In March a boat smuggling fifty cans was leaving Grisebåene when a cruiser fired a warning shot and then twelve live rounds. One of the shells went straight through both of the guys in the boat. The two deaths sent shock waves through most in the trade, but the Customs & Excise action also raised prices.

The lighthouse on the island of Torbjørnskjær looks like a red stone church with the light as the spire. Several families are said to live there. As always, he wonders how people get to and from this place with sheer rock faces and the sea in constant motion.

Soon the lighthouse is behind him, and he wonders whether he should make for fru Arbostad in Skjeberg-kilen bay now or drop in on the return journey. Jack regularly goes to fru Arbostad and gives her money. Her husband was the skipper of a fishing smack that Bjerke used to transport booze to the harbour. When Bjerke stopped smuggling and sold the smack, Arbostad was left unemployed, but was the obvious person to be the mechanic when Jack bought *Gloria*. From then on they worked together on every single trip, until one day in February. It was cold, a really freezing, brutal day — one of those that casts a sense of lifelessness over land and sea, a day when the sparse light is as blue as ice, and drifts swirl over snowed-in fences and roof ridges that look lost for ever in a world you would not believe could reawaken. Strangely enough, Oslo's internal harbour was still open, but would soon freeze over. Jack had no idea how cold it was that night, but it was bitter enough for *Gloria*'s engine to stall and drift towards Jomfruland and Kragerø. There was thick ice on the railings and the foredeck. Jack couldn't restart the engine and finally poked his head down below, to where the mechanic was.

'Aren't you working?'

Arbostad was on his knees, big and pale, holding his chest. 'It's bad, Jack. I'm in real pain, but it'll soon pass. It always does. Hang on a bit.'

The boat was drifting fast. Without an engine there was no chance of turning the boat and meeting the swell. Hanging on was out of the question.

'You'll have to hold the tiller while I try and get the engine started.' With that Arbostad trudged to the tiller, bent double, while Jack saw to the engine. When it failed it was usually because of condensation, and he would be able to fix that if he inspected the filters, but in these temperatures this was a shit job. Not only that, the boat was rolling in the heavy sea. The cold bit at his hands, and he dropped the screws on the deck while he was blowing on his fingers. The screws rolled under the hatches, where water was sloshing around, so he had to go down on all fours and shine the torch on them. Eventually he managed to start up the reserve engine and yelled to Arbostad that he could give it some throttle. Arbostad didn't. So Jack climbed back up. Arbostad was sitting at the tiller, but could neither see nor hear. The boat was already heading for the rocks in the waters outside Portør. Arbostad was dead. Jack realised that when he nudged him aside and his body almost slid into the sea. However, at the last minute, he managed to lay him on the deck and steer the boat away from the rocks. Jack couldn't stop thinking that he had killed Arbostad, that he had allowed the poor man to freeze to death at the tiller. He begged God for forgiveness all the way to Skjebergkilen, but the doctor from Sarpsborg said it had been his heart. Arbostad had had a bad heart. Everyone knew that.

'Don't blame yourself,' said Evelyn, Arbostad's wife.

191

'My husband knew what he was doing. We needed the money.'

Everyone needs money, and since then he has often dropped by with a small contribution for the widow. There are two women he maintains now: Arbostad's widow and his mother. The latter is becoming more and more fragile. Jack would like his mother to live in a flat in town, so that he can keep an eye on her, but she refuses to move from her house in the forest. She wants to hear birdsong in the morning and sit at the window, seeing deer roam around the edge of the trees. Jack can't get her away from the window. All he can do is give her money, so that she has food and wood and whatever basic help she needs.

★ ★ ★

Jack runs the aircraft engine at a moderate rpm and doesn't notice his pursuer at once. What gives them away is the noise. It is a speedboat, and when the contours of the boat are revealed against the grey sky, he can clearly make out more than two men on board. It must be *Rappen*.

Gloria rises from the water as he accelerates. The bow hits the waves hard and the spray drenches him in seconds. *Pull yourself together*, he tells himself. The important thing now is to invite the heavy sea along for the trip instead of fighting it. This is a challenge. Without a backward look, he makes a decision: he turns to port and ramps up the speed of the aircraft engine, but he has the sea almost alongside him and has to work harder with the tiller. Jack thumps the hull with his fist and tells her she is good. When he finally does look over his shoulder he can't see *Rappen* anymore, but he can make out what may be a black cloud to the east. It might be the smoke from a big boat. It could be the customs cruiser. Jack holds a steady course west.

A warning shot crosses his bows. It is the cruiser. Jack knows he is up against it now, but he is not about to let the customs officials board *Gloria*. So there is only one thing to do: give the aircraft engine everything it has got. The boat is heavily loaded, and he is short of a mechanic; nevertheless the weather is too bad to race with the extra power. He has one single aim: to cross the fjord unscathed. Somewhere between Sandø, Hvasser and Tjøme it should be possible to find shelter and a hidden quay.

Fully concentrated, he carries on and sees a projectile plough through the sea only a few metres to port a second before he hears the explosion. How much luck can he have, he thinks, and knows in his heart that the boat will not escape the third shot, but he doesn't look back. When at last he does, neither the cruiser nor *Rappen* are anywhere to be seen.

It is too early to breathe out though. Jack senses rather than hears the surf breaking over the rocks by the shore as he scans the area for Røsse Sound. Finally, he realises that he has passed it and turns starboard. He has land on the starboard side. It must be Tjøme. Nonetheless, he doesn't dare believe that he is out of trouble, but soon espies well-known landmarks in the twilight. He has been here before. The boat glides forward into calm waters, with rocks and islets on either side. The engine is almost idling, but the boat is still doing five knots as he searches for a place to hide. Ahead of him there is a small boat rowed by a solitary figure. Too late he sees the boat has a fishing line in the water, and he turns hard starboard not to get it tied around his propeller. A woman is rowing the boat and she is angry. He doesn't hear what she shouts, but says it to himself anyway: 'Watch out, you clumsy clot!'

Jack waves to her and turns between two rocks. Here he finds the perfect place. The islets form an atoll encircling some metres of beach in such a way that the water inside is as calm as a pond. A ring bolt has been hammered into a crack in the rock sloping gently down into the water. First, he drops anchor. Then he cuts the engine and clambers up onto the foredeck. Stands with the rope in his hand, as *Gloria* glides into land. Perfect. As the anchor holds the boat back with a little jerk he jumps onto the rock and makes it fast. Then he jumps back on board, goes under the bow deck, changes into dry clothes and takes a packet of cigarettes from the jacket hanging on the pantry door. It is chilly, but he will soon be warm. His jumper is made from fine-meshed wool and wadmal frieze. Pleased with himself, he slaps the bulkhead and thanks *Gloria* for the part she played. Leans back at his ease and looks at the goods. A little later he hears the sound of oars.

As he pokes his head out to check, he sees a woman with thick blonde hair in a ponytail kneeling down and mooring her boat to the same ring bolt. She is wearing a woollen skirt, high boots and a thick jacket. It is the woman who was rowing the boat.

'This is private,' she says, standing up.

'Am I in anyone's way?'

'It's good manners to ask, isn't it?'

'I didn't think I was in anyone's way.'

'This is where I moor my boat.'

'I'm sorry,' Jack says. 'I just wanted to wait until the wind fell, but I'll find somewhere else.'

He jumps ashore and is about to untie the mooring rope.

'Never mind,' she says.

'So I can moor here for the night?'

'Townie, are you? From Kristiania?'

'Oslo. It's called Oslo now.'

Jack grins. She smiles back.

'There's only me,' he says. 'I'm from Oslo and I'm going back.'

'With a boat full of bootleg.'

'Who says so?'

'Do you dare deny it? You aren't the first smuggler to seek refuge in the bay here. I just saw *Rappen* going through the sound. They were searching for someone.'

'My name's Jack. And you?'

Her eyes are critical at first, but then she seems to make up her mind.

'Kristin.'

'Is it a long time since you saw it — *Rappen*?'

Kristin shakes her head.

'They went past?'

'Towards Veierland.'

'I'm happy to pay for the berth.'

'If you pay with booze.'

Jack hesitates. It is his turn to look at her now. The woollen clothes do their best to conceal her figure. Kristin isn't tall, reaching only up to his shoulders, but the evening light reveals attractive features in a face with two ice-blue eyes flashing with life and intelligence. Jack cannot convince himself that this woman drinks. Presumably she wants the alcohol to sell it on, but she has seen the boat and she might talk.

'I don't snitch,' she says, as though she can read his mind. 'And I can run up and fetch you some supper.'

Jack still hesitates.

'Something savoury now and porridge early tomorrow.'

'With syrup and sugar?'

'If that's how you like it,' she smiles.

'You like syrup and sugar on your porridge too, don't you?' he says.

Kristin shrugs, still smiling. She has a nice mouth.

'I hope I didn't destroy your fishing line,' he says.

Kristin shakes her head, turns and raises a zinc bucket onto the rock. 'I caught some mackerel.'

Mackerel in May was early, he thinks, and looks in the bucket, but she is telling the truth. The bucket is almost full of the black-and-blue striped backs of mackerel, coiled around one another.

'I'm going to sell them,' she says. 'To fru Appelsvold in Oterstig. The hotel.'

'I fancy a fried mackerel this evening,' he says. 'You can have the booze,' he says when she hesitates. 'The spirits you get from me will give you good money at the hotel. They won't miss a poor little mackerel.'

'We'll see,' she says, turning away and going.

Jack stands watching her. She has a springy stride and her ponytail bounces against her neck. A real wild rose: a woman who fishes for mackerel and sells it to survive. *I wonder what her husband does?* he thinks, jumping back into the boat. The weather is beginning to brighten up, but he is already looking forward to her return.

OSLO, 1938

I

After getting up, Paaske first folds his pyjamas and makes the bed, then goes into the bathroom and washes and trims his beard. He likes distinct lines and uses a cut-throat razor to define the beardline on his cheek, under his nose and under his chin. Then he cleans his teeth, puts on his underwear and his garters and attaches his socks. Recently he has taken to wearing a net vest. It is constructed in the same way as Viking chainmail. A Norwegian army commandant, Henrik Brun, is supposed to have spent years researching clothing that insulates the body against the winter cold. The secret is a layer of air between the skin and the garment, and the coarse knitting pattern provides precisely this layer.

In the kitchen he puts the coffee on to boil and goes back to the sitting room. Here he slips into a white shirt with a starched chest and collar. His shirts are delivered by the laundry every two weeks and lie neatly folded in a pile in his wardrobe. Cuff links always cause him problems, and he prefers the type made of material. Then he plugs in the electric iron so that he can restore the crease in his trousers. He watches the iron heat up while keeping an eye on the coffee. Then pulls the pan off the ring to let the coffee brew.

He splashes a few drops of water over the crease in his trousers. Puts them on, buttons up his waistcoat and checks his watch. He isn't hungry so early in the morning, but enjoys his coffee in the sitting-room armchair as he fires up his first pipe of the day. Soon he is ready for the new day, but perhaps the most important part of his routine remains: his shoes. Paaske puts on an apron to protect his shirt, takes the tube of shoe polish and brushes it lightly into the leather, then uses a rag to shine it. It is not only the sight of gleaming shoes that appeals to him but the smell. It is the smell of order and discipline.

★ ★ ★

It is a bright morning. The sun is rising behind the tenement blocks in Bogstadveien when he parks his car and walks the last few metres to the steps leading up to Majorstuhuset. In the kiosk by the entrance to the Holmenkollen Line he buys the morning edition of *Aftenposten* and skims the headlines as he waits for the lift. The main feature is the robbery and murder in Oscarshall. The article doesn't tell him any more than he already knows.

It is half past seven when the lift attendant slides open the scissor gate on the third floor. Paaske can see from a distance that the office door is unlocked. Jack is sitting behind his desk with his nose in the paper. Both mumble a good morning. Paaske hangs up his light coat and lays his hat and newspaper on the shelf. He still has his back to Jack as he says:

'Front page. Murder in Bygdøy.'

Paaske turns to Jack, who responds with raised eyebrows.

'I've been told by a secure source that you're well informed about the case. Taking a risk coming here, aren't you?'

Jack doesn't answer now either.

'You have a Nagant, don't you?'

'That's correct.'

'Where is it?'

'Here.'

Jack rummages in a leather bag on the floor and places the revolver on the newspaper. Paaske takes it and sniffs. It smells of oil, not cordite. Jack leans back and eyeballs him with a mocking smile on his face. Paaske checks the chamber. Counts the bullets, examines the percussion caps before replacing it on the desk.

'The victim the paper describes is the man you photographed getting out of a car in Carl Berners plass. He was shot.'

Jack says nothing.

'You were at the scene before, during or shortly after it happened.'

'Says who?'

'The police. They contacted me yesterday and showed me the corpse.'

Jack sighs. 'I've seen the corpse too.'

'When?'

'Shortly after his heart stopped beating.'

'Was it you who shot him?'

'What does the gun tell you?'

'I have to ask, Jack. And I think you should answer.'

'It wasn't me.'

'The police can't get hold of you.'

'They want to throw me in the jug.'

'The police think a robber — you — shot him down to steal his wallet.'

Jack just shakes his head.

'What were you doing in Bygdøy?'

'Amalie, the woman calling herself Vera Gruber, told me to go there.'

Paaske sits down.

'It transpires she was married to a German, some-one called Von Schiller. Last night she appeared at my place. Read me the riot act and drove off, but a little later in the evening she rang, apologised and said she wanted to talk, but refused to talk over the phone. Wanted to meet me in Oscarshall. Told me to be there at ten.'

Jack leans back in his chair and tells Paaske about the ferry trip from Skarpsno and the meeting with Werner Krause. 'I had some misgivings, but the ferry left with the guy on board and I was supposed to meet Amalie, as I said, so I went into the garden and up to the main building. When I reached the gravel area I tripped over a body on the ground. It had begun to rain, so I pulled him under cover.'

'You moved the body?'

'I didn't think he should lie there in the rain.'

'How far did you walk before you tripped over him?'

'No idea.'

'Think.'

'From the top of the steps? Ten metres perhaps. Twelve?'

'How far did you drag the body?'

'Twenty metres? Thirty? Why?'

Paaske doesn't answer at once. Werner Krause is a German policeman. If he shot the man it is not unlikely that he used his service pistol, a Luger. It ejects a cartridge, but the police haven't found it. As Jack dragged the body under cover, it is possible that the police didn't know where to look for it.

'I felt his neck,' Jack says. 'No pulse. Went to the gate-keeper's and knocked on the door. I had to inform the police and asked if I could use a phone, but the woman who opened the door slammed it in my face and didn't open up again. Then I heard the sirens and made off.'

'The dog,' Paaske says. 'When the police found their dog, it was dead.'

'It attacked me. It was self-defence.'

'How did you kill it?'

'With a rock.'

Jack lifts his trouser leg so that Paaske can see the bandage.

It's the leg of a miserable wretch, Paaske thinks immediately. His shoe isn't polished and his stocking isn't straight. 'Amalie von Schiller. When and where did you get to know her?'

Jack takes a deep breath and leans back. 'She was eighteen. No parents. Living with her brother and some relatives in Enerhaugen. Amalie was a girl with no money and only one aim in life: to escape from poverty. There wasn't much I could do about her aims, but she was still flesh and blood. Our paths crossed a few times.'

'You were her boyfriend?'

'Amalie would never have a boyfriend.'

'When was this?'

'When I worked for Arvid Bjerke.'

They exchange glances. Jack smirks. Paaske understands. He has never forgotten the case against Bjerke, and he never accepted the final outcome.

'Amalie was a maid in their house. That was doomed, too.'

'Why?'

'He humiliated his wife. Bedded the maids and she knew it.'

Paaske reflects on what Jack has said. It is news to him that Arvid Bjerke was unfaithful, and he wonders if things would have been different if he had known. Wonders if he would have done anything differently — had he known. But, he thinks, taking a deep breath, this all happened a long time ago; it is water under the bridge.

'You think Arvid Bjerke's relationship with this Amalie could've been the reason for Julie to go to the police?'

'I know Julie Bjerke wasn't happily married, that she contacted you and told you what her husband was up to in addition to passenger transport. I'm pretty certain about why she did it, but surely you must've had your own theories.'

'I was surprised, that's right, but Julie was young and came from a good family. She told me personally that all she wanted was to extract herself from a situation she could no longer tolerate. Living with shame and constant fear of what her husband's illegal activities might lead to made her desperate. The only way out she could see was to inform the police.'

Paaske gets up, walks over to the window and looks out, remembering Julie Bjerke with some tenderness. At the time it had been a mystery to him how such a wonderful creature could choose such a crook as her husband. Again he catches himself wondering if anything would have been different if he had known how tormented she really was.

He can see Jack's reflection in the window; he's smiling patronisingly. He turns back to him.

'When Bjerke was on the run, Julie bit the bullet

and ran the bus company,' Jack says. 'Gossip to her was like water off a duck's back. When the scandal was at its worst, she had me drive her in an open saloon down Karl Johan. Julie liked people talking about her. She felt powerful. When she gave me the boot, I could see she enjoyed doing it. Julie simply wanted her husband convicted. That was the reason she served him up to the police on a platter.'

Paaske looks outside again, annoyed by this know-all sitting at the desk. Down on the street the patisserie door opens. A tram trundles into Bogstadveien and stops. Passengers stream out. Paaske doesn't only dislike Jack's know-it-all attitude; he also dislikes his assistant's negativity and scepticism about other people. As far as Julie Bjerke is concerned, Jack is decidedly wrong anyway. She was in dire straits when she asked for help. Had he known, he would have gone further — much further — for her. He can feel that in his heart.

'Bjerke got off the hook because I didn't testify,' Jack says.

'So they were going through a crisis, Julie and her husband; so what?' Paaske can feel that he is sick of this talk. 'We busted the smugglers and were happy.'

'Were you happy?'

'Actually we *were* happy.'

'Why didn't you tell her to take the witness stand? Julie knew all about the business. She would've got you a conviction.'

Paaske meets Jack's eyes. The irritation he feels at his assistant's attitude grows afresh. 'They were man and wife. The condition she set at that time was that she wouldn't testify against her husband, and I kept my word.'

Paaske sits down. Glances across at Jack, who still has a condescending smile on his face. 'What's the problem?'

'Nothing.'

'This Amalie, you weren't in a relationship at the time, but...?'

'Amalie was probably never in love with me. The door was open for men with fat wallets, and they always found their way to her. When she was here a few days ago, I hadn't seen her for at least twelve or thirteen years.'

'You should go to the police.'

'Maybe, but not yet.'

'What are you waiting for?'

'Krause. I want to have a serious word with him. You can come along, too.'

'Now?'

Jack stands up. 'I don't feel like deferring it for much longer.'

★ ★ ★

When they get in the car, Paaske passes the newspaper to Jack.

'I've read enough about this story.'

'Not that one. Look at the bottom right.'

Jack folds the paper and finds the article. 'I read about this yesterday as well. The boat that sank off the Jutland coast.'

'It's not just any old boat.'

'What's so special about it?'

'The name. *MS Claus Böge.* German ship. It's the same one that was being loaded in Filipstad, where I photographed Bernhard Gruber and the man who no

204

longer draws breath.'

Paaske starts up and drives. Takes the Bogstadveien route to the city centre.

Jack sits with the paper in his lap. 'Do you think that's a coincidence?'

Paaske shrugs. 'It's definitely interesting.'

As he turns into Karl Johan, the Freia clock on the corner of Øvre Slottsgate shows time has moved on to a quarter to nine. Paaske parks outside Hotel Westminster.

'I'll go in alone,' he says. 'The police know he's staying here. They could be nearby.'

Paaske gets out. Crosses the pavement and walks through the swing door. There is a queue in front of the counter in the lobby. A group is checking out. The receptionist — a man with a greasy hairstyle and a pencil moustache — counts money, writes invoices and hangs keys behind him.

When the group moves towards the swing door, Paaske goes to the counter and asks after Herr Krause.

'Herr Krause has paid and left.'

'When did he do that?'

'Yesterday.'

'Did he leave a forwarding address?'

'I'm afraid not.'

'Shouldn't you just check the register to see?'

The man doesn't make a move to check the register, just stares at Paaske and says: 'I've already checked. You're not the first to ask. The police were here an hour ago.'

Paaske nods, goes back to the car and gets behind the wheel. 'Bad news,' he says. 'Krause has upped and gone. The police have already been here.'

'That suggests they're investigating other suspects

as well as me?'

Paaske isn't so sure of that. 'As far as I can see, there's only one way out of this hornet's nest for you.'

'And that is?'

'Amalie von Schiller.'

'Why would she help me?

She's the one who set the trap.' 'She's the only person who can give the police information about Werner Krause. Her version of events regarding the man's shooting is important.'

Jack shakes his head. 'The police were at my door only hours after the man was shot. They knew who they were looking for. No one else but Amalie could've known I was going to Oscarshall. It must've been her who tipped them off. I went to her place yesterday. I wanted to know what she was doing, but she didn't answer the door. Just stood behind the curtain and watched me. Do you think she's changed her mind and will open the door now?'

We can't have the police chasing you. We have to talk to them, get them to see you have nothing to do with this case.'

'I don't want to go back to prison,' Jack says earnestly. 'I'm not going to the police of my own accord, only for them to lock me up.'

'The police listen to reason too.'

'If they don't have enough on me to arrest me for the murder, they'll use the dead dog. I'm not going there voluntarily.'

Paaske glances at his assistant. The situation seems hopeless, and he is suddenly unsure whether Jack realises how hopeless. 'Have you somewhere you can lie low for a while?'

Jack nods.

Paaske starts up. 'Then we'll go there.'

Jack shakes his head. 'You can drop me off in Majorstuen. I've got my motorbike there.'

'We have to get you out of this fix,' Paaske says. 'Perhaps I ought to know where you're staying in case I need to get hold of you.'

'Let's use the office as a meeting place,' Jack says. 'I'm not keen on you having to lie if the police ask.'

II

A hen treads lightly over the gravel. Someone must have dropped seeds on the ground. Its comb falls like an unruly fringe whenever it pecks and kicks backwards. She is reminiscent of a secretary, bowing and scraping her way through life.

Paaske strolls over to the covered walkway in front of the tall window on the palace's western side. A dark stain is visible on the concrete base. It has to be remnants of the victim's blood.

He walks back to the gateway and steps aside for a group of people coming up from the ferry jetty. They wander down to the road leading to the Folk Museum. When they are out of sight, he walks back to the steps. Acts as if he is coming up the steps and strides through the gateway, continues onto the gravel while counting his strides. Stops at eight. He makes a mark in the gravel, crouches down and studies the ground around the mark, but sees nothing but fine gravel. Then he takes two steps forward, makes a new mark, crouches down again and sifts through the gravel with his fingers. Then he repeats the process.

The black hen comes closer. It pecks and every time its beak touches the ground a little stone jumps up and rolls away. Paaske remains on his haunches as she slowly struts past him. When he is about to straighten up he hears a different sound as the hen pecks. Paaske follows the hen, which takes fright, flaps its wings and runs off. He crouches down and sees it at last, trodden deep into the gravel. Paaske takes out his penknife and coaxes it out. It is a spent cartridge and it has been trampled flat. The cartridge was fired and it landed on the ground. Then someone unwittingly trod it into the gravel. It could have been Jack, a policeman or a tourist.

He puts the flattened case in his jacket pocket and walks back to the gateway beside the tower. Carries on through the gateway and down through the garden to the jetty. Soon the ferry appears. A young man clambers over the railing, moors the boat and pulls the gangway into position as the engine idles. Paaske waits until all the passengers are ashore before boarding and nodding to the skipper.

'Could I ask you a few questions?' he says.

The man steps back and examines him.

'It's about the tragic death up there. I've been engaged by close family.'

'A kind of solicitor?'

Paaske nods. *A kind of* solicitor is a flexible concept.

'Terrible business, but I think they'll catch the bastard. I saw him. He caught the last ferry.'

'Did you hear any shots fired?'

The skipper shakes his head. 'I told the police. There's a lot of noise around here in the evening. All the machines at the exhibition are going full tilt. There are stands where people can shoot at targets and win prizes. We may've heard a shot, but we didn't notice it.'

The skipper nods to the youth who has just moored the boat. The young man is pushing the gangway back and untying the ropes. Paaske passes the boy a coin and is given a ticket.

'After you'd dropped off this man, were there any other passengers?'

'One man. A foreigner.'

'How do you know he was?'

'Because he spoke English when he bought the ticket.'

Paaske produces the photograph of Werner Krause from his inside pocket. 'This man?'

Both the boy and the skipper nod when they see the picture. 'So?' the skipper says. 'Has this man got anything to do with the case?'

'No one knows. Do you two remember which ferry he caught from Skarpsno to Bygdøy? Which departure?'

'No idea,' the boy says. 'There are lots of people. We shuttle to and fro all day. No chance of remembering a face. It might be quiet now, but generally speaking there are a lot of passengers wanting to cross. Remembering a face from the crowd is impossible.'

Paaske takes another photo from his inside pocket. The picture of the victim. 'What about this man?'

Both of them examine it.

'Possible,' the skipper says, tossing his head as he turns the wheel and hits the throttle. 'I may've seen them both. Can I have another look at the photos?'

Paaske waits until the skipper has set the right course, then he hands him the photographs of the murder victim and Krause.

The skipper nods to himself. Taps the photos with the mouthpiece of his pipe. 'It was the same evening.

They were talking, but it was more like an argument. Mr Game-Leg seemed angry.'

'One of them had a game leg?'

'The man who returned with us. That's why I remember. They went ashore, and Mr Game-Leg turned and shouted at the other man. There was something strange about them. As they were tourists, I tried to tell them to keep an eye on the time if they were returning, but they walked off without letting me finish my sentence.'

Paaske thanks them.

They are approaching the jetty in Skarpsno.

'Who engaged you?' the skipper asks.

'A woman,' Paaske says. 'I'm afraid I can't say who.'

The skipper nods. Seems happy enough with the answer.

The ferry docks. The youth jumps ashore and moors the boat. Paaske follows him and carries on over the jetty and up onto the road. Here he turns. They are both watching him, the skipper and the deckhand.

III

From the jetty he walks back to his car, which is parked in Drammensveien. If Bernhard Gruber is still away, he intends to have a serious conversation with his wife, the real Vera Gruber.

As soon as he is there, he grabs the newspaper and gets out of the car. He sees Johnny Moe's black Chevrolet as he is walking along the pavement, but passes it without acknowledging him. Goes to the front entrance and climbs the stairs two steps at a time, then rings the bell. No one answers. There is total silence behind the door.

210

He knocks and rings the bell again. It is still as silent. However, he hears the neighbour's security chain rattle. And the click of a lock. An elderly lady pokes out her head.

'There's no one in,' she says. Her hair is thick and grey. Her narrow face is as lined as a chopping block. Her eyes are large and watery, and she is missing a tooth in her lower jaw. 'They've moved.'

'Who's moved?'

'Vera and her husband. The Grubers. They drove off at around three in the night. They kept me awake until then, with all the noise they were making.'

'Do you know where they've gone?'

The lady shakes her head and closes the door.

Paaske walks down the steps and out onto the street. Goes over to the black car parked by the pavement. He bends down and bangs on the window, which rolls down.

Johnny Moe is sitting there, chewing. In his hand he is holding a half-eaten custard tart.

'And here we have the man who's never been here,' Paaske says.

Moe tries to swallow at the same time as evincing his displeasure.

'Are you waiting for Gruber?' Paaske asks.

'Valentine,' Johnny Moe says.

'Sorry?'

'God knows what his real name is. Here he calls himself Gruber. One thing we'd like to know is precisely that: who is he actually, this weirdo who calls himself Bernhard Gruber?'

'His neighbour said Gruber and his wife have moved.'

'I know they've moved.' Moe stuffs the rest of the

211

tart in his mouth, chews and swallows. 'They've done a bunk, but I hope they haven't told all their fellow conspirators. As soon as you shift your arse, I'll carry on with my surveillance.'

'What do you actually know about this man?' Paaske says.

'Why do you ask?'

'It was why I was here the day you followed me. I had a job connected with Gruber, but it's finished now.'

'Someone paid you to spy on Gruber?'

'That's one way of putting it.'

'Who?'

Paaske says nothing and Moe's face flashes annoyance, but the policeman represses it and instead asks:

'What was Gruber doing when you followed him?'

'Several things. He contacted the man lying in the Anatomical Institute with his stomach cut open, for example.'

'Why didn't you tell Sveen that?'

'He didn't ask, and you refused to acknowledge the existence of Werner Krause.'

'Where did they meet, Gruber and the victim?'

'In Filipstad, among other places.'

Moe leans across and opens the passenger door. 'Jump in, Ludvig.'

Paaske walks around the car and gets in. Inside, the car smells of a bakery. Moe disposes of the bag and turns to Paaske. His eyes are serious. 'They met at the harbour?'

Paaske nods. 'Gruber talked to the dead guy and some stevedores.'

'Were they loading a boat? Could it by any chance have been a two-thousand tonner from Hamburg?

MS Claus Böge?'

'It could.'

'It might interest you to know that *MS Claus Böge* sank off Esbjerg. The boat was lost forever the same day it sailed from Oslo. The captain went down with the boat. The rest of the crew survived.'

Paaske lifts the newspaper. 'I read about it. My understanding was it hit a mine from the war.'

Moe shakes his head. 'I had a man in attendance during the maritime inquiry. No mines that have moved in the sea since 1918 could have caused such damage to the ship. The crew blame the stevedores in Oslo. They say there were two explosions that blew holes in the hull — from inside.'

'The newspaper says something different. It says the ship was probably laden with arms as it was German and bound for Huelva in Spain.'

'The boat wasn't laden with arms.'

'Huelva is a war harbour, Johnny. No German ship sails unladen to a harbour in war-torn Spain. If the ship had arms on board, it's not improbable that it was the cargo that blew it up.'

'The boat was carrying nothing but ballast.'

'Who says so?'

'I know so.'

'How can you know?'

'The boat was going to Huelva. The stevedores loading it must've known that.'

'So?'

'So, they wanted to stop the boat from getting there.'

'Why would they?'

'Because Norwegian stevedores have been infiltrated by communists.'

'So?'

213

'The boat sank, Ludvig.'

'You seriously mean to say that Norwegian stevedores have something to do with the sinking? The boat
sank in the North Sea off the Danish coast. Whether
they are communists or right-wingers, Norwegian
stevedores live in Norway, not Denmark.'

'Geography's no argument. The fact is that Germany and Italy support the rebels in Spain. This has
meant that Joseph Stalin has singled out Germany
and Italy as the enemies of communism.'

Paaske shakes his head in resignation. 'Are you
sure? The last I read about this in the paper, Stalin
was supporting the non-intervention policy of the
League of Nations.'

'That's what he says, not what he does.'

'You're a policeman in Oslo, Johnny. What Stalin
says and does is nothing to do with you, is it?'

Moe doesn't answer.

'By the way, you were a little evasive when we were
talking with Sveen. Tell me about this German policeman, Werner Krause.'

Moe heaves a heavy sigh. 'You aren't in the force,
Ludvig. Have you forgotten?'

They look each other in the eye. Paaske braces
himself, waits for the sarcasm, ready to rebuff him if
it comes. But it doesn't.

'I went to Hotel Westminster,' Paaske says at length.
'The receptionist said Krause had paid and left. He
also said the police had been there, asking after the
guy. That was you, wasn't it?'

An angry flush appears on Moe's cheek as he raises
his index finger. 'You call yourself a private investigator. But you're playing at being the police. You can
carry on as far as I'm concerned, so long as you keep

well away from things that have nothing to do with you.'

'Are you saying the police are investigating Krause?'

'Are you hard of hearing? Keep well away. Forget Valentine. Forget Krause.'

'The next time you meet Werner Krause, ask him what he was doing outside Oscarshall,' Paaske says. 'Ask him what he was doing when the man you haven't identified was shot. Krause was with the man when it happened, you see. The ferry skipper has just confirmed that to me. Krause and the victim caught the boat together from Skarpsno to Oscarshall. Krause was alone when he returned. What does that tell you?'

'As I said—'

'I heard what you said.'

Paaske grips the door handle. 'Perhaps it's about time you also started listening,' he says and gets out.

IV

Jack rides with the sun in his eyes, and pulls in next to the petrol pump at the grocery in Lysaker. A man dressed in Standard overalls stands at the ready as Jack dismounts from his bike and pushes it onto the stand. Jack asks him to fill the tank and goes into the shop. A bell rings above the door, and a woman wearing a white apron comes from a stockroom behind the counter. Jack asks for some bread, eggs, meat, some tins, a few bottles of beer and a packet of coffee. The items soon occupy a lot of space on the counter. The bell rings again when the man in the overalls opens the door and says he has put in four and a half litres. The woman makes a note. Her face is narrow with a sunken mouth, and she has her hair gathered in a net.

It looks like a beret shoved to the back of her head. Her thin fingers are crooked and slightly deformed. Presumably she suffers from arthritis.

The woman notices his eyes and moves. Hides her hands and continues to ring up his items on the till. Jack walks over to the big shop window. Behind him the woman pours the coffee beans into the grinder. The smell of freshly ground coffee spreads as the grinder does its job. In the window there is a grocery backpack. He buys it, pays, stuffs the shopping items into it, swings it onto his back and leaves. Starts up the bike and waves to the man on the pump. Rides down Drammensveien, turns off by Høvik and carries on down to Villa Strand. Here, he leans the bike against the broad front steps, unhitches the pannier bag and unlocks the front door.

As soon as he is inside, he takes off the backpack and places it on the floor. At that moment he freezes. Something is different. Once the thought is in his mind, he knows he can smell tobacco smoke. All his senses aroused, he comes to the realisation that there is someone in the house. The living-room door is ajar.

Momentarily paralysed, he stands listening, but the silence is total. Then comes fear. It slowly creeps up his spine, wanting him to turn round and run out, but he stays where he is. Trying to rein in his panic. He has just unlocked the front door. It hadn't been broken open. If someone has entered the house, they may have smashed a window, but wouldn't he have seen something as he came in? The person who is here, or has been and gone, must have a key. It must have been Arvid Bjerke, he supposes. Bjerke has been sniffing around.

Still with his eyes fixed on the open door, he calms

216

down, now that he is thinking rationally. His fingers are about to open the pannier. The buckle clinks as he lifts the lid. His hand closes around the shaft of the revolver inside. Then he treads softly as he makes for the living-room door. The floorboards creak. Can't be helped, he thinks, stopping by the door and pushing it open with the gun barrel.

The light from the window casts a rectangle on the table. The shadow of a person is outlined in the corner by the light. Jack takes a deep breath and cocks the revolver.

TJØME, 1925

I

Jack no longer lives in Oslo. Few people, other than Kristin, know that he is staying in Tjøme. The police officers tasked with fetching him to testify in the appeal case against Bjerke drive to Grønland, to the little flat he left ages ago. They don't find him there. The newspaper makes an issue of it. The leader writer criticises the police for not having guarded the witness, for not having arrested this man who had also palpably chosen to ignore the previous trial.

Jack goes to the train station in Tønsberg to buy a newspaper and read about himself and Bjerke. He discovers that Bjerke has been acquitted. The defence had created chaos and confusion by arguing about which articles of law had actually been broken when the confiscated contraband outside Bjerke's house had obviously been smuggled into the country by a German sea captain. The jury believed the engineer when he said he had been tricked by the German, whom the police had never managed to locate. The jury decided: Arvid Bjerke was not guilty.

Jack couldn't care less. The engineer no longer smuggles, but Jack does, filling his speedboat with spirits from German and Polish smuggler boats anchored by Grisebåene. Then he races at thirty knots towards Tjøme, where Kristin runs barefoot over the hills.

When Kristin was sixteen she got engaged to a sailor from Tønsberg. This fellow was two years older

218

than her, and she promised him eternal fidelity when he went to sea. Her fiancé wrote letter after letter during the first year, but died as the result of a crane accident in the ship's cargo hold in Port Said. That was four years ago. She kept his photograph and letters in a box, which she shifted into the loft when Jack moved in. The little house nestling behind a cliff has a sitting room, a bedroom, a kitchen and a little corridor with stairs up to the loft. Kristin fishes for the meals they live on, and she can handle a catfish just as easily as she does a pollock or coley. Kristin knows how to set lobster pots and can get so excited when a mackerel bites that the flat-bottomed boat almost capsizes. Kristin and Jack eat fish every day of the week and meat soup on Sundays, after she has been to the butcher and bought a piece of chuck or brisket. She adds flavour with Hamburg parsley, cabbage, celery, carrots and flour balls.

There is always laughter bubbling under the surface with Kristin. She picks up lobsters by their hard shell and holds the claws in front of his face. When one pinches Jack's nose, she falls over laughing, drops the lobster, which attaches itself to her, and she screams in panic. Then it is his turn to run after her, brandishing a black lobster-cracker in each hand. The hardest part of dealing with lobsters is boiling them. Kristin refuses to do it. So Jack has to, but when the water boils, she is ashen-faced and puts the poker in the fire under the pan of boiling water until it is red-hot, and then places it in the water to be sure that death is quick. Afterwards she runs out and doesn't want to see or hear anything. Only when he has emptied out the hot water and the lobsters are on the plate, red and delicious, does she return. By then she is over her distress and bakes white bread and prepares a feast.

Kristin can name lots of different varieties of butterfly and explain the differences between them to him. Such as the Small Tortoiseshell's ring of blue spots around the edge of its wings and its mainly reddish-orange coat, and the rich colours of the Camberwell Beauty's coat with the yellow border.

She grows potatoes and other vegetables in a plot behind the boat shed. It is a shallow piece of land developed in a fairly long hollow between the rocks, but it gives a good yield because the sun warms the rocks in the evening, and because she fertilises everything with seaweed and the compost she makes from old plants, leaves and more seaweed. When she harvests the potatoes, leeks, parsnips, Jerusalem artichokes and carrots, she digs everything up with her fingers. Kristin isn't frightened of getting her hands dirty. She says the soil smells good, and she really means it. Plunging her hands into the greasy humus, she provides evidence of how good it is: fat worms wriggling in the palms of her hands.

Jack loves Kristin also because she is incapable of dissembling. Because she cries as easily as she laughs, because she makes love with the same passion as she lives. Because she protects herself against the stormy winds and weather in thick, shapeless clothes, and, when he divests her of them, turns into the greatest creation in the world. Because she walks barefoot or chooses practical shoes over fragile, ornate high-heeled footwear. And because she isn't embarrassed to kneel by her bed and pray with the same intensity and sincerity every night.

The times she joins him on a trip to Oslo, she

doesn't want to go to Grand Café, Engebret or posh places like that. For Kristin, going to a restaurant is as alien and risky as walking into a room full to the brim with precious porcelain. She just wants to be outdoors again. Kristin doesn't want to reform Jack either: she offers him her life. The condition is that he finds an alternative activity to smuggling. And that is also the plan, but she will not let him sign up to go to sea. Kristin has already lost one man to working overseas.

The problem is that there is still widespread unemployment. In that regard, it is as hard in Vestfold towns as in the capital. Not even in the archipelago outside Tønsberg is there any work. Jack could possibly invest in a cheap boat and start fishing, but that is a last resort. Because he has another idea. Based on keeping the speedboat. Jack has an idea that there is a need for transport between the mainland and the sparsely populated islands. A taxi boat would be the thing. Kristin rejects the idea, saying that no one but tourists would use the transport.

'And tourists are only here for a few weeks every summer.'

Jack lets her laugh, but he has another idea, one that he hasn't yet run by her, but if things go the way he would like, he might be able to lure his mother to live here in the future. The sea air would do her such good. If she lived closer, he could be at her side and give her a hand as soon as any illness threatened, but this is a new thought, freshly conceived. Before he discloses his plan to anyone else, he will have to talk more with his mother.

★   ★   ★

During this time, Jack barely sees Amalie. She works as a dancer now, at the revue theatre, Chat Noir, in Klingenberggata in Oslo. She has introduced him to the director there, who buys spirits from him. The theatre boss has a delicate, vulnerable face with an aquiline nose, wavy, combed-back hair and a goatee, and walks with his chin in the air. The boss holds the rear door in Munkedamsveien open while Jack carries in first a case of genuine French cognac and then a case of apple liqueur from Normandy. The man salivates and mumbles French words as he studies the bottles and the text under the medals on the labels.

This particular day Amalie drops by too, wearing her dancing outfit and thick woollen stockings up to her knees. Amalie, with two cups of steaming-hot coffee in her hands, brushes against Jack's arm and remarks: Aren't you going to invite me out soon?

Perhaps it is her directness, perhaps it is his conscience that makes him open up, but he tells her about Kristin. It all comes out in a flood, the passion he feels. He continues even when he can sense her irritation and dark humour, and despite knowing in advance that she would react in this way. Amalie doesn't like to hear about other women. And least of all about women such as Kristin, but Jack doesn't want to be cowed by her acerbity. Indefatigably, he describes the new joy he has found in his life.

'Finished, have you?' she asks. 'Bedtime prayers!' she snorts in a contemptuous tone. 'Butterflies! You're going soft.'

'I've found someone I never knew I was searching for.'

'A grubby little girl who digs up worms with her hands.'

222

Jack grins. 'I never imagined I'd live to see the day you were jealous, Amalie.'

'I am not!'

Her eyes flash, and her face assumes the calculating expression he has never liked.

Amalie taps the director on the shoulder. 'There was something you wanted to say.'

Her boss is still admiring the bottles. The man wipes his mouth with a handkerchief he takes from his waistcoat pocket.

'Oh, yes,' he says, as though he has just remembered something. 'There's a driver who'd like to meet you. This man apparently knows his way around engines, and you were after a mechanic, weren't you? He'd like to move into your line of business.'

'I don't know,' Jack says, heading for the exit. 'I'm on my way out of all this, and the profits are getting smaller with every trip.'

At the exit Amalie is standing with a coffee cup to her lips.

The man with the goatee hurries over to her and says: 'Talk to him, will you.'

'Me?' Amalie says. 'It's probably best if I don't say anything. If I do say something, Jack does the opposite. That's how it's always been.'

OSLO, 1938

I

Jack stands, revolver raised, staring at the shadow outlined on the table. It still isn't too late to make his escape, but could this be the police? Could this be the police ambushing him in an empty house? No. This isn't the police. Jack takes a step forward, and one more, then opens the door wide.

A woman is sitting in the wicker chair in front of the panoramic window. Her black hair hangs down loose to her shoulders. Her dress is purple, and her stockings are skin-coloured. Her legs are crossed, and she is bobbing a shoe up and down. In her hand she is holding a cigarette in a long mouthpiece.

'You frightened me,' he says.

'And you me,' Julie Bjerke says, tearing off a matchstick and lighting her cigarette. 'Would you mind putting away the obnoxious object you're holding in your hand?'

Jack puts the revolver back in his pannier. Enters the living room and looks around. There are two cigarette stubs in the ashtray. She has been waiting a while.

'You're alone?'

She nods.

Jack leans against the door frame. 'What are you doing here?'

'This is my house, Jack.'

'So, you do remember me. Do you want something from me?'

'I've been asking myself how it could even occur to Arvid to lend you the key to this house. You of all people. What could the reason be?'

'It wouldn't be right of me to say.'

'Will you be disappointed if, in point of fact, I know why?'

'Try me.'

'The whore's back.'

He sits down in the chair opposite her.

'This is almost like the old days,' she says, taking a drag of the cigarette. 'Arvid and I, and the whore and Jack.'

'I saw her onto the train to Copenhagen back then,' he says. 'She had a ticket to Berlin.'

'Where she met her husband,' Julie says. 'Jürgen von Schiller. Rich man from a fine family with an aristocratic 'von'. He works for the German government. Race issues. They don't talk about anything else but race down there. Von Schiller had studied Norwegian and was enthusiastic about everything Norwegian, especially the whores. He married one of them.'

Her top lip curls and reveals her sharp teeth. Jack has always been fascinated by precisely this angular smile, and now he smiles back.

'You didn't know, did you. Some of us know. Because she has this crazy brother of hers, of course. She never quite cut herself off from her homeland.'

Julie stretches out an arm and flicks the ash off. 'Arvid knows the man she married.'

Jack nods. 'He said they met in connection with the building of the new airport.'

'Arvid travels to Germany now and then to watch car racing or just to do some business. On the odd occasion I used to go with him. I stopped going when

225

we were invited by the whore and her husband.'

Julie lifts the cigarette holder and studies the glow. 'Jürgen von Schiller divorced her recently. She doesn't want any children, you see. He couldn't accept that. The reason he chose her was so that she would raise some tiny, pure-bred Nordic trolls. When he booted her out, she moved back to Norway and is threatening to stay here now.'

'Have you got any children?'

Julie doesn't answer at once.

'She doesn't *want* any. I can't *have* any,' she says at length. 'I saw you when you were standing outside the window. You were watching her, weren't you. You might've seen that Arvid took Jeppe with him on his way to hers?'

Jack nods. 'It wasn't a very cordial reunion.'

'She'd crossed the line again. She'd gone way over. It's one of the things I'd like to talk to you about.'

Jack leans back in the chair, ready to listen to what she really wants.

With a downcast expression, she says: 'She almost succeeded in ruining my life then. Do you remember when I asked you to come here?'

'It's not easy to forget such an incident.'

'You were strong. You saved me then. As strange as that might sound. It made me so strong that I've been able to endure.'

'You've been able to endure what?'

She stares at him without answering. Then she smiles her oblique smile again. 'And now you're lying low in this house. You haven't changed much. You're hiding from the police, aren't you?'

Jack nods.

The light from the window casts her face in shadow.

When she takes a drag of her cigarette the red glow is reflected in her eyes.

'Now we're here once again. You and me. Perhaps I should go to the police?'

'Why?'

'I could bring a charge against you, for example. It would be my word against yours. Which of us would the police believe, do you think?'

'Now I don't understand what you mean.'

'You broke into my house, you accosted me. I can lay it on with a trowel, if I want to enough.'

'Anything I can do to change your mind?'

'I'd like you to do something for me,' she says, and the wicker chair creaks as she leans forward. The smell of her perfume wafts over to him, and he recognises it — a scent of carnations and Mediterranean fruits. 'Because you know her.'

Julie rests the cigarette holder on the edge of the coffee table. The cigarette sends up a grey ribbon of smoke coiling in great spirals to the ceiling. After a long silence she stands up, comes close to him and strokes his hair.

Jack looks up and meets her inscrutable gaze. Two bracelets she is wearing around her wrist jangle softly every time her hand strokes him. It is an attractive hand, and she is good at stroking. Now and then we are hard put to gain any insight into our existence, he thinks. We work like oxen and bear our yokes for as long as we are able. We allow ourselves to be led by the star called morality and, after long searching, set a course according to the answers we find to profound ethical dilemmas, but sometimes a man searches more for tender loving care than intellectual nourishment, and sometimes a man is no more than a man.

Jack looks down at his hand. It finds her calf. Feeling the smooth silk against his fingertips, he immediately wonders how far the stocking goes. Julie holds her breath as he determines to find out.

Silence fills both of them, meets the winding ribbon of smoke from the cigarette on the table and encompasses the sound of fumbling hands.

★ ★ ★

He wakes with a gasp of pleasure as his body gives a start. The evening sun hits the mirror on the wall and casts a gleam over the hair cascading over his stomach.

When, a little later, she raises her head, they lie looking into each other's eyes.

'You're attractive when you sleep,' she whispers. 'You look so innocent.'

Julie gets out of bed and starts getting dressed.

'I'm going to tell Arvid where I've been all day and how we passed the time,' she says. 'Can you take that?'

Jack rolls over and supports himself on his elbows.

'Actually, I'm more interested to know if *he* can take that,' she continues, attaching her stockings to her suspenders. Holds up her dress, but waits before putting it on. Instead, she sits down on the edge of the bed.

'How long have relations between you two been so cold?'

'All married couples have problems. Ours are just much bigger, and there are more of them than others have to deal with.'

'Why don't you leave him?'

'Do you believe that yourself?' Julie's smile is con-

228

descending. 'That life is so simple.' She looks down, immersed in some memory. 'Arvid's been elected as an MP to Stortinget, did you know?'

Jack shakes his head.

'Aren't you interested in politics?'

'I was at sea for a long time. I signed off last year. It's not so easy to follow everything that's going on at home.'

'You don't need to apologise. The point is merely that you were lucky to find Arvid in the depot. He's had an office in Stortinget for two years. He's one of many there. Arvid eats and drinks well and is always in agreement with the last speaker. What I'm going to tell him when I come home will be a challenge.'

She stands up and steps into her dress. Hooks it over her shoulders. Turns away from him and crouches down. Jack pulls up the zip, and Julie walks over to the mirror and straightens the creases.

'Isn't that what politics is all about?' she says, facing the mirror, then bends down for her bag. Takes out a brush and drags it through her hair. 'Swallowing camels. I mean always looking for solutions and finding ways out instead of feeling humiliated? The end justifies the means, I think it's called.'

She puts the brush back and takes out a lipstick. Goes close to the mirror to paint her lips.

'Which party does he belong to?'

'Høyre. Right-wing.'

Julie presses her lips together, parts them, pokes at the corner of her mouth with the nail of a little finger until she is happy, and then drops the lipstick into her bag, straps on her shoes and kneels by the bed.

'It's come to my ears that you work with a mutual acquaintance,' she says.

Jack has to smile.

'How can that be?'

'You could say that Paaske and I have sort of kept in contact, after the business in this house.'

She angles her head enquiringly, and Jack lies back down on the bed.

'When I signed off last year we happened to meet. By chance he needed an assistant and he thought that with my background I was suitable. How did you find out?'

'The telephone directory,' she says, stroking his hand. 'As I said, there's something I want you to do for me. Arvid pays her money. I want to know why.'

'You call her a whore. Perhaps that's where the answer lies?'

'This is a lot of money, Jack. A huge amount. You know her. If anyone can find out why, it's you.'

'Is it something to do with her crossing the line, as you put it?'

Julie deliberates. 'I think it is.'

'Have you asked him? Asked him why he pays?'

'As I said, marriages have their problems. We have ours.'

'Surely you must have a suspicion?'

'She's got something on him.'

'What?'

Julie looks down. 'I don't know.'

'If she's got something on him, it's probably connected with a specific object. What do you suppose? A document, a contract, a photo?'

'I know it's something serious. There are some photos. I want to get them from her.'

'What should I do with these photos if I find them?'

'Destroy them,' she says, chewing her lip. 'No, give

them to me.

I want to know for certain that she no longer has them.'

'So, you know what she's got on him?'

She doesn't respond.

Jack takes her chin and turns it until he can look into her eyes.

Julie looks back without ceding ground.

'You said she'd crossed the line. What did you mean by that?'

She ignores this question and kisses him on the mouth instead. 'Will you do this for me?'

'I can try.'

'Thank you,' she says and stands up.

Jack lies on the bed with the taste of her lipstick on his lips. It is as though something of Julie is still with him, even though he can hear her footsteps on the stairs. He waits to hear the front door close behind her. Time passes. He slowly counts in his head. Then it closes and Jack wonders why it took her so long to leave.

He gets up naked and walks downstairs to the ground floor. Goes into the living room, where she had been waiting for him. Nothing seems to have changed. Nevertheless, he lets his eyes wander from the door to the chair where she was sitting. Then he turns and goes into the hall. Ditto. His cycle pannier is where he left it, and then a suspicion forms in his mind he wishes hadn't.

II

Julie Bjerke waits until the street is quiet again. Then she walks down the flagstone path to the front door, but stops and observes the house where she lives.

231

The light in the windows tells her that Arvid has been waiting for her, that he is still waiting. So, he can wait a bit longer.

Julie turns again and walks down the street, in the opposite direction, away from her own house. Once at the house close to the crossing, she stands before the front door, wondering if the woman inside can sense that she is here. Finally, she takes a deep breath and knocks. Nothing happens. Then she notices the doorbell and rings.

Nothing happens now, either. She steps back a few paces and catches sight of Amalie in the window. They study each other for a few long seconds. The woman in the window disappears. Her steps can be heard on the stairs, then the door opens.

Again, they eyeball each other. Julie breaks the silence.

'Aren't you going to invite me in?'

'By all means.'

Amalie steps aside and holds the door open. Julie enters. The hall is surprisingly similar to her own. Julie continues towards the staircase and goes up to the first floor. The living room is big — bigger than hers. It is open with a sofa and a low coffee table in the part facing the garden. The parquet floor is in a fishbone pattern. There are two armchairs adorned with velvet cushions by the wall in front of a bookcase with no books. From the dining-room window the view south is magnificent. Julie turns to her former maid, who has now come up the stairs and is leaning against the balustrade with her arms folded in front of her chest.

'It's late. What do you want?'

'I think you know.'

Julie walks over to the bookless bookcase and runs

232

a hand over the wood. 'And I think you've misunderstood the purpose of this piece of furniture, Amalie.'

'I still haven't got the house in order. Please tell me why you're here.'

'I want you to give them to me.'

Julie's former maid is true to herself. She composes her expression. 'Give you what?'

'The photos, Amalie.'

Now there is no pretence, only haughty contempt. 'That wouldn't be very clever of me, would it.'

Julie doesn't answer.

'Try and put yourself in my shoes.'

'I'd prefer not to.'

Amalie sighs condescendingly. 'You understand, of course, that I'm not going to give you them. Go home to your husband.'

Her arrogant, self-assured attitude is provocative, but the worst is the way she articulates the words: 'your husband'. As though the two words are dirty. Julie looks at her own two hands. One is holding a bag. The other hand opens it and takes out a revolver.

Amalie shakes her head. 'Julie, you don't mean this.'

As though anyone, Julie thinks, least of all this woman, can know what she herself means or doesn't mean. Julie raises the revolver.

Amalie takes a step towards her.

'Don't move.'

'Julie. Put it away. Go home to Arvid, and we'll forget all about this.'

'Give them to me.'

'The answer's no. You're not having them.'

'You have to do as I say.'

Amalie shakes her head.

Both stand with an arm outstretched. Julie with

a gun in her hand. Now it is heavy. Her shoulder is beginning to ache, and Julie doesn't want to do this anymore, she doesn't want any more of this, not for a second longer. Closing her eyes, she squeezes the trigger. Nothing happens. Julie squeezes as hard as she can, but the trigger won't budge.

'Give it to me,' Amalie says. 'You won't be able to do it.'

'Why won't I?'

Julie opens her eyes. And meets a gaze filled with such condescension that all she can do is lower her arm. Feeling so exhausted that she barely notices Amalie taking the gun from her.

'Because you have to cock the hammer first,' Amalie says, and shows her how it is done. 'Like this,' she says.

They glare at each other, and Julie doesn't recognise Amalie. The woman with the steely gaze, cocking the hammer on the gun, is not the person she remembers. Julie can feel her legs buckling beneath her and has to take a step towards the wall. Leans against it and closes both eyes, concentrating now on staying upright. Opening her eyes again, she sees Amalie standing with the revolver in one hand and the telephone in the other.

Julie slumps down. She sits on the top step of the stairs as she fights a sudden feeling of nausea. In the distance she hears Amalie asking to be put through to Arvid Bjerke.

'Arvid, it's me. Come here and fetch your wife. I don't think she's very well.'

Amalie rings off. Strides across the floor. She disappears into the kitchen and returns not with the revolver but a glass of water. Amalie takes two steps down the stairs and kneels, holding out the glass. 'Here, drink.'

Julie struggles to her feet without answering. Sways. Finds her balance and staggers down the stairs. Carries on out, leaving the door open behind her. Sees Arvid in the distance. He is in the middle of the road, regarding her with terror in his eyes. Julie walks past him, into her house and upstairs, to Jeppe, who jumps down from the chair and runs towards her, wagging his tail. Julie sits down on the sofa. Jeppe whines. Julie pats the seat next to her. Jeppe leaps onto the sofa and curls up beside her.

'Don't you say a word,' she says as Arvid comes up the stairs.

'What were you doing there? What business did you have with her?'

'What do you think?'

Julie can't bear to look at him and closes her eyes.

'Where are all the shopping bags?'

'I haven't done any shopping.'

'Where have you been all day?'

'In Holtekilen.'

Arvid doesn't ask any more questions.

'I went to bed with him,' she says. 'We were there until an hour ago.'

'Have you been on the juice, Julie?'

'Until just now it'd been a nice day. I felt like a normal woman. It's a long time since I've done that. I'm sure you appreciate you weren't missed.'

Julie thinks about Jack's revolver. She forgot about it and can't give it back now.

She gets up and goes into the bathroom. Leaves the door open behind her. Pulls up her dress and crouches down over the toilet and pees. The stream murmurs against the porcelain as she exchanges glances with Arvid through the open door. Julie drops a sheet of tissue into the bowl, gets up and straightens her dress. Looks into the mirror. Has to straighten her stockings and waist.

Now it is Arvid who has a telephone receiver in his hand. Even though he seems annoyed, she can't hear what he is saying. His voice is drowned when she pulls the flush, turns on the tap and washes her hands. When she emerges from the bathroom he has finished talking, but she carries on over to Jeppe, who comes to meet her with his head and back lowered.

'My only friend in the world,' she says, and gives the dog a big hug before slumping back on the sofa. Stupid, she thinks, utterly stupid to have left the gun there.

III

Jack opens his eyes. There must have been a noise, but this old house is full of sounds. The walls click, and the floors creak as you walk on them. His eyelids close and he goes back to sleep. In the distance he hears other sounds, but he only wakes up when the bedroom door slams against the wall. A powerful torchlight blinds him as he is dragged from the bed onto the floor. He lies naked on the floor, gathering splinters, as an officer knees him in the back and attaches handcuffs. The smell of sweaty uniform and nerves is the same as the previous time he was cuffed in this house. The panting is the same. Jack might have thought he was still dreaming, but for the pain in his back, chest and chin.

It is dark, and the torchlight wanders across the

walls. One of the uniforms lights the paraffin lamp in the ceiling. Jack looks up. There are three of them. Their faces shine white against the black uniforms. No one says anything. Footsteps resound on the stairs. The man joining the foot soldiers this time is a broad-legged individual in civilian clothing. He is so tall he has to duck to avoid hitting his head on the beam when he steps over the sill. The man has a serious, almost sad, expression on his face. His short hair is white, and he has a large birthmark on his forehead. His coat is long and unbuttoned. In his hand he is holding a hat, which he smacks against his thigh, apparently to dust it down.

The officer sitting on Jack stands up and pulls at the handcuffs. It feels as if his arms are breaking and Jack groans with pain as he struggles back to his feet.

The civilian introduces himself as Reidar Sveen, the police inspector.

'You're Jack Rivers?'

'Will you go away if I say no?'

'Funny man, are you, Rivers?' Sveen says. 'You can get dressed.'

'Shouldn't *you* dress me? Thought that was why you cuffed me.'

The policeman holding his arm rewards him with a slap.

Jack reacts instinctively. Twists round and head-butts him. The man holds his face and sinks to his knees. Another man kicks Jack in the leg. Jack falls. His head hits the floor, temple first. He sees stars, almost, but through the mists he can see the policeman who got a taste of his skull. Blood is streaming from his nose. It runs into his mouth and forms stripes between his teeth.

The man is spitting blood and gazing at the floor, dumbfounded. 'The bloody bastard,' he gasps. 'The fuckin' arsehole.'

The man struggles to his feet. This time he kicks. Hard. Iron-capped boots hit Jack in the diaphragm, and he has no chance to defend himself. A boot hits him in the head. Everything goes black.

'Enough,' Sveen says. 'That's enough.'

Jack throws up and lies on the floor shaking.

'Loosen the cuffs so that Rivers can get dressed.'

In a second he has his hands free, but the pain just grows in strength as he gets onto all fours to clear his head.

'Onto your feet, you bloody shit.'

It is the man with the blood-stained chin who lashes out. With his knee this time. Jack falls to the floor and hits his head again.

'I told you that was enough!' Sveen yells.

Jack has to be counted out again before he can stand. Nausea surges through his body as he pulls on his trousers and shirt. He looks for his jacket. A policeman is holding his pannier. Jack goes to take it. The policeman empties the contents. The jacket falls on the floor. Jack picks it up.

Sveen holds out a hand, peremptorily. 'The revolver,' he says.

Jack has to swallow the vomit in his mouth before he can answer. 'Who says I've got one?'

'You have a revolver.'

Jack doesn't answer.

'Search the place, but don't destroy anything,' Sveen says. 'You're looking for a handgun. Rivers will go with me to number nineteen.'

Sveen turns his back on Jack, who makes the effort

238

to shout after him: 'Am I under arrest?'

Sveen turns and smiles wryly. 'What do you think?'

'On what basis?'

'Let's call it burglary for the moment.'

'I was given the key.'

'According to Bjerke, you were told you couldn't stay here and stole the key.'

Jack stumbles down the stairs with one officer in front and one behind. Outside, they wait for the police vehicle to turn and slowly reverse to the steps.

'You work with Ludvig Paaske,' Sveen says.

'Correct.'

The car stops. Sveen holds open a door for him. 'Has he told you why he had to stop working for the police?'

'Why he stopped working?'

Jack wriggles onto the seat.

'No, Rivers, why he *had* to stop,' Sveen says and slams the door.

IV

Using a magnifying glass, he manages to identify the similarities in the brushstrokes in the part constituting the sky, but there are so many pieces, and details. At length he puts down the magnifying glass and instead lifts his coffee cup. It has made a little wet ring on the table. There is something about it. He puts the coffee cup back down and locates the piece. A little circle. It is the dome of the street lamp on the bridge over the Seine. The piece fits.

When there is a ring at the door, he gets up, goes to the entrance hall and opens the door. Outside, there is a pretty woman dressed in a woollen coat with a belt. On her head she is wearing a fetching Alpen cap at an angle over blonde curls. Paaske holds the door open and steps aside.

The real Vera Gruber, née Halvorsen, shakes her head. Says he should come with her and is already heading towards the stairs. She casts a glance over her shoulder and says she has a car waiting.

Paaske puts on his outdoor shoes, grabs his hat from the shelf and hooks his coat over his shoulder. Opens the door again. Remembers what he has forgotten and hurries into the sitting-room to fetch his pipe and tobacco.

Vera Gruber stands waiting in the yard, under the chestnut tree. The branches are thick, and the buds are ready to burst, erect like brown nails on arthritic fingers.

'You've moved,' Paaske says.

Vera Gruber doesn't answer, but continues towards a taxi idling by the kerb. They get in at the back. Vera asks the driver to go to Kjelsås School.

Paaske is about to ask about her husband, but she motions to him to be quiet.

They pass Sagene church, cross the Akerselva. Drive up Kjelsåsveien. Vera Gruber occasionally glances through the rear window.

Kjelsås School appears.

'You can pull in over there,' she says, pointing.

They get out and stand on the pavement, watching the taxi drive off and disappear around the bend. Then she leads the way. A hundred metres further ahead there is another car parked by the kerb. They get in the back. There is no driver behind the wheel. The car is chilly and must be quite new, because there is a strong smell of leather.

The minutes snail past, so Paaske takes out his pipe. 'Do you mind?'

'Not at all. I like the smell of pipe tobacco. I grew up with it. My father smokes a pipe.'

When Paaske lights up, she raises her nose and sniffs theatrically.

'Who are we waiting for?'

She doesn't answer.

Paaske rolls the window halfway down, draws on the pipe and looks out. The street is dark and quiet. The windows of the scattered houses are like yellow squares in the darkness. Paaske sees a little girl move from one window to another in one of the houses. She turns and talks to someone, then goes into a room and disappears from view.

At last, the driver's door opens. A man dressed in sports gear and a peaked cap gets in without a word of greeting. Just inserts a key in the ignition, starts up and drives off.

The trip takes them into Maridalen. A car comes towards them, and their driver dips his headlights. Flicks back to main beam. Tree trunks and a deserted road is all there is to see. It is a long journey. They drive without meeting any other traffic. Eventually the driver pulls into a stopping place. Vera Gruber says Paaske has to wait here.

He gets out. The car drives off, and he is left there. It will soon be pitch-black and he can just make out a turn-off to a cart track leading up the mountain alongside a river. Only the sound of running water, mixed with an indefinable noise from the forest, is heard as he kills time by pacing to and fro and counting his steps.

At long last a car comes towards him from the north.

241

It turns in and stops. The passenger door opens. A light comes on inside the car, but the man behind the wheel has his hat pulled down over his face. Paaske doesn't recognise him at once. It is only when he lifts his head that he sees it is Bernhard Gruber.

'Get in,' he says in a distinctly German accent.

Paaske gets in and closes the door. The light goes out.

Gruber holds the wheel with both hands. 'So, finally we meet face to face.'

Paaske doesn't answer.

'You contacted my wife and told her about some deception,' Gruber says.

Paaske waits for Gruber to put the car into gear, but there is no sign of him wanting to start up. 'The man I observed talking to you at the harbour,' Paaske says, 'do you know that he was shot and killed?'

Gruber nods.

'Who was he?'

'Can you first tell me who was pretending to be my wife?'

'A woman called Amalie von Schiller. She's Norwegian, but married a German some years ago.'

'Jürgen von Schiller? Who works for Alfred Rosenberg?'

Paaske shrugs. 'I know nothing about that. I know the woman got married in Germany. She and my assistant have a shared past. That was how we were able to identify her. My assistant knew her real identity. He saw her together with a German policeman by the name of Werner Krause.'

Gruber nods. 'That's how Krause operates, via a third party. You're a private investigator. Through you the Gestapo could follow what I was doing here in

Oslo. You photographed people I met. You exposed my circle of acquaintances to Werner Krause.'

Gruber looks straight ahead while he is talking. The explanation he gives for Amalie von Schiller's deception is interesting and Paaske knows there will be more.

'My assistant confronted her,' he says. 'That led to her asking to meet. They were due to meet one evening in a deserted place. My assistant went there, but she didn't show up. Instead, he found your friend, dead.'

Gruber stares into the darkness.

'I know that Werner Krause and your friend caught the ferry together to Oscarshall,' Paaske continues. 'Krause caught the ferry back alone. The police see the case as robbery with murder. They found an empty wallet at the crime scene.'

Gruber sighs, his mouth contorted into a smile. 'The man who was killed is called Ingmann. Heinz Ingmann wasn't a wealthy man. The empty wallet is Krause's signature. Murder camouflaged as aggravated violence.'

Gruber looks straight at Paaske as he continues. 'I knew the Gestapo were in Oslo, but I thought they were groping in the dark. When Heinz Ingmann talked to you it was clear that they were not groping in the dark at all. We were forced to find out how much they knew. Ingmann took on the job. I told him to be careful and said you'd photographed us. It's very likely that Krause had seen the pictures and would recognise him.'

'I'm fairly sure that Krause got to see the photos of Ingmann,' Paaske says. 'I delivered the photos to Amalie von Schiller. I'd imagine she passed them on to Werner Krause.'

Gruber nods. 'Heinz Ingmann waited for Krause outside his hotel and followed him that evening. Heinz thought he was incognito, but unfortunately Krause knew who he was.'

'What are you frightened the Gestapo will discover?'

Gruber spreads his lips in a wry smile. He clearly has no intention of answering that question.

'You live in Norway under the guise of being some sort of businessman,' Paaske says. 'As soon as you're out the door, you're afraid you're being followed. You employ diversions and a whole bag of tricks. You're at odds with the German police. What exactly is your business here in Norway, Gruber?'

Gruber ignores this question too: 'Have you wondered why Amalie von Schiller told your assistant to meet her that evening?' 'My assistant happened to see her with Werner Krause. This woman had told me that she was your wife. So, I became curious to see who the gentleman could be and photographed him. I think Krause found out. As my assistant also knew Amalie von Schiller's real identity, Krause must've felt threatened.'

Gruber turns to him again. It is impossible to see his eyes because of the darkness. 'Krause turned up with a weapon. The bullet was actually meant for your assistant, but unfortunately Ingmann was shot instead.'

'Why would a German policeman want to kill my assistant?'

'Werner Krause cannot risk his cover being blown.'

Paaske realises that Gruber means what he is saying, but he doesn't want to have the wool pulled over his eyes. This cloak-and-dagger stuff is too airy-fairy for him to take seriously. Paaske wants to move on, to reconstruct what actually happened that evening.

'After Heinz Ingmann was killed,' he says, 'Krause must've decided to pin the blame on my assistant for the murder. Amalie von Schiller knew Jack Rivers was on his way to Oscarshall. She or Krause contacted the police and said that a man had been robbed and murdered in Oscarshall, and that the perpetrator was Jack Rivers and he was at the crime scene.'

'Why would they do that?'

'Krause and Ingmann attracted attention during the ferry crossing. They had some kind of argument. On the way back, Krause was alone. If the police arrested someone other than Krause on suspicion of murder, the ferry crew's observations would be of less interest. With my assistant in prison, he would also be prevented from making trouble for Krause. The plan almost worked. The police arrived while my assistant was at the scene, but he fled and got away. There's only one thing I don't understand: what are Krause's and Amalie von Schiller's plans? What insanity is driving them to kill?'

Gruber dons a patronising smile.

'What are you smiling at?'

'Don't you understand what the plan is? Murder is the plan.

Nothing else. Werner Krause had orders to kill Ingmann.'

'I find it impossible to believe that a policeman would receive such orders. I find it even more unlikely that a policeman would travel to a foreign country to liquidate people.'

'Then you'll have to get used to the idea quickly. This isn't the first time this has happened and it won't be the last.'

'Who would have given Krause such an order?'

'The German authorities did. His superiors. Believe me, Paaske. The sole reason for Werner Krause being in Norway is to eliminate German citizens the German authorities want out of the way.'

'Ingmann was that kind of person?'

Gruber nods. 'I'm also the kind of person German authorities intend to neutralise.'

'That's why you moved from Båhusveien?'

'When Ingmann was murdered, going underground was the safest thing my wife and I could do.'

They sit for a while in oppressive silence.

Paaske breaks it: 'I think Krause's left the country. The man isn't staying at Hotel Westminster anymore.'

'Then he's staying somewhere else in Oslo. His work isn't done. Krause still hasn't killed me.'

'This conspiracy theory is crazy,' Paaske says. 'Tell me why the German police would wish to see you dead.'

'The German police view me as dangerous. I damage Germany, which I'm not ashamed to say I do.'

'Who are you?'

'I'm Bernhard Gruber. A very ordinary man, like you.'

'Who's Valentine?'

'Where have you got that name from?'

'I talked to a high-ranking Norwegian policeman, who told me that the police are investigating a certain Valentine.'

'Valentine is a construct, a myth, an enemy image, which Nazism nurtures. Every civilisation cultivates its enemy images: Satan, migrants, religious minorities, communists or people of a different colour.

Believe me, Valentine doesn't exist, but as long as the Nazis insist that he does, they'll hunt him down.'

'Why?'

'The real Valentine was a martyr in ancient Rome, arrested for practising his Christian beliefs. When Emperor Claudius asked what Valentine thought about the Roman gods, he answered that they were demons. Then he was executed. The story of Valentine is not unlike what's happening today. Constructing enemy images is the method the Nazis use to legitimise the persecution of people who think differently. All Hitler's actions have to be seen in the light of his thirst for power. Four years ago, he had several party members, who dared to contradict him, killed. It happened in the course of a single night. Since then, he has managed to convince the majority of my countrymen that Germany will achieve its past greatness with him in power. The recipe is simple: Hitler is always right. Everything should be done as he determines. Those who think differently are to be regarded as parasites. Such parasites have to be eliminated. If not, the door is open to the Great Conspiracy, people like Ernst Thälmann, Marinus van der Lubbe or the Zionists attempting to plot Germany's ruin.'

'You fled Germany to escape from the police?'

'Correct.'

'What did you do that was illegal?'

Bernhard Gruber smiles. 'In Germany? Nothing. My Germany's become a country where people are imprisoned for no justifiable reason. Jews have their possessions confiscated and are made to scrub the streets for the Nazis' delectation. Undesirable elements are killed or hidden away in concentration camps, but what is at least equally as bad is the acquiescence of other countries' political leaders. The heads of government in France, England and your Norway act as if they can't see Hitler's abuse of power or his imperialism. Hitler can bomb Spanish women and children without provoking any kind of reaction. He's just annexed Austria. Not even that has produced a reaction. Soon he'll annexe Czechoslovakia and get away with it as well. Hitler lies systematically and no other countries confront his lies. This political cowardliness is as bad as Hitler's own politics, because other countries' acquiescence visibly legitimises Hitler's actions and increases his aggression and thirst for power. My crime against Hitler's regime is that I believe in justice, I believe in equality for all, and I believe many people in this world suffer because a few enrich themselves at the cost of the many, and I've spent my life in Germany using my talents in an attempt to fight injustice.'

'You're a communist.'

'Call it what you will.'

'What do you do to ships?'

'Which ships?'

'*MS Claus Böge* sank after leaving Oslo Port.'

'It was a German ship on its way to a Spanish war harbour. It was a target.'

'Why didn't the ship arrive?'

Gruber ponders before answering. 'It was blown up,' he says finally.

'By whom?'

'I'll tell you, Paaske, but I have no confidence in your ability to understand. I'm leaving Norway this evening, but I'm at war, and we're only at the start of this war. My friend Heinz Ingmann has fallen. If I go back home to my dear fatherland, I'll be arrested at once and duly executed. Hitler's aggression and Chamberlain's and Daladier's defeatism will sooner or later lead to the rest of Europe joining the war I'm already fighting. Our people stationed in Narvik receive dynamite stolen from mines in Kiruna, Sweden. We use this dynamite to carry out our operations. We put dynamite in delayed-action bombs. We place bombs on German and Italian ships before they leave harbours in Norway and Sweden. The bombs go off in open sea.'

'So, the crime is committed while the perpetrators are far away. How does a delayed-action bomb work?'

'With chemicals. The mine is in two parts. One consists of dynamite and the other of acid. When the acid has corroded the partition, an explosion will detonate. I run a big organisation. Heinz Ingmann was one of many soldiers. Werner Krause might imagine he won a battle by killing Ingmann, but he didn't. When Ingmann fell, another officer was already taking his place. Krause doesn't know that. Krause doesn't even know where the next battle will be.'

'That's quite a war you're fighting,' Paaske says contemptuously. 'Innocent seamen are the ones who die. The *Claus Böge* was a cargo ship, not a warship.'

'The ship was on its way to Huelva, a war harbour. No ship docks in such a harbour without serving a master.'

'You're mistaken,' Paaske says. 'The boat was carrying nothing but ballast. What you do isn't war. It's terrorism. The Norwegian police are after Valentine and they'll find their way to you. It's only a question of time before they do.'

'Your naivety's charming, Paaske. I feel no need to defend my actions to you, but I'll say this anyway: my organisation fights for equality and freedom. Today the fight is for the Spanish Republic. In a year or two it'll be for Poland or France or the Netherlands or Belgium, or maybe this country, your Norway. Hitler's Nazi regime has one aim above all others: to create *Lebensraum* for what he calls '*das dritte Reich*'. In this empire the *Herrenvolk* march in step, obeying the orders of a self-appointed elite. In the Third Reich every independent thought is to be considered a cancer, a malignant bacterium or a virus that has to be extirpated at all costs. The path to the Third Reich goes through fire and death and pain for all free-thinking people. It's Hitler's megalomania and other European leaders' lack of spine you have to understand in order to appreciate the fight that today is for the Spanish Republic. Anything that can delay or destroy the German and Italian war effort in Spain means saved lives, and it's one stage on the way to peace. Hitler is bombing Spanish towns today. Killing mothers, children and the elderly. The killing is blind and it is without mercy. In the Great War soldiers fought soldiers from trenches. In Hitler's and Mussolini's warfare, soldiers, airborne bombs and other explosives are directed at defenceless children, women and the elderly. In this context the captain of the *Claus Böge* means very little. It's the ships we hit, not the seamen. The crew of the *Claus Böge* was saved. The captain died because he was an idiot, a stubborn old mule who refused to leave the ship when he had the opportunity, which in turn tells us that our attack was successful. The captain wanted to protect the weapons the ship was carrying, and fortunately it went to the bottom.'

Paaske shakes his head. 'I don't understand you.

You accuse people of killing innocent people, yet you do the same.'

'When you were a policeman you fought for the individual. You worked on the basis that anyone who caused injury to others should be punished. Probably you're still governed by the same morality. I do the same, but on behalf of a class, on behalf of the people.'

'Those who suffered were innocent seaman.'

Gruber smiles wearily. 'Imperialist powers suffer damage and genuine losses. On top of that, ship-owners and war-profiteers suffer. That's the main point. Do you actually think, deep down, that evil can be fought with good?'

Paaske has to think before he can reply. 'I hope so,' he says and immediately regrets his answer. He has no idea how evil can be fought. He isn't even sure if evil exists. Paaske can feel he is tired. 'Will you drive me back to town?'

'I don't trust you. You're an ex-cop. Besides, you suffer from spineless, petit-bourgeois chivalry. My guess is you'll run to the police with my information as soon as you get the chance. I've told you this solely out of consideration for Heinz Ingmann, the man who fell in the fight against the Nazis. I'm leaving Oslo this evening and will be out of the country before you can pass on what I've told you.'

Gruber leans across Paaske and opens the door on his side. 'Goodbye, Paaske.'

The door closes behind him, and Paaske can do nothing but watch the tail lights disappearing over the brow of the hill. He feels immense unease in his whole body. Bernhard Gruber is an unscrupulous man who doesn't shy from using terrorist tactics to achieve his aims, but what unsettles him is that Gruber's inter-

251

pretations resonated with the letters Edna wrote to him. It is five or six years since he replied, urging her to come to her senses; since he sent her the letter that silenced her. His response must have angered her. Now, perhaps, Paaske understands why she reacted as angrily she did. He wasn't there in Berlin. Nevertheless, he could sit at home in Norway, thinking he knew what was best for her while her friends experienced the Nazi abuse first-hand.

Now his only option is to walk back to town, but it is late and pitch-black. There are no buses; there is no traffic at all. The road in front of him is very long, and he can barely see a metre ahead of him. His thoughts are with Edna as he comes to terms with the long trek, and he can see it would be a mistake to write to her. He will have to go there. Once this business is all over, he will have to book a ticket to Paris. They have to meet and make up.

TJØME, 1925

I

It is still night when Jack is awoken, but he lies awake, listening, because something is different. The south-westerly wind whispers around the corner of the house. There is a wheeze coming from the vent on the wood stove. Yes, there it is: the chug of a two-stroke engine. A boat lying still in the darkness of the night. Someone is down by his boat. His hand gropes for the matches on the bedside table to light the paraffin lamp, but he changes his mind. If this is contraband raiders on the prowl, it is best not to reveal his presence with a light.

Jack lifts the duvet. Sits up. The floor is cold. Kristin's breathing is even. He moves soundlessly towards the door. The night is black, and he holds out his hands in front of him so as not to collide with anything. One of the floorboards always creaks, and of course he treads on it. He freezes, but there is nothing to suggest that Kristin is awake. Jack fumbles his way forward along the wall. He finds his clothes hanging on a hook. Takes everything. Opens the door carefully. Closes it after him. The moon casts light through the kitchen window. Here, he puts on his jumper and trousers. Goes into the cold hall. Finds his boots. Pulls them on and takes the revolver from the pocket of his jacket hanging by the door. Rotates the cylinder. Presses the release mechanism. The bullets gleam dimly, one after the other.

253

A cold draught enters the room as he opens the front door and tiptoes out. The sound of the engine becomes louder. He carefully closes the door. The wind ruffles his hair and jacket as he creeps forward through the willows, sweet gale and gnarled trunks of pine trees towards the sea. Jack crouches low. Stays sheltered by a crag. Peers over the edge. The moonlight has turned the sea into a shiny surface.

There are at least two of them. One silhouette is in the boat tied alongside *Gloria*. The other is on board her. This man is lifting a liquor can. Jack doesn't hesitate. He stands up, cocks his gun and holds the weapon with both hands. Stretches out his arms. Has the can in his sights. Pulls the trigger. The gun recoils. For a moment he is blinded by the flash, but sees the man jerk and drop the can. It falls in the water with a splash.

Jack cocks the gun again, but there is no return of fire. So, they aren't armed. Jack fires the next shot in the air. The robber in Gloria rushes to and fro. He is big and fat with short hair. His head is like a ball. He climbs over the railing, searching for safety, but the other boat has already begun to reverse out. The robber is splashing in the water. Jack holds fire. No reason to waste ammo. He watches the man thrash around and scramble onto the raiders' boat. Jack doesn't move as the boat turns and accelerates towards the sea. Two-stroke. Open boat. Two men who probably live in the vicinity. Two crocks of shit who have been monitoring local activities, who know what he does and have targeted a smuggler under cover of night darkness.

As he steps on board he is met by a sorry sight. Of the fifty cans there are fewer than twenty left.

'Jack?'

He sticks his head out and catches sight of her silhouette. Kristin is standing on a rock with only a blanket wrapped around her. The wind pulls at the blanket and her hair.

'Contraband raiders,' he says, jumping ashore, again struck by the beauty of this child of nature standing there. Suddenly he is unable to understand that this is his world and she is part of it. Kristin is still warm from bed as she allows herself to be hugged.

'They took so much that I'll have to go out again tomorrow and get more.'

★   ★   ★

Kristin doesn't want to leave him alone. Wrapped in the blanket, she sleeps on the floor while Jack keeps watch. As the sun rises, the ridge of the mountain is like a sharp blade. Above it rests a reddish-yellow aura that pales into blue. Jack stares intently eastward to capture all the hues of the kaleidoscope as the day awakens. For this reason, he doesn't immediately notice that Kristin is awake and watching him.

'This place must be the bit God saved till last,' he says, 'to round off the job perfectly on the seventh day.'

Then she sits up to see as well.

'They probably won't come back,' he says. 'They're happy. Thirty-odd cans of booze is a better catch for them than a bucket of red cod trapped in nets.'

Kristin stretches and says she wants to go to bed.

'You've been asleep.'

'*You* haven't,' she says, holding his hand.

OSLO, 1938

I

Paaske places the newspaper on Jack's empty desk. A man suspected of robbery and murder in Oscarshall has been arrested. The individual concerned is an 'old friend of the police', and Reidar Sveen praises the tenacious, systematic work of a force determined not to leave any stone unturned. There is nothing else. Paaske has already been trying to decide whether to contact Sveen or not. Both the cartridge he found and the eye-witness account ought to count in Jack's favour.

When there is a knock at the door, he is still standing by the office window, looking down at the traffic on the Majorstuen crossing while considering what he should do. Paaske walks over to the door and opens it. Standing there is someone he hasn't seen for many years.

'You?' he says, both surprised and unable to conceal his excitement.

'Nice to see you again, Ludvig,' Julie Bjerke says and walks in. 'You do agree with me that it's been much too long, don't you?'

Paaske stands by the door, admiring her. Julie is almost more attractive than his memory of her. She removes a light coat with a belted waist. Beneath, she is wearing a slim skirt and a tight-fitting pullover to enhance her figure.

She lays the coat over the back of the client's chair,

and her eyes are shining as she turns to him. 'So, this is where you end up when you leave the police.'

Paaske closes the door. The modest girl he once got to know has developed into a self-assured, mature woman with deep secrets in her eyes.

'You must be doing quite well, Ludvig. I don't think the rent here is the cheapest in town.'

'Business comes in waves,' he says. 'Some periods are hectic; some are quieter than others. It's like that now.'

He pulls up the chair for her. Julie sits down, and he takes a seat behind the desk. They sit gazing at each other, both with faint smiles on their faces.

'How long has it been?' she asks.

Paaske gesticulates. 'What is time?'

What he would like to say crosses the line, but Julie presumably senses what he means because she casts down her eyes.

'I hope I don't seem as naive as I did then.'

Paaske is silent, content that it is she who makes their shared experience the subject of the conversation.

She looks up at him, her eyes suddenly filled with uncertainty. 'Do you think I went too far that time?'

'You did the right thing. You were in a crisis.'

She seems happy with this answer. There is no longer any uncertainty in her blue eyes. 'It could've gone quite differently,' she says.

Paaske makes no comment. Just shrugs. He has spent far too much time fretting over what went wrong back then.

'It was what I wanted,' she says, looking him in the eye. 'I wanted my husband to be in prison and out of my life, but he was acquitted. It happened because we

257

had a very loyal employee.'

Her admission puts him out. 'He works with me now,' he says. 'Rivers. Jack's my assistant.'

Julie's eyes widen. 'A police officer and a crook, that's quite a combination.'

'You knew that he works for me?'

Julie nods.

'A rumour?'

She shakes her head.

Paaske leans back in his chair, realising that this visit is more special than he at first imagined. He rummages in his pocket for his pipe, thinking that perhaps he should refrain from saying any more, but he decides to be equally open: 'Jack's been arrested. This won't exactly be a good advertisement for my business, I'm afraid.'

'I don't think you're the type to worry about your good name and reputation, Ludvig.'

'Did you know he'd been arrested?'

She nods.

'May I ask who informed you?'

'The police.'

'And now you're here,' he says, and realises she can also see the parallel with the conversation they had the previous time. 'What can I do for you today, Julie?'

'This is about my husband,' she says. 'He's paying money to someone called Amalie von Schiller. Don't get me wrong; this is not about loose living, but Arvid's paying her a lot, and he's using the inheritance my father left me.'

Paaske opens the tin of Capstan and tamps his pipe. 'So, these are payments without a reciprocating service, if I understand you correctly?'

'You understand me, Ludvig.'

Paaske leans back in his chair and regards her through half-closed eyelids. Her slightly veiled gaze doesn't deviate. He likes this, her will-power, the strength it signals. He likes the way she gets straight to the point. It also did something to him to hear her mention the name of Amalie von Schiller. Thereby opening a new path for himself and the impostress. On top of which, he likes the idea that the job involves her husband, that his activities are causing problems — and last but not least that she has come to him and is asking him to do something about them. However, the situation today is different from before. Today he is free, without the obligations of a public post or anything else. Now he doesn't intend to do anything that might lead to undesired consequences, either for her or him.

Paaske takes a deep breath and weighs his words. 'It's my understanding that this relationship you and your husband have with Amalie von Schiller goes back some years, in fact to the time we met.'

'Did Jack tell you?'

Now it is Paaske's turn to nod.

'Amalie knows how to get on in the world, and she usually does it in a vulgar and sordid manner.'

'You want the payments stopped?'

'First of all, I want the cause eliminated. Then the payments will stop, too.'

'So, you know why he's paying?' 'Yes.'

Paaske tilts his head in an enquiring manner.

'There are some photographs involved.'

'Are we talking blackmail?'

'That's one way of putting it.'

'What kind of photographs?'

'I don't know. I really don't know.'

'Blackmail is a police job.'

'I've come to you, Ludvig, because you are who you are, and because this is a matter of life and death, literally.'

Julie collects herself. When she raises her head again her blue eyes are blank with tears. 'If you wish to involve the police, I'll leave this minute, and we'll forget this meeting ever took place.'

She jumps up and turns for her coat.

He leans across the table and grips her hand. 'For God's sake, sit down, Julie.'

Her small, warm hand rests tightly in his as she stands with her back to him, ready to leave.

'Have I your word of honour?'

'Of course you do,' he says. 'You have my word of honour.'

Only then does she let go of his hand and sit down.

Something has happened here. They glance at each other, both somewhat confused, unsure what it actually was. Nevertheless, the quiver of electricity between them is so strong that Paaske has to look down and swallow. He sits like this for a while, looking down at his hand, before straightening his back. Then they look each other in the eye until he finally clears his throat and asks her to tell him everything she knows about the relationship between her husband and the woman known as Amalie von Schiller.

II

Jack lies down on the bed and stares up at the prison-cell ceiling. Tries to think rationally. The police don't have his weapon. They have no proof. They have nothing. It isn't easy, either to resist the pressure or to convince himself, even if the police are barking up the wrong tree. Time passes, and he simply has no idea how much time has passed since the police took him from Bjerke's house in Holtekilen. Then he thinks about Ludvig Paaske, about what Reidar Sveen told him about Paaske's errors of judgement, and he wonders why Sveen would tell him this. What has Sveen to gain by speaking ill of his employer and friend? It must be part of the policeman's strategy, but he doesn't buy it. Jack was once a criminal. He knows what it means to be guilty and serve a sentence. He isn't the type to change his opinion of a person because of gossip. On the other hand, what Sveen told him is interesting, and Jack speculates on how this will change their relationship when he meets Paaske again.

Rolling onto his side, he finds himself looking straight at the latrine bucket in the corner of the cell. It hasn't been emptied yet. The stench is probably worse than ever, even though he barely notices anything other than that the air is heavy and stale.

He has already given a statement several times, but it is like banging your head against a wall. Sveen doesn't believe him when he tells the truth. Sveen doesn't believe him when he doesn't.

Such are his thoughts as the lights are turned off; he is unsure whether they do it to annoy him or because it is late at night. The neighbouring cells are quiet. After a while he falls asleep. Sleep is a black well of emptiness. Often he wakes with a start, out of the well, but unsure where in the world he actually is. Until he smells the prison air. Then he places a hand on his chest, breathes evenly and calmly to lure his body back into sleep's liberating darkness. When the

261

door bolt rattles, the light is still off and he has no idea whether it is morning or still night.

Another round of questions, he thinks, swinging his legs down onto the floor. At least this is a change from the monotony. Something is happening. When the door bursts open, he is standing in the middle of the cell, squinting into the light from the corridor. Obediently, he follows the broad-legged warder and realises it is a new day as he crosses the Bridge of Sighs and glimpses strips of sunlight breaking in through the narrow windows in the wall.

The warden opens the door and pushes Jack into the room, where the crime division head is sitting. The warder stands by the door. Sveen points to the chair on the other side of the table.

Jack sits down.

'We've been through this do-si-do several times,' the policeman says. 'What did you do with the money you stole?'

'I haven't stolen any money.'

'Why did you shoot and kill a man then?'

'Let me tell you again: I didn't. I *found* a dead man. I knocked on the door of the elderly woman who lives in Oscarshall. I did it to inform the police.'

'If you really wanted to inform the police, why did you leg it when the police came?'

'You came with full sirens blaring. That had to mean someone had already talked to you. I assumed you were hunting a murderer. I didn't wish to be the prey. I was innocent.'

'What did you do to the dog the police let loose when you ran away?'

'I don't know anything about a dog.'

'You've got bite marks on your calf.'

Jack is silent.

'What were you doing in Arvid Bjerke's house?'

'Bjerke gave me the key to his house. We once knew each other. I worked for him as a driver. Bjerke said I could use the house for a few days and gave me the key.'

'You have a revolver. Bjerke gave it to you as a present many years ago. A Nagant he once won from a policeman at cards.'

'I've told you before and I can tell you again: Julie Bjerke dropped by the house. We once knew each other. After she left, I discovered the gun was gone. Julie Bjerke took it with her.'

'How could she take a revolver from you without you noticing?'

'I don't know, but I went out for a while. Had to go to the toilet.'

'Why would she take it from you?'

'I don't know. Ask her.'

'Why would she drop in on you at the house?'

'I don't think she came to visit me. I suppose she came for some other reason, because she was surprised to see me, but I told her that her husband had said I could stay there, as was the truth.'

'You say you happened to stumble over a man who'd been shot. Then you run off when the police arrive, hide all night and use an abandoned house as a bolthole. And you justify this behaviour by saying you're innocent?'

Jack eyes him in silence.

'Julie Bjerke says she gave you the key to the house. You say you got the key from her husband.'

'I didn't want to put his wife in a difficult position. That's why I said her husband gave it to me.'

'Julie Bjerke says she dropped by the house to pick up a few things from the kitchen, chatted to you, but took nothing apart from the kitchen utensils.'

'So, it's her word against mine.'

'Who should I believe?'

Jack doesn't answer.

'You're even lying about who gave you the key.'

Jack has nothing to add.

'You're going to have to pay for killing a man. Your revolver is a murder weapon. You used it to rob and kill a poor tourist. After shooting him, you got rid of the weapon, but I'll find it. We're going to do a finger-tip search out there. I'll find the revolver you shot the man with — and you'll be behind bars for life.'

Jack doesn't feel any need to add anything to this tirade, either.

'Do you know what I learn most about in this job, Jack? Liars. A liar balances on a bridge without railings. A liar has no experience to support himself; he's always searching for something to hold onto, but there is nothing, because sooner or later time makes the liar forget what he's said. So, sooner or later, the liar will contradict himself. Always.'

Sveen beckons to the warder by the door.

Jack follows him out of the room, but this time they don't go to the Bridge of Sighs.

'Where are we going?'

'We? You.'

'Where?'

'Out.'

Jack doesn't ask any more questions. Just does what he is told. Stands behind the yellow line as the fat uniformed policeman behind the counter lays out his possessions. The man has dandruff. His shoulders

264

are flecked with grey. Now he makes a big deal of how worn Jack's shoes are. There is almost a hole in the leather sole. Fatso finishes the job, puts his finger through the sole and laughs out loud. The man is a comic. The finger through the sole is like the nose of a shoe puppet. Now he puts on a voice as well.

When the prison gate slams behind him, Jack walks out into the sunlight, lights a cigarette and stands looking ahead. Free, he thinks, rubbing his chin. Free for as long as it lasts. He feels the bristles of his beard. He has no idea how long he has been banged up.

OSLO FJORD, 1926

I

Jack is sitting in the mess, drinking a toddy from a large mug while the crew loads the cans under the foredeck of *Gloria*. It is a privilege to have experience. He doesn't have to handle the cargo himself. A man is standing by the railing and passing the cans down to a man in his boat. There are several people watching. Two boys, of twelve and fourteen, have come in a rowing boat with home-made rigging. The mast looks like a hay-drying pole. It has been stuffed through a hole cut in the middle thwart. Even the sail looks home-made. Both boys have red hair. The older of the two is wearing a ragged suit jacket and black trousers. His shoes are battered and worn. The younger one is barefoot, in breeches and has freckles over his nose. The boys are here to do business, and Jack asks them what their parents will say when they see the boat loaded with spirits. The older boy says their parents aren't alive. They died from Spanish flu.

'Who takes care of you?'

'We live with our Gran.'

The younger boy shows Jack a matchstick box filled with dried tobacco leaves. The lad grew them himself and asks Jack if he wants to buy some tobacco.

'How much?'

The young boy gives this some thought before looking up and taking the plunge: 'Fifty øre.'

Jack gives him a krone and puts the box in his

266

pocket.

Afterwards he watches them go down the rope ladder and over into their boat. They have four cans and will earn a few kroner for food when they sell them. Both of them have sea legs, and the weather is good.

Jack leans against the railing, waves to the boys, who set sail, and thinks about the previous day, which Kristin and he spent in bed. There was something panicked about it, as though they were both frightened this was the last time.

In a way, the two men who had sneaked up on them during the night and robbed them had destroyed their dream existence. They were two local men who did what they liked, who saw nothing wrong with stealing from a law-breaker. Kristin and he had met reality head-on — the reality that he was regarded as a stranger, someone it was fine to harass. Perhaps it was that realisation that lay behind the vigour of her passionate embrace? A desire to drive out reality and retrieve the dreamy state of living on love and air?

★   ★   ★

There is almost no wind, and the sea is as calm as a pond as Jack makes his way down the fjord, and the customs boat races in from the east. Jack looks over his shoulder and discovers they are gaining on him. Only one thing to do, he thinks, ties the tiller up, goes under the deck and grabs a couple of cans. Resurfaces and throws them overboard. Checks his course. It is steady. He makes three trips down. Fetches the cans and throws them overboard. On the third he can feel the boat's speed increasing. Now he can leave them in his wake. Jack cheers. He screams at the wind and sea,

267

glances over his shoulder and sees they have given up; they have slowed down and are letting him go.

Later he finds an islet off Vesterøy and decides to lie behind it until darkness falls.

Again it is evening as *Gloria* glides past Drøbak and he sets a course for the sound west of Håøya. No trouble there, and he accelerates up past Nærsnes and Slemmestad. Then he sees the contours of a ship. It could be one of the cruisers the customs use. Its silhouette is large and tranquil, like a guard dog. Jack keeps to the west of it. Continues towards land. Casts a glance over his shoulder and sees the cruiser is closer now. He assumes they want to check him over. Accordingly, he speeds up, heading for the skerries outside Sandvika. Turns starboard before he reaches the cluster of islets and skerries, and heads full throttle for Nesoddtangen. *Gloria* races away, and the cruiser has no chance of keeping up. It is lost in the darkness. Jack laughs into the wind.

Afterwards he winds around the island of Hovedøya and sets a course for Bjørvika to enter the mouth of the Akerselva. He lowers the lantern mast in preparation for the low bridges. Finds the river flowing quietly behind Nyland's workshop. The silhouettes of cranes and the hull of an unfinished ship are outlined against the sky as *Gloria* enters the Akerselva. The boat has enough power to counter the current with the engine in neutral.

Soon he approaches the railway bridge. Clears it. The echo of the engine booming against the stone walls. Boats moored nose to tail on either side. *Gloria* glides under Schweigaards Bridge. The lights above make the water sparkle. Here, too, the boats are moored close together on the port side. On the starboard side, broad steps hove into view, leading up to Grønlands torg. The boat moves forward, now under Vaterlands Bridge. On the other side of the bridge small boats are moored beneath the tumbledown wooden houses. The façade advertising Holter & Borgen's skins and pelts can just be discerned, and soon he passes the hoarding for Lilleborg soap. As the boat makes for a free mooring post, he cuts the engine.

A glance at his watch tells him he is early. So he sits behind the tiller and waits. The message has to be that he doesn't need a mechanic, he doesn't need anything, but as this client wants to move into the business, the guy can make a bid for the boat; anything is possible if he has enough money.

After approximately thirty minutes a lorry stops above him. A door closes and the driver comes down under the bridge. A lanky type wearing breeches, an anorak and a peaked cap.

Jack jumps ashore. The man shakes hands and says Vilda sends her regards. That is the password, but the guy is the taciturn sort and in a hurry. He is probably nervous, but Jack likes it that he has brought the lorry as promised. There is something familiar about him, Jack thinks, but he doesn't pursue the matter. They work quickly and in silence. Jack unloads the cargo and the driver carries the cans in pairs up to the lorry.

Afterwards the driver climbs up on the flatbed to move the tarpaulin. Jack helps him to tie it down. Then they both get into the cab. When the man takes a wallet from his inside pocket, Jack is struck again by the familiarity of the profile. 'Where have I seen you before?' he says.

The man stops counting and glances up for a few short seconds, shrugs and passes him the wad

269

of notes. Jack puts them in his inside pocket. When he is back on the pavement watching the lorry drive off, he is even surer. He has met the man before, but where? Besides, this man had expressed a wish to be a mechanic, so why didn't he say anything about it? Once the thought is in his mind, he feels a chill grip his shoulders, and he walks down under the bridge to the boat. As he is about to take the rope to slip his moorings, he remembers where he has seen the man before. It was in Møllergata 19. He was photographed by this man, whose name was Johnny. At that moment the fo'c'sle door opens.

Jack is taken aback.

'Nice to see you again, Jack,' says Ludvig Paaske and raises a hand. In it he is holding a pair of handcuffs. Paaske guffaws at Jack's open-mouthed stare and dangles the cuffs in front of his nose.

Jack casts around, but then they appear. Four uniformed men just waiting to grab hold of him.

OSLO, 1938

I

When Jack walks through the prison gates, Ludvig Paaske is sitting in his car, a little unsure whether to make his presence known or not. Jack looks drained — so bowed that Paaske wonders if Reidar Sveen has had him beaten up. Of course, it is possible, but there could also be other things weighing on the poor man. The past, for example. Old ghosts are rarely delicate when they come visiting the world of reality.

Jack stands smoking without seeing the Opel.

It is spring. The sun is higher now than a few weeks ago. Jack should get out of town, Paaske thinks. If for no other reason than to be out among nature. To see the farmers doing their spring work, to find a place so tranquil that you can hear the command-like honks of the geese as they fly in a V-formation northward. To inhale some fresh air. To get back on his feet.

Then he asks himself: is this possible? Has Jack got what it takes? Or has this man standing there always been the type to go to the dogs at some point?

Once this last question has been formulated the next comes of its own accord: was it really wise to take Jack on in his business? An assistant means outgoings, but he has to be able to repay investment, to add value. The problem is that Jack's past lurks in the

271

background, like a black cloud, sending out poisonous tentacles that devalue Jack and everyone around him. It was his past that made the Amalie von Schiller job different from routine, which involved them in a murder, which led to him being beaten up and to coming into conflict with the police — and which later brought about a situation which now seems hopelessly deadlocked.

Paaske realises that Jack is a burden, and that he is better off working alone. He is a little put out that this didn't occur to him before. It is so obvious. What does this man contribute, apart from debasing their work?

A mother and her two children are walking on the pavement. A boy and a slightly younger girl, jumping and hopping and laughing and nudging each other. Both are wearing low, lace-up shoes, one of the signs of spring. Paaske can recall that feeling — being a child and not having to wear heavy winter boots, at long last. Walking in summer shoes for the first time in spring feels like flying.

Jack steps aside for the three of them and watches them as they pass. Only then does he notice the car.

Paaske opens the door and gets out. 'Welcome back to freedom. Fancy a lift home?'

Jack gets in without another word.

Paaske sits behind the wheel again. Closes the door and looks across at him.

Jack stares ahead.

'You look exhausted.'

Jack is silent.

'What are you thinking about?'

'I'm wondering why they let me go.'

Paaske shrugs. 'They haven't got enough to hold

you.'

'Cold comfort.'

'Perhaps you should go into the country for a few days. Take a break from all this.'

'If I go anywhere they'll think I'm running away and I'll be back inside.'

'Imagine you hiding in the Bjerke family's old house,' Paaske says.

'Arvid gave me the key.'

'He wanted you behind bars for burglary.'

'I didn't break in.'

'Why did he claim you did?'

Jack gazes into the air. 'Do you remember when you arrested me by Hausmanns Bridge?'

'What about it?'

'Actually we've never talked about it much.'

'What's made you think about that now?'

'Who set me up?'

'I've told you before. It wasn't me that got the tip-off.'

'Who did?'

'The man driving the lorry, Johnny Moe. He's still in the police. Works in Surveillance now.'

'This guy had a lorry and money. There must've been quite a bit of organisation beforehand.'

'I organised it, but it was Moe who had the contacts. I joined the party because your name came up. I knew you were smuggling. You'd failed to testify in the trial against Bjerke. Twice, in fact. I wanted to give you a slap in the face as thanks. I approved the action because it was your name that came up.'

Jack takes a deep breath and seems annoyed. 'You must've known. You were in charge of five or six men. You had money, a lorry. It must've been more than my name that formed the basis for such an action.'

'There was a woman. Johnny was working in Vice at the time. I think it was one of the girls he knew from there.'

'How do you think he knew her?'

'It's a long time ago, so I may be mixing things up, but I seem to remember that Johnny Moe had picked up this girl for stealing underwear and silk stockings from Steen & Strøm. She was referred to as a dancer. My guess is he was willing to drop the charge against her if she gave him something. So she bought her freedom by telling them about you. But why are you wondering about this now?'

'I've always wondered. It's good to know.'

'I never met any of Johnny's snitches,' Paaske says. 'He vouched for them.'

'How could he vouch for some girl who pinched stuff from shops?'

'As I said, my understanding was that he knew her. But so what? Why are you thinking about this?'

Jack shakes his head. 'Forget it. My weakness. I'm much too hung up on the past.'

Jack opens the door and gets out, but hesitates before he closes it.

'Don't you want me to drive you home?'

'Thanks, but no thanks. You're right. I need some air. It's not far. I'll stretch my legs.'

With that, he closes the door. Paaske sits watching him turn into Youngs gate and disappear from view. The feeling that Paaske has in his bones doesn't disappear though. Still, he breathes lighter now that he is alone again. He has had his instinct confirmed. Jack has become a burden. When all this is over, Paaske thinks, I will have to figure out how I can tell him that we can't continue working together.

II

The sun is setting and bathing the countryside in soft light with long shadows and sharp contrasts as Ludvig Paaske gets out of his car and stands looking out over the Oslo fjord, towards Nesodden, the islands and the urban spread in the Oslo 'pot'. A car comes. Paaske steps aside and lets it pass before crossing the road.

A sports car is parked by the fence. Amalie von Schiller is at home. Paaske walks past the car to the front door. The doorbell is mechanical. He pulls and waits. Nothing happens. Finally he steps back a few paces and scans the house front. All the curtains are drawn.

Well, he can wait. Sooner or later she will appear. So he walks back to his car and gets in. As usual, he is prepared and has equipped himself with a Thermos. It is full of coffee, which will stay warm in the insulated Bakelite container. He pours some coffee into a pewter mug and rests it against the back of the seat to let it cool. Soon darkness descends. Strips of light shine through gaps in the house's curtains, but she doesn't show her face.

Julie Bjerke is nowhere to be seen, either. Paaske knows where she lives. Now and then he glances over to the ridge of the roof that is visible further down the street and thinks about her. He remembers her hand squeezing his, thinks about how providence has brought them together again and the fact that Julie is in conflict with her husband. A fantasy takes shape as he sits like this. Could he possibly ask her out? Would it be wrong to do that? She is married, true enough, but the sense that she wants something else is irrefutable.

Having once made so bold, other, bolder fantasies quickly follow, and he has to restrain himself. The right thing to do would be to wait, take one step at a time. Be patient. Nevertheless he can't let go of the mutual understanding that arose in his office, the trust and all the inexpressible thoughts that can be sensed at such moments.

An occasional car comes up the road. Few leave. Two boys jog by, passing a ball to each other. One picks up the ball and runs with it under his arm as they go to their respective houses.

The quiet street has fallen silent, and the evening has become very dark when another car drives past, turns and parks in the road. Its lights are switched off. This is a residential area, Paaske thinks, so why would a driver sit inside and not get out?

Soon it is so dark that the car is no longer visible. A little later he thinks he notices a movement and sits up. He focuses and concentrates. On the outline of a bush at the edge of the road. Did a branch move? Paaske could have sworn it did, but he continues to stare intently. The dim illumination from the town below casts a dull sheen upward. A man crosses the road. There is something unusual about his gait. He drags one leg.

Carefully, Paaske opens the car door and gets out as the man approaches the house. The light above the front door falls on the man, who activates the bell pull and knocks on the door. This time the door opens.

Immediately the man backs away. Amalie von Schiller comes out of the house, pointing a revolver at Werner Krause.

The two of them speak German. Krause tells her to take it easy; she tells him to go away; she seems determined and business-like, holding the gun in her outstretched hand. The man doesn't move. The woman repeats that he should go away, but he doesn't move a millimetre from the spot. It is as though the man has decided to challenge her, and she no longer seems so sure of herself.

Paaske cannot allow anything to happen and coughs. Krause clocks him. Amalie von Schiller stands her ground, still pointing the gun at the man's chest. A car engine starts up. Two headlights blaze out. The car drives slowly towards them and stops. Krause turns away from the woman, hobbles towards the car and gets in. Gravel is sent flying as the car roars off.

Only then does she lower the revolver and glance at Paaske for a few brief seconds as she backs into the house. The door closes with a bang.

The next move is obvious. He hurries back to his car. The beams of the other car's headlights sweep around a hairpin bend further below. Paaske grips the steering wheel with both hands and presses his foot down hard on the accelerator. The tyres skid as the car screams around the bends on the way down.

The distance between the cars hasn't narrowed as they pass Gressbanen stadium and carry on towards Smestad. The driver in front must know that he is being followed.

By Volvat the unfamiliar car bears right. Paaske hangs on. They pass Frogner stadium and bear right again. A tram sets off at a snail's pace. The tram forces

Krause's car to slow down. Paaske catches him up. The black car has a reserve wheel mounted on the front wing, and there is a star on the boot lid. It is a Mercedes Benz. It turns off again and accelerates. Overtakes another car in a risky manoeuvre. Paaske can't get past and has to brake, and the gap with the Mercedes widens again. The car in front turns off, and Paaske puts his foot down. The Mercedes turns off again. Paaske does the same, but when the Mercedes enters the gates of the stately house, Paaske drives past. He knows this building. It is the German embassy.

He heads home, unable to get the thought of the episode in front of Amalie von Schiller's house out of his head. What would have happened if he hadn't made his presence known? One thing is clear: Amalie von Schiller must not be under-estimated.

As soon as he is at home, he rings the operator and asks to be put through to Amalie von Schiller. The telephone rings for a long time before she answers, and when he introduces himself she says nothing.

'The two of us have quite a bit to discuss,' he says. 'About the job you entrusted me with and other matters. I'm ringing to arrange a meeting.'

She still doesn't say anything.

'I know you're in a tight spot,' he says. 'I saw that with my own eyes a short while ago.'

She rings off, and for some seconds he sits with the receiver in his hand before he calls her again. This time she doesn't answer.

It is well past midnight and time to go to bed. Yet he mentally enacts what happened outside her house again and again. Amalie von Schiller defends herself against Werner Krause. The two who had been allies

278

are now enemies, and she is living in fear behind her own locked door. She doesn't want to speak. It is obvious that she has ended up in a very difficult situation. It will be a challenge for her to extricate herself. Precisely that fact should give him an advantage.

OSLO, BOTSEN PRISON, 1926

I

The sun shines through the window set high in the prison wall, penetrates the hall and paints a yellow rectangle on the floor. Jack is standing by a lathe with his leg in the bright sunlight and can feel its heat as the shavings rain down over his hands. He likes this job: the smell of wood, seeing the miraculous evolution of the timber as the chisel bites, following the structure of the birch as it changes and is shaped. There is something comforting about this activity — placing your body weight against the chisel in an attempt to make your hand and the material one, to draw out the finished chair leg. The closer he gets to its final form, the more convinced he is that the end product has been there all the time — formed and ready. It is just a question of finding it. His job isn't to turn wood; it is to reveal what is already there, wrapped in superfluous packaging.

The work allows him to think about other matters than being in prison. It also allows his mind to switch to other matters than his mother's death. He doesn't have to speculate about how it happened. Being busy means he doesn't have to think about whether she was frightened or lonely when she drew her last breath; it means he can think about other matters than the funeral, what the priest might have said by the coffin, or muse on who accompanied her as she was laid to rest, because he himself was prevented from attending. He doesn't have to brood over who exchanged glances and whispered because he wasn't there. Nor to dwell on life outside — on Ole's wedding, for example.

He thinks only about Kristin. He spends a lot of time imagining life after prison. In one fantasy he has begun work as a fisherman and sails every morning to the island of Jomfruland to fish for cod, saithe, pollock and whiting. In another he has started up as a wholesale buyer, borrowed money to buy a second-hand lorry and buys fresh produce from local fishermen, then drives inland and delivers fresh fish to shopkeepers who used to buy spirits from him.

Jack stops the machine and releases the piece of wood. Strokes it to check it is smooth enough. Perfect. Then he puts down the sandpaper and throws the chair leg into the box on the floor. Another leg finished. Soon there will be a chair. Soon four chairs. Soon a table leg, four table legs, a new table. Soon a kitchen eating area will be finished. With a practised hand he inserts another piece of wood in the lathe. He passes time by counting table and chair legs. If he can do ten sets a day, that will be sixty a week, as Sunday is a holiday. That is two hundred and forty sets a month, and in a year that will be…

His train of thought is interrupted when Bendiksen slaps him on the shoulder. 'Rivers.'

Bendiksen is holding an envelope, and Jack takes the letter. He recognises the big letters with the intricate loops, but is immediately struck by a sense of doom and hears himself say: 'I'd like to read this in peace.'

Bendiksen stares at him.

'Come with me,' he says, inclining his head. Bendiksen rattles the keys and opens the door.

Bendiksen is a great guy. He has been around the block a few times. Two large, sunken, watery eyes float calmly above dark bags. His skin is pale, and his jowls are like a bloodhound's. His cap is threadbare. He looks as though his black uniform has been draped around him; he looks like a bedraggled parcel waiting to be collected. You can pay Bendiksen a small sum, and he gets you things, such as cigarettes or nude photos, but only if you have the money. Jack has none. The money he had was confiscated, along with the boat and the liquor cans, when he was nabbed under Hausmanns Bridge, but it doesn't matter, because now his existence is in parenthesis. When the gates finally open he will have his life back, and it will continue in Tjøme.

Jack sits down and tears open the envelope while Bendiksen pretends he is busy by the opposite wall.

Dear Jack,

It is a cold winter, but there's enough wood. And I have something to tell you: Sverre has come into my life. You know each other. Sverre brings the post by boat. He has asked for my hand in marriage. It hasn't been easy, but now I'm going to be a bride this summer. The priest says that life is a house. When one door closes, another opens. Sverre advised me not to write, but I have to tell you the truth. Dear Jack, you will always have a place in my heart.

Kristin

Jack stares at the piece of paper in his hand. It is cheap lined notepaper; the words are written in pencil. There are rubber marks on the lines. This could be a memo, he thinks, a shopping list, and he watches as his hands rip the paper into pieces. He goes to great lengths to make sure the pieces are so small that not a word can be read. His hands tremble as he does so. As soon as he has finished, he starts on the envelope.

Bendiksen leans against the wall watching him.

For the first time in prison Jack can smell the stench. The stale air of the barracks; rooms and halls that are never ventilated. The place is sullied by people who breathe the same air several times, and he feels sick from inhaling it. Even more sick. Then he gets up, turns to Bendiksen, who holds out a wastepaper basket. Jack sweeps the bits from the table into the basket.

The door closes behind them.

On the way back Bendiksen takes a packet of Golden West from his pocket and passes it to Jack, who taps out a cigarette. His hand is still shaking. Bendiksen holds up a lighter. Jack puts the cigarette in his mouth and bends down as Bendiksen flicks a flame into life.

'You're not the first to get a boot up the arse,' he says. 'Not outside and definitely not inside, in prison. Keep it,' he says when Jack hands him back the packet. 'It's cold comfort, but it is a comfort.'

Bendiksen unlocks the second door through the security channel to the workshop and holds it open for Jack, who takes a last drag and pinches the end of the cigarette. The stub breaks as he tries to put it back in the packet. He hides this from Bendiksen and stuffs the packet and the loose tobacco in his pocket.

Back in the workshop he no longer sees men working; he sees only stooped, cowed backs. When he starts up the lathe, it is mostly because he knows Bendiksen is watching. The piece of wood begins to rotate. Jack

283

takes a chisel and places it on the tool rest. There is a bang as he does so. The wood flies off and bits hit him in the face. A hand shoves him away and stops the machine.

Jack stands motionless. It is the others who are looking at him now. All of them. They watch. He feels an urge to sit down and curl up.

OSLO, 1938

I

It is light but quiet outside; quiet on the stairs, quiet on the river, quiet in the yard. Still he doesn't move. The few times anyone uses the stairs, the front door bangs softly against the frame. The door is in the same state it was when the police came here and kicked it open. You soon get back into bad habits. A few days in a cell and you do what prisoners have to do. Nothing, zilch.

The years have passed and he has lived apart from them: Amalie, Julie and Arvid. He has lived his life without them, had experiences that have reshaped him while the three of them have gone in circles around each other with the same intrigues, the same contempt and the same sick passions. They were stuck in the same bowl of filthy dishwater, he thinks, and meeting them again has left him feeling grubby.

In the end, it is this sense of grubbiness that hauls him to his feet. He takes out the last clean clothes he has, rolls them into a bundle and leaves. Strolls up Åkebergveien to Enerhaugen's public baths. The small brick building in front of the baths themselves is a pentagonal annexe with tall, narrow, rectangular windows like arrow slits. Jack ambles up the stone steps and into the men's entrance. Goes in. Hands a coin to a woman in huge clogs, holding a mop, which she runs across the floor. She leans the wooden handle against the wall, then goes behind the counter and gives him a rolled-up towel and a locker key.

Jack goes in and undresses. The heat hits him as he opens the sauna door, and he establishes that he is the only customer. No surprise perhaps. It is the middle of the day. The sauna is dark. The planks of the benches are almost black. The stove rumbles. He kneels down, takes the little shovel and heaves in some more coke, then climbs up to the top bench, where it is hottest. Unfolds the towel on the bench and lies full length. The heat stings his skin and his muscles relax. He has longed for this. To sweat. To cleanse his pores of the dirt. To go into the shower afterwards and scrub himself as clean as it is possible.

On the way back, freshly washed, in clean clothes, he spots her car as soon as he turns into Rødfyllgata. For a moment he wonders what she wants, but he doesn't stop. Just crosses the road to avoid being seen. Manages to walk another fifty metres before the engine starts. The car drives past and stops, this time on his side of the road. When he sets off to cross the road again to avoid her, she opens the door and steps out.

Amalie is radiant as always, in her smart, pink outfit that emphasises her hourglass figure. Here, in Vaterland, she stands out like a lily in grey stone scree, but her eyes don't belong in this glossy photo. They are nervous, searching.

'I've thought about what you said,' she says. 'It's important we talk.'

'Last time you wanted to talk, I had a rather horrible experience,' he says, trying to assess the magnets that are activated when she is near, but feels nothing. Only that he is sick — of her and himself, because he is standing there like a valet.

'Werner Krause,' Jack says. 'Who's he?'

'A German policeman.'

'Who's the man he shot?'

'I don't know.'

'Why do I think you're lying?'

'It's true. I don't know.'

When she goes on, it is with downcast eyes. 'I lived in Germany. For a long time. So long that in a way I see myself as slightly German. Especially after getting married. But we got divorced, and I've moved home. Werner's a man I went out with before I got married. He suddenly appeared on my doorstep a few weeks ago. Asking me to do him a favour. I would never have agreed if Werner hadn't told me how dangerous and cunning Bernhard Gruber is. Gruber receives direct orders from the Soviet Union. I don't know what he does, but I know he has lives on his conscience. Innocent people lose their lives because of criminals like Gruber. I didn't use Paaske's services to hurt anyone. I did it to save lives. It was a little favour for Werner.'

'Why didn't he go to the Norwegian police if he was going to hunt criminals here?'

'Something to do with politics. Werner said he couldn't reveal his presence here in Norway. Norwegian authorities are politically neutral. That's why he couldn't ask the police for help. The job I gave Paaske was simple and perfectly harmless. Your boss just had to follow Bernhard Gruber, and find out who he met and spoke to. I didn't know you worked with Paaske. Had I known, I would've asked Werner to find someone else to give Paaske the job.'

'What were you using for a brain?'

'I don't understand what you mean.'

'A foreigner asks you for help to find a person in

Norway — to go behind the authorities' backs in this country. What did you think he wanted to do with the people he singled out? Do you think he wanted to play cards with them? Or ask them to join a choir?'

'No, Jack, but he assured me it was information-gathering, that was all.'

'Information? Paaske photographed a man Gruber met in the harbour. You gave the photo to Krause. He shot and killed the man in the photo, emptied the poor blighter's wallet and threw it away. That was what the information was for. And you knew. The police think I killed the guy. They think that, because you arranged for me to meet you in the place where he was lying belly up. Someone told the police I was there. No one else but you knew. Why did you tell them I was there?'

'I didn't.'

'You never showed up, Amalie.'

'Because he refused to let me go.'

'Who did?'

'Werner.'

'He couldn't stop you, because he was there, in Oscarshall. He boarded the ferry when I went ashore. Why can't you just tell the truth? It was Krause who told you to arrange to meet me, and he went there earlier with a weapon. It was my luck that the other guy appeared and had a fight with Krause before I arrived. That was why he got a bullet that night and I didn't, but it was meant for me.'

'He'd never have hurt you, Jack. Werner wanted to talk to you. Make you listen to reason. Make you understand.'

'Understand? What?'

'That Gruber's dangerous. Why it was important that I commissioned Paaske.'

'Krause could've told me that in daylight. Or he could've invited me to a cup of coffee, but the meeting had to take place at night in a deserted area away from people. Krause went there armed with a gun.'

'He would never have used it.'

'But he did. Luckily, he shot someone else. As I managed to escape with my life intact, you didn't mind contacting the police and accusing me of killing a man.'

'What do you think he would've done if I'd refused?'

'Who?'

'Werner. What do you think he would've done if I hadn't made the call?'

'I don't give a damn what Krause might have done. I care that you sent me to prison. The only reason I got out is that the police have no evidence, but as they're still convinced I killed the man, they'll continue to hound me for God knows how long.

'There's one thing you can do to convince me that you're not rotten right through, and that is to go to the police and tell them everything. You can go to the police and tell them about Krause, tell them you told me to meet you in Oscarshall, say you failed to turn up and instead rang them and falsely accused me of killing a man. Do that now. Telling the truth isn't dangerous. If you're nervous I'll go with you and hold your hand.'

'I can't do that, Jack.'

'Why not?'

She is silent.

Jack takes a deep breath.

An answer still isn't forthcoming.

'I hadn't counted on you doing me the favour anyway,' he says and turns to go.

Then she grabs his arm.

Jack stares down at the white gloved hand. It reminds him of Johan. Her brother also grabbed his arm, but he doesn't need to loosen her fingers this time. He just stares down at them until she lets go.

'Jack, you and I had something once. It might sound pathetic, but we have memories. Shared memories are stronger than chains. We should be happy about what happened then, we should honour the memories. That's what we have, Jack. They bind us together.'

'What do you mean?'

Amalie gives a start and looks at him slightly disconcerted. 'I mean that we two, we're special for each other.'

'How's that?'

'You know. It's always been this way.'

Jack angles his head and meets her nervous eyes. It is as though she is waiting for some kind of confirmation.

'Why are you saying all this?'

'Because I'm frightened.' Her eyes are imploring.

'What are you frightened of?'

She hesitates.

'Has someone threatened you?'

'I'd hoped I could persuade you to come home with me.'

She looks down and again she searches for words. 'I'll pay you.

Just say what it costs.'

'What do you want to pay for?'

'Protection.'

'Who are you frightened of?'

'My life's under threat.'

290

'From whom?'

She hesitates once again, so he isn't able to believe her, even though he would very much like to.

'Why can't you just look me in the eye and answer honestly? Who are you frightened of?'

'I'm frightened of Werner Krause. I'm frightened of Bernhard Gruber. I'm frightened of your boss, Paaske. I'm frightened of Arvid Bjerke's twisted wife, Julie. But no one will hurt me if you're there.'

'Why are you frightened of Krause? The last time I saw you, you were out dancing together.'

Once again no answer is forthcoming.

'Why are you frightened of the man?'

'It said in the paper that you'd been released.'

'By name?'

Amalie shakes her head. 'It said the suspect had been let go. Werner's special. Werner sees ghosts in bright daylight. As the police have released you, he'll be thinking they're after him instead.'

'So?'

'So I've become dangerous for him. I know what he did.'

He almost feels as if he wants to put a protective arm around her narrow shoulders. Almost.

'Has he threatened you?'

'I know how his mind works. Please come with me.'

'Bjerke gives you money,' he says. 'Why does he do that?'

She deliberates for a fraction of a second. It is a fraction too long. He knows her so well.

'Who says he does?'

'His wife.'

'So? Arvid's kind. He helps me, and gives me money. I'm divorced and unemployed. I have no income.

Julie can't stand it that he's helping me. So she uses threats. Please come with me.'

'You already have a helper.'

When she starts to object, Jack refuses to listen anymore. 'Let's go back a few years. You danced at Regnbuen, but then Chat Noir took you on. The boss there used to buy booze from me.'

'What about it?'

'It was a few months after you started at the theatre. A Thursday.

I told you I'd got engaged to Kristin. Do you remember?'

'No.'

'You knew a guy who wanted to be a mechanic on a boat smuggling bootleg, but you didn't say so yourself. You got your boss at the theatre to tell me. That was pretty smart, because for all those years I thought the theatre boss was the driving force. Now, recently, after you almost got me killed and then arrested, you've made me reconsider what happened. You see, I told your boss that, yes, I could meet the guy, so he went away and arranged a rendezvous. Your boss even made up a password for us, but he didn't do that on his own. It was all channelled through you. This guy was apparently interested in illicit booze. The agreement was that he would buy the stuff, and we would discuss him working as a mechanic on my boat. I met him.'

Jack can see it all now, it is dawning on him, and he can see that she doesn't like what he is saying.

'This so-called mechanic was a policeman, who is still on the force. His name's Johnny Moe. This policeman had arrested a young woman, a so-called dancer who had stolen stockings and underwear from Steen & Strøm. This young lady bought her freedom by promising a bigger catch. So Moe dressed up in breeches and a peaked cap, pretended he was a worker and drove a lorry to Hausmanns Bridge. Five other officers stood by and watched me sail into the trap with a full load of hooch. You would've got a fine and perhaps a little warning, like a conditional sentence, if you'd accepted the punishment for the shoplifting at Steen & Strøm.'

'I would've lost my job.'

'Alright. So you could've lost your job.'

'Julie Bjerke sacked me. I didn't have a reference, nothing. Dancing was all I had. Without the theatre job I would've had to go on the street.'

'But you kept your job and made sure I got fourteen months inside. While I was behind bars, my mother died. She died alone. I was denied permission to go to the funeral. Another six months passed. Then the girl I was going to marry dropped out of my life while I was sitting in prison, unable to do anything about it. You've never needed protection, Amalie, least of all from me.'

Jack turns his back on her and walks away. Feeling her eyes burning into his back, all the way to the gates, but he doesn't turn round, just keeps going to the yard and up the steps. The door is half open because of the draught. Jack goes in without bothering to close it behind him. Goes over to the window. Looks out and down. Amalie is no longer there. Both she and the car have gone.

II

The SP09 clubhouse in Dælenenga smells of sweat and resounds to the shuffle of feet and blows to the

293

body and to punch balls. Paaske has to plough his way past a group of teenage girls admiring a training fight between two welterweights. The two boxers dance around each other, one in a singlet and shorts; the other in overalls. The girls are cheering them on. Paaske knows, of course, that women in Oslo East prefer boxers.

Four young boys are skipping on mats, concentrating, and behind them, at the back of the gym, are two boys wearing shorts down to their knees and leather headguards. They are swinging away at each other, but a man suddenly breaks up the fight. It is Reidar Sveen instructing one of the boxers, a thin rascal with boxing gloves so big that it seems the gloves have put him on and not the other way round. Sveen is wearing training gear, elasticated trousers that reveal bum cleavage as he kneels down and tells the boy that attack is not always the best form of defence, because the counterpunch is all you have to hide behind.

'Do you understand what I'm saying?'

The boy nods. His headguard tips over his eyes.

Sveen winks at Paaske and gets up. He pulls up his trousers and pushes the young boy towards his opponent, a much stronger, sturdier number in blue shorts. The two of them fly at each other. The littl'un is energetic. His arms churn like the blades of a water mill, but it seems the fatter one has learned from the instructions and keeps his guard up. When the littl'un gets tired of windmilling, Fatty launches a haymaker, and it rocks the littl'un on his feet.

Sveen stops the fight. 'Take a break, boys. I've got a visitor.'

'Your wife said you'd be here,' Paaske says as they walk to the exit.

'The best crime prevention there is,' Sveen says. 'Open the boys' eyes to the noble art of self-defence before idleness and bad role models reach them. Boxing's a metaphor for everything these boys will meet in life: conflict, class struggle, becoming someone, being seen, getting a job and a salary, and having respect for who you are and where you come from. By the way, you were a competent middleweight once, weren't you? Which club? Pugilist?'

'Ørnulf, but that's a few years and a few kilos ago now,' Paaske says, patting his stomach.

Sveen stops and shakes hands with another coach, a thin fellow in his fifties. Paaske recognises him. It is the legend, Haakon Lind, one of the club's most acclaimed boxers. Sveen and Lind exchange a few pleasantries before Sveen leads the way, with Paaske behind. They go out onto the front steps with a view of the sports ground. Sveen takes a half-smoked cigar from a pocket in his training pants and lights it with a slim lighter from his other pocket.

'I seem to remember Lind was in the 1928 Olympics,' Paaske says. 'Didn't he get all the way to the semis?'

'That was Sverre Sørsdal,' Sveen says. 'The heavyweight. Haakon didn't get that far, but you didn't come here to talk about boxing, Ludvig.'

Paaske nods pensively. 'The man who was shot in Oscarshall was German apparently. His name was Heinz Ingmann.'

Sveen takes a drag of the cigar. Blows out the smoke and takes another drag, all while looking at Paaske through narrowed slits. 'Where have you got that from?'

'My theory is that Ingmann was shot by the German policeman, Werner Krause.'

'Your theory,' Sveen says acidly. 'Wonder what it's based on.'

'The German police use a Luger P08. It ejects cartridges.'

'We've searched and didn't find an empty shell. That tells me the guy was shot with a revolver.'

'What would you do if you met someone who'd found a cartridge in the area outside Oscarshall?'

Sveen has a suspicious frown on his forehead. 'Are you telling me you've found such a cartridge?'

Paaske doesn't answer. They eyeball each other.

'May I remind you that you aren't a policeman, Ludvig?'

Paaske doesn't answer now, either.

'Shall I tell you what I'd do if you'd found this shell? Nothing. Do you know why? Perhaps because it's you who found it.'

Paaske swallows, surprised by Sveen's jeering tone.

'Also,' Sveen says with the same narrowed slits, 'because a cartridge is a cartridge. You could've picked it up in the forest during a hunt or on the firing range in Skytterkollen. An empty shell proves nothing unless I found it myself.'

Sveen goes quiet, and Paaske is shaken. He actually thought Sveen was mature enough to put the past behind him, to let bygones be bygones.

'How did you get the name of the murder victim?' Sveen asks in a gentler tone.

Paaske has to clear his throat to make his voice carry. 'You would also have continued investigating in my place, Reidar. So you don't need to take that tone.'

Now it is Sveen's turn to refrain from answering.

'I've seen Werner Krause being driven around in a car belonging to the German embassy. You can contact the embassy and ask to speak to Krause. Find out what he was doing the night Ingmann was killed. You can ask Krause what he's doing in Norway and if it's true that he works for the German police.'

Sveen is still looking at him through narrowed slits.

'Once you've done that, I might be ready to discuss the case further with you.'

'What's that supposed to mean? Have you more to offer?'

'A tip-off, Reidar. Talk to the embassy. It won't hurt to make enquiries, will it. Or you could put Johnny Moe on the case?'

'Why would I do that?'

Paaske goes down the steps before answering. 'Werner Krause's keen to meet a man called Bernhard Gruber. Last time I talked to Johnny, he was also keen to speak to Gruber. It seems that Johnny already knows a good deal about this Krause. It might be advantageous to let him talk to the embassy.'

Paaske lifts his hat and leaves. He can feel Sveen's displeasure clinging to him until he rounds the corner, but this displeasure is a trifle compared with his own fury. Paaske has a clean record. Sveen's innuendo is nothing less than contemptible and below the belt.

III

The newspaper is lying beside the chess board. Jack makes sure once again that he has set out the pieces correctly. Checkmate should be possible in three moves, and he still hasn't given up on solving the problem when the sound of the door banging against the frame downstairs tells him someone is on their way up. Jack listens to see if whoever it is carries on to the next floor. The footsteps are heavy. They come to a halt. There is a knock at the door.

The door is shoved open when he shouts, 'Come in.' And, of all people, who is it but Ludvig Paaske? It is so rare that Jack's boss visits that he can't remember the last time it happened. Now he is examining the damage to the door.

'What happened here?'

'The police came when no one was at home.'

'Aren't you going to do anything about it?'

'It's not so easy to get hold of carpenters and locksmiths from a prison cell.' Jack gets up and takes a couple of beers from the window sill. Places the newspaper on the floor and sets the bottles on the table while Paaske hangs up his coat.

He fetches the stool from the kitchenette for himself and offers his guest the chair.

Paaske looks at the table. 'Chess,' he says, leaning over the board.

'Checkmate in three moves,' Jack says. 'It's white's move.'

Paaske moves the knight to d4, and then Jack sees the solution.

Paaske gives a sardonic smile and Jack grins back, both surprised and impressed.

'What brings you here?'

'Your ex-girlfriend, Amalie.'

Paaske's expression tells him a good deal. He isn't smiling anymore. Whatever it is about Amalie, it must be serious.

Jack prises off a cap and passes him the bottle. They say '*skål*' and drink.

'I think her life's in danger,' Paaske says. 'She knows what Werner Krause did the night the police were after you. Now you've been released. The police are still searching for the murderer, and she knows who he is. Her testimony can bring Krause down.'

Jack shakes his head. 'The police are searching for evidence against me. Nothing else.'

'Krause doesn't know that. I was watching her house last night. Krause turned up.'

'Really?'

'When she opened the door, she was holding a revolver in her hand.'

'What happened?'

'I think he intended to intimidate her, but shied away when I showed my face. He drove off in a car belonging to the German embassy.'

'What did you do?'

'I followed him, to no avail, but the point is that she'll feel threatened now if he reappears.'

'He got off lightly then.'

'Amalie von Schiller was carrying a weapon to protect herself. Now he knows she has one. He'll try again, definitely, and he will succeed.'

'Why were you there?'

Paaske takes a swig and shrugs. Jack knows him. A shrug of the shoulders is all he will get in answer to that particular question.

'Did you see what kind of revolver she had?'

Paaske shakes his head.

'Could it have been mine?'

'How would she have got her hands on yours?'

'When I was staying in Bjerke's house in Holtekilen, Julie Bjerke came round. She stole my revolver. She and Amalie live in the same street.'

'Came round? Why did she do that?'

'I don't know.'

'What did she say she wanted?'

The question produces a reaction in Jack. 'That's nothing to do with you,' he says coolly and meets Paaske's eyes.

Paaske is pale and his mouth contorted.

'I know Julie, and she knows me,' Jack says to change the topic of conversation. 'The head of police, Reidar Sveen, said that Arvid Bjerke called them and told them where I was staying. That happened a few hours after Julie went off with my revolver. They've always had problems, those two. Don't forget it was her who whispered in your ear what illicit activities her husband was up to during the Prohibition days. Lady Luck was smiling on me when she stole my gun. It meant the police didn't find the murder weapon they claim I have.'

Paaske is still scowling, his eyes dark. It makes Jack tilt his head in surprise.

'Why can't you just say why she visited you?'

Jack leans back with a smile playing on his lips.

'What are you grinning at?'

'I think I know why Julie Bjerke didn't testify that time.'

'What do you mean?'

'Arvid Bjerke would've been convicted as a smuggler if you'd put Julie in the witness box. You decided against it.' Jack can't hold back a grin. 'You were in love and wanted to spare her. You were so taken by Julie that it was more important for you to spare her than to get a conviction. What did you think when Julie stayed with her husband afterwards?'

Paaske's eyes are still as dark and his fists are

clenched. 'Wipe that grin off your face, will you.'

Jack has never seen his boss like this, and he is unsure whether he likes this side of him. So he holds back. There is nothing Jack has to stand to account for. Not to anyone.

It appears that Paaske doesn't like the atmosphere that has arisen, either. 'OK,' he says at last, breathing out. 'So, she dropped by the house where you were staying, but why would she steal your revolver?'

'I don't know. Ask her.'

Paaske takes a swig of the beer and licks his lips. 'Are you sure it was her who took it?'

'It was there before she came. After she left, it wasn't. I think she stole it for a purpose.'

Now it is Paaske's turn to smile condescendingly. 'I very much doubt that.'

'Why would she steal a gun if she didn't have any plans to use it?'

Paaske doesn't answer.

'And now you think Amalie's life's in danger?' Jack says. 'So?'

'I was thinking of asking you to talk to her.'

'I already have. Today. She came here. She claimed she was frightened.'

'Frightened? Of who?'

'Several people. Krause was one of them.'

'Who else?'

'Bernhard Gruber, Julie Bjerke. You.'

'Me?'

'Amalie pulled the wool over your eyes when she asked you to spy on Gruber. Perhaps she thinks you want to get your own back. Have you threatened her?'

'No.'

'But you were outside her house last night. It might

not be so surprising that she's sceptical about you in particular. Today she wanted to hire me for a job. To protect her.'

'What did you say?'

'I said no. She's caused me enough trouble.'

'Amalie von Schiller's life is in jeopardy. She isn't bluffing.'

'You said yourself she chased Krause off with a gun. It doesn't sound like she needs any protection.'

'I think Krause opted to clear off because I was there. Until I appeared he didn't seem very afraid of her. It's true enough, though, that Krause and Gruber have a score to settle with Amalie von Schiller. But Julie Bjerke doesn't. I can't believe that.'

'Wrong,' Jack says. 'Amalie's blackmailing the Bjerke family.'

Paaske looks at him again. The same furious eyes. The cop look, Jack thinks. Once a policeman, always a policeman.

'Blackmail,' Paaske says. 'Where have you got that from?'

'Julie Bjerke told me when she was in the house.'

'Did she say what the blackmail was about?'

'I had the impression it was about some photos. What are you thinking?'

Paaske leans back on his chair and looks around. 'A fine bolt-hole you have.' He nods towards the dust in the corner. 'You need a woman.'

'You manage well enough without one, too.'

'You're still young, Jack. No one on the horizon?'

Jack shakes his head.

'You were engaged, weren't you? Seem to remember she visited you once in jail.'

'She found someone else.'

Paaske smiles. 'You've never struck me as the type women break up with. You're more the sailor who slings his hook.'

'I must be the exception that proves the rule,' Jack says in response. This is chit-chat now. Paaske has presumably said all he is going to say.

Paaske gets up. 'Do you mind checking on von Schiller tomorrow? Just pop by, make sure everything's in order. You and I will benefit. You might find something out.'

'Find something out?'

'What she has on Bjerke. Something to do with photos, you said. Julie Bjerke's hired us to do a job.'

Now Jack thinks about Julie Bjerke. The slightly gauche girl has developed into a self-assured woman in many ways. Somehow or other she has managed to manipulate Paaske. She has sent him here. Made him aggressive, made him hassle. Jack can feel in every muscle how much he hates manipulation and being hassled.

'There's money for us in this,' Paaske says. 'If you find the photos that are allowing Amalie to blackmail substantial sums from Arvid Bjerke, you'll be contributing more than you have so far.'

That comment produces another reaction in Jack. 'What do you mean by that? Don't I make a contribution?'

Paaske ignores the question.

Jack can't let this go unchallenged. 'What do you mean?'

Paaske takes a deep breath before opening his mouth to speak. 'She's asked you to go there, after all. Why not go?'

Jack eyes him in silence. Hesitant. What can you

say to a hypocrite who only sees himself? A man who dismisses Jack's efforts, who waves a moral flag while keeping mum about the skeletons in his own cupboard? Should he tell him face to face what Sveen told him about Paaske's exit from the force?

'You know her, after all,' Paaske says with an expression worthy of a travelling salesman. 'She came here and invited you home. Of course she'll open the door to you. You're the one person who can find out what sort of devilry she's up to.'

'I did,' Jack says ruminatively. 'Now it's so long ago it's as if it were a different life, but once I thought I was in love with Amalie. We were a kind of alliance. Us two against the world. Which was really a figment of my imagination, a mirage that disappeared the moment she was no longer there. I realised when I left her today that I'd been fooling myself. My feelings started out as a kind of bewitchment. It was probably mutual. Because it was like we were playing games whenever we were together. While we were playing, the special feeling intensified, regardless of what happened, regardless of what she did, regardless of whether it was good or evil. It's only today that I've been able to plumb the depths of that feeling. Because I'd never understood that hatred can burn as brightly as love, not until today, when I was talking to her. Can you understand that?'

Paaske looks at him blankly. 'No,' he says at length. 'I can't.' He grasps the door handle. 'Love or hatred, so what? This is about a job. We have to find out what she's up to. Will you go and see her tomorrow?'

'I can if you come along.'

'OK, I'll join you then. When?'

Jack shrugs. 'At ten?'

'See you there,' Paaske says.

When Jack finally looks up at the door, Paaske has left. He hears the footsteps on the stairs fading. Once they have gone he feels a wave of energy wash through him and he decides he has to make his way to Høvik and pick up his motorbike.

IV

Paaske is sitting, staring at the half-finished puzzle. Soon he will have the full image of Margrete leaning against the railing over the Seine. Edna has painted an excellent portrait of her mother. Not just her posture — one leg straight as she leans over the bridge — but also her face, profile, eyes and forehead bear a striking resemblance. Paaske is also fascinated by her expression. Margrete is looking down into the water, at a bottle floating down the river. There is a message inside. She seems to be anxious. Margrete is not only wondering what it says, she fears the contents, but he is no longer able to focus on this. His mind keeps going back to Jack and Julie Bjerke. So he doesn't react at once when the doorbell rings, only when it rings a second time, and he is actually somewhat relieved that he can concentrate on something else.

Standing at the door is Reidar Sveen. The crime division head is wearing his light-coloured suit and holding a paper bag. Inside there are the contours of a bottle.

'Come in,' Paaske says, going back to the sitting room to clear a space for his guest. He places a forearm on the table and pushes the puzzle carefully aside without destroying any of the parts he has already assembled.

Sveen puts the bottle on the table and stands looking at the jigsaw pieces. 'Where's the original?'

'This is the original,' Paaske says, fetching two glasses from the vitrine cabinet beside the window.

'You mean you don't have a template, nothing to check? Is it possible to do a jigsaw puzzle without a picture to help?' Sveen is clearly impressed.

'It's no different from doing our job in the police,' Paaske says. 'You never have a clear picture until you've pieced it together.'

This is a jibe, a tit for tat, but if Sveen realises, he doesn't show it. Sveen looks around the room and notices two other water colours hanging on the wall. He studies them. 'Who's the artist?'

'Edna, my daughter. She lives in Paris now.'

'Talented,' Sveen says. 'There's no doubt about that.'

They sit down.

Sveen undoes the top of the bottle. It is Vat 69.

Paaske goes into the kitchen and finds some seltzer water. They each pour their snifter and say 'skål'.

Sveen puts down his glass. 'I've spoken to Werner Krause.'

Paaske raises his eyebrows.

'Krause has a diplomatic passport and cannot be touched.'

Paaske's eyes widen even further.

'Issued two days ago by the German embassy.'

'They're protecting him,' Paaske says. 'Krause's been in the country a long time. When Ingmann's body is found, he moves from his hotel. You arrest my assistant as a suspect. As soon as you let him go, Krause is given diplomatic immunity. What do they say at the embassy?'

'They don't comment on cases. Krause left the country today. I accompanied him on board the boat. Stood on the quay and watched the boat sail off with him.'

'What about Bernhard Gruber?' Paaske says. 'Have you located him?'

'Should I search for a man called Gruber? Has he done anything illegal? If so, I'd like to know.'

'I have reason to believe that Gruber is an accessory in the sinking of a ship.'

'A ship? Was the ship at sea? The seven seas do not fall under my command, Ludvig. Please don't give me any more political conspiracy theories. I get enough of that from Johnny Moe.'

They sit in silence, weighing each other up. Paaske breaks the silence: 'You know something about this Gruber. Why not come clean?'

'I know where Gruber is. That's all. Gruber and his wife live in Copenhagen now, and so he's a case for the Danish police, if indeed there is one.'

'What do they say at the embassy about Ingmann?'

'No one by that name has been reported missing in Germany. The embassy won't accept that the murdered man is a German citizen unless I can prove it.'

'What happens to the body?'

'Presumably it'll be donated to science. If we can't establish a formal identification, trainee doctors will cut it into small pieces and preserve them in jars at the Institute of Anatomy.'

Sveen puts down his glass.

'So what's the police position on the murder case?'

Sveen gives himself time to think before answering. 'Someone doesn't want there to be a case, but I don't accept that.'

Personally, Paaske is relieved. Both Krause and Gruber are out of the country. That means Amalie von Schiller is safe. That is the most important thing right now. She can be reassured and subsequently the job of acquiring the compromising photographs will be easier. '*Skål*, Reidar,' he says. 'It isn't often a murder case parks itself in this way.'

'It isn't parked, Ludvig.'

Sveen takes a slim cigar from a case he removes from his inside pocket, lifts his glass and drinks, then lights the cigar and wanders across to the pictures on the wall with it in his mouth. 'I seem to remember this.' He lifts the diploma down from between the watercolours. 'You were famous for your one-two combo.'

'That was a long time ago,' Paaske says, stroking the bump at the back of his head. It has almost gone now. 'Recently I found out how long ago; but to change the subject, do you remember when we arrested Jack, my assistant?'

Sveen replaces the diploma and takes the cigar out of his mouth. 'The old days? Many years ago?'

'Yes.'

Sveen nods, with a suggestion of a smile on his lips. 'I liked chasing the hooch runners. It was a great time.'

'Johnny got a tip-off from a woman. Do you remember her name?'

Sveen shakes his head.

Paaske nods. 'There should be a name and photo at the station, shouldn't there?'

'I doubt it. It was petty stuff. Shoplifting. It's strange that Johnny managed to force her to snitch on Rivers.'

'I suppose Johnny made up something or other.'

'No one made anything up. Rivers broke the law and had to pay for it, simple as that.'

'Are you still convinced it was Rivers who shot Heinz Ingmann?'

'Convinced? No. But he's a clear suspect. When I find the weapon he used, I'll know more. If he did it, he'll be sent down, and for life.'

'Why would he kill the man?'

'My guess is the poor man was killed for money, but I don't care why. I care about punishing the criminal. That's my job. That's what my life's about.'

'Do you think I could've worked for a whole year with an unscrupulous murderer?'

'As I said, for the time being he's a suspect, but I don't understand how you can all allow yourselves to be duped.'

'All? Yourselves?'

'You aren't alone in thinking the best of your assistant. When a man rang to accuse Rivers of breaking and entering, the man's wife wasted no time in undermining her husband's story.' Sveen sighs in desperation. 'Women who are attracted to crooks. I'll never understand them, but, hey, it was generous of you to give Jack Rivers another chance. He's a likeable guy, with everything you and I like about fanatical criminals: charm, style, courage, a sense of justice, dynamism and, as I said, he's a hit with the ladies. He's also got this thing about him that you didn't see then and don't see now either — the mark on the forehead that says he'll sink when the boat springs a leak. Heinz Ingmann was an innocent tourist visiting Norway. He was first robbed, then killed. I suspect Rivers of being an ice-cold, unscrupulous murderer. If he's innocent, it will come out. What's the matter?'

Paaske suddenly conjures up an image of Julie Bjerke and Jack together, a kind of nightmare. He immediately closes his eyes and forces Julie out of his mind, and then he sees Jack alone, coming out through the prison gates. That is the image he wants. The loser. This was the stigma he could see so clearly when Jack came through the gates.

'What's the matter?' Sveen repeats, putting down his glass.

'Oh, nothing, nothing at all.'

V

It is late evening when Jack dismounts from his motorbike, drags it onto the stand and walks deeper into the cover of the forest, right up to the wall behind Amalie's house. The window is a cinema screen again. The curtains are open. So she must feel more secure, and he wonders why she is suddenly doing this.

Amalie comes into view, presumably from the kitchen. All she is wearing is a housecoat with a belt around the waist. Her red hair is combed flat and has a dark tone. She is holding a cup in her hands. It is so hot that she puts it down on the low table and blows on her fingers. Yes, indeed, she does feel secure. Why does she feel so secure?

She sits on the sofa. Wraps the sleeves around her hands and grips the cup through the material to protect them from the heat. Blows into the cup between sips. Puts it down again. Raises her legs and rests them on the edge of the table. Bare legs.

A door closes and footsteps can be heard in the street. It is Arvid Bjerke out for a walk. Without the dog this time. The shadow lengthens as he passes in front of the light from a window further down the street. The footsteps stop. Amalie tightens her belt before going downstairs.

A sharp intake of breath from Jack. He can see Amalie has the protection she wanted. He should feel honoured, Jack thinks, as she asked him first.

Bjerke is a man of action. Soon the housecoat is on the floor and the two of them walk hand in hand through the door to what must be a bedroom.

Jack waits until he is sure. Then he walks through the garden and over to the house. Stops in front of the patio door, which has four small panes. He crouches down and squints through the keyhole. There is a key in the lock. At the edge of the house, around the flower bed, he finds a big stone and smashes the glass in the pane nearest the door handle. There is a tinkle of glass and he freezes. He listens for a reaction inside. Hears nothing. Starts loosening fragments of glass with gloved hands. When the hole is big enough, he sticks a hand inside and unlocks the door. Goes in. Stands still listening, continues through an open door and into a large hallway with a staircase leading up to the first floor.

Slowly he tiptoes up the stairs and stands motionless on the top step. Now he can hear them in the bedroom, and waits. Looks around the living room, which he had earlier only seen through the window. Two closed doors. One leads into the bedroom, the other maybe to a bathroom. An open door leads to the kitchen. He goes in here. Opens drawer after drawer until he finds what he is looking for: a long knife with a strong blade, and an even stronger meat cleaver. While he is weighing these utensils in his hand, he turns to the living room and sees a familiar object lying on the telephone table. It is his own revolver, the one Julie stole from him. Jack feels an unarticulated happiness at being reunited. Without a moment's hesitation, he puts the knife and cleaver back. Then goes into the living room and grasps the revolver. Rotates the cylinder, checks that all the chambers are loaded and cocks the hammer.

The bedroom is silent now, and for a few seconds he wonders whether they have heard him. No. Low voices carry from behind the closed door. He tiptoes back to the staircase. Hears Amalie laugh, as she usually does after making love, and he imagines her, in a mock blush because she has made such a racket.

Without making a sound he descends the staircase. When he reaches the ground floor, an upstairs door opens. It must be the bedroom door. Jack turns and looks up through the bars of the railing at the top. He can see Arvid through them. Arvid is carrying a pile of clothes under his arm and walking through the door that probably leads to the bathroom. A fat, white, hairless torso mounted on two rigid legs. Jack thinks he can see a horn on his forehead. The sight stuns him. Because he realises that actually it wasn't Bjerke he just saw but a pictorial representation of him, his inner self.

The bathroom door closes and soon he can hear water running.

Jack is standing at the bottom of the stairs in someone else's house and experiences a moment of life's impenetrable logic. He sees various events passing before him, ones that have led to this moment — to him being here in this house now. Being here is only the beginning, he thinks; there is a longer sequence to come, there is a decision to be made. The two horizontal lines drawn under an arithmetic calculation are missing.

No, he thinks, as in the very next moment he feels the weight of the revolver. He has left this state of mind behind him. He is no longer led by spur-of-the-moment impulses. He has to get out of here before he does something he will regret later. However, he doesn't move.

Again a door opens upstairs. Amalie comes out of the bedroom. Naked, she bends down and picks up her housecoat. Puts it on without tying the belt. Then she goes over to the record cabinet and opens the lid. Only her head and back are visible as she places a record on the turntable. Soon music streams into the room and she is lost from view.

A draught, a current of air makes him turn to the patio door.

Julie Bjerke has come inside, dressed in a worn anorak over a woollen skirt. Her hair is tied in a bun. On her legs she is wearing tall boots. She, too, is standing with her face raised. She has seen the same thing he has.

They exchange glances as she takes off her boots, soundlessly. Then she pulls the hood of her anorak over her hair. She comes towards him in her stockinged feet. Her hands seize the revolver. He lets go. Her hands are small and white against his black gloves. The weapon she is holding seems larger now than it did. She looks down at the cocked hammer and her lips extend in a little smile before she places her foot on the first step.

Jack stands motionless. The slightly bent figure silently ascending the stairs resembles a stooped old crone, and it strikes him that this is the epitome of death, a shadow that sneaks up the stairs the day you least expect it. While thinking this, his mind is elsewhere. He can see Amalie sleeping in the bow of a little sailing boat, feels the water licking at his right hand, watches the wind play with her hair, the breeze lovingly wafting her locks under her nose, her chin and over her eyes. When the shot is fired, he sees her sinking into the black, bottomless depths, down, down deeper, until she has completely disappeared. The cold, he thinks, she can't feel it. Because it is in him now and makes him tremble uncontrollably.

How long he stands like this, he has no idea. What he notices eventually is that upstairs the song has finished playing. His hand is no longer shaking, and the house is filled with a heavy stillness that isn't broken until Bjerke's faint voice is heard from inside the bathroom.

'Amalie?'

'Answer me, Amalie!'

A sound comes from the bathroom door. A key turns in the lock. Arvid Bjerke has locked the door.

Then Julie reappears. Now she is making for the record cabinet. She puts the stylus back to the beginning of the record. When the music starts she goes to the bathroom door. She stands in front of it with the gun in her hand. For a long time. In the end she falls to her knees. When she gets up, she no longer has the gun in her hand. Julie turns to the stairs and walks down. Her steps resound on the staircase this time. They glance at each other and Jack can feel himself raising his eyebrows although he doesn't understand why he does this.

Julie nods affirmation and sticks her feet into her boots. They walk out together and he asks her why she has left the gun.

'So he can find it,' she says. 'Perhaps he'll do the right thing now, but somehow I doubt he's strong enough. Go home, Jack. This is no place for you.'

Then she leaves. The figure lumbering off in boots that are much too big for her merges into the darkness.

Jack is stunned, unable to think of anything except that he bears some guilt for what has just happened. He broke into the house and the gun was his. What would he have done, if she hadn't come and taken the revolver from him?

No, he thinks. What counts is what happened. She is the person who fired the gun. Even though he knows this is the truth, he can't bring himself to believe it. Julie has captured him, tied him to her in a macabre union while she gambles on her husband tidying everything up by doing what she calls 'the right thing'. This story is far from over. It is also the reason he doesn't leave the area but goes back into the garden, over the wall and between the trees where he had been a few minutes ago.

VI

The window is a scene in the theatre. A sofa, a table and two chairs. On the sofa there is a body. On the floor there is a weapon. The play's next act will start soon: the bathroom door will open and the actor will make his entrance. When the bathroom door does eventually open, Jack holds his breath. The door slides open slowly, but the man doesn't show himself. He heard the shot; he called without getting an answer. He must have heard the footsteps on the staircase as well.

315

At last a figure walks through the door. Arvid is dressed. A white shirt over dark trousers. The figure bends down and picks up the revolver from the floor. Then he sees the body on the sofa. He sinks to his knees.

He remains like this for minutes. At length he stands up. Wanders around restlessly. Realising that there is nothing he can do to help.

Jack waits for Bjerke to go to the telephone and sound the alarm. He doesn't. Arvid Bjerke is motionless. Still holding the revolver in his hand. Now Arvid remembers the footsteps on the stairs, Jack thinks; now he is absorbing the facts: he is alone in a house with a woman who has been murdered and he was in the house when it happened.

Bjerke doesn't pick up the telephone now, either. Instead, he crouches down, opens a cupboard under the bookshelves and rummages, but he doesn't seem to find what he is looking for. Finally Bjerke goes into the bedroom and stays there, for quite a while.

At last he comes out again, wearing a jacket now, but not holding the revolver. The fat man crosses the floor and disappears down the stairs. The front door closes, and shortly afterwards there is the sound of running feet. Jack waits until the fat man has hared, head down, along the street and back into the house where he lives.

Why didn't he ring the police?

Jack walks back to Amalie's mausoleum. He is keen to see if Bjerke found what he was after, because he has a suspicion that the man didn't know where to look. Jack has shared a room and a bed with Amalie for many nights and knows where she hides things she holds dear.

Jack climbs the stairs, continues over to the body

and looks down at her. Her body is white and there is no elasticity about her skin now. Her mouth is half open; her eyes are staring at something in the ceiling above him. The bullet went into her left temple. Standing over Amalie, once again he is paralysed by a sense of guilt, but at this moment, more than any other emotion, he feels horror. He forces himself to back away from the body on the sofa. Turns and continues into the bedroom. Glances briefly at the unmade double bed.

The revolver is on the duvet.

Bjerke has ransacked the bedside table and her wardrobe. The doors are open and there are clothes on the floor of the room and of the wardrobe. Jack looks for the drawer containing her stockings and underwear. Finds it. At the bottom he sees a brand-new and apparently unopened packet of silk stockings, a packet that is a little fatter than the others.

He removes his gloves and opens the packet. Between the stockings there is an envelope. Jack walks over to the dressing table with the mirror. Sits down on the stool in front and opens the envelope. It contains two photographs. He examines the pictures before using a corner of the duvet on the bed to wipe everything thoroughly. Slips the photos back into the envelope. Wipes that, too. Once that is done, he puts his gloves back on. Then he opens the dressing-table drawer. Pushes a hair brush and some cosmetics jars aside and places the envelope in the drawer, in full view.

Finally he meets his eyes in the mirror, gives a start and looks away at once. Gets up. Rushes out of the bedroom, past Amalie's body on the sofa, down the stairs and out.

317

OSLO, 1926

I

Her suitcase is on the handcart, which he pushes in front of him, as they walk side by side down Tomtegata towards Oslo East station. They have spent some wonderful weeks together at the Stadshotel in Strømstad while waiting for this day. It is only now, as they are approaching a farewell, step by step, that he believes he understands why there has been such harmony between them.

Jack has to move into the middle of the road to manoeuvre the cart around a parked car. They pass either side of the car and steal a look at each other. Amalie smiles, and he winks at her. He realises that it's the uncertainty of this trip that has given her the composure she's needed to enjoy being with him these past three weeks.

Her travel fever has meant that they are early. There is still an hour to go before the train departs as Jack coaxes her suitcase up onto the luggage counter. Afterwards they go to the railway café. Amalie finds a table by the window and takes the chair that gives her a view of the room, as she always does. When he expresses his admiration for her, she lowers her eyes becomingly. The lipstick on her heart-shaped mouth is thick and red. The grey dress, stockings, the beige boots and the skin-coloured gloves are a perfect match.

When the waiter comes, Amalie says that she would

like a glass of white wine. 'Even if it's a bit early in the day. One glass only. To calm my nerves.'

Jack orders the same.

The man points out that all customers have to eat in the railway restaurant.

Jack looks at her, but she isn't hungry. 'Then I'll have an open sandwich,' he says.

The waiter goes. Once more she starts speaking about the letter she has received from the theatre in Berlin. While she is speaking, Jack is struck by the thought that he will be seeing her off on his own. There will be no friends, men or women, no Johan or her grandmother. Not even Arvid Bjerke has come.

The waiter brings two glasses of wine and half a bread roll with white cheese. They wait until he has left before raising their glasses and taking a sip.

'How will you travel on from Copenhagen?' Jack asks, even though he already knows the answer.

'There's a direct train to Berlin. Apparently it goes on the ferry as well. With all the carriages. What I'm most nervous about is Berlin. I don't speak any German, as you know, but I have the address of a Swedish dancer I can stay with. I just have to get a taxi there.'

'Are you still nervous?'

Amalie laughs out loud and reveals a line of white teeth. 'And how. I hardly slept a wink last night.'

'Will you come back?'

'I can't stay away from Johan, can I,' she says, grim-faced. 'Johan's in an asylum now,' she adds, as though trying to convince herself that her decision to travel will not be at the expense of her brother. 'Gaustad. I'll be back for Christmas and then I'll visit him. Perhaps he'll be well by then.'

Jack conceals his scepticism by taking another sip.

'After all, it is a hospital,' she says, and suddenly seems a trifle depressed.

Amalie is always depressed when she thinks about her brother.

'Will you write?'

Deep down, he doesn't know if he will, but asks anyway, mostly as a pleasantry, something you say out of politeness to someone embarking on a long journey when you are left behind.

Amalie shakes her head. 'Don't take it amiss, but I want to make a new start now. To do something completely new.'

'I won't write to you then, either,' he says, and can hear it came out wrong. He sounds sullen, but he doesn't want to give that impression.

'Besides, you're going to sign up again, aren't you?' she says. 'You'll be away for ages and have a girl in every port.'

She says the latter with a little smile, but silence has both of them in its thrall. There is so much left unsaid, and he can feel that he isn't in the right frame of mind to do anything about it.

'When I'm rich I'll come and visit you,' she says.

'If you're rich, I won't recognise you. I won't open the door to you.'

She grabs his hand. 'Promise me one thing, Jack. Keep the door open for me when I come. Do you promise?'

Jack nods.

'Say it.'

'I promise.'

'Do you promise to forgive me, too?'

'Forgive you for what?'

'For everything.'

Jack has to smile again. 'I promise to forgive you. For everything.'

Amalie glances up at the clock on the wall. There is still half an hour before the train departs, but she can't sit still.

'Drink up,' he says, 'and we'll go and find your seat.'

OSLO, 1938

I

The sun is shining from a cloudless sky as he alights from the Holmenkollen Line at Besserud Station. He hears rhythmic thuds and follows the noise.

It is a boy of ten or eleven kicking a ball against a garage door. He is wearing breeches and cloth shoes. The ball thuds against the door and rebounds. The boy kicks it back once again. The ball spins to the left. Jack is there, controls the ball and kicks it against the door. The boy traps it and kicks it back against the door, from which it rebounds to Jack. They play like this for a while until the boy mishits it and has to run and fetch it. According to the rules, the boy is out. The young lad wants to carry on, of course, but Jack didn't come here to play football with young lads. Besides, it is time. A familiar Opel comes round the bend and down the hill. Jack takes a deep breath. Starts walking. He can see Amalie's house. The windows are black and dull despite the sunshine. His legs don't want to obey him, but he forces himself to walk. As he is about to turn into the road, Paaske drives past and parks behind her car.

They nod to each other. Paaske walks to the entrance and rings the bell. Behind him, Jack waits with his back to the front door. Looking straight ahead. He hears nothing. Only the ball thudding against the garage door. That and the sound of the bell ringing inside the house when Paaske yanks the bell pull.

Then Jack goes to the corner of the house. 'Look,' he says.

They walk together to the open patio door where a corner of a beige curtain is flapping through the opening.

Paaske steps across the smashed glass and enters the house. Jack follows. They continue across the oak parquet and into the hallway. Here, Paaske stops and gazes up at the floor above.

At length Paaske sets a foot on the first step and carries on up the stairs with Jack hard on his heels.

A strong smell of corpse hangs between the walls and a clicking noise is heard. It is the gramophone. Jack goes over to the cabinet by the wall. The record is going round, but the stylus is jumping up and down on the last groove. Jack raises the tone arm with the stylus and puts it on the rest. The record stops rotating, and he lowers the cabinet lid before making for the open bedroom door and peering in. The revolver is still on the duvet.

Then he turns to Paaske, who is examining the body on the sofa. Paaske raises his head and looks outside.

'There's a man in the garden,' he says.

Jack tears himself away. Stops by the sofa and looks down at the murdered woman. Death has spent the night taking a firmer grip. Her lips are distorted into a grin, and her eyes are wide open. He forces himself to look out of the window. 'That's her brother.'

'Go down,' Paaske says. 'Make sure he doesn't leave before the police come. I'll stay here.'

Jack hesitates. It will be a liberation to leave this room, but he doesn't like leaving Paaske to his own devices.

Paaske tosses his head angrily, and Jack goes downstairs. Outside, the ball is still thudding against the garage door. The sound fades as he turns into the garden. Some steps lead up to the dry-stone wall cutting off the forest. Johan is sitting on top, chewing his lips.

Jack ambles over and sits down beside him. Neither of them speaks. After a while Jack breaks the silence.

'Why are you here now, Johan?'

'My sister lives here.'

Jack nods and looks at the house. Remembering that Johan stops stammering after he has received a shock.

'So you visit her now and again, do you?'

Johan nods, and Jack catches himself wondering if the poor fellow has realised how alone in the world he has become.

'Shall we go, Johan. Home to Gaustad?'

He shakes his head.

'You don't want to go home?'

'Can't leave her, not now.'

Jack can fully understand that, because he remembers Johan as a nice man, unsure of himself, but full of consideration for others, particularly his sister.

A coltsfoot is growing outside the flower bed, where the earth is black. A small weed is turning green in the black humus.

'Want a fag?' Jack asks, fishing a packet of cigarettes from his breast pocket and lighting up a Blue Master.

Johan shakes his head. The conversation has petered out. It doesn't matter. Jack will have to brace himself for the turmoil to come, and he steals a glance at the poor devil beside him.

Johan is following an insect with his gaze. It is a fly, he tries to catch it in his hand, he closes his hand around it, clenches his fist, then opens it to see, but the fly has already flown away. Jack takes a drag of the cigarette and hopes Johan hasn't touched too much inside the house. At any rate, he hopes he hasn't touched the gun. That would give the police an open and shut case.

II

Ludvig Paaske stares at the dead woman. Her skin is marble white and her nail varnish blood red. The contrast could not be greater, he thinks, as he kneels down and grips her hand. It is cold, and rigor mortis is well established. There are no remnants of skin under the filed nails. There are no signs of any resistance. She was lying on the sofa listening to music and was shot through the head. So, she must have known the murderer well, or she just didn't see what was going to happen.

He stands up, goes into the bedroom and stops by the bed. Sees the revolver. Bends down and sniffs it. It has been fired, but what concerns him most is that he has seen this weapon before. Several times.

On the floor beside the bed there is a used condom. Amalie von Schiller had sexual intercourse and was killed afterwards — before she could put on any other clothes than the housecoat.

Both Gruber and Krause are out of the country, he thinks, and notices that a bedside-table drawer is open. There are several packets of condoms and a bottle of sleeping pills inside. Paaske doesn't touch anything. He opens the wardrobe. Closes the door again.

Someone has been looking for something. However little he wants to articulate the thought, there is

325

one name forcing itself to the front of his mind: Julie Bjerke.

Paaske wonders if Julie found what she was looking for and walks over to the dressing table with the large mirror. Opens a drawer. Here Amalie keeps her make-up, a hair brush, a fountain pen, a closed bottle of ink and an envelope. There is something inside. As he opens it, two photographs slide out.

He slips the envelope, with the photographs, into his inside pocket and stands for a few seconds in the doorway, looking at the gun on the bed.

If it was Julie Bjerke who broke in, when did she do it? Before or after the lover had gone? The time aspect, he muses. Check the sequence of events. Amalie von Schiller goes to bed with a lover. Then she leaves the bedroom, wearing a housecoat and puts a record on the gramophone. Lies down on the sofa in the living room and is shot in the head. The lover can't have been in the house when that happened. So she must have stayed in bed after her lover had left her. When the pane in the patio door was smashed, she must still have been in bed. If she had heard glass breaking she would never have reclined on the sofa to listen to music.

Julie must have waited until the lover had gone. Then she broke the pane in the door and gained access. Is that likely? Could she have been so calculating? So bold? Who else but Julie would shoot this woman first and then riffle through the drawers and cupboards? Her husband? Arvid Bjerke? That is more likely. Bjerke was one of the country's most unscrupulous criminals during the Prohibition years. Bjerke has the qualities, the daring and the uncompromising nature.

Paaske keeps looking at the revolver. Julie stole it from Jack. It was either her or her husband who brought it here, shot Amalie, put it down and started to search. Which one was it?

Will Reidar Sveen ask himself that question? Isn't it absolutely obvious who will fall under suspicion? The person who stole the weapon from Jack must have intended to use it. After firing it, she started to search, but didn't go through the drawer in the dressing table. Why not? Did she panic?

No. It can't have been her. It must have been her husband.

Paaske takes a deep breath. Still staring at the revolver. Speculating on whether he can stand by while suspicion falls on Julie. Paaske weighs up the pros and cons. If he is going to act, it will have to be now. Finally he picks up the gun and drops it into his deep coat pocket. Then he goes back to the room where the corpse is lying on the sofa.

The gun weighs heavily in his pocket. It makes him hesitate. Could it have been the lover who shot Amalie? No. She was killed by the gun that Julie stole.

Paaske walks over to the telephone. Rings the switchboard and asks to be put through to the police, but cradles the receiver without waiting for an answer. The noise outside tells its own story. The sirens. Someone has already informed the police.

Paaske walks back to the sofa and the dead woman. Her housecoat is open and he is ashamed to see her like this, unprotected and naked. He remembers how bowled over he was the first time she entered his office. He feels he ought to cover her up, but it would be wrong to do that so long as Sveen hasn't been here.

On the floor there is a cushion with a hole through

it and Paaske imagines what happened. It is still Julie Bjerke he has in his mind's eye. Sees her coming up the stairs. She has the element of surprise on her side. On the chairs there are lots of cushions. Julie reaches the top of the stairs, grabs one of the cushions, walks towards the sofa with the cushion in one hand and the gun in the other. The woman on the sofa can't see the gun. She sees only the face appear, a face she knows well. Accordingly, she doesn't react until Julie presses the cushion against her head and fires.

Does evil exist? Paaske asks himself. It is a question he has asked himself many times since he got out of Bernhard Gruber's car. Now he thinks that if someone commits an act that causes pain to others, you have to analyse the reason why the act was committed before you judge them. Gruber has no scruples about sending civilian ships to the bottom of the sea — provided that the owners are in alliance with the enemy. On this particular point Gruber is right, Paaske thinks now. The phenomenon of evil cannot be exclusively tied to one consequence of an act. Pain or suffering is only one side of the coin. All the rest is equally important — the motive, the cause, and not least the system the act forms part of. A ship is a link in a larger system. The war in Spain is more than a civil war if German and Italian weapons are actively employed in the conflict on one party's side.

Amalie von Schiller's death has to be viewed in the same way. The pain triggered by one act has to be measured against the pain that persists — or arises — if the act is not performed. For this reason, Paaske forgives Julie, from the whole of his being, for everything she has done in this house.

Once again he leans over the dead woman. The exit

wound is large. Fragments of the skull and wet tissue lie under the head stuck to the back of the sofa.

The sirens are coming closer. Paaske gets up and walks to the window. From here he looks down on Jack, who is sitting on top of the wall beside her brother. As though Jack can sense him, he turns his head and looks up at Paaske in the window. Paaske doesn't like the way he looks and turns back to the room. The lover, he thinks. Who is her lover? Could Jack have been in the house last night?

This question prompts him to take the revolver from his pocket. He weighs it in his hand, knowing he has to make a decision and that, whatever the decision is, it will have a fundamental significance for several people for a long time, for an eternity.

Finally he stuffs the gun back in his coat pocket. His coat hangs at an angle. When he views himself in the reflection from the window and shrugs his shoulders, the lopsidedness disappears. Then he goes downstairs and opens the front door. By the time the first car has slowed down and stopped, Paaske is in the doorway, thinking that now the die is cast.

III

As Reidar Sveen gets out of the car, Ludvig Paaske raises his hand in greeting.

'You came before I could ring, Reidar.'

'What are you doing here?'

'The dead woman employed our services.'

'Where's the body?'

'Upstairs.'

Sveen passes him and goes inside.

'I came in through the patio door,' Paaske says,

following him. 'It was open. A pane in the door was smashed.'

Sveen doesn't answer. He single-mindedly mounts the stairs in a few strides with his fists clenched. In silence he absorbs the scene: the perforated cushion on the floor, the sofa and the body lying on it. At last he turns to Paaske.

'Have you seen the weapon?'

'There's no gun.'

'Why on earth are you here?'

'We made an arrangement.'

'Who did?'

'Rivers and I arranged to meet here at ten.'

'What kind of arrangement?'

Paaske motions towards the dead woman. 'Amalie von Schiller feared for her own life. It looks as if she had every reason to.'

Sveen steps aside for three officers coming up the stairs dressed in civvies. Paaske nods to one of them; he remembers him from his time in the force. The three of them stop for a moment as they take in what has happened, but soon they are busy preparing themselves.

'Does anyone else live in this house?'

'She lived alone.'

Sveen comes closer to Paaske. 'Could you perhaps tell me who threatened her?'

'That's precisely what we intended to ask her about when we came. Neither Rivers nor I have called you. Who raised the alarm?'

'Arvid Bjerke. He lives in this area.'

'A long time ago?'

Sveen looks at his watch. 'Twenty-four minutes ago.'

Paaske consults his own watch. 'I entered this house twenty-four minutes ago,' he says. 'Arvid Bjerke wasn't here. How could he know the woman was dead?'

'That's one of the things I intend to ask him.' Sveen heads for the staircase. 'Don't go anywhere, Ludvig. We have more to talk about.'

They go downstairs. Outside, Paaske watches Sveen walk to the house where the Bjerke couple live. Paaske thinks about the fact that Arvid Bjerke rang the police. What does it mean? Could he have shot Amalie? Will he open the door to Sveen and confess? Or has Julie confessed to him? Was it a mistake to remove the gun from the crime scene?

Paaske longs to follow Sveen to the house to find out what is happening now. Julie Bjerke is his client. He could use that as his excuse. On the other hand, all clients have to be handled with discretion until they clearly express a wish for anything different. Besides, he knows Sveen. The policeman is already very annoyed that he wasn't the first man on the scene.

Paaske hopes that Julie is well enough prepared for what is to follow.

Some rubbernecks have already made their way to the house. A uniformed officer cordons off the patio and the front door. Another car parks in the road. It is the press. Paaske knows the people getting out. They carry huge cameras and flash lamps. He has no wish to talk to them. So he strolls around the house and over to the two sitting on the wall.

'This is Johan,' Jack says. 'Her brother.'

Paaske nods to him.

'I've seen you before,' Johan says.

Paaske tries unsuccessfully to smile. He always feels slightly uncomfortable meeting the mentally ill.

'You're a policeman.'

'Kind of policeman.'

'I know who did it.'

Paaske nods. 'That's good, Johan. It's good to talk about it. Who was it?'

Johan looks at Jack, but then he hesitates, and Paaske realises the poor fellow has a stammer.

'It was the mm-ma-ma-man.'

'Which man?'

'Hi-him,' Johan says, still eyeing Jack.

'Him?'

Jack smiles at the simple soul's suggestion, but Johan nods energetically.

'Him,' Johan repeats, his eyes flickering under half-closed eyelids. 'He did it.'

IV

There is a crush in front of *Aftenposten*'s windows in Akersgata. So many people want to read about the murder in Holmenkollen. The police have arrested a leading member of society. This person is claimed to have shot and killed his lover. Of all the *Aftenposten* readers Jack is probably the only person who knows that the leading member of society is Arvid Bjerke, but soon everyone will know, and he thinks about Julie and her husband as he wanders towards the metro station. He buys a ticket from the window and continues down to the track, where a train is waiting to depart. There are not many people in the compartment. An elderly man is smoking a cigar. Another is reading a newspaper. The conductor whistles. The rear door closes, and the train moves off with a jerk.

Jack stands by the doors. Still thinking about Julie and her husband.

He gets off at Majorstuen and takes the stairs up to the third floor. Ludvig Paaske is sitting in the office with his nose in the paper. Jack asks if there is anything new he should know about and sits down behind his desk.

Paaske says he has just spoken to Reidar Sveen, who was able to inform him that Arvid Bjerke denies having killed Amalie.

'What does Julie say about what happened that night?'

'What does his wife say.'

'What do you mean?'

'Julie Bjerke is Arvid Bjerke's wife, not just any old hussy you can talk disparagingly about.'

Jack's eyes widen and meet Paaske's. 'What does Bjerke's wife say?'

'Julie Bjerke confirmed that they'd had a row when her husband left her that night. Her husband said where he was going and told her he would stay at Amalie's that night. She says her husband came home sometime in the night and she woke up. Her husband was completely out of his mind, his hands were trembling and he sat drinking instead of coming to bed. Apparently he refused to say what had happened. Moreover, she wasn't aware that he'd rung the police, in fact she didn't know until Reidar Sveen was standing at the door and asking how Arvid Bjerke could know that Amalie von Schiller was dead. Things don't look good for Bjerke. He simply doesn't have a leg to stand on.'

Jack imagines the scene at the Bjerkes' home that night: Arvid pouring himself a dram with trembling hands while Julie is standing there in her nightdress and has to accept that her husband hasn't had the courage or the will-power to do what she calls 'the right thing'.

'The patio door was open,' he says. 'We both saw that.'

'The police think Bjerke shot her first and then went downstairs and smashed the glass in the door. Bjerke wanted to have the police believe there'd been a break-in.'

'What does *he* say?'

'Bjerke says he and his lover went into the bedroom. He can't tell them how long they were in bed. Afterwards he went to the bathroom and had a shower. When he left the bathroom he saw her on the sofa, dead from a gunshot wound.'

'Did he hear the shot?'

Paaske shakes his head. 'Bjerke says he heard a bang, but thought she'd dropped something on the floor. When he came out of the bathroom, he found her dead on the sofa, as I said, and he says he ran home. Then he began to drink because he had no idea what to do. He says he couldn't sleep all night. Then he saw us two outside her house and decided to call the police.'

'Strange he didn't hear the shot.'

'Bjerke's lying,' Paaske says. 'If he was in the bathroom, as he claims he was, he must've heard the shot, but he's a lying bastard, a murderer with no defence whatsoever. If it were true that he didn't hear a shot, why didn't he raise the alarm when he found her? Why did he rummage through her things? Why did he drink instead of calling the police? Why did he wait until he saw people entering her house?'

334

'What would his motive be?' Jack says. 'Why would he have killed her?'

Paaske eyes him in silence.

'What does the murder weapon tell us?'

'The police haven't found a murder weapon.'

Jack angles his head. 'I saw one in the bedroom. It was on the bed.'

Paaske looks him in the eye. 'You must've been seeing things.'

Jack leans back in his chair, speechless. They sit weighing each other up, and in the end Jack has to accept that not only has Paaske removed the murder weapon when he was alone with the dead woman, but he is also sure that he can get away with this. What on earth is he up to?

'No weapon,' Jack says at length. 'That reinforces suspicions of a break-in and murder with intent to rob.'

Paaske shakes his head. 'There was a used condom on the floor beside the bed. The poor woman had only just got up and wrapped herself in a housecoat. It couldn't be anyone else but the man she went to bed with who shot her.'

Jack observes his boss, still with incredulity.

'I took a liberty when I went through the flat,' Paaske says with a rigid expression. 'While you were with her brother in the garden, I found this.'

Paaske opens the desk drawer and takes out an envelope. Shakes it. Out falls a photograph he pushes across the desk. It shows a naked Bjerke with an equally naked girl on his lap. Arvid is big and fat, and she is young — maybe thirteen or fourteen. The girl's breasts are developed, but she is a slip of a thing, tiny, with plaits.

'You found this picture?'

'There was another one too, but I burned it.'

'It was lewd?'

'Very.'

'At least we know how Amalie managed to blackmail Arvid Bjerke,' Jack says. 'How could she have got her hands on such photos?'

'They're probably from Germany. Bjerke's supposed to have gone there quite often. My guess is that Amalie von Schiller set something up with this girl when Bjerke was there, and then she had the photographic evidence.'

'I know she was aware of this side to him,' Jack says. 'Many years ago she played the role of a little girl for him several times. When you raided the house in Holtekilen, they escaped as father and daughter. Have you told Julie about these photos?'

'No.'

'Really? When are you going to?'

'Never.'

Paaske takes a matchbook from the drawer. 'The police have confirmed that Arvid Bjerke transferred money to an account belonging to Amalie von Schiller.'

'So the police know Amalie was blackmailing Bjerke?'

'They do.'

'Have you shown the photos to the police?'

Paaske shakes his head, tears off a match and sets light to the photograph. 'As I said,' he says. 'I've already burned the viler of the two.'

They both study the flame licking up the photograph. Paaske drops the burning photograph into the ashtray.

Jack clears his throat.

Paaske looks up.

'Why are you destroying evidence in this way?'

'The world doesn't need to be burdened with this filth. Julie Bjerke's a woman in her best years. A woman with her future in front of her, who doesn't need to be spattered with his shit.'

The photograph curls into an unrecognisable flake of ash. When the flame dies Paaske uses the end of a pencil to stamp the ash into powder.

Jack doesn't buy what Paaske has said. He sees in his boss a poor soul who is still enamoured of Julie Bjerke, a poor soul who still believes he has the immense power he once had.

'Is this what you did when you were in the police?'

'This?'

'Arvid Bjerke's in clink. You're crazy about his wife and you suppress evidence vital to the case.'

They glare at each other, then Paaske speaks up: 'Julie Bjerke has nothing to do with this case. Julie Bjerke only wanted to stop her husband's payments to Amalie von Schiller.'

'I never imagined I'd live to see this,' Jack says. 'To see Ludvig Paaske so under the spell of a woman that he'd tamper with evidence in a murder case.'

Paaske looks up. 'This isn't evidence. It's filth! And filth has to be got rid of.'

Jack shakes his head. Takes a packet of Blue Master from his jacket pocket and lights up. 'Have you asked yourself why Reidar Sveen won't let Bjerke go?'

Paaske looks up, eyebrows arched.

Jack takes a drag of his cigarette. 'If you're right, the police don't know what Bjerke's motive was for killing Amalie. Yet Bjerke's still under arrest — although no weapon has been found and a pane in the patio door was smashed. There's something wrong with your train of thought.'

'What do you mean?'

'The police know Arvid Bjerke paid money to Amalie. From the outside that might of course look like blackmail, but it could also be gifts from a wealthy man to a practised courtesan. If the police think it's blackmail, they must have a basis for their theory. In other words, the police have to know about the photographs. If they were unaware of a motive, they wouldn't have any reason to hold Bjerke.'

'How could the police know about the photos? I found them. I've destroyed them.'

Jack's smile is condescending. 'If the police know about the photos, there must be more than the two you've burned.'

'I found only two. Where would the police get other photos from?'

Jack shrugs. 'Let's say there were four photos, for example. Let's say Amalie had all four of them, but then — to make Arvid pay the first time — she sends or shows him one. Arvid's furious. I know him. He has the temperament of a raging bull. So he refuses to pay and rips up the photo in front of her, but Amalie has a head for business. She just waits a few days, then she sends another photo. This one she sends to Julie Bjerke. When Julie sees it, the marriage takes a nasty list. Julie confronts Arvid. Perhaps she threatens to leave him. Arvid has a lot to lose. He's in Stortinget and married to a woman from a fine family with a lot of old money. Not only that, he's invested in a new site in Skøyen, has plans for transport licences and needs eminent friends and his wife's money. Now he knows that Amalie's actually prepared to ruin him. So he bows his neck in submission and pays up. His wife finds out and knows what's happening. The marriage suffers, but Julie doesn't want a scandal. Accordingly, she keeps up appearances and endures. There's a cold front at home though. Amalie has both herr and fru Bjerke under her thumb.'

'What are you trying to say?'

Jack takes another drag of his cigarette before going on. 'Only the obvious. Arvid and Julie Bjerke must've known there were more photos. And so the days pass. Until the murder outside Oscarshall. The police are after me. I go to Bjerke and use his house in Holtekilen to escape the attentions of the police. Julie's there and sees me get the key. The following day she visits me. Julie knows I know Amalie well and asks me to find what it is she has on Arvid. Julie tells me there are some photos so that I know what I'm looking for. While she's there, she notices I have a revolver and steals it.

'That night I'm arrested. I can't do what Julie asked me to. So Julie comes to you and commissions you to find whatever it is Amalie's blackmailing her husband with. But the police let me go and Amalie becomes a threat to Werner Krause. Amalie herself is the first to see that. The police have released the man she served them up as a scapegoat. Krause might now think the police will be after him instead. Amalie knows she's vulnerable because she's sitting on crucial information that could send Krause to prison, but she can't turn to the police. If she does, if she tells the truth about the Oscarshall murder, she'll be arrested as an accessory.'

'OK,' Paaske says angrily. 'So she goes to you and

asks for help. So what?'

Jack nods. 'Amalie asks me to stay with her. So that I can protect her against those she fears most. That's Krause, that's Gruber, that's you and that's Julie Bjerke. I refuse. Amalie's still desperate. So she turns to Arvid, asks him to come over and hold the fort at night, which he does with pleasure, because she's a fantastic lover, and because then he will have access to her house and a chance to get hold of the photos.

'Arvid tells his wife where he's going. Julie has to sit tight and watch what happens. Now her husband's spending the night with the woman who is black-mailing him, and it's only the first night, probably of many. Bjerke's thinking of protecting Amalie for some time. If we now follow your idea of what happens, Arvid and Amalie go to bed. Shortly after getting up, he shoots her. Why would he do that?'

'It's obvious. Bjerke demanded the photos, but she refused. He shot her, panicked and scuttled home.'

'But where's the logic in that?' Jack says. 'Why would he shoot a woman he's just been to bed with, and where did the weapon come from?'

'I think she was shot with your revolver,' Paaske says. 'Julie stole the gun from you when she visited you in Holtekilen. The gun was in the Bjerke family home. When he went to see Amalie he took it with him to pressurise her into handing over the photos. At first, he tried gentle persuasion and went to bed with her. Afterwards, when he tried to force her, she refused to give them to him. So he shot her. He searched for the photos, but without luck. Afterwards he smashed the pane in the door to make it look as if there'd been a break-in. Then he ran into the field and threw the gun into a bog. And went home, where he sat drinking.'

Jack shakes his head. 'Amalie and Arvid had just been to bed. Amalie had relaxed on the sofa. If they'd rowed over the photos, don't you think she would at least have been upright when she was shot? Why wasn't she found lying on the floor, or on the staircase, or in a pose that suggested something quite different from reclining on the sofa?'

'The police are happy, Jack. That's enough for me.'

'Well, what happens next is that you and I find Amalie dead. Her brother's sitting in the garden. I go out to see him. You search for and find the photos Julie wanted destroyed. The police arrive. Bjerke gives his statement and is locked up. While this is going on, Julie waits to hear if you've found the photos, but she hears nothing. Julie knows the police are searching Amalie's house. Julie's convinced the photos are there. Perhaps the police will find them, perhaps they won't, but the fact is that her husband's lover has been killed. Her husband's admitted to the police that he slept with the victim immediately before she was shot. In other words, her husband's statement means that Julie Bjerke is the person with the clearest motive for killing. Julie also knows that I — when I was under arrest — told the police that she stole my gun. She knows that because Reidar Sveen confronted her with my allegation. At that time she denied taking the gun, but the situation now's a little different. Her husband's lover is dead and someone's claimed that she, the man's wife, has stolen a gun. What does she do in this situation?'

Paaske stares back without answering.

'She wants to deflect suspicion,' Jack says. 'At the same time, she sees an opportunity to get rid of her husband for good. The press depict him as the suspected murderer of his lover. So far, the journalists have been considerate and haven't revealed his name, but it's just a question of time before they do. That's certain. Then the scandal will be a fact. Julie wants to go on the offensive and have her husband convicted, but she doesn't want him getting off like he did fourteen years ago. So Julie goes into her own, deep bedside-table drawer and takes the one photo Amalie did send her. She shows this to the police.'

Jack takes another drag. Flicks the ash from his cigarette into the ashtray, with the burned photograph.

Paaske gulps and makes no comment on Jack's reasoning.

'I think this is perfectly obvious,' Jack says. 'The police have to know about Bjerke's motive for killing Amalie. I'd imagine they must have at least one compromising photo, and my guess is that Julie gave it to them.'

Paaske stares vacantly into middle distance. 'You're wrong. Julie Bjerke hasn't given the police any photos.'

Jack tilts his head. 'If she didn't give Sveen a photo, you must've done,' he says. 'You just told me you'd burned the second photo, but for all I know, you could've given it to Sveen. Perhaps you're tampering with the evidence to play David to Bjerke's Uriah?'

They glare at each other without speaking.

The silence is oppressive, and only the vague noise of traffic outside carries into the room, where the spiral of smoke from Jack's cigarette rises to form a grey mist beneath the ceiling.

Paaske swallows. Both of them hear it.

Jack smiles wryly, stubs out his cigarette in the ashtray and continues. 'If you did give the photo to the police, why would you do that? Why would you wish to tamper with the evidence in this case at all? It must be because you want to steer suspicion away from someone. Perhaps someone you have a passion for. Perhaps because deep down you believe it was Julie who killed Amalie.'

Paaske shakes his head.

'Julie Bjerke stole my revolver. Why would she do that, if she didn't intend to use it?'

Paaske shakes his head. 'Let me ask you something,' he says. 'What are you trying to say with all this?'

'Isn't it obvious? What Arvid Bjerke maintains is the truth. He and Amalie went to bed first. Afterwards he went to the bathroom. Amalie was killed while he was in there. Perhaps he heard the shot, perhaps not. If he did, he must've realised it was his wife who fired the gun. It would never enter Arvid's head to say that to the police. Arvid's a man of honour and would never accuse his wife of murder to get off the hook. Julie left the crime scene before her husband came out of the bathroom and found Amalie dead.'

Paaske angles a look at him as if he is being tortured by an unpleasant truth. 'You mean that Julie broke into the lover's house while she and Julie's husband were having fun in the bedroom?'

'You don't need to act surprised. The thought has been in your mind, too. Julie Bjerke was upset and furious because her husband was paying money to Amalie. She's been trying to put a stop to this for a long time. Besides, she knew that her husband and Amalie were in bed together. From that point of view, she has a much stronger motive for killing Amalie than the man who sleeps with her.'

Jack feels banal as he answers in this way. He knows

Paaske has covered the same ground. After all, Paaske removed the gun from the bedroom. He must have done that to save the woman with whom he is in love.

Paaske shakes his head. 'No, Jack. That doesn't hold water.'

'It's not certain that she'd psyched herself up to kill,' Jack says. 'Perhaps she was just sick to death of being a spectator in the other two's drama. Julie Bjerke was defiled by someone she'd despised and considered a cheap tart for years. So she broke in that night, wanting to catch them in the act. Perhaps that was the confrontation she wanted. If only to get a divorce. Once she was in the house, she heard them in the bedroom. It was only then she knew what she was going to do. I don't think Julie planned the murder. I think it was an act triggered by hatred, by many years' pent-up fury, the effrontery of it, the humiliation and the circumstances of the moment.'

'The circumstances of the moment?'

'What do I know? Perhaps she saw a weapon and was roused to action?'

Paaske shakes his head. 'I simply don't believe that Julie can have wanted to kill anyone.'

'Why did she steal the gun from me then?'

'We don't know if it was your gun that killed Amalie. The weapon hasn't been found.'

'Perhaps she shot Amalie and left the gun there,' Jack says. 'Perhaps you found it when you were alone in the house. Perhaps you took it, kept it and hid it from the police to save the woman you love?'

Jack wonders whether he has gone too far. Paaske's lips are white. So be it, Jack thinks, and presses harder:

'Perhaps you removed the gun from the crime scene

344

first and then gave the police the photo to show that Arvid has a motive for the killing?'

Paaske doesn't answer now, either. Jack will soon be as sick of Paaske as he is of herr and fru Bjerke. The hypocritical manipulator. What he and Paaske are doing now is playing verbal catch. They are tossing arguments to and fro, both mindful that they don't give themselves away in the process. From the corner of his eye, Jack notices Paaske watching him.

'What's up?'

'There's someone you haven't included.'

'Who?'

'The murderer.'

'Which murderer?'

Paaske shrugs. 'The man.'

Paaske imitates Johan. 'H-hi-hi-him. The mm-ma-ma-man who killed her.'

Jack stares at him open-mouthed.

'I think you're wrong, you see,' Paaske says. 'I'm an old cop. You can say what you like about being in the saddle for a long time, but when you leave, there's one thing you take with you: intuition. It wasn't Arvid Bjerke who shot Amalie. It wasn't Julie either.'

'Who was it then?' 'Someone else.'

Jack has to smile. 'Who could it be? Werner Krause was on board a ship in the Skagerrak when the murder took place. Bernhard Gruber was in Copenhagen.'

Paaske isn't smiling. 'I saw Amalie von Schiller with a revolver in her hand when Krause was standing in front of her door. The weapon that killed her was already in the house. I think the murderer was a man who broke in, a man who found the weapon there, a man who used the revolver to kill the woman he's hated all his life.'

345

Jack can barely be bothered to shake his head in disbelief at the insinuation, then gets up to leave, sick of all the discussion.

'Are you sure it's worth the effort?' Jack asks, buttoning up his coat.

'What do you mean?'

'Honour's as capricious as women, they say. Are you sure Julie will be waiting for you at the end of the rainbow when all this is over?'

This takes Paaske's breath away and he can't answer.

Jack goes to the door, opens it and turns back to Paaske for a last time.

'Sveen told me why you had to leave the police,' he says. 'You were tampering with evidence. You were caught, and you resigned before you were given the boot, but take it easy; I know what it means to make a fool of yourself. I've also done illegal things. I did a stretch and I've kept to the straight and narrow since. It doesn't seem that you have.'

Jack doesn't wait for an answer. The door closes after his last word.

⋆ ⋆ ⋆

Paaske sits looking at the door close behind Jack. Focuses again on the nature of evil. What if Jack says to the police what he's just postulated here? What if Jack makes accusations about evidence tampering, for example? Wouldn't that be a purely evil act?

Paaske's hand finds a desk drawer, pulls it out and lifts the object lying there: a flat cartridge. He places it on the desk. Then he opens the other drawer and takes the revolver he removed from Amalie von Schiller's bedroom. He lays that on the desk pad.

For some time he stares at the two objects while swinging to and fro on the swivel chair. In the end, he grabs the cartridge and throws it in the wastepaper basket in the corner.

V

The electric mini-train whistles and Jack steps aside. Carriage after carriage rattles past. The passengers are parents with children. Everyone is dressed up. The adults look a little bashful while the children laugh and cheer with their hands full of sweets. The little train with rubber wheels is on its way to the carousels. Jack follows and glances at his watch. There is still a good half an hour until he has to meet Ludvig Paaske.

He isn't sure what Paaske wants from him. But Jack doesn't mind meeting up, if only to tell the man he intends to find himself another job.

Soon he passes the sculpture that the architect Arne Korsmo called *The Knife*, a concrete colossus clad with silver sheets, thirty metres high — at least. The space in front of the sculpture is a natural meeting place. There are several people standing around and waiting. Jack walks on and passes the pier with the roller coaster. The queue for it is long. Jack stops and gazes at the construction, the framework that supports the switchback railway. Another train is on its way. There is a clacking sound as the train is pulled up the first hill. People in the train scream as it rolls down. The site for the VI KAN exhibition is immense. It stretches all the way from Framnes by Filipstad almost all the way to Skarpsno station. Jack strolls through the area and takes in the crowds of people on the carousels and by the stalls where customers can perform a variety of feats in the hope of winning a prize. The pavilions have been designed by leading Norwegian architects, and several of the exhibition sectors are filled with Norwegian products. There is fashion, sportswear, food and drink. The stalls are staffed by hostesses wearing either the latest fashion or skirts and blouses, all with cash satchels over their shoulders. The food stalls serve samples. There is beer and pop; there are cured meats, legs of mutton, ham, dried reindeer, pickled herring, smoked salmon, pancakes, cream porridge and tinned goods — an Eldorado for the unemployed.

The three masts of the museum ship *Lingard* tower above the buildings. Jack considers going into the boat for a look, but decides to save the visit for another day. The year is 1938, unemployment is coming down, and the future is bright and promising. 'VI KAN' — we can, the exhibition says to the ex-seaman as he slowly wanders around. So, Norway is more than fishing and merchant shipping, and Jack can both hear and see that, but still feels he is on the margins of everything, without dwelling especially on why that is. When he reaches the end of the covered exhibition area, he goes outside and walks the last few metres to the ferry jetty. A crowd of curious onlookers are staring at the Bygdøy side. As he approaches the quay, a young man steps towards him from the crowd. He stretches out an arm.

'We're closed.'

'Why's that?'

'The police are busy out there.'

Jack looks across at the quay by Oscarshall. There is a big boat moored, a kind of barge. A huge box and an even bigger winch tower up on the barge. A thick cable leads from the winch down into the water. Two men are standing on the deck, staring down into the sea.

When Jack spots Paaske's back in the throng of people, he walks over and taps him on the shoulder.

'There you are,' he says.

They look at each other, reserved and affected by their previous conversation. At length Jack clears his throat. 'What's going on here?'

'Diving. The police have a man underwater. The guys on the boat are running a pump so that the frogman has enough air to work.'

'What's he doing?'

'Who?'

'The frogman.'

Paaske doesn't answer.

They walk along the quay towards some small rowing boats moored nearer the end of Frognerkilen.

Something is happening by the barge. There is shouting. A rowing boat with uniformed officers has come alongside. What looks like a thick cable is being wound up on the winch astern. There is frenetic activity. One man is staring down at the sea while another controls the winch. The sea is bubbling and frothing. Then the water sprite appears. The cable is attached to the frogman's helmet, which has a lid and a grille. He looks like a monster rising from the deep.

Paaske shades his eyes with one hand and watches closely. 'Let's find out what's going on,' he says, untying the ropes of one of the boats and stepping down.

Jack jumps in. 'Have you read the paper?'

'With reference to what?' Paaske says, battling with the oars.

'The case against Arvid has been dropped.'

Paaske shakes his head, places the oars in the row-locks and rows. 'There won't be a case.'

'What do you mean?'

'Arvid Bjerke's dead.'

Jack arches his eyebrows. 'When did he die?'

'Yesterday. I spoke to Sveen a couple of hours ago.'

'How did he die?'

'It happened in his cell.'

Paaske pulls long and hard on the oars. Soon they are more than halfway to the quay on the opposite side. Paaske looks over his shoulder and adjusts his course, then rests on the oars.

'He hanged himself.'

'How did he manage that?'

Paaske resumes rowing. 'I don't know, but he isn't the first.

Committing suicide is smart.'

Jack thinks about the grumbling braggart — dead. It is unreal. Again he feels the pressure from over his shoulder. The feeling of guilt that streams through your body like poison, a drug that renders your muscles impotent before it lodges itself like a knot somewhere in your diaphragm.

'Why's there nothing about it in the papers?'

'Newspapers don't write about suicides.'

'Why did he kill himself?'

'No one knows, but he'd just been confronted with the evidence and the charge, which is that he killed Amalie von Schiller to stop her blackmailing him. They also showed him the proof that he'd been black-mailed.'

'Did he get to see the photos?'

Paaske nods. 'The first thing he does afterwards, when he's alone, is kill himself.'

'So the whole business is over?'

'No trial. No new scandal, no dirty linen washed in public. I think it was a wise decision on Bjerke's part.'

They approach the barge. 'He did the right thing,' Paaske says, and repeats himself: 'The right thing.' And aims for land.

All Jack can think is that an innocent man has died, and the same claw of guilt is squeezing his innards.

'You look pale, Jack.'

'Have they informed his wife?'

Paaske smirks. 'They have.'

'I bet she liked what she heard.'

'Why do you say that?'

'She's off the hook.'

They are alongside the barge. Paaske rows past and over to the quay, where the two boats from before are moored, and there are several uniformed officers waiting to receive them.

Jack tosses the rope up to a policeman, who holds it while they clamber ashore.

'Let's find Reidar Sveen,' Paaske says, walking ahead through the gate and up into the garden.

Jack glances over his shoulder. Two uniforms are walking right behind them. All four enter the gravel drive towards the palace at the top, but before they get that far they meet Reidar Sveen waiting in the square between the fountain and the smokers' pavilion. Sveen is standing with his hands behind his back and a half-smoked cigar in his mouth. He nods to them. Apparently in a good mood.

'Have you found anything?' Paaske asks.

Sveen frees an arm and points. Five columns with a steeple support the pavilion roof, a little pentagon. Inside, he has set up a kind of makeshift office. 'Please come in.'

Sveen allows the two of them to walk ahead. There is a package lying on a table inside. It is wet. Something is wrapped in white canvas. Twine has been tied around it and cut with a knife.

Sveen unfolds layer upon layer of white to the side. His expression is nigh on jolly when he peers up, as though a huge surprise is in store.

'Jack Rivers,' he says.

Jack inclines his head.

'Seen this before?'

The last layer is removed. On the white canvas lies a revolver.

Jack shrugs.

'Nagant. Check it carefully,' Sveen says.

'It resembles one I used to have.'

'Any distinguishing features?'

Jack glances over at Paaske. 'It may be mine,' he says. 'Mine was stolen. We've talked about that before.'

'It was never stolen from you,' Sveen says in the same cheery tone. 'It couldn't've been. You see, this revolver has been in the water by the quay since the day you robbed and shot a tourist here.'

The accusation draws a deep, patronising sigh from Jack.

'We found it a few minutes ago. It's been fired. One shot. Jack Rivers, you're under arrest, on suspicion of having murdered a German citizen.'

Sveen beckons peremptorily. A uniformed officer steps forward. Jack has seen him before. The click as the cuffs close around his wrists is familiar. The pain, too.

Paaske and Sveen exchange glances.

Jack notices and makes a lunge towards them, but

the policeman holds him back.

Jack points at Paaske. 'You did this. You took the revolver from Amalie's house.'

Paaske shakes his head. 'There was no weapon in Amalie von Schiller's house.'

Jack turns to Sveen. 'You started the search by the quay because someone tipped you off. That person was Paaske. He removed the revolver from Amalie's house and threw it in the water here so that you would find it.'

Sveen shakes his head.

'Julie Bjerke stole it from me.'

'No, Rivers. I have her word that she didn't.'

'Paaske saw that I had the revolver the day after the shooting in Oscarshall,' Jack says. 'In the office.'

He turns to Paaske. 'You asked to see my revolver, and I showed you. You were able to verify that it hadn't been fired.'

Paaske sends Jack an icy look, and his eyes are black as he speaks. 'Murderers have to be punished, Jack. That's the way it is.'

Jack then takes a step forward, towards Paaske. 'I deny any culpability,' he says. 'There'll be a trial. What will you do then? Will you turn up and lie? Or will you abscond perhaps? Hide?'

The police officer jerks the chain. Nevertheless, Jack turns for a last time to Sveen.

'If I threw it into the sea, do you think I would've wrapped it up first? It was bound in white canvas so that you could find it. Don't you realise?'

That is all he manages to say before being pushed away.

★ ★ ★

Ludvig Paaske stands watching Jack and the officers disappearing through the gates at the top of the hill, until he notices Sveen's eyes on him.

'Is there anything in what he says, Ludvig?'

Paaske struggles to concentrate and refrains from answering. What can you say to such questions? So he ignores both Sveen's expression and the significant fact that the policeman is shaking his head.

Paaske turns to the sea. Trying to persuade himself that he has done the right thing. His assistant's self-assurance and Sveen's attitude have, however, cast a shadow of doubt over the arguments he uses on himself. Then he hears a low sound. It is the fountain starting up. Paaske stands admiring the slim jets of water arcing in the air. The sunshine makes the droplets glisten. He chooses to interpret that as a good omen and walks back to the quay.

★ ★ ★

It is afternoon when he drives into Doktor Holms vei and parks outside the house where Julie now lives alone. Before getting out he looks at himself in the mirror, straightens his tie and hat and takes the roses.

As he closes the door, a car pulls up a few metres behind him. It is a black Chevrolet Master.

Paaske ignores it and strolls the last few metres to the front garden adorned with two hedges that still haven't sent out any green shoots. A deep toll can be heard from deep inside the house when he rings the bell. Soon he hears footsteps behind the door and when it opens, he is ready with a broad smile. Great is his surprise, therefore, to find himself looking into the face of an elderly woman with pronounced wrinkles

354

and thick make-up around her eyes.

'What do you want?'

'I was hoping to see Julie Bjerke,' Paaske says, taken aback. 'Who are you?'

'Her mother,' the woman says, taking the bouquet from his hands. 'Name?'

'Paaske. Ludvig Paaske,' he just has time to say before she closes the door and he is left staring at the teak wall, still hoping it will be opened again and by quite a different person from the Fury with the sagging jowls. Disappointed, he has to confirm that his dream has not been fulfilled.

The Fury is back, and now she seems even more agitated than before.

'My daughter is a woman overwrought with grief,' she says, handing him back the roses. 'An honourable woman. She's asked me to say that she does not wish for your attentions. Goodbye, herr Paaske. Please be so kind as to remove yourself and do not show your face here again.'

Once again he finds himself looking at a closed door. For a few seconds he is rooted to the spot, recovering, then he leaves the bouquet on the doorstep, turns and walks back to his car. There is a man in the black vehicle parked behind his own. Paaske walks over to him.

Johnny Moe rolls down the window.

'Sveen would like a few words with you,' Johnny says. 'I'll lead the way.'

He twists the key and starts up.

'A few words? What about?'

'Fingerprints,' Johnny says. 'There are loads of prints on the revolver we found — but none of them belonging to Jack Rivers. For procedural purposes we need to have yours, too, so that we can eliminate you

355

from our enquiries.'

Paaske nods and goes to his car. Sees green shoots at the side of the road, a sign of spring and the sad march of time. Now and then one could wish that time wasn't so damned headstrong, he thinks. Sometimes it should be possible to wake up to the previous day, walk out in the sunshine and do things in a very different way. Then the world would be a better place, he reflects, and gets into his car.

We do hope that you have enjoyed reading this large print book.

Did you know that all of our titles are available for purchase?

We publish a wide range of high quality large print books including:
Romances, Mysteries, Classics
General Fiction
Non Fiction and Westerns

Special interest titles available in large print are:
The Little Oxford Dictionary
Music Book, Song Book
Hymn Book, Service Book

Also available from us courtesy of Oxford University Press:
Young Readers' Dictionary
(large print edition)
Young Readers' Thesaurus
(large print edition)

For further information or a free brochure, please contact us at:
Ulverscroft Large Print Books Ltd.,
The Green, Bradgate Road, Anstey,
Leicester, LE7 7FU, England.
Tel: (00 44) 0116 236 4325
Fax: (00 44) 0116 234 0205

THREE WOMEN AND A BOAT

Anne Youngson

Meet Eve, who has departed her thirty-year career to become a Free Spirit; Sally, who has waved goodbye to her indifferent husband and two grown-up children; and Anastasia: defiantly independent narrowboat-dweller, suddenly vulnerable as she awaits a life-saving operation.

Inexperienced and ill-equipped, Sally and Eve embark upon a journey through the canals of England, guided by the remote and unsympathetic Anastasia. As they glide gently — and not so gently — through the countryside, the eccentricities and challenges of canalboat life draw them inexorably together, and a tender and unforgettable story unfolds.

MRS ENGLAND

Stacey Halls

West Yorkshire, 1904. When newly graduated nurse Ruby May takes a position looking after the children of Charles and Lilian England, a wealthy couple from a powerful dynasty of mill owners, she hopes it will be the fresh start she needs. But as she adapts to life at the isolated Hardcastle House, it becomes clear there's something not quite right about the beautiful, mysterious Mrs England.

Distant and withdrawn, Lilian shows little interest in her children or charming husband, and is far from the 'angel of the house' Ruby was expecting. As the warm, vivacious Charles welcomes Ruby into the family, a series of strange events forces her to question everything she thought she knew. Ostracised by the servants and feeling increasingly uneasy, Ruby must face her demons in order to prevent history from repeating itself.

THE TALENTED MR. VARG

Alexander McCall Smith

Spring is coming slowly to Sweden — though not quite as slowly as Detective Ulf Varg's promised promotion at the Department of Sensitive Crimes. For Varg, referred by his psychoanalyst to group therapy at Malmö's Wholeness Centre, life now seems mostly a circle of self-examination: something which may or may not be useful when it comes to the nature of his profession, and the particularly sensitive cases that have recently come to light.

One of his new investigations involves fellow detective Anna Bengsdotter; it will require every ounce of self-discipline he has in order to remain professional. The other, more curious case is centred around internationally successful novelist Nils Personn-Cederström. According to his girlfriend, Cederström is being blackmailed — but by whom, and for what reason?